Praise for
Painted Dresses

"*Painted Dresses* is both wise and witty, full of living, breathing people, rather than cardboard characters. I'm *sure* I went to high school with Gaylen, dated Braden, partied with Delia, and ran away from Freddy—that's how convincingly they leaped off the page. Amusing at one turn, sobering the next, *Painted Dresses* captures life in all its messy glory. A wonderful novel from a uniquely gifted storyteller."

—LIZ CURTIS HIGGS, best-selling author of *Grace in Thine Eyes*

"Gaylen is the responsible sister; Delia the impulsive younger. With only parentage in common, and a vague but troubling memory, the two find themselves thrown together, chasing clues to their childhood angst while staying two steps ahead of a hired killer. Patricia Hickman writes from the heart. I could not put it down."

—LAWANA BLACKWELL, author of The Gresham Chronicles

"With engaging characters—quirky, flawed, but endearing—a vivid sense of place, and a wonderfully droll, tell-it-like-it-is narrator in Gaylen Boatwright, *Painted Dresses* is the ideal book to lose yourself in on a rainy—or any—day."

—NAEEM MURR, author of *The Boy, The Genius of the Sea* and *The Perfect Man*

"Don't miss *Painted Dresses*! Through Patricia's pen pours passion and playfulness. The energy in her writing alone will sweep you off your weary feet and into an adventure that you won't soon forget!"

—PATSY CLAIRMONT, author of *I Second That Emotion*

"I can still see those painted dresses in my mind…sensing the hidden pain behind the layers of paint. As usual, Patricia does an artful job of developing realistic characters, transporting them to those somber places where it's not always easy to travel."

—MELODY CARLSON, author of *The Other Side of Darkness,*
    Finding Alice, and *Crystal Lies*

PATRICIA HICKMAN

A NOVEL

PAINTED DRESSES

WATERBROOK
PRESS

PAINTED DRESSES
PUBLISHED BY WATERBROOK PRESS
12265 Oracle Boulevard, Suite 200
Colorado Springs, Colorado 80921
A division of Random House Inc.

Scripture quotations or paraphrases are taken from the following versions: King James Version. New American Standard Bible®. © Copyright The Lockman Foundation 1960, 1962, 1963, 1968, 1971, 1972, 1973, 1975, 1977, 1995. Used by permission. (www.Lockman.org).

ISBN: 978-1-4000-7199-9

Copyright © 2008 by Patricia Hickman

Published in association with the literary division of Ambassador Agency, Franklin, Tennessee.

The songwriters of "Digging Up Bones" are Paul Overstreet, Al Gore, and (deceased) Nat Stucky; Scarlet Moon Records, Screen Gems/EMI Music, and Tree International. All rights reserved. Used with permission from Scarlet Moon Music Inc., www.pauloverstreet.com.

Published in the United States by WaterBrook Multnomah, an imprint of The Doubleday Publishing Group, a division of Random House Inc., New York.

WaterBrook and its deer design logo are registered trademarks of WaterBrook Press.

Library of Congress Cataloging-in-Publication Data
Hickman, Patricia.
  Painted dresses : a novel / Patricia Hickman. — 1st ed.
    p. cm.
  ISBN 978-1-4000-7199-9
  1. Family secrets—Fiction. I. Title.
PS3558.I2296P35 2008
813'.54—dc22

                                                              2008008378

Printed in the United States of America
2008—First Edition

10 9 8 7 6 5 4 3 2 1

To Elissa.
You are the best.

All men whilst they are awake are in one
common world: but each of them, when
he is asleep, is in a world of his own.
—PLUTARCH

Awake, sleeper,
And arise from the dead,
And Christ will shine on you.
—EPHESIANS 5:14, NASB

1

I INHERITED DELIA by default. My younger sister works the night shift at Hamby Furniture Factory. Furniture is big business in North Carolina. Delia, however, lives a small life. But it is often the small life that brings the rest of the world to its knees.

Delia and I grew up in the house owned by my father, who inherited it from my grandfather. Poppy stole it in a poker game.

We are of the age—our late twenties—when most sisters lay down their feuds and settle for an equitable peace. But Delia, not one to go quietly into the rules of southern female engagement, failed to recognize my white flags of surrender. Long after I had burrowed myself into a love match with a Wilmington pilot, Delia continued living a life of discontent. I managed to move around enough the first three years of our adult life to curb her phone calls to me and send her running back to my father to bail her out. He bailed her out of simple crises, like when she ran out of gas or was about to be evicted.

I was artful in avoiding my sister's dirt. That was why Delia seldom called me, especially before eight in the morning.

"It's Delia, Gaylen. Daddy's doctor, Doctor Weiss, has called in the family. You best get on the road to home. Weiss says Daddy won't be long on this earth."

Home. Boiling Waters, North Carolina. Population 2,972, including quite a few Sylers, some living and some dead. Some of the living counted among the dead. Not a town that wooed me back. Boiling Waters was slow in coming out of the chute, so to speak, like the Sylers. It is part of the town's oral history that the main drag of Fifty Lakes Drive did not see real pavement until the last day of 1959. Technology, pavement, and integrated schools all came late to Boiling Waters, the residue of change seeping across our sleepy borders. Color TV, it was believed, sent radioactive waves straight into the body. Accompanying the thrill of talking heads, Amity once told me, was the intoxicating gossip that circulated whenever a Boiling Waters family snuck a color television into the house. Then word spread from Raleigh that color TV was not radioactive at all, but quite nice for seeing Lucille Ball in flesh tones and electric red hair.

My mother loved Lucy reruns. Fiona Chapel Syler. My mother. She grew up in the town next to Boiling Waters. I never knew the name of that town, but it was called The Bay, a spot on Highway 17 rowed by bungalows and a divergence of snaking dirt roads, no mailboxes. On the porch, a washtub and sundry pots kept for starter plants like begonias. The letter carrier delivered house to house, perhaps twice a week, but it was a surprise to the family when a letter arrived, according to Mother.

Our house in Boiling Waters imitated that house on Highway 17, minus the washtub. Begonias were loved like children.

My mother worked at insulating the days of my childhood in as much sentiment as she could muster while describing her own childhood as bleak as bleak could be.

Down in a bureau drawer, when I was on one of my many sleuthing expeditions as a curious girl, I found a photograph that time had sifted to the bottom. A group of neighbors living close to my grandmother gathered for that photograph: ladies in checkered blouses and faded jeans, sunburned around the eyes, and children perched on their mothers' hips. My mother looked to be about five. She was shyly hugging a porch pillar, standing next to no one in particular. Her eyes carried a perpetually surprised look, hair pulled back into a braid that encircled her head. One hand was grasping a finger on the other hand, as if she was unsure of whether or not she was supposed to be in the picture.

My mother described herself as spirited and strung high like a kite, the opposite of her sister-in-law, my Aunt Amity. Mother often compared their differences, along with the things they held in common, suggesting a sisterhood had silently formed between them. Both Amity and Mother joined their flesh to the clan of Syler unwittingly. By that I mean that before the I-do's were said to each respective husband, neither of them knew firsthand about the tomcat-like fighters making up the clan of Syler. But Amity caught on to her in-laws and each woman's divisive nature by watching the criticism that followed my mother into her marriage to my father.

Amity overcame my aunts' speculations about her through charm. Mother could have benefited from such a talent. The Sylers hated her, though, and she returned the sentiment.

After her stroke, Mother was never herself again. She passed away a year before Amity.

When people die, things get shaken loose. After my mother died, my father fell ill too.

———

I drove my aging Neon to Boiling Waters. Braden's Dodge truck, still parked next to my space, the one marked "Resident Manager," needed new tires, and I couldn't pay for them until my next paycheck. Daddy had squirreled away some money to leave to Delia and me, but even after his mind was touched with the dementia initiated by painkillers, I would not touch a penny of it, not a single penny for myself.

I stopped for gas and to call home. Aunt Renni answered and said, "Fanny is here already," and then added in that up-and-down voice so characteristic of southern women, "They've upped your father's morphine." Fanny was Renni's daughter and a trusted cousin. In the Syler clan, a trusted relative is rare, like Flamenco-dancers-in-Arkansas rare.

"Is Delia holding up?" I asked.

Whatever Delia blurted out, Fanny stifled with a laugh. I had not spoken to Delia or heard her low, grating voice in over a year. Perhaps that was the reason that my sister's voice was frozen in that instant, in midair.

Memory foamed up like waves washing to land: the algae stink of Sharon Creek and how the two of us squatted on the creek bank behind my father's house, watching ants straddle boat leaves.

How do I describe my sister's voice? Low like our mother's, an embarrassed alto, at least her speaking voice was. Mother had an uncontrollable vibrato. She sang an octave above her range, her tiny hands poised in front of her, red from dish soap. Not once did I ever hear Delia sing. I recalled how she sighed on Sunday mornings when Mother sang. She pushed one foot out of the sheet, allowing it to drop down from the mattress over my head. We crawled out of the bed on our knees, shuffling across the hardwood floor, peeking around the corner to watch our mother stage a performance in front of the gas stove. Mother sang every Sunday morning. In winter, she warmed in front of the gas stove my father installed in our living room. Daddy was not a good fix-it man, so our house functioned through his primitive inventions and screwed-together widgets, air ducts outside of the Sheetrock, a bathroom sink hanging off the wall with naked pipe elbows perched perfectly so that Delia and I could stand tiptoe on them to brush our teeth.

Delia and I slept in a bunk bed in my mother's bedroom across the hall from Daddy. The quiet of Sunday was always wrecked by the *Sunday Morning Jubilee,* a gospel music TV show populated with a cast of family quartets, most from the Carolinas or Tennessee. Mother threw back her head, her hands on her hips, her small elbows drawn back like wings. TV was substitute church for my mother. Mother turned it up loud, singing, "I'll fly away, oh glory." Delia wanted to know who was Glory. She watched Mother, grinning. But her small, bowlike lips never mouthed a single lyric. Not to the eighties Top 40 and not to "I'll Fly Away."

Mother took us to a Church of God service when I was five, a Baptist church when I was seven or eight. Once we visited a Mormon church, a trip she said was a mistake—she'd taken a wrong turn trying to find a Catholic mass. Her mother warned her that she was bringing up the spawn of Satan if she neglected her children's religious upbringing. We ended up back home on Sunday mornings, singing with the Greenes.

Delia threw off my mother's religious accouterments as fast as our little toy dog threw off the jingle-bell harness we fastened to him one Christmas. As soon as Delia turned fourteen, she flatly refused to go to church. When the visitation committees paid a call following our respective visits, Delia rejected Mother's cues. Mother sat poised in her brown chair as if she herself was from the women's missionary committee. But when she cued Delia to say something nice about church, Delia would say, "WE NEVER GO TO CHURCH, PEOPLE, SO WHY LIE LIKE THE DEVIL?" I couldn't blame her. Mother thought of religion as something you lay in front of children like a doormat. To Delia that was the same as a suspicious option she was glad to walk around.

My sister never left Boiling Waters, its small department stores, the town boys growing up to drive bread trucks, girls coming of age and congregating on Saturday nights at the Blue Water Café and Raw Bar.

Some people believe that you can come back and relive your life until you get it right. I assume that "right" is what you get free of regret. If I could relive my life, saying that I was given a choice, push this button to return to age seven, what have you, I'd relive high school. But not the bad grade I got in Mrs. Juarez's algebra class or the first time I got felt up by an ugly eleventh grader underneath the water's surface at the city pool. I would rewrite my life with Delia.

People talked about Delia for saying the wrong thing in polite company or impolite company. She could take an average conversation down to the English language's bottom-most parts. If my classmate Ellie and I waited out in front of BW High for the bus, talking about Gilda Freeman's new push-up bra, Delia said things like, "I think I have a brain tumor." I got mad at Ellie for laughing, not because it might hurt Delia's feelings. I didn't want to advance Delia's campaigns. Laughter was affirmation to keep up the antics. Delia was an affirmation addict. She fabricated wild fictions, but in a manner so subtle that the unwary bystander might stop and give her a serious listen. Ellie laughed at Delia, the same as our cousin Fanny or Aunt Amity did. Delia made people laugh when she responded to the misfirings of her disorderly neurons. She did believe a brain tumor grew on the left side of her cerebellum. Mother got a call from the school counselor saying that Delia complained that her family was neglecting her tumor and why wouldn't our family take her for treatment.

I believed that Delia could be fixed the same as me. If I made an asinine statement that caused all eyes to look away or, worse yet, to stare, I composed a new thread to lead the listeners into a more sobering topic. Then I returned quietly to the herd to graze on teenage silage, the things we pretended to like so we'd coalesce: a boy making it above the popularity blip or beautifully wrecked jeans. I blended. Delia followed her own voices. She raised her voice twenty decibels in a hushed room. If the topic was clothes, she blurted out, "I WEAR THE SAME T-SHIRT EVERY DAY, PEOPLE. CAN'T YOU APPRECIATE WHAT YOU HAVE?" She brought the conversation to a frozen state, all eyes fastened on her and our mouths hanging open.

I rehearsed a conversation I might have with her after I arrived in Boiling Waters. I was gassing up the car, so I practiced. "How is work?" I imagined the wink I would give her when she answered, "I think someone is putting cocaine in my coffee." I practiced laughing. A woman across the fuel island averted her eyes.

Delia was not a trophy sister. She was the girl my father called "a brick shy a load." One nut shy a pie. When school was in session, she was not my worry. But summer's lottery with Delia fell to me, her personal guide through and around the small troubles she elevated to tragedy.

One June when we were girls, we collapsed on our backs in clover. While I wistfully looked for four-leaf ones, she picked three-leaf specimens and handed them to me, at first with glee. Then she tossed them at me until I screamed. She had no sense of what was common and what was rare.

I topped off the gas tank and hurried back into the warmth of my car. I checked my phone for messages. Braden still hadn't returned the call I left him about my father. His suitcase was missing, but I was almost certain he stored it outside in the apartment storage closet. He wasn't really leaving. What a joke to act like he really meant it! He was funnier than Delia.

Raleigh was gray like Wilmington. As the Neon coasted onto the interstate ramp, white tufts blew across the interchange and stuck to the window glass. The sky unrolled like a towel, shaking snow onto us mortals.

2

TOO MUCH COLD RAIN washed mud onto the surface of the lake by the hill where they buried Daddy. The banks turned into a slough. The brown water spilled all the way into the longleaf-pine woods where pig's-eye-sized grapes once grew in our summers. Water breaking to shore, brown as dung by day but always, always beautiful again by night, lapping against the little bluestem. Pitcher-plant fronds parted to lie limply on the stony shore, languishing on the moss.

I divided up the jobs it took to plan Daddy's funeral. I helped his sisters, Renni and Tootie, select the floral casket drape, a rug of red roses, and then took a half hour to collect my thoughts and write my father's eulogy.

I called Braden again on Wednesday. Three days had passed since our fight, and he wasn't answering the phone at the airstrip. Finally he answered, sounding as if he had just crawled out of the sheets.

"My father died," was all I could think to say. He didn't speak for a few seconds and then said, "Gaylen, you asked me to leave, so I left."

"I didn't say leave." It was a fight, so how could he remember?

Didn't he know emotional memory wasn't dependable? "You're coming today, aren't you?" I asked.

"I flew the Weyerhaeuser executives to Phoenix."

"But you came back, right?"

"No, I got drunk. My head's not on straight. I got a room and stayed until I could think straight. Did you say James passed? Are my parents there? They're not answering the phone." I was still holding my breath when he asked, "When's the funeral?"

"An hour from now," I told him, not wanting Renni to overhear.

He let out a long sigh as if reeling in the miles between Phoenix and Boiling Waters.

He asked, "What are you going to tell the Sylers? That I up and left you in the middle of your daddy's funeral? I wouldn't have, you know." He then said, "Don't you tell them this is all my doing. You know better."

"Didn't you check your messages?" I'd left three. "Call me! Emergency!" I had said each time. When I tried to form the words about Daddy, the only thing that came out was the breathing you do when hiding behind poise. "Are you saying you didn't check your phone?"

"Not until this morning. I thought you were calling about the fight. I wanted time to think. Can you postpone the funeral?"

"The aunts leave tomorrow." I wiped my eyes. Didn't he know what he was doing to me, leaving me to deal with the Sylers without the shield of an objective outsider beside me?

He asked again. "Did my parents come?"

"They're in Jamaica, their housekeeper said." I had talked to Anita before breakfast. She worked for his father and helped his parents out around the house. She hadn't come in until this morning when she found sixteen unheard messages on the Boatwrights' answering machine.

Braden's voice broke. He cried easily. I listened to him saying nothing, as if I knew that he was about to ask me, "Are you holding up?"

"Delia's not doing so well. She fell apart when we picked out the casket," I said.

I paid tribute to my father's love of hunting—the minister had told me that when you don't know someone well, you talk about the person's hobbies. The field outside the church was frosted over, the grass resistant to every human step. The relatives and neighbors seated in the little Assemblies of God church my mother attended on occasion sat nodding and agreeing to the polite things I read about Daddy.

According to Renni, Daddy was not high on church until he saw the end was near. "Two days before he died was the first time," Renni said, "that he mentioned matters of religion. He mumbled until I brought my ear close to his mouth. Then your daddy told me, 'I got some things off my chest with the Big Guy. Ask the preacher to say grace over me. I'll make it good on the other side.'" She whispered that all to me as the pallbearers wheeled Daddy down the aisle. The front wheel got stuck, though. My cousins all looked at one another until Tim Grady, Uncle Tommy and Aunt Renni's boy, came forward, fiddled with the wheel, and got it moving again.

Daddy told me, Delia, and anyone who would listen that when

he was buried next to my mother behind their house, to let the men from the Masonic Lodge serve as pallbearers. Then Renni told me how horribly her cousin's funeral went when the Lodge Masons took over. So my male cousins filled in as pallbearers, wheeling my father's remains out of the church and into the ice blue limousine. Delia and I rode behind in the family car. The funeral-home chauffeur led the caravan out to the acre behind the house where Delia and I once buried a dead pet cat.

The Masonic Lodge officers showed up but hung back, whispering and cutting their eyes at my sister and me.

Delia and the aunts and their husbands shivered in the cold shade of pines under William Hawkins' funeral-home awning. The cousins traversed the clearing north of the deer woods to deliver James Syler in a rose-suffocated pine box. Tim Grady took the head pallbearer's job. The guys surprised us by dressing in duck-hunting camouflage, branches sticking out from hats, leaves hanging about their ears. Tim made everyone laugh. Even Delia laughed. Sweet relief that Tim had taken charge! Sweet boy to ferry Daddy back to the earth like the exultant hunter he knew.

Twelve cars were parked on the sticky mud-and-grass acre like rows of coffins below the hill where my father was buried.

The cold mud clotted the streets from downtown Boiling Waters to our family farm. Laudus, my father's first cousin and only bachelor cousin, gossiped about my father Wednesday after the funeral. He collected old coins the same as my father and talked about the gold and silver market as if the world were about to end, also like my father. He and the other veterans gathered on the lawn, talking over the women's chatter. They swapped stories about

Daddy, prompting Laudus to say, "Winter came early for James Syler."

I remember Daddy telling the old man, "I'm goin' to die just as I come into the world—at winter's onset. Mark my words."

James Syler came into the world by midwife in the room that eventually became the place where Delia and I slept.

"He got his teeth early and could whittle by five," said Laudus after the service. He knew those things. "I grew up with James down on Sharon Creek and was still living there until urban renewal bulldozed the place down in the '60s. But James, he got the luck of the draw. The interstate missed his land entirely by a good twenty miles. James was lucky, lucky like that his whole life."

The veterans nodded and lit cigarettes off one another.

Laudus found God a year earlier than my mother. Daddy called it queer the way Laudus had taken to reading religious books and the Bible. But he liked the old man in spite of it. After the peeved men from the Masonic Lodge left the cemetery, driving off in matching Cadillacs, Laudus stayed behind, lingering, maybe praying.

The American Legion guys folded up the flag on my father's coffin and presented it to Delia and me. Afterward, they gathered in a circle on the hill with their hands in their pockets. They laughed, telling a funny story about Daddy.

I memorized Laudus standing over my father's grave, his hands clasped in front of him, and the serenity of his gaze. He was the last to leave my father's graveside. I envied what he knew about Daddy.

My father told me things over the phone his last two weeks that I did not notice until after he was gone like, "Make sure the house is fixed for winter, the plumbing wrapped beneath the house. Be sure to watch after the plumbing, the roof, the Ford, the light bill, and Delia. Take better care of yourself. You're bad with money, so don't spend any. Take care of the place, check the water pipes," he said again. He did not ask me about Braden, but he was never one to ask about my husband. "Delia needs looking after," he said again. "Don't let her get pregnant or anything."

Laudus's tires spun in the mud, and then he disappeared into the curve of Winding Lane.

Red clay coated the relatives' car tires. "Bad for the alignment," said Uncle Carl, my great-uncle. He asked the great-nephews to run a hose across the field to wash mud from the cars. "Give ye a dollar a car wash," he told them as though the boys would gasp. He threw in a movie ticket each to attend the opening of the Royal movie house Friday night in downtown Boiling Waters. He was a retired cabinet-maker but was given free passes when he installed the countertops for the theater's concession counter. He called it a genuine downtown movie house, not like the one-theater building shut down last summer. The Royal boasted four different theaters. "Don't let the water run like that!" yelled Uncle Carl. The hill hardened into an icy knob.

The constant flow of cars driving in and out rutted the acre surrounding the farmhouse like a bird held too long by the neck.

By the end of the day, Renni was pale. I was the only one who saw her kneel on the floor near my father's bed. She cried and kept touching a pack of his cigarettes. It was the only time I would hear her say, "I miss you."

Wednesday came and went. The funeral behind us now, it was "happy Thursday" and "good morning" and "we ought to not take so long to gather as a family and sorry for the circumstances." The

trio of aunts, Renni, Lilly, and Tootie, were a cloud of gossip and
Camel tobacco smoke. The women bobbed and teased their hair into
what might have been perfectly opaque helmets were it not for the
parlor lamps shining through the thinning fringes. Renni, who was
Tim's mother, smothered Delia and me in big-armed hugs until we
slipped away to the front porch. She followed close behind.

"Lousy to crash your husband's plane, and what with you all doing so well, Gaylen." Renni meant it in the best possible sense. "You
staying outside, Gaylen? It's getting cold out on this porch," she said.

"I'm fine," I said. I took the rocker with the creaking leg. None
of us could bear to sit in Daddy's chair. I pulled my knees up into an
oversized sweater. Delia rocked beside me for only a moment and
then trailed Renni back into the house.

The fog kept most of the men out of the deer woods, all but a
few cousins promising one last hunt to honor Uncle James.

"When you hear the first round, Gaylen, that one's for Uncle
James," Tim Grady told me. He held Daddy's rifle over his head. So
good of him. Sappy but good, but Tim never shied from sentiment.
Delia and I grew up playing with him and his sister Fanny, down by
the stream running east of where Daddy kept bees. Tim was the boy
who swathed Delia in a surplus of kind words. When at age twelve
she babbled like a six-year-old, Tim told her, "You ought to be a
comedienne, Delia."

Daddy called Tim big for his age and a chump for taking teas-
ings from us Syler girls. After neglecting his earlier studies for the
outdoors, he finally got his payoff when he made forest ranger for the
state of Colorado.

"You'll have the whole woods to yourselves," I said. Out of respect for my father's death, none of the neighbors had inquired about deer hunting on the Syler land. Word spread throughout Boiling Waters that James Syler's prostate had finally given out.

"Try not to shoot each other," I told Tim and the guys before they headed into the deciduous woods. Two-hundred-year-old trunks and a milky mist hid the quarry. But Tim and a nephew, Fanny's son, claimed to have spotted a white buck at dawn, sight enough to whet their appetites.

"I'd forgotten how warm it still is in November in North Carolina," yelled Tim. "Woo-hoo!" He gathered our other guy cousins, all tall as pines now, most gainfully employed, at least as far as their mothers knew, and led them into the woods. Five red vests turned pink as salmon in a morning fog that swallowed them whole.

"It ain't warm to me," said Renni, stumbling through the doorway rubbing both arms.

"Tim's in Colorado now," I told her. "North Carolina would be warm to him."

"I'd not be out on this cold porch, but it's loud in the kitchen. Didn't Fanny have a lot of children?" asked Renni.

I turned my chair back toward the mound of fresh burial dirt.

Renni dropped into the chair evacuated by Delia. She moved the rocker closer to mine. "I've done good this week not to ask, Gaylen. You ain't said a word about Braden. Now that we're alone, you can trust me. I won't tell." There was no escaping her.

"We're working things out. He did have a big client to deliver to Phoenix, though." Renni wasn't wrong about the cold, so I zipped my jacket closed. "Braden had to take the only good plane left to Arizona. What else was he supposed to do?" It was his way of punctuating his anger, of making me feel guilty after I crashed the new Embraer—and for sleeping with the professor from the university.

Renni stubbed out her cigarette in the tin ashtray I had won for my father at a county fair.

The more I thought about it, the more the affair seemed like something that had happened to another woman in another place. Like I was someone else watching me like my sister watches the war on TV. Instead, I kept the talk light. "Braden doesn't want the family mad at him," I said.

"Braden loved your daddy as much as you. It don't make no sense," said Renni. She kept saying, "It don't make no sense," and staring down at her red cuticles. She and Aunt Lilly had just sliced beets for soup. "Your daddy told me he wanted Braden to have one of his guns. So's he coming in later? Is that the grand plan?"

A shotgun discharged in the woods. Fog was a heavy piece of weather turning noise to deadwood.

"Delia never could keep a husband. But you and Braden calling it quits...I'd have not believed it."

"I didn't say 'quits,'" I said. *Quits* is a final word. It means you've taken off the gloves, so to speak. I didn't believe in quits for the time being. Braden would make me suffer for a while. That was to be expected. He was coming around, though.

Renni was the talker out of all of the aunts. She said, "Aunt Tootie, you know, she was saying this morning how you got the best life out of the Syler women. I told her, told all of your aunts and cousins, 'That Gaylen, you can count on her to do what's right.' That's why you got Braden and got it so good. You always did right by your mother, your daddy, all of us Sylers." She whispered, "Not like Delia." She muttered something inaudible about Delia.

It was time to change the subject. "Tim said he saw a white deer," I said. "Did Daddy ever talk of seeing a white deer in our woods?"

She could not be sidetracked. "You and Braden will get it worked out, you'll see. If it's about that plane, why it's only a scrap of metal after all. I hope you give up your flying license now. Your daddy said all along you wasn't cut out for such things. 'Women are too emotional to fly,' he said. What was Braden thinking? The things he could talk you into."

Braden had not talked me into getting my pilot's license. I said that from the beginning. I got the idea in my head that it would be the thing that Braden needed from me that I had not been able to give him. A partner. He used that word often. He had lifted it from his mother and father, Clemson and Daurie Boatwright.

The toes of Renni's black loafers lifted gently up. The rocker back tapped the wall restored by my grandfather. Down came the toes.

I catalogued my aunt as I saw her in the moment. Black loafers, knit pale green slacks. Hair by no means completely styled, silvery strands glistening like a web by morning. Pretty when she smiled, but not as pretty as my mother. Renni had a slightly crooked front tooth that gave her face a bit of character.

"In all my years here, I never saw a white deer. I think Tim's wrong," I said. He and his nephew told Fanny's other children about the white deer standing out in Syler's Field before the sun had come up.

Delia squeezed out of the door to keep her dog inside. He was a half lab, half something-or-other pup brought along, she said, to play with Fanny's kids. She called him Porter, after her boyfriend's favorite steak. By that, she meant porterhouse, I thought. Delia named her animals according to her men. The chicken she kept in a birdcage in her kitchen she called Least One. Her second beau was only five two, thus the name. A set of canaries called Dee and Lee, the pet names she and her first husband had given to one another, slept most of the day. They were thin-necked little birds, their mouths gaping open when a human moved too close to the cage. Delia had loved Leland, but he was the swine who taught her a hard lesson: don't name a pet after a man who might disappear when the money is cut off. Once Daddy realized why he hung on to Delia even after she had shown up with her wrist in a suspicious cast, he stopped giving her money. Leland disappeared.

So she named the pets according to things that reminded her of whoever happened to be the man of the hour.

"I told you to leave that dog at your trailer, Delia," said Renni.

"Fanny's telling a funny. I think she's got it wrong," said Delia. "Gaylen, you see if I don't have it straight. We was all riding a raft down the creek one summer when the water was up. Remember, the water was spilling over the banks?"

I remembered the creek being up that summer. Delia never had to wait for agreement, though.

"We all nearly drowned." She laughed.

"Not us," I said and then, catching my words too late, added, "was it?"

I coaxed Delia that day onto the pallet that washed ashore. I called the pallet—a set of planks nailed to three thick two-by-fours—a raft. A lumber mill seven miles from the farm habitually kept timber stacked near Sharon Creek. Rain washed the pallet into the stream during the storm, and fate deposited it beneath our tall pine wonderland. Fanny and I helped Tim hang three swinging ropes from the treetops. I took Tarzan's role, and because Tim said Jane was a patsy, he had to play Cheeta. He mostly sulked, sitting up a tree, refusing to pick his fleas and eat them. He grew bored. The pallet created a new trove of possibilities.

"You came home looking like a drowned rat," said Renni. "I about whipped Tim for letting you get in the creek and what with it so high from the rain. But what does Fanny know about it?"

"She was there, like Tim," said Delia.

"I thought your mother would die," said Renni.

Mother nearly beat Delia to death. Delia looked perplexed.

"Renni is telling it right, Delia," I said.

My sister was stunned. "That's not how it goes."

"It was a long time ago. Who could possibly remember?" I laughed, so as not to send Delia into a rage.

The pallet carried her five miles downstream; the water sucked her under a fantastic pipe and then spit her out where she finally swam to shore.

Delia stared out toward the pond.

"It doesn't matter," I said.

Being right mattered to Delia. She stomped across the porch. Her right foot hit the fourth plank from the door. It squeaked. That squeaking always irritated Mother. I learned to step over it in the same manner that I developed the art of missing the two squeaks in the flooring outside my mother's bedroom on those afternoons when Mother napped. To awaken her was like stumbling into a cave of bats, wings flailing, hands slapping. It fell to Delia to take the brunt of Mother's rage, mostly, Mother said, because Delia did not have the common sense I had gained to avoid a quarrel.

Delia jiggled the door handle for a millisecond as though someone had locked her out. A pang of guilt hit me. I imagined Delia rising from the sand hills of her resolve and telling me, "Your assumptions of me, as usual, have missed the mark!" leaving me stunned and happy. Some girls have imaginary friends. I created an imaginary Delia who could banter and poke fun, throw in a four-syllable word every now and then to throw me off balance. I never knew how to make Delia laugh. We could never have fun with each other, not like Fanny and Tim.

Instead, Delia opened the door.

"Don't be sad, Delia," said Renni.

My sister's foot crossed the entry. Renni obsessed at how the temperature continued to drop. The door slammed behind my sister. Porter could be heard scratching the paint off the doorpost. A high tenor whimper followed as though the pup had been winded.

Fanny cut out from behind the house to a silver compact car parked in the muddy field.

"Is she leaving?" I asked. "We haven't had a chance to talk."

Fanny grinned and waved, her arm a flag in the November wind.

Renni's loafers came down flat. She cupped her coffee mug. "I'll check on the soup, see what condition your family's kitchen's in. And," she said heavily, "I'll see to Delia." She went inside.

Uncle Carl helped Fanny navigate to dry footing. Fanny, more prone to flashing livelier colors than we Sylers, wore a purple pantsuit, the jacket splayed open. Her breasts strained out of a V-neck knit top of a malachite color. She had grown a full set of boobs by age nine. At age twenty-seven she had put on a pound or two.

I met Fanny out on the lawn. She hefted a bag of preschool toys.

"What's it like in there?" I asked. I stared past her through the front windowpanes into the living room.

"There's plenty to eat. You hungry?" she asked.

A Canada goose chose that instant to crash-land six feet out from the porch where Fanny and I stood. "Stupid bird," I said and carried the toy bag behind her.

Fanny's hair blew forward and stuck to her cheeks. "What with Thanksgiving and all coming, I had to grab what I could get. It's hard to know how much to bring the week of a funeral. It snowed Monday for just an instant, Mother said, just as your father passed." She sounded melancholy when she said, "It never snows in Boiling Waters. Least not that I remember."

"The aunts are still making soup," I said. We climbed the stairs to the porch. "Let's talk." I offered her the rocking chair.

Fanny said whatever came to mind, as did Delia and most of the Syler women. "That Delia's got tangled up with some bad business, Gaylen. That guy she's dating, Freddy, he's never held down a job for long. She attracts the wrong man like nobody's business."

My younger sister had gone to the emergency room twice after a series of fights with Leland. Her second man, the short live-in name of Ray, had the unfortunate hobby of growing weed in the backyard. After an interview with the Boiling Waters deputy, Deputy Bob, Ray was fixed up with a fine set of wrist jewelry and new living arrangements. He had lived with Delia for a solid month.

Fanny said suddenly, "Gaylen, your arm. I heard you broke it in the crash. You were all over the evening news. You crashed in Charlotte, right?"

"I crashed into a Wal-Mart north of Charlotte," I said. "Is that funny?" I asked, for Fanny was laughing so loudly it set the dog inside to howling. Better that Fanny laughed about it. She was the first to laugh, me confessing how Braden's fairly new Embraer took a nosedive into Big Box heaven. Fanny snorted through her nose. I laughed with her.

"When I heard it on the news, I nearly died. Your daddy about had a fit over it. You know how he ranted. Like my daddy. Are you scared to fly now?"

"I'm grounded pending the investigation. I hadn't been in the air more than five minutes, started losing altitude."

"Wal-Mart. You didn't kill anyone, did you? Land on anyone, I mean?"

"I hit the garden center. It wasn't such a big deal. November's not a big gardening month," I said. I had flown too low to the ground, truth be told, and stalled out.

A woman in a blue smock started screaming. You can't remember exactly what happens when you crash. I don't care what people say. But I could hear her voice, the screaming, and she was yelling, "Drag out the insecticide, or we'll all blow up!" She kept yelling until I was shoved into the ambulance. I could see her face as the attendant closed the ambulance doors. She was eating cheese nachos, shoving one tortilla chip after another into her mouth. And then I was driven to NorthEast Medical Center.

"Your husband must have nearly died when he heard the news," she said. "Did he almost die hearing it?"

Made Braden tender, perhaps, but the distance between us was exaggerated by the accident. "He was relieved that I made out so well," I said. I was almost positive he said he was relieved.

"I'll bet he was sick to hear your father had passed. Everybody said that Uncle James loved your husband as much as his two girls. Who told me that? Anyway."

Two shots exploded from the woods.

"Oh, those men are out shooting guns so early. I hate the sound of it," she said.

Her mother opened the front door. "Lunch is ready in five minutes," she told us and shut the door. The front windows vibrated.

A minute passed and the door opened again, only slowly. Delia peered out. "Did Aunt Renni call you two to lunch? I guess you heard, Fanny, that Gaylen and Braden are splitting the sheets." She ducked back inside when Aunt Renni yelled for her to bring more chairs into the dining room. "It is getting colder. Wonder if it'll snow?" She closed the door.

I sat staring into the deer woods. A faint drizzle blew across the porch. My jacket was too thin for the worsening weather.

"Gaylen," Fanny said, leaning toward me, "I know how the family talks. But I don't listen unless I hear it straight from the source."

That made five times I was asked, once by each aunt and then Fanny. "Braden might leave me. Temporarily."

"And you with a broken arm! Is he crazy?"

"He doesn't mean it."

Fanny had a comforting tone. She extended her enameled nails, lifting the tips, tapping my arm.

"I've missed you," I said.

"Me too." She clasped my arm. "We live too far apart." She and her husband, Dill, had moved to Durham.

"You're looking fine."

"And you, Gaylen. Like the hair color. Auburn is back," said Fanny. "You're a little on the thin side, but I'd expect it, considering. I did remember you as much shorter." She did not ask about Braden again.

"Five eight is short by Syler standards," I said. "I finally stopped growing. Not like Delia. She's almost tall as Tim."

Delia stuck her head out the front door once more. She blinked without saying a word.

"We're coming," I said.

"Come in for soup, and see my new dog do a trick," Delia told Fanny. "I'm gon' train it to dust things."

The aunts had packed up and left all their baggage by the door.

Fanny hefted the bag of toys and the diaper bag inside. I glanced across the field. The interior light of her car was on. She had not closed her car door all the way. I walked out to the field and shut the door. Then I walked behind my father's garage to cry. I waited at the corner of the garage until I was certain no one was watching. I slid along the back garage wall until all I could see was the deer woods out in front of me. I sobbed convulsively.

The air turned callous. Sleet and rain sifted like salt into the uncovered trees. A vertical sheet swept across the pond and into the woods. Tim and the guys were completely out of earshot. A buck bolted from a copse of trees, the rack and hooves lifting fluidly, the eyes aimed straight at me and then vanishing. It seemed as if I had seen a ghost, but that's how your eyes play tricks when you see a white animal flying through rain. Tim's deer was gone as quickly as it had come.

3

TIM CONDUCTED TWO male cousins, hands in pockets, across the lawn and toward the house. Grass blades, stiff icicles, snapped underfoot. My other two cousins, Blaine and Andy Pearson, weathered the cold to take in a movie and then go off for drinks. Boiling Waters' only hot spot was a bar fixed like a lantern on the town limits. Tim served the Blue Water Café as bartender one summer, home from a California college. He could not take the long trek home without haunting the local dive. "I'll catch up with you later," he promised as the guys split off.

The firmament darkened as the cold front took hold, leaving a dusting of stars exposed through a small window of sky. The front dragged a tail of arctic weather into the county. The black sky was dense as though the air holes to earth were shut off.

I wanted the house to myself, but to Tim I said only, "I'm so tired." My forearm ached from the pangs.

"I'll make you some coffee," he said, carrying his gun aimed at the ground. "Heard from Braden?"

I shivered and avoided his question. Porter's paw prints dappled the muddy ground. By morning the predicted hard freeze would turn the ruts into frozen cavities.

Since the aunts all offered their good-byes once the soup bowls were washed and put away, the house was stilly silent, as if nothing but moths lived inside. Lilly left for Raleigh. Renni and Tootie retreated into the hamlet two towns away called Siphon. Fanny drove Delia back to the trailer to feed her animals.

The back porch light illuminated the walk the rest of the way. I pulled open the screen door. A coarse wind blew sleet into my eyes. I squinted and the wind took the screen door out of my hand until Tim grabbed it and helped me inside.

"Finally. Quiet," he said. He carried my father's rifle to the gun cabinet behind the dining table and locked it inside. He put the key atop the cabinet, as was my father's habit.

The kitchen remained as my mother had left it. A framed photo of Delia and me was wedged between a loaf of bread and a nearly empty cereal box on top of the refrigerator. Mother had cleaned off the top of the appliance one day, wiping away the dark kitchen residue that forms in places above eye level. The photo snapped by Aunt Renni was the last one taken of Delia and me together. Ever. We posed on the diving end of the small square dock's north shore. Delia's two front teeth had not grown in. My hair was pulled into double braids. We wore identical pink bikinis. Delia had taken a growing spurt and outgrown me by a good inch. Her shoulders stooped forward, her two small hands covering her stomach. Her eyes were cast toward the water.

She had learned to swim and took to it so well I called her the Mermaid of Syler's Pond. She won first place in a swim race at the city pool. I was both jealous and astounded when her hand slapped the pool ledge and the whistle blew. She was a natural at water sports but couldn't stick out the class to finish Red Cross training the summer I became a lifeguard.

To look at us in that photograph, we were a genial pair of sisters, swapping pokes in the arm.

Tim saw me looking at the photo. He had known me long enough to know the pain between Delia and me.

"Sorry you didn't bag your deer," I said.

"That Blaine. He's an awful shot. Shouldn't have taken him. Never could hit a moving target. He's nothing but a big dumb nut." Tim laughed as he always did when he did not know what to say. I had known him to laugh when his baseball team lost a game. It was a nervous laugh.

"You see that white deer again?" I asked.

"I'm not lying. I got up early to go walking in your daddy's field. The rest of the house wasn't up. Right smack in the clearing, he came down for a drink at the lake. Pale brown spots on his rump. You know, like a photo negative. Stop looking at me like that."

I debated whether or not to tell him I had seen his deer. Truth be told, I was not certain what I had seen.

He jabbed me under the arm.

"Stop, I'm not in the mood," I said.

"I see something in your eyes. Want to tell me what it is?"

I ran my finger over one lid. "Is it a smudge?"

"I mean inside you." Tim was still standing against the door. "You got this funny look. I can't get anything out of Fanny. You women are all bullheaded, like you got this club and no guy can come in."

I fished a can of coffee from out of the dish cabinet.

"Where's Fanny?" he asked.

"She wanted to see Delia's place."

"Too depressing to stay around here," he said, pulling out a chair for me and then one for him.

"I think that's why. That and she didn't believe Delia kept chickens in her kitchen." I dug out the can opener. The coffee hissed open.

"You and Delia still go at it?" The funny tilt of his head was his way of telegraphing that he was not all about goading me this time.

"Delia? No. At least, I don't take the bait. I let her win is what I mean." I wanted to let Delia win would have been more truthful, but the emotional issues took too long to explain. This week was the first time I had seen her in over a year. If I admitted that, he'd call me inhuman for staying away so long.

"She's not so nuts like everybody says," said Tim. I spilled the coffee grounds but kept talking as if I hadn't. "I don't mind her." Tim was always one year ahead of me in school, thus two years older than Delia. The distance helped his perspective.

I kept sifting grounds into the coffee filter. "I'm glad you see good in Delia." I wasn't lying. Delia got to me only when she scared people around her, usually a stranger who did not understand her ways.

He took the filled filter, hefting it one-handedly. "I said I'd make the coffee." He gave me one of his annoying redneck hip bumps, nudging me away from the counter.

"Don't treat me like an invalid," I said. I didn't like him coddling me. Delia took to Tim's indulgences better than I did.

His belt buckle flashed, silver chrome shaped into the face of a race car driver. He dressed in boot-cut Levis, faded and straight as a razor. He'd thrown on a rumpled plaid shirt, unbuttoned and, under that, a screen-printed T-shirt. Across his toned chest, a largemouth bass fishtailed into the air.

I pulled two cups out of the dish drainer. "You haven't said much about Meredith. How's the wife, Tim?" Fanny mentioned Meredith had taken ill.

"I'm calling her tonight. I hated leaving her. But she's got this idea in her head she can cure herself through herbs and whatnot. Then there's her tedious budget. She wants us to build this dream house. It's a bungalow really. Nobody is building bungalows in Colorado. Then she found me this low-budget flight, said I ought to come, but that she'd stay home and heal." He peeked into the water-well lid on the coffee maker. "She'll do it too. Meredith's got, like, these steel guts."

"I've flown those budgets before. Six layovers…go up…down."

"Thought I would be sick."

"I'm glad you have Meredith."

"You didn't exactly marry a slouch yourself." Tim forgot to fill the coffee well.

I flushed the glass coffeepot under the hot-water spigot. "I'm making a full pot."

"The night's just started."

Beads of water hissed under the carafe. Tim put me at ease. Made me want to confess. He had had that effect on me since adolescence. "I want to ask you something. Do I seem uptight?"

He squeezed my good upper arm. "If you were wound up any tighter, you'd spring."

"I don't mean to be."

"Who's been saying you're uptight, Syler? Not Braden. He wouldn't." He thought highly of Braden. During the NASCAR season, my husband would fly Tim and three of his buddies to Concord, where they would gather for beers at the racetrack.

"No one's said that," I said. I hadn't been called Syler in five years. I grew tense but couldn't say why. Several Bundt cakes had been left sitting out on the counter. "Who bakes all these anyway?"

"You have to get caught up on your funeral traditions. When Dad died, Bundt cakes were stacked all over Mom's kitchen," said Tim. "It's what people do when they don't know what to do."

"Maybe they stand for something. They're circular. Is that spiritual?"

"No."

"Think people bake them because they're trying to express the hole they feel," I asked, "when they lose someone?"

"It's a cake with a hole. You think too hard. You'll give yourself one of those headaches."

I swung the conversation away from me, headaches, or broken arms. I was back home where I was known as one of the Syler girls, the unsung women whom neighbors whispered about on porches, yet smiled and waved at when Mother drove us past. Tim's persistent questions still hit my vulnerabilities so I changed the subject. "What's different about you?" I asked. There were dark circles under his eyes, but he had stayed up late the night before.

"I feel old."

"Coffee's ready." I filled the two cups and placed the carafe back under the filter to finish brewing. I set a cup in front of him. "Hard to believe my mother kept this old Formica table."

"It's a classic. Can you say yet how you're holding up?"

"I can't say for sure," I said. My crying jag that afternoon left me feeling ashamed, as if I were responsible for Daddy's death. I was ten again and responsible for my family's pain.

"You're like your mother, not wanting a morsel of sympathy. I remember that about her too," said Tim.

I reached for the headache medication. The large bottle stayed in the middle of the kitchen table next to the hot pepper vinegar. I popped two capsules and swallowed coffee to wash them down. Tim and I split a wedge of cake. He stuffed several bites into his mouth, overfilling his mouth until his cheeks ballooned. He laughed. Crumbs blew out of his mouth.

I got up, laughing, to find the dustpan.

"I'll get it later," he told me. "Stop cleaning, will you?"

"This house never smells clean. Maybe if I light a candle, it won't smell like a pharmacy." The hospice-care women had poured Daddy's leftover medications down the disposal, but the medicine stink hung in the air. "Something about this old house, Mother used to say, was hard to keep up."

Without a bit of hesitation, Tim said, "I talked to Braden."

The news silenced me. I couldn't breathe or cuss.

"Just now." He came up with a fast excuse. "I got depressed when we didn't bag our deer. Braden was always good for a laugh, so I called him." He touched the rim of my cup. "I hate it when you look at me like that."

My spoon clanked inside the half-empty cup. I pushed it away with both hands. "I should check the thermostat," I said. Tim often lied to annoy me, or at least he did when we were kids. So when he confessed about calling Braden, I pretended not to care. "Aren't you meeting Blaine and the guys at the Blue Water?" I asked. "They'll be out of the movie soon."

"Stop changing the subject," he said, put out with me. His knee hit the table leg, causing the hot pepper vinegar bottle to tremble.

"Why did you call him, Tim?"

"I was worried about you. You look awful."

"Did you say that to him?"

"No."

"What then?"

"He told me what happened, but I didn't ask."

"Shut up, Tim! He wouldn't. He told me I couldn't."

"You two are not over. I know Braden. He's decent. Not like those other guys you dated."

"What did he tell you?"

"That you've drifted as a couple."

"That's what men say when they don't know what to say," I said, angry. Tears slipped down my face.

"I can't stand to see you like this," he said. He touched the cast on my arm. "You always kept ahead of the others." The dim naked bulb overhead turned the whites of his eyes yellow.

I walked to the sink and leaned over the porcelain. The sleet had subsided. The wind whistled past the house. Through the window, nightfall seamed the sky and land together, thin and hard. The moon was covered entirely.

"I'm an idiot," said Tim. Both of us fell quiet, and then he said,

"Meredith says I can't stay out of other people's business. She says it's because I live in the South. Not that she hates the South. She likes it better than Pittsburgh."

The ibuprofen was like a pebble in my stomach. The polite thing to do would be to forgive him. But I stared into the space that swallowed Syler Acres. The dark could hide me entirely, and I'd be as happy as happy could be. "What else did Braden say?"

"Was there something else he could say?"

I stared at the empty cup.

Tim muttered that he was filling my cup again. Then he got down on one knee and used a napkin and fork to clean up the cake crumbs.

His breathing was audible as he walked on his knees to the open trash container. I sprinkled cleanser into the sink to whiten the scratched porcelain. I kept my back to Tim until he finally said, "When you were small, we'd stay over, Fanny and me."

I nodded.

"Most nights I was the last to fall asleep. You girls had it so good. The three of you would curl up next to the gas stove in your folks' living room here. I'd be jealous. All of you slept warm as kittens, all rolled up in your mother's quilts."

I still owned one of those quilts. I allowed him one accepting look, liking him better telling a story.

"I was the only boy. So I'd sleep sitting up in that plastic chair."

"No one made you sleep in Mother's chair, Tim." It was actually her mother's chair passed on, called Naugahyde, but I didn't correct him.

"Then right about the time I'd be nodding off, you'd have a bad dream."

"Is there anything about me you don't remember?" I stared at my feet. Sleet had dissolved on my suede boots. I slid out of them.

"I was scared when you had those bad dreams. Delia and Fanny, they'd sleep right through it. The two of them could sleep through heavy artillery fire."

I slipped back into the chair. The hot coffee tasted strong.

"You still have those bad dreams?" he asked.

I stayed too long out on the porch that morning, and my throat was raw. The coffee warmed my throat.

Tim's voice was soothing. I closed my eyes. He said, "When you met Braden, I knew he'd take good care of you, that I'd not have to worry about you anymore."

"I'm not nine anymore, Tim." He had Meredith to play Mother Hen to now. That ought to have satisfied him, but he kept prying. The headache spiked through my skull. I remembered something I'd overheard in the kitchen at noon. "I heard you enlisted in the National Guard. Is that right?"

"It was awhile back, even before the war. I've still not gotten called up. Maybe because I'm a park ranger. Could be I'm on some list. We needed the extra money. I want Meredith to have her house."

Headlights moved across the window glass above the sink. Two car doors opened and slammed closed. Fanny's laugh spilled out across the drive. Delia was yelling, "Who's the ice queen? Me, me!" A bit of moon showed through the clouds like a mustard streak on a child's face.

"What is it you want?" Tim asked. He leaned toward me. Our privacy was drawing to a close, so it was his last chance to pry me open. "I'd buy it for you if I could."

"What are you going to do? Knock over a gas station?"

"I'll have to think about it. Don't know if I'd go to jail for you."

"Best you don't. You'd be the worst candidate for jail. You were never good at being the girl, and you'd definitely be the girl in jail." Since he wouldn't laugh for me, I said, "I want to finish school, I guess. I've made a lousy pilot." I didn't know if that was the answer he wanted.

"What's to finish?" He acted impressed with me. Considering his soft spot for Delia, I measured the validity of it. "I think you and Braden really want to make a go of it. But you made his life yours. Meredith says that if you really love each other, you can have a life of your own and a life you share."

Tim's mosquito-persistent probing was softening my resolve not to spill my guts to a man who still had my ex on speed dial. "I feel as if I've had a fill-in-the-blank question hovering perpetually over my life."

"Say that to Braden."

"You saying that if I make my life my own, Braden will return to me?"

Tim never knew it all. But what he said brought comfort. He called it his conduit from heaven. He blinked, which was what his father had taught him to do when at the dead end of manly advice.

The girls made it to the back door, stomping their feet on the back porch rug, laughing raucously.

"We're being invaded. I have to go to the airport tomorrow. You want to give me a lift?" he asked.

I nodded. "Sure."

Fanny burst through the door. Delia followed close behind, yelling the punch line to a dirty joke. She was snorting. Her arms high in the air, my sister brandished a couple of wine-cooler six-packs and said hoarsely, "Drinks for the house."

Too many women underfoot sent Tim off for the Blue Water Café.

Fanny got the idea to dress for bed before coming back to my father's house. They drove home like that, Fanny wearing a T-shirt and blue lounge pants under her coat. I put on Felix the Cat pajamas. Braden had not liked them, so the store folds were still new.

"It's high time for a pajama party," said Fanny. "We changed at Delia's and drove over here like nincompoops. Delia kept lookout for Deputy Bob."

"I'll show him the bird, is what!" said Delia. "How I'd love to moon that man after all the grief he give me."

"I was literally hooting," said Fanny.

"You was farting," said Delia. She turned off the back porch light.

"No lie!" said Fanny. Her expression was one of mock shame.

"If her old man back at the motel, trying to bed down all those kids, could have seen her out tomcatting down Cornell Street in her pink nightie, well, it would have been all she wrote." Delia dropped an empty wine-cooler bottle into the waste can.

"But Delia, she wouldn't do it," said Fanny.

"My clothes are my pajamas." Delia excused herself to go out for a smoke. "Tim forgot the drink we brung him. I'll finish it." She screwed off the lid and pressed the bottle to her lips. Tiny dog hairs pirouetted through the air behind her. She forgot her coat. The second I hesitated to remind her, Delia stepped out into the cold. A cloud of smoke blew past the door glass.

"Delia does have live chickens in her kitchen," said Fanny. "Here's how it goes. She has this birdcage, right. So she takes wire cutters, and she cuts the front out of the birdcage, lays it open, makes this, I don't know what you call it, a drop bin for the chickens."

"Drop bin?" I said.

"So the chicken, Least One, right, will lay an egg for her breakfast. The egg, she says, rolls down the ramp—that's what you call it, an egg ramp! So when she gets up to make her breakfast, she says, the egg is waiting for her."

"Sounds made up," I said.

It was not the first time Delia had thought up an elaborate scheme to shortcut household duties. Once she cut the tops out of popcorn tins, left them all over her house. She did it to cut down on the time it took to empty the seven glass ashtrays her boyfriend brought home one night from a shooting gallery.

"You really think she's got that chicken trained to do all that?" asked Fanny. Then she fell facedown on the kitchen table. She laughed, slapping the tabletop.

I leaned forward, whispering as if my mother were still alive and sleeping down the hall. "If she cut open the birdcage, won't the chicken get out?"

"This chicken sits there on this little pile of hay like it don't know it can run away," said Fanny.

"Then there's got to be a big mess."

"She changes out the newspaper underneath, like it's a freaking parakeet," said Fanny.

"You're lying," I said.

Fanny held up two fingers and crossed her heart.

By midnight, Fanny chucked six-pack carton number one under the table. She pulled carton two out of the refrigerator. "I'm good," I said. Delia went out for her last smoke.

"Hurry and close the door!" Fanny said. "I can't believe how fast the temperature has dropped." I loaned her a bathrobe to warm up. She still wore her red rain boots and wool socks. After Fanny gulped down half her wine cooler, she got up from her chair and fetched an entire Bundt cake. I told her not to cut me a slice, so she cut one for Delia and one for herself. Fanny had seldom eaten anything sweet throughout her teen years. She was bulimic in high school, so I often found her up in my bathroom giving up what she had just ingested. After discovering she was pregnant with her first child, though, she followed in her health-conscious husband's footsteps. Dill was a vegetarian. She said she would never date a construction guy. But the promise to herself was dropped when she saw him for the first time. He was fit and muscular, utterly sinewy and brown from his job as a roofer. I could not imagine Fanny throwing up vegetables. She glowed like a girl on a ski slope, her skin the color of pink carnations.

"I'm sorry I talked about Delia awhile ago," said Fanny. "If I were to go out the door, I'd hate to think you'd talk about me. If I was an idiot, forgive me."

"My headache's finally subsiding," I said. I put on another pot of coffee. I didn't know how to answer Fanny. Most people who talked about Delia seldom apologized.

"No one thinks you're an idiot, Fanny," I said.

She arranged bottle caps in the plate border around her cake. "I do." She laughed quietly.

Delia coughed outside from her perch on the second step. She blew out a stream of smoke. The wind blew the haze back into her face. She closed her eyes and took another drag. Her hair had grown down her back. The dark strands lifted and spun in the wind. It was magical the way the moon and the wind changed her looks.

"Gaylen, my mother says you're going to stay at Aunt Amity's," said Fanny. "Is it snowing up there yet?"

"I hope so," I said. "The pines look pretty in the snow."

"Dill and I stayed at Amity's one summer when she was off visiting her sister. We started a family after that and haven't been back," said Fanny. "I guess they might have sold the place after she died. But none of the family could agree on a price."

"Did you know her well?" I asked.

"Not really," said Fanny. She poked my cast.

I flicked her cheek. We started gouging each other, laughing, until Fanny came up out of her chair as if she were coming after me.

Delia threw open the door. "Tell me what's going on!" she yelled. She made a run for our small mob.

"I'm beating up your sister," said Fanny.

"Hit her hard!" screamed Delia.

Fanny and I just stared.

"There's someone else not here besides Braden," said Fanny.

"A whole bunch of Sylers are missing," I said. It was the only job I gave to Delia, calling family members to invite them to Daddy's funeral. She did not call a soul on the list Renni gave to me.

"I'm talking about your brother," said Fanny. "His name was Truman, wasn't it?"

"He wasn't Daddy's son, so he wouldn't be here," I said and then remembered, "Delia, you called Truman when Mother died. Did he say anything?"

She sat tinkling a long strand of necklace, one I had not noticed her wearing until now. It made a soft swishing noise, like the sleet outside. She flipped it behind her, causing the single silver charm to fall down her back. "I didn't want him showing up at my mother's funeral wearing handcuffs and under prison escort," said Delia. It was strange to see her suddenly so full of herself.

"That's not what you told me, Delia," I said. I had asked her to call Angola Prison, my mother's last known address for him. When Mother passed away, Delia's job was to call the prison and see if they would send him by escort to the funeral. Maybe it was my nosy curiosity, but I wanted to meet a half brother I scarcely remembered.

"It's like everyone forgets your mother had a son," said Fanny.

"Truman had a different daddy than us," said Delia.

I had not thought of Truman, not during Daddy's illness nor even throughout the funeral preparations. He was my mother's boy, the boy never mentioned, not even at Christmas.

"Delia, you told me that Truman wasn't allowed to come to Mother's funeral, that he was in a maximum security prison." Now that I thought about it, it did seem odd that Truman would be locked up in a max-security prison for stealing cars.

"Medium security, I said," said Delia. I couldn't tell if she was lying or if my memory was lagging.

"You kept Truman from coming to Mother's funeral?" I asked. I didn't know if that was why I was mad or if it was because she had made a decision without asking me.

Delia kept fiddling with the wine cooler caps.

"Don't prisons allow their inmates to attend a parent's funeral?" I asked.

"Of course. They make arrangements," said Fanny.

"How do you know that?" I asked.

"My father's cousin's son," said Fanny. "He had a friend who was in prison for tax evasion. He got to go to his mother's funeral."

The wine cooler and the painkiller were going to my head.

"Like, how would they do that?" I asked. "Escort him in with a prison guard? Wouldn't that be odd?"

"That's why I told him no," said Delia.

After all this time, she was finally telling me. It was a rare power play for Delia.

Fanny chucked a third empty into the waste can and then examined the wedge of Bundt cake in front of her. "How did I get cake?"

I had never stopped to count the years. Truman was fifteen, or so they said, when he took off. I might have been four years of age. "Has it been twenty-five years?"

Delia said, "Somebody peench me."

I could never tell when she was trying to be funny.

"I got rigermordus standin' too long out in the cold," she said.

Fanny laughed.

"Delia, you said that when they told Truman his mother had passed, guards had to restrain him," I said. "But that wasn't the reason, was it? It was because you denied his leave, wasn't it?" I could feel my ire rising. I hated it when she lied to me.

Delia didn't answer.

"Gaylen, has it been that long?" asked Fanny. "I mean since you saw your brother?"

The clock over the sink hit twelve thirty.

"Half brother," I corrected her. "I never knew him, Fanny."

"Tim says he remembers Truman," said Fanny, pinching off a bite of cake and stuffing it in her mouth.

"I remember him returning to our house once," I said. "Maybe I was eight. It's hard to say."

There was a faded photograph of a boy, large dark eyes, full lips, in my mother's bureau drawer. "Maybe it was because of his picture, but I have this image of him only as a boy." I kept his picture. Mother never framed any of his photos, but she was never that kind of domestic, setting many framed photos around the house. She was a busy woman working her job at Weyerhaeuser, not so full of children and husband as to make little photographic tributes for others to notice.

"Who we talking about now?" asked Delia.

"Truman, your brother," said Fanny. "Do you remember him?"

Delia shrugged. "Hot coffee!" She poured a cup.

My headache came back strong in the front of my skull. Truman was never brought up at family gatherings, so hearing Fanny fire off one question after another was agitating.

"What do you remember about Truman?" asked Fanny.

"I asked my mother about him once," I said. The pain medication relaxed me. I lifted my feet and rested them on the crossbeam beneath the table.

"It was because of one of those…what do you call it…regressive memories," I said. By age seven, my arm bones had the extension capabilities of a small rhesus monkey, so stretching between the door frame of Mother's room to touch the opposite door frame of Daddy's room was proof that I was growing and not, as one aunt incorrectly speculated, the family midget. It was at that exact point, my right hand touching Mother's entry, the left pointer finger pressed against Daddy's, that I remembered.

"I can see him plain as day," I said to Fanny, "a tall boy in that same hall space. He walked Delia and me to my father's bed." Because the mental snapshot had bubbled up from my memory from when I was age three, I surprised my mother when I told her about it. With the picture of this boy so lucid in my mind, I picked her brain. "It annoyed my mother when I brought up Truman's name, but that was all the more reason to ask. My mother walked in at that same instant that I remembered, her arms holding a bundle of warm linens fresh off the line. It was morning, the windows open, a warm breeze blowing the curtains back a few feet out from Daddy's bed. I told Mother, 'I remember something. A boy standing here, tall and a teenager.' She dropped the linens onto the sofa."

"What did she say?" asked Fanny.

"She said, 'That's impossible,' and 'You were too young.'"

"It was Truman," I said, but still didn't know how I knew. "He showed Delia and me a biology kit or some such, like a dead frog. Mother explained that it once belonged to Aunt Tootie, so she even remembered the very day I recollected. Mother said she told him not to bring the kit into the house."

"Like a dissection kit, sounds like, like from Aunt Tootie's biology lab at school," said Fanny.

"I told Mother, 'You whipped him.'" Mother kept repeating that he deserved it. Her voice was shaking. When she was defensive, I felt a deep and abiding sympathy for her, too much to persist when she had had enough. That was Delia's weakness, not knowing when to back off from Mother when she had had enough.

I expected Delia to respond, but she kept drinking.

Fanny glanced toward my mother's bedroom. "You know I loved Aunt Fiona, Gaylen. But my mother said she wasn't good to Truman back then."

"You don't know what to believe. The two of them didn't get along. Besides," I said, "Mother married Truman's daddy too young and had him when she was only sixteen. She got into disagreements with everyone over him because she was so young."

"He was a bad kid," said Fanny.

"I don't remember him as bad," I said, keeping my voice low, my eyes fixed on Delia in the event she decided to blurt out something. "I don't know why she beat him that day, but he must have done something to set her off like that."

"It's hard to remember back to age three," said Fanny, swigging the last drink of her cooler. "I can't remember seventh grade. What else do you remember?" she asked.

"He cried." While I stared into my father's bedroom, the picture of the three of us faded. A pain spiked through my head, but there was plenty of ibuprofen.

"I don't remember," said Delia, her brows knitting together in confusion.

"You were a baby, too young," I said.

"Then so were you," said Fanny. "Delia's a year younger than you, right?"

"I remember," I said. My mother was angry with him. She rushed into the room. She took Truman by the arm. She hit him and then kept hitting. He screamed.

"Are you all right, Gaylen?" asked Fanny. "You don't have to tell us any more."

"I've stayed up too late." I rubbed my temples. "I shouldn't have had that wine cooler." The headache was back. "I don't even drink. I don't know what's wrong with me."

"Mother said Truman was a runaway," said Delia.

Fanny glanced away.

"He's our brother, Gaylen, and we ain't even tried to write him," said Delia, her voice cracking. The wine coolers were making her emotional.

"Should we?" asked Fanny. "Do we know what prison?"

"Angola. He could be out by now. Or back in." I pulled out my bottom lip, thinking. "We don't know him."

"My mother used to call him the boy erased," said Fanny. We all sat in silence for the time it took the coffee maker to beep and go off.

"Maybe Renni knows more," I told Fanny.

"Don't bring me up to Mama, Gaylen," said Fanny, leaning

forward and whispering. "And don't tell her we were all sitting here talking about your mother. She's finally at peace about your mother and all of the Syler squabbles. Let sleeping dogs saw logs and all that."

The house creaked. Fanny and Delia kept laughing, arguing over the last wine cooler. Fanny started a game with Delia and me, challenging us to make a list of the top ten things you can do with Bundt cake.

"Am I drunk?" asked Delia. "Or are there twelve of them circle cakes sitting in a row? How in god's name do people expect us to eat all them things?"

I set to work stacking up the girls' empty plates with my one good hand.

4

A BAD DREAM came full blown right at dawn Thursday. I blamed Tim for talking about my nightmares, like he had summoned a bad dream right out of the night. I shot up out of my mother's bed. The sheet was wrapped around my feet. My pajama top was soaked in cold sweat. Since I could not fall back to sleep, I got up to clean.

Fanny left with Dill and their four children. I drove Tim to the airport. It was along the way he got a call from Meredith. They were talking all the time, it seemed—when Tim woke up, during lunch, and again at midnight. Finally, after four years of trying, she announced right then over the phone that they were pregnant.

I told him, "You ought not to have signed up for the National Guard. If you get called away, what will Meredith do?"

"I'm getting too old to get called up," he said. He kissed me good-bye. I drove home.

Delia slept late.

I cleaned Daddy's bedroom using bleach water to get rid of the medicinal smell. Then I sat down at the small desk in front of the window and pulled out Daddy's bank statements and the will. He had always paid bills at that desk, yelling at Mother when he balanced the checkbook. It was their game. Mother was supposed to keep the pantry filled and clothes on our backs without the expenses showing up on the bank statement.

Renni said Mother once sold plasma to buy a Thanksgiving turkey. I remembered Mother raising a turkey right out in the garage, but it did not cost her a penny. That bird somehow worked his way off a poultry truck. Mother found it wandering the roadway, stunned, she said, as if addled by the fall off the truck. She threw Daddy's fishing net right over its head and dragged it all the way down our driveway, corralling it finally in the garage. She never said anything about selling plasma. But Delia was telling it now for truth as if she herself sat at Mother's side watching the blood fish down the tube.

I read the most recent bank statement. Daddy had saved up a quarter of a million dollars. In his will, he left me the executor, as well as the newly appointed guardian of Delia's trust. Since I had been paying his bills for a year while he withered away to a pencil of a man, I knew about his stash. But having grown accustomed to his treatment of me as a clerk, I felt like a crook laying claim to it.

Delia crept down the hardwood floor in the hall and stuck her head inside the room. She wore only a long T-shirt ornamented with NASCAR driver Kyle Busch's face. "You cleaning?" she asked.

I was bent over a baseboard beneath the windowsill. "I'm cleaning," I said. "Smells like a nursing home or a hospital room around here."

"Did you make coffee?" she asked.

"A half pot."

She looked away.

"You want to move into the house? I mean, it's empty. You might as well," I said.

"I figured you'd want to live here, what with you and Braden splitting up."

I came up on one knee and then stood. "We're not splitting up," I said, not so much defensively as to the point. It wasn't her business. "I can help you move into the house." Then I thought about her animals. "But maybe you ought to leave the chickens outside."

"Sure, sure. It's a good house and all, not for inside chickens. You mean it? I can live here?"

"We need to wrap the pipes for winter. I can help you do that."

"This'd be my house then?" She kept asking, "You sure?"

"We'll both own the house, of course. But you might as well live in it. Keep it up." She was in a fix after her last bout with Leland. Her carpet had been pulled out after a sewer backup. She was walking around on the bare subfloor. That was when I moved her into the trailer. It was the last time I saw her until Daddy's funeral. "I can make you a list of what to do. You'll have to keep up the taxes. It's not much," I offered.

She yawned. "We got anything to eat around here? I'm starved."

I kept cleaning until, bored, she left me to finish. I swept the baseboards and then pulled off the bed linens to launder. I was about halfway up the hall, holding the load to launder, when I heard a sound coming from the guest bathroom. I knocked on the door. "Delia? You in there?"

Cigarette smoke escaped under the door.

Mother hated smoking in the house so much that, after she

died, my father continued taking his smokes outdoors. "It's okay to smoke. I mean, if you're going to live here, you can do that."

She opened the door, grinning. She blew out a stream of tobacco smoke. "That's right. It's my place now." She strutted out into the hallway, her cigarette dangling from the side of her mouth. She extended her arms as if she was about to dance. She was always a graceful girl, rather artful when it came to dancing. She twirled. Then she lifted her arms into the air, the wide grin never leaving her face. "My place, my place, Gaylen!"

"Houses are harder to keep up than trailers. You can't let the lawn go to pot or leave garbage out." She was bad about not carrying garbage out to the dumpster.

"I swear I'll take good care of this place."

"We've got some money from the inheritance. You can use it to fix up the house, if you want," I said.

"Money?" She looked as if she didn't know about the inheritance. She could have been playacting. It was her way. She would get this honest-to-goodness look about her of utter surprise, even when she knew the truth full well.

"We can go to the bank today if you want." Daddy wanted the money split between us. But her trust was dependent on my agreement to make small deposits into her account each year.

"A new house and money all in the same day? What am I, rich or something?" She twirled again in her sock feet and then leaped, this time both legs extended in midair, landing nearly in an arabesque. Her heel slipped on the hardwood floor, and she fell backward. Her feet went up in the air and she yelled, "I broke something!"

I helped her to her feet. "You got any clothes you want to move over?"

"I know what I want. One of them aboveground swimming pools. Do I have enough for that?"

I didn't know how to explain the trust fund without setting her off.

"I been needing me a suntan. This is the life, Gaylen. A house and a swimming pool and all the money I'll ever need. I can quit my job at the furniture factory." Hamby's was the only employer willing to keep Delia on in spite of her outbursts and flights of fancy. She never knew that Braden had talked a friend of his into hiring her. "You need to keep your job, Delia. Besides, you'd get bored sitting around the house doing nothing."

Her eyes drooped at the corners.

"You like the people at Hamby's," I said.

"I do," she said. "We go out to the Waffle House at three in the morning, all us late shifters."

Delia's reputation around town was legendary. A lot of the stories about her tantrums and rages came from the Hamby employees, I realized, but she didn't act as if she knew.

When we were girls, the town character was Ned Guillame. He climbed up onto the water tower after a group of high school boys told him that naked sorority girls could be seen each summer night performing a wiccan ritual on the twenty-yard line of the high school football field. After his death in 1985, Delia picked up his baton as blithely as an Olympic torchbearer.

I stuffed my father's linens into the washer. Then I packed my suitcase, my overnight bag, and said, "Let's go and take a look at your place. We can decide what you can move to the house and what you can sell off."

She slid into a pair of jeans while I started the load of linens. When I joined her, she was dragging an old steamer trunk through the kitchen. She wanted it, so I told her to take it, mostly because it was unlike her to care for family items of sentimental value. She shoved it into my car trunk. I placed my bags in the trunk too. We drove off, headed for her trailer.

We passed through downtown. Delia said, "I heard you yell early this morning. One of your bad dreams. What was it about?"

I had nearly forgotten about the nightmare. "Usually, I can't figure out what I'm seeing. It's as if I'm straining to see in the dark and something is scaring me, only I can't see it. This one was different." The shadow was crawling into my bed. "Usually I believe in my sleep I know what I'm seeing. Then I wake up and it's washed away."

Delia waved at the theater owner sweeping the walk in front of the new movie theater.

"But I remember this one. I was a baby again. Isn't that odd? It was as if I opened my eyes and saw myself as an infant lying on a table."

"Was you hurt?" she asked.

"I don't know. I was afraid, and then I woke up screaming."

"It's your psychic self trying to tell you something."

I was exhausted, though, as if I had not slept all night. "You'll have to tell me when to turn. I haven't been out to your place in a while."

She directed me onto a country lane. There were few of that type of road left. So many roads in Boiling Waters were under renovation, being widened while new subdivisions sprang up on both sides of Fifty Lakes Drive. We drove past a horse farm and then turned again onto an unmarked and unpaved road. The road sign had gone missing, and the lane was shadowed by sycamore and oak that hid an old cemetery. The road snaked past three mobile homes, all of them prettily decorated with concrete yard art and circular flower gardens. The pansies were still blooming, but down South, even if the weather brought a melting snow, winter pansies' faces lifted like little girls frozen in the ice.

"Turn right into this next drive," she said.

I drove around the mailbox that was off its perch and lying beside the drive. Two bare lawn-chair frames sat starkly out in front of the trailer. A flattened tire lay propped against the front porch steps. Empty beer cans were piled in a ceremonial heap at the foot of the stairs. Delia pushed them aside with her foot. She carried the long empty trunk inside, she said, to use for packing.

The sparse lawn out front was pungent as if spring was trying to sneak up from the soil. Not a bird sang overhead. I craved a sausage biscuit but not from Delia's kitchen.

The single-wide was dark. I reached for a light switch.

"My lights was shut off for nonpayment," she said. "I had the money, but it got took out of my purse. I don't know by who." She waved her hand in the air.

I knew that Freddy had taken it, the same as Ray and Leland. But when Delia was in the early stages of being dumped, denial was her pacifier.

I decided that I would show her a budget and how to plan out her spending so that she put aside enough money to pay the utility bills. I was lit up by the thought. My father had picked at Delia so much, I decided, that she had fallen into despair. What she needed was training. If she could train a dog to dust her tables, she could keep a checkbook balanced.

"If you're careful, I can show you how to save a little aside every month so you can have your swimming pool," I said.

She beamed. "You'd do that, Gaylen?"

"It takes time," I said. I opened the window blinds, but yanked too hard. The blinds came loose from the frame and clattered to the floor.

"Who cares? The landlord can burn it all down, far as I'm concerned." Delia lifted another blind and looked out. "My neighbor kept Porter overnight. I couldn't stand to leave a new pup here in the dark. I'll fetch him after I get my things." She pulled her clothes off the hangers in her closet. She handed each piece to me, I assumed, so that I could fold them. I held up the first shirt. "This is a man's shirt, Delia," I said.

"I been living with a man. Freddy, he wouldn't let me buy a stitch of clothes. That left me to wear nothing but his things." She unzipped her jeans and opened her fly. "But I love him, so what was I to do?"

"You're wearing men's underwear," I said.

"It's all I had," she said. "All he give me."

"Are any of the clothes in this closet yours?" I asked.

"Nothing but a few bras." She held up a bra, yellowed and stretched thin.

"We'll go shopping then."

A loud noise shook the trailer. I braced myself against the wall, thinking the entire place might cave in.

"Someone's beating my door down, sounds like," said Delia.

I told her to keep throwing out the men's clothes, that I would get the door.

A woman about thirty, black, and about to pound the door down stepped away when she saw me.

I looked at her inquisitively, trying to smile.

"I come looking for Delia Cheatham." Cheatham was Delia's name by her first husband. "Am I at the wrong place?" She was frowning, trying to see around me. Suddenly a burst of feathers and clucking from inside the trailer startled her. She backed away. Least One wanted to escape the dark trailer prison.

"It's a pet," I told her. I let Least One out the door and into the yard.

She was a spare woman, dressed too thinly for the chilly weather. When I didn't answer her question about Delia, she backed down the stairs looking at me mistrustfully. "If you see her, she's the ho tried to take my husband. He been living two lives, one at my place and one here until today. But it's over now, tell her."

Glad to hear it, I was about to close the door, but the pain in the woman's eyes made me continue to stare after her. It was the kind of curiosity that made my expression appear obliging, but really, my fascination with Delia's life made me stare. Here was a woman I might have never met if I had not been placed at that instant on my sister's threshold. "If I see Delia, may I tell her who asked after her?"

"Sophie Deals, Freddy Deals's wife. Delia knows Freddy, that's for sure."

Delia whispered down the hall, "Tell her to get lost!"

"Delia Cheatham! You come face me!" Sophie cocked her head to one side. She smirked and planted one clear acrylic heel on the first porch step. "You hiding, ain't you? You know you broke up my marriage."

"Shut up, Sophie!" Delia yelled, but she wouldn't come out.

Sophie tromped back up the stairs, her long arms pulling her up by the porch rails toward me. I wanted to calm her and send her on her way. "Please, Mrs. Deals, I'm sure Delia's got no reason to fight with you. If you'd just take some time to cool off, I'll talk to her and see what she can do to make it right."

Sophie's eyes softened. She pursed her lips, pausing, still straining to see around me. "You think you can get her to make things right?" she asked, as surprised as if I was fresh as flowers off the farm. "Only way she can do that is to keep away from my Freddy. We got four kids to bring up, and she don't care nothing about that. Maybe you can talk to her."

"I will," I promised. "She's moving away, if that helps."

Sophie acknowledged me with a slight nod. "Good, then. Can't believe my husband got tangled up with the likes of her anyhow." She was standing out in the yard and was pretty well on her way off Delia's property when she muttered, "Everybody knows she's crazy. Who knows why Freddy went slumming?" She turned to walk back to her car.

Delia yelled from inside, "Shut your face, Sophie! He don't love you anyway!"

Sophie turned and yelled, "Your life ain't worth squat from this time on! You watch your back, Delia Cheatham."

I walked out onto the porch to be certain she was leaving. I took the steps down to the last boarded landing, continuing to force a smile any time Sophie glanced back at me. I didn't see the door come open and the butt of my father's rifle lift over my head. Delia yelled, "I'm not standing for this!" and then pulled the trigger. I fell onto the bottom porch step. The rifle fire was as deafening as it had been out in the deer woods with Tim. But overhead, it seemed to take all of the sound out of the air, out of my ears, as if no sound was left in the world. Sophie fell against her car.

I clambered up the steps before Delia could unload a second round. I forced the rifle butt into the air. Delia was laughing. Sophie gunned her engine, pulling out onto the dirt road, gravel spangling my car like wedding rice.

Reassured that Delia did not just murder her boyfriend's wife, I said, "What a relief! I thought you got her." I leaned against the railing, trying to regain my senses.

"I did. She was bleeding like a knifed hog."

I stared after Sophie, but she kept driving until her car was out of sight.

"She won't come messing around here no more!"

"How'd you get Daddy's gun in the first place?"

"Tim stored it in the gun rack, and I put it in back o' your car, bent inside that steamer trunk you give me. I heard she was coming to whip me."

"You'll go to jail, Delia!"

Her smile disappeared. "Sophie's brother's a low-life drug dealer. The Freemans don't go to the cops for nothing."

I had heard of Mason Freeman; back-page-of-*The News and Observer*-Mason Freeman. He did time in prison after turning down a deal with a Wilmington judge to snitch on a fellow drug-dealing relative.

Dust lifted from the unnamed lane in front of Delia's trailer. "Go and pack what little you need, Delia. We've got to get you away from here. Go, go!" I meant to the police. But the road never took us in that direction.

❧ ❧

Still driving, I called the rental office where I worked. A leasing agent, a college student named Kimberly I hired out of the university, was manning the phones. I oversaw a small-time rental operation. The couple who owned the apartments had given me a week's leave to go to my aunt's cottage. But Daddy died and the leave turned to bereavement. Either way, I was supposed to be back by Monday.

Kimberly said, "I leased out a unit today. He's divorcing, but drives a BMW. He checked out fine, like, he's maybe well off. We're going out tonight. You didn't say I couldn't date clients, did you? You holding up all right?" and "Sorry about your dad."

Delia sat beside me. She pointed to a hot dog stand. "That'd be a good place to stop for suds and a dog."

"Kimberly, I'll try to make it back Monday. But stuff has come up, you know the little things that come up after a death," I said, getting increasingly better at lying than Delia.

A customer came in, and she had to cut the call short. "I got exams coming up. Monday would be a stretch."

I knew with her parents' recent divorce Kim needed the hours for school bills. "But if I don't get back until Tuesday, you could cover for me?"

She was breathing into the phone.

"You'll get a bonus. I'll buy you a blouse."

"Okay, then." She hung up.

I was watching the mirrors for a tail. "Delia, there's a good chance that Sophie's gone to the hospital. They call the cops for bullet wounds, no matter what. I think we ought to go straight to the police. You can tell them you were mad, you didn't mean it. She threatened you." With Delia's track record and Daddy's death, we could claim all sorts of mental anguish.

She stared out the window, watching the passing stores and shops along Fifty Lakes Drive. A road sign advertised concert tickets for an underground band.

"If we go straight to the police and you tell them that you didn't mean to shoot her, that you were, I don't know, just fooling around or something, maybe you'd get off with probation."

She cocked her head. "Them cops, they got it in for me. You know since Ray got caught growing weed in the backyard, they drive real slow past my place now, like they're watching me."

"They're not watching you, Delia. Why would they?"

"Ever since then, they watch me."

You could never tell by looking at Delia whether she was in the present or in her fictive world. She never showed it, not in her mannerisms or body language. But since she was a little kid, her bottom lip jutted out when she was off script. As we drove out of town, but onto the highway and not onto the interstate, she was wide-eyed and her bottom lip could hold dime tips.

I said, mad as bees, "Getting back to the present, let's talk about shooting people. Most of us don't shoot people, so maybe you shouldn't either."

Delia's fingers curled into tight balls. When Daddy lectured her, I saw that same tight-fisted response. She told me, "I been wanting to kick Sophie Deals's butt since Freddy told me how she treated him. She don't love him, so I don't know what her problem is anyway."

"But he's married to her, not you."

"He talked about leaving her."

"They do that."

"How would you know anyway, like, you've had this perfect husband, and now you're throwing him away."

She had a point. "No man's perfect, Delia."

"There's that new restaurant, Bojangles. They got chicken. You crying, Gaylen?"

I wiped my eyes. The tears hadn't flowed since the day after Daddy's funeral. "It's been a tough day, Delia. We just buried Daddy. My sister's shooting people."

She laughed. "Life's like a big nut, ain't it? Hard to crack and such."

5

I COULD NOT DISCERN the quiet of Boiling Waters that afternoon. No sirens going off, not even a cat stuck up a tree. The bare trees shadowing the highway seemed to turn their backs to Delia and me; a few dying wheat fronds—the kind you see sparsely growing along the highway after a grain truck drops seed on the road—listed in the wind. All at once, every little mom-and-pop business storefront looked large to me, as if I were seeing each shop newly. I knew most of the buildings by memory, even though the ownership changed hands as often as the economy fluctuated. A single American flag hung in the front window of a café. A mobile sign out by the road advertised coffee better than Starbucks; a yellow ribbon tied to one leg of the sign explained the caption under the coffee ad that said, "Until Bill comes home, we pray." I had been away from Boiling Waters too long to know whose son or daughter had enlisted and gone off to the Middle East.

Delia dug through her purse for a cigarette.

"You can't smoke in my car. I'll find a place to stop for lunch, though."

She tossed her purse onto the floorboard.

"You like Wendy's?" I asked.

"Anything with a smoking section," she said.

We parked on the back side of the parking lot. Inside, I led us to a booth in the center of the fast-food restaurant away from the story-tall plate-glass windows.

She picked out another booth and sat down, expecting me to buy her food. "Just get me a hamburger, ketchup, fries, large Coke," she said. She looked like my father lighting a cigarette. The cigarette hung sideways out of her mouth, flopping up and down when she spoke. I had seen Daddy do the same thing, sitting on the back porch after breakfast.

I ordered and brought Delia her lunch on a tray. She still seemed out of place in a restaurant. Except for the Waffle House, she had never been one to go out and eat much, not in the light of day at least. I thought that over time, as she worked and earned her own keep, she'd ease into the social graces of ordering food. But come to think of it, I had never seen my father order a meal in a restaurant either. Eating-out culture had come up around them both but had evaded their simple daily practices.

"They got any ketchup around here?" She unwrapped her burger and set her cigarette in the ashtray to smolder.

I pointed to the condiment island. She could get her own ketchup.

She got up wearing the same pouty smirk that dimpled her cheeks as a girl. Delia could never walk across a public room without drawing attention, not since she could walk. I assumed it was her way of trying to look cute for the adults, to make the aunts fawn over her, or to make my father take notice. But Daddy did

not notice us girls in that manner. Even when we bought new swim-
suits and Mother had us parade out in front of him for approval, he
would glance at us as if we were distracting him and then glance
down at the floor. Delia skipped to the condiment island. The
smirk was in place, as if she was playing her hand again at age six;
only at age twenty-eight, cute was not in her deck.

The restaurant was filling up, mothers toting infants and a paint
crew stopping for lunch. No one noticed Delia dancing to the condiment island except one Latino employee pushing a broom outside
the women's rest room. He glanced at her and then looked away as
if he were being polite, as if he would look back and this woman
would have somehow composed herself.

Delia picked up a round empty condiment container and held
it under a ketchup pump. She filled it with a flourish, pumping
wildly, giggling, and glancing up and down to see who was watching. I looked down at my food.

She filled a second one and carried them both back to the table,
holding two condiments out at arms-length as if she were deliver-
ing something mysterious back to the table. "I like those ketchup
gadgets," she said. "It's like, all-you-can-eat ketchup, no end to
ketchup."

"I'm glad you like it, Delia, but do you have to draw attention
like that? I mean, you should think about a low profile from now on
until we figure out what to do about Sophie."

She took a bite and rolled her eyes as if tasting burger for the
first time.

"Don't you and your friends go out?" I asked.

She dipped a fry in ketchup. "Ain't got the money. I do got a friend, though. Juanita. She's not Spanish, though, except her name. We went out for a beer once after I got paid. Freddy, he got mad, took the rest of my money and said he'd save it. I never saw it. Said he paid the bills, but they shut the lights off after that."

"Delia, you got to take care of your own money," I said. "How'd you meet this Freddy anyway?"

She reflected on the shape of her fry and then said, "He worked the assembly line at Hamby's. We sat and talked each day over lunch. The more we talked, the more he liked me. He told me I was funny. Then we went out for a smoke during break, a drink after work, one thing led to another." A smile spread slowly across her face.

A squad car pulled up outside. One of two officers sat in the car talking on the radio, looking down at something, perhaps a computer screen. The other got out and waited at the door for his buddy to join him. His face was a pumpkin, wide and nearly yellow. His head tilted in the cold wind, causing him to step more quickly to gain balance.

Delia turned her face away from the cops.

My food tasted the way nothingness would taste if served between stale buns. I swallowed a bite with soda that was more carbonation and less syrup.

She leaned toward me and said, "Should we make a run for it?"

The second cop got out. He stopped in the doorway behind his partner.

"Delia," I whispered.

She looked at me. Her nose freckles had faded, but under the fluorescent lights they were suddenly visible, and she looked nine again.

"It's Deputy Bob. Keep eating and don't look up," I told her. He was the same Bob who arrested her boyfriend Ray for growing weed. But he had told Delia to come along too for questioning. When he frisked her, he slowed down over the vulnerable places. Delia slapped him, and he dragged her out to the car. She cried so loudly that he stopped the squad car and made her get out. She skipped back to the trailer, she told me later, not believing that he had let her go.

"Look what the cat drug in, Johnny." Bob spotted Delia right away and crossed the room to walk up to our table. He stood alongside her, looking down at her. He got this look where his mouth opened and faintly smiled at her. Delia might not have known why Deputy Bob let her go that day, but it was then that I knew.

"I ain't botherin' you, Bob," said Delia. "And I ain't looking at you, neither."

He was standing close enough that she could see her face in his belt buckle if she would only look up. His right hand moved down away from his waist and tapped the set of handcuffs linked to his belt. "You seen any mischief out around your place, Delia?"

The big-faced deputy, Johnny, stood with his feet apart next to Bob, listening to his partner but also checking out the lunch deals on the overhead marquee.

My sister finally looked up at me.

"We've been at my father's house, Deputy," I told him. "He passed this week."

Bob said, "Yes'm. Heard the news about your daddy. Sorry to hear it." He glanced back at Delia and then slowly returned his gaze to me. "Neighbor called from out your way, Delia. Said she heard gunfire in the neighborhood," he said. "I figured it was boys out hunting too close to home."

"It is, after all, hunting season," said Delia. She wrapped the remaining wedge of burger in the aluminum paper. "I ain't got much of an appetite. Let's go, Gaylen," she said. She slipped on the thin hooded green sweater left in her closet by Freddy.

I expected the deputy to grab her and haul her out kicking and making a scene, but Delia walked out free. Deputies Bob and Johnny fell in line to order lunch.

I followed her out of Wendy's and to the car. I sat staring out over the steering wheel until Delia said, "Time to go."

The parking lot had filled up. Two more cops pulled in next to Bob's squad car. "They're meeting for lunch, I guess," I said. I had to make a choice right then and there. I imagined Deputy Bob putting his hands on my sister.

"This place we going have a TV?" she asked. "I like to watch the war."

❧ ❧

Highway 74 would be less trafficked than Interstate 40 and give us a view of the towns. We drove out of Wilmington and crossed the Brunswick County line. A white cupola surrounded a clean white steeple pointing to the sky. Delia pulled on a loose green string hanging from her sleeve.

"You need your own clothes," I said.

We drove off the James B. White Highway, a strip of road shadowed by a row of naked bay trees, the fruit long eaten by mockingbirds. A ladies' dress shop called Kramer's advertised a sale. I parked and led Delia inside.

The store catered to a mostly retired set, women who bought the brightly adorned clothing only to hang, tags still attached, inside long closets against their everyday drab attire. Delia was fascinated by the riotous colors. She pulled out a dress and held it against her.

"Jeans are more practical," I told her.

"Ladies wear this kind of thing to mass," she said.

"When have you ever attended mass?" I asked.

"Freddy's Catholic."

"Do you want a dress then?" I asked.

A shop lady watched her from the counter. Her eyes raked over Delia, every light in her eyes scrutinizing Delia's grating voice and ungainly movements. Delia could not simply walk, of course. She galloped rack to rack, excitedly pulling out items of clothing like an adopted foreign orphan.

"I'll show you the dressing room," the woman said blandly.

Delia disappeared behind the hand-sewn curtain. I rummaged through a pile of women's winter sweatshirts.

A choked gasp emanated from the dressing room.

Another salesclerk appeared from the back. She held a coffee cup and was looking curiously toward the dressing room.

"Delia, are you all right?" I asked as if cued. I knew that she was fine, of course, but unfolding a small plan to draw attention.

She threw back the curtain, strutting onto the sales floor. The dress was not well suited for her frame. It was a fuchsia and white print with a full skirt and long sleeves. She twirled. The skirt fanned out like a parasol spinning in a geisha dance.

The clerk covered her mouth and glanced at her friend who still had not come out from behind the counter.

"I want this," said Delia. She stared in the mirror at the long skirt hanging in chiffon fingertips above her bare toes.

I held up a blue sweatshirt and a pair of jeans. "Try on?" I suggested.

She complied, however reluctantly. The jeans and sweatshirt fit her perfectly, giving her more of a shape than Freddy's jeans and hoodie. I handed her a pair of sneakers and socks. She carted them into the dressing room.

"Do you carry lingerie?" I asked the clerk. They did.

She helped me select a half dozen pairs of panties. "Mind if I give her a pair now?" I asked.

The woman looked troubled, as if shoplifters were afoot on her watch. She acquiesced and asked if she could get me a coffee too. I accepted and handed Delia a pair of panties through the curtain. "Hand me the tags off those," I said, "and put them on."

The clerk appeared with the coffee and gave it to me. "Everything all right?" She smiled in a painful way, as if the training she had gotten her first week was the only scaffolding sustaining her composure.

Freddy's underwear flew over the top of the curtain and landed at our feet. "She's done with those then, I guess," said the clerk.

We drove out of Whiteville, past the yards dotted with purple pansies. The day was nearly gone. A band of pink dimmed on the horizon like a fading influenza fever.

"I wish you'd stop making everyone stare. Everywhere we go, Delia, you have to make everybody in the whole place look at you," I said.

"Why you got to criticize me, Gaylen? There you go, like always, picking me apart." Her tone was deep and full of pain.

"All I mean to say is that if you have a mad drug dealer on your tail, why do things to make people remember you?"

"I was only having a little fun. Can't a body do that without being criticized?"

I wanted to understand her. "Are you trying to be funny?"

"Maybe I am funny. Other people seem to think so, other people who ain't you."

"Funny and silly are not the same thing. You don't act your age, Delia."

She pulled a cigarette out and then, remembering not to smoke in my car, sat tamping it against her knee. "Ever heard of being young at heart?"

"That's not what that means. It's like people who have a good attitude about life, that's all, Delia. It's not permission to act a fool in public places. Teenagers do it, but not grown women."

"You sound like Mama. Pick, pick, pick."

"Mother wanted to help. She didn't mean to pick. Besides, she's dead. Have respect," I said.

Delia shook her head. "She didn't love me." She held the vowel in *love*, almost yodeling. "You don't know how she did me, Gaylen, at the end. You wasn't around."

"Mother loved you."

"The day she died, I went over to her bedside to tell her 'good-bye,' like you're supposed to do when someone is dying, right?" she paused. "She slapped me."

"Her sister told me how Mother was that day before I arrived.

She had been singing a song about Jesus, Delia. That doesn't sound like a woman who slaps her daughter." I halfway believed Delia but wanted to talk about something else.

"She was slapping at my face, over and over. What was I supposed to think?"

"That she was a woman on morphine," I said.

"You didn't know her. Why do you think I'm lying?"

"Delia, it's hard to know when you're telling it straight. If you would remember right, then people would believe you."

"I remember the truth. I say it like I see it."

Delia was a revisionist. I knew that, but she never admitted it. "Do you say those things about our mother so people will sympathize with you? Like, you know, when we were ten and we wanted sympathy so that adults would lay off us?" I asked, thinking that if I used a gentler approach, Delia would finally admit something, allow me a minor concession.

"She treated me like she treated her son, Truman." There was a familiarity in her tone, as if she knew Truman better than I did. That was impossible. She was too young.

"What do you remember about Truman?" I asked.

"Aunt Tootie told me all the dirt on Mama. I asked and she told."

Considering we had just talked about Truman over wine coolers, I doubted her. "You didn't say anything about him the other night?"

"I knew if I told Fanny, she'd squeal to Renni."

Since when had Delia cared what anyone thought? "Tootie hated her, Delia. Why would you sit gossiping with her about your own mother?" I watched for a highway sign. The meandering maze of

Highway 74 was easy to venture off of. It could spit us off into South Carolina and we wouldn't know it for miles.

"Tootie knows because she knew Mama before she married Daddy."

Even if she was making it up, she had me curious. I didn't want to talk anymore anyway. I wanted to get us as far as Charlotte before stopping. Listening to Delia's chatter calmed me more, I realized, when I stopped arguing with her. I took a deep breath.

"Mama, Tootie said, moved away to California. Truman was young. Like, not in school yet. She lived two apartments down from Aunt Tootie. That's how they met, Daddy and Mama."

"Tootie introduced them?" That was news to me. I fingered the bottom of the steering wheel with my one good hand. That was not the story my mother had told me about how she met Daddy.

"Tootie said that little Truman would go door to door, knocking and asking the neighbors for food," said Delia.

"She lied."

Delia was nervously tapping the cigarette against one palm. "He was covered in filth, not taken care of by Mama. Naked, he was, and neglected."

"Delia, our mother was meticulous. Remember how she sewed for us, kept our clothes starched and ironed, our hair curled?" My frustration grew. "Does that sound like her?"

"Tootie said she had Truman too young."

"Why, Delia? Why would she change that much?"

"Ask Tootie."

Tootie was not like Renni. She was my father's quieter sister, a brooding woman who seldom made an appearance at the Syler house until Daddy's death. Even then, she said almost nothing to me. "I never see her. When did you see her, come to think of it?"

"She's Catholic."

"I see. And Freddy's Catholic, and apparently, now, so are you."

"I like the priest. He's nice."

"Are you saying that Tootie told you all of this at mass?"

She hesitated. "I saw her at mass, and she invited me over for supper."

"Why did Mother never mention any of this before, that she lived next to Tootie in Salinas or that she met Daddy there?"

"You were born in Salinas."

"They were married two years when I was born, Delia." Mother had made a huge deal about it.

"You ever see the marriage certificate?"

I looked for it once, but never found it. One hot summer I stayed inside to keep cool and teach myself how to sew. Mother's electric sewing machine was difficult to thread, so she let me practice sewing on her grandmother's Singer treadle machine. The smell of machine oil was suddenly alive in my memory. While digging through a drawer for thread, I found a work card. It was for a factory where she had worked in Salinas. Her name was wrong, typed as Fiona Polette, so I asked her about it. She told me I ought to be an attorney.

"Was she ever named Polette?" I asked.

"That was her second husband," said Delia. "Tootie told me that too."

"So she was married to Polette in Salinas?" I asked.

"They was divorced, and she moved away from Boiling Waters to get work in Salinas."

"It's still not right, Delia. I was born in Salinas and my name is obviously not Polette but Syler."

The sky was the color of ash. The sun slipped out of our sight as we drove toward the west. Delia did not talk for the next couple of miles. She was not the kind of woman who liked the quiet or allowed silent spaces in the conversation, so it was a clumsy silence. Finally she said, "Mama was two different women. The one she wanted us to believe was her and then the real Fiona Syler."

"You don't know that, Delia." Whether or not she was right was not plainly obvious at the time. But what we both knew, or felt we knew, was most likely some combination of the truth of the matter; who my mother was before I was born and why my version of her was so different than Delia's seemed best left untouched. But Delia could get her facts confused within minutes after having heard the truth.

"I've heard people say that everyone is really two different people," said Delia. "Not me. What you see is what you get."

She was finally right about something.

Uncle Malcolm, Amity's husband, liked singing a Randy Travis song.

I'm digging up bones, I'm digging up bones.
Exhuming things that's better left alone.

I did not know why that song stuck in my head the whole trip to Cashiers.

6

DELIA SLEPT LIKE a newborn kitten in the Charlotte Sleep Inn. The continental breakfast the next morning was tasteless, but she said it tasted a lot better than the instant grits Freddy made her cook every morning.

"You don't sleep much, do you, Gaylen?" she said over her doughnut.

"I keep expecting a drug dealer to bust through the door, Delia, guns a-blazing. I don't know why I'd think that, though," I said, not hiding the sarcasm too well.

"I woke up, and you were standing in front of the window, looking out like you was watching the stars. The streetlight was shining right down on you, like you was being pointed down on from the finger of God." She laughed. "You know, like when a person in a movie is supposed to suddenly know everything she needs to know and it seems like she's getting it all transmutated from heaven."

I watched her eat for a while, guileless and not once looking over her shoulder at the quiet black guy sitting behind her watching her talk. "Do you ever worry about anything, Delia?"

She thought for a moment. "Going to hell. You believe in heaven?" she asked.

"Of course I do," I said.

"I worry about that sometimes. If I go on a good day, I guess that's where I'll be. But if on a bad day, then hell, I guess."

"Lately, I don't think I'm headed for heaven," I said.

"You always are," she said. "That's what Mama liked best about you. You was good. Delia was bad."

"Maybe I'm two women too," I said.

"I doubt that, Gaylen. The last thing I'd believe about you is that you'd mess up. I never seen you make a mistake your whole life."

"You're not around every minute of the day. No one sees every minute of all we do," I said.

"I couldn't be as good as you if I tried."

"Delia, life isn't always about being bad or good. Sometimes people get stuck in situations and no matter which way we choose, it turns out wrong. I get stuck just like you."

"I feel like that every day of my life. Like no matter what I do, someone's going to be mad. I make people mad without meaning to."

I told her, "Everyone does that from time to time."

"But every day I do." She pushed away her coffee cup. "Before today is gone, you'll be mad at me."

The black customer picked up his luggage and left.

"So work on not making me mad."

She threw up her arms. "It's like a big mystery to me, Gaylen! I don't even know I'm doing it when I'm doing it. So how am I going to work on it?"

My phone rang.

Delia said, "Hah!"

By the time I dug it out of my purse, the caller had hung up. Finally, though, it was Braden. I would call him when I got to Cashiers.

Delia talked the whole way between Charlotte and the town of Clayton, Georgia. We stopped for lunch. She wanted ice cream and was pointing to a small freestanding mom-and-pop stand. I turned around and pulled into the small lot. I paid for her mint chocolate chip cone.

"I appreciate you buying my food," she said. "I know I'm broke and not helping out with the expenses."

"It's Daddy's money," I finally confessed. "And you're not completely broke. He left us money, you know."

"When you going to tell me how much?"

I didn't answer right away. "I planned to tell yesterday, only you shot a person, and we've been busy since."

"How long you going to make me feel bad about it?" she asked. She followed me out into the parking lot.

"It's a surprise to me that you feel bad about shooting Sophie Deals."

"What kind of monster you think I am?" She was indignant. "Besides, I barely scratched her. She put a Band-Aid on it and forgot about it."

I remembered standing over the pool of blood at the end of Delia's lawn. "What if she died, Delia?"

"You're getting mad already. See how I don't even see it coming?"

"When will you admit anything? Do you ever do anything wrong in your eyes?"

"Everything I do is wrong, Gaylen, according to you!"

A woman guiding four children into the ice cream shop stopped and stared at Delia.

I unlocked the car doors. Delia clambered inside, still stewing.

We drove out of Clayton toward Dillard. "I need you to navigate for me." I handed her the atlas. "Aunt Amity showed me this back way up the mountain to Cashiers. It's easy to get lost, so try and keep us on the right road for once."

"See. That's what I mean. You got to get your digs in, like Mama." She slapped the atlas against her lap. As we meandered through Dillard, I saw the signs for the ski resort we would travel past to get to Cashiers.

She was quiet for the longest space of time, and then finally she said, "How much money did I get?"

"You won't get it all at once," I said.

"How much?" she giggled.

"It's in a trust."

"Are you going to keep me in suspense?" she laughed.

"Ten grand a year for a while," I told her. "But he left us a quarter mil. So we divide that; then your part will come to you once a year, ten thou at a whack."

"I'm rich, is that what you're telling me, Gaylen?"

"Not rich. You'll still need to work, Delia. But the house is paid for, and this will give you extra each year to help out with what you make at Hamby's."

She shouted all the way up the mountain, rolling down the window, hanging her head out and whooping, "Woo-hoo!"

The temperature was dropping to below freezing. "Get your window up, Delia," I muttered. "You'll catch something."

A cold November front followed us up the mountains.

Every few yards, we were in a different state. Delia yelled, "Welcome to Georgia!" and then "Welcome to North Carolina!" all the way up the steep slope that snaked along the state line.

The last vestiges of autumn had died, leaving leafy graves underneath the naked tree huddles in the mountain town of Cashiers. Fog lather-white rolled into the deer woods from Lake Glenville. Amity's cabin sat in a blanket of fog.

Delia and I hauled my bags into the cabin.

Amity's pantry was sparsely kept by the relatives: a half dozen cans of Campbell's soup, and, in the refrigerator, a half pound of cheese, a tub of margarine, and a bag of coffee rolled down to the bottom and clipped shut with a clothespin.

I grocery shopped down the mountain, leaving Delia to stay inside the cabin out of sight. I added a bag of apples, one loaf of bakery bread, a bottle of milk, and some lunch meat to the pantry.

Delia examined the small bags and said, "Why be such a cheapskate?"

My aunt's cabin was not typical of most of the getaways bought by retirees in Sapphire Valley. You see a lot of curios in those parts, like wooden carvings of black bears and wedding ring quilts, as well as the endless shelves of locally canned salsas and pickled okra.

Amity decorated her walls with dresses. The paintings were formed from actual dresses, dipped in paint, fastened to canvas, and then framed and hung on the wall. Primitive brush strokes left swirls in the dried paint that caught the light from overhead. There were specific designs painted onto the fabric, perhaps overlaid on the paint to give the dress back its original character yet not its original design. The designs were larger than textile art, more like the curlicues and paisleys were dropped onto the fabric rather than having been run through a factory stamp.

When my mother was alive, she and her friend Effie talked about Amity's cabin out of jealousy, so I had never quite sorted out the details about the paintings. But I had heard them tell about Amity's process. My aunt and her best friend, Cally, would pour paint into a washtub and then dip the dress. It would hang to dry for days on a clothesline she had strung across the garage. A line of paint splatters across the concrete garage floor alluded to that fact. She and Cally ran coat hanger wires through the dresses to give them a shape, like the blue and green one over her sofa that appeared to be waving. The dining-room piece was a wedding dress dipped in pink paint and adorned with beads. The dress was fastened to the canvas through some means invisible to me. In the corner was Amity's fine, cursive pencil explanation: *Boo's wedding dress. The beads are from my grandmother's necklaces.* That one appeared to blow in the wind from a backyard clothesline.

"What do you make of these things?" asked Delia.

I went room to room. Every room was decorated thematically to contrast its dress painting. An art dealer had tried to buy them once. Renni and Tootie wanted to sell them, Tootie especially, since she was always having money problems. But my father put his foot down and would not part with them. With Daddy gone, I expected that the dresses would soon disappear.

The dress framed and hanging over Amity's bed was the one that held my eye the longest. I put my things in that room and told Delia she could take the loft room, an arrangement that made her giddy

since the loft was the only room in the house with a TV. Lying flat
on my back, arm in a cast, I studied the careful folds of fabric fastened to the canvas, the tiny spatters of paint—yellow, blue, green,
ochre—dripping down a backdrop of burnt umber. The child's dress
was blood red. Amity's competing color choices contradicted the
palette for a young girl.

I fell asleep, and when I awoke, a smell seeped under the door.
Delia was burning something. "Delia," I yelled. "What's going on?"

I found her in the kitchen stirring soup.

"I was warming peas," she explained. "But they burned. I'm
making soup. You got bread and cheese and apples. That's dinner
where I come from."

I ate the soup and then scoured the burned pea pan. Mother
never wanted us girls underfoot while she cooked. Yet I picked up
cooking tips over the years like girls do. But not Delia. Southern
women pass that stuff around like little boys trade baseball cards, but
she couldn't cook beyond the warming of canned goods. I learned to
cook Braden's mother's potato casserole and my neighbor's mother's
jambalaya dish imported from New Orleans. Braden never wanted
warmed-up soup. He expected me to cook a meal every evening like
his mother did. There was the first tense moment when we sat down
to eat each evening. I would not eat a bite until he had given me the
thumbs-up or -down. When he hated my cooking, he tensed up. I
could see the disapproval first in his face. He would lay down the
fork and say, "I'll go and get something edible for me." He did not
offer to buy dinner for both of us. He would put on his coat and
walk out of the apartment, jangling keys and covering his thinning
hair with a ball cap. He'd bring home a sack of fast food and sit down

in front of the TV alone to eat it. I would sit at the table frozen, as if I had to wait for permission to join him on the couch.

"The soup is good," I told Delia. "I like the taste of hot soup with cheese. Like, it warms up the cheese and sort of melts in your mouth with the hot vegetables."

"My special recipe," Delia lied.

I laughed.

"Finally, I made Gaylen Syler laugh."

I didn't correct her for calling me Syler.

I tried to call Braden but got no response, so I bathed after dinner. When I dressed, I noticed pencil writing scrawled in the corner of the red dress painting. Amity had written, *Dress found in Fiona's burning barrel last week*. The painting was dated May 1981. I was four years old.

I tried to see into the neck of the dress, but, of course the dress tag was coated too.

"Almost every dress is from a member of the family." Delia was standing at the foot of the bed. "Who's that one from?"

"From Mother's leaf burning barrel," I said. It must have been before she learned to compost. Once a leaf burning project turned bad when she set the yard on fire. The fire chief was mad at her for interrupting the men's bowl game.

"My dress or yours?" She came around to the side of the bed and examined the dress. "Mama's burning barrel?" she asked.

"Is it yours?" I asked.

"Ruffled hem. I hated those ruffles. Eventually, it could have been. I wore your hand-me-downs."

My mother burned the leaves at the end of autumn. But she never burned our clothes. She and Daddy argued when she bought the fabric to sew those dresses. I studied the lace around the collar, now made stiff by the paint. "Who did she give our dresses to after you?" I asked.

"Girl cousins."

"Amity and Malcolm never had children."

"Coulda been torn or maybe stained," said Delia.

I could not find a tear, at least on the front of the dress but, since the dress was covered over with paint, who could tell? "She didn't pass it on. Must have been worn out."

Delia rummaged through the books in Amity's bookcase, selected a romance novel, and disappeared up to the loft bed to watch the war.

On either side of Amity's bed were nightstands, both white, but with tole paintings on the drawers; Amity may have painted the flowers on the drawer fronts. I dug through the drawers looking for an ink pen. In case the paintings disappeared, I planned to record the notes Amity had written on each one. I decided I might buy a disposable camera and snap photos of the paintings. Things disappeared from my mother's kitchen following her funeral. I could never say that it was Tootie looking for a pawnshop item to sell, but she had keys to the cabin the same as Renni and me.

That is when I thought of taking the red-dress painting while it was still to be had. Amity had used either my dress or Delia's on the canvas, so either of us could lay some sort of claim to it. I took it off the wall. That is when I found a note taped securely to the back of the painting. It read, *Please give this painting to my niece, Gaylen Boatwright.* My old address was written under my name. Amity had left me the painting, but to my knowledge no instructions to inform me of the bequest.

It occurred to me then that no one, not my father or his sisters, knew that Amity had left the painting to me.

I walked around the cabin, pulling each painted dress off the wall and finding another of Amity's notes. Behind the canvas of another dancing dress hanging in the living room were instructions to give it to Amity's friend, Luce Dawson. Luce's telephone number was included with the address. I had never heard Amity talk about Luce. Renni never brought her up, nor did my mother. I took down each painting, and arranged them around the living room.

Delia looked curiously down at me. "Redecorating?" she asked.

"Amity left instructions on the backs of the canvases. She left the red dress to me."

Delia ran down the stairs. She took one off the wall. But she was disappointed when she did not find her name taped to it.

"It's only because she didn't have one of your dresses," I told her.

"So the red dress was yours," she said.

"Must have been," I said.

Delia asked, "What made you look?

I thought about telling her that I was dusting it, and then I said truthfully, "I was thinking about taking the one over Amity's bed."

She forced a laugh.

"She's clearly left it to me," I said.

"But you didn't know that at the time."

"I do now." One of the framed dresses measured over five feet in height. "We might get a few in the trunk, maybe one in the backseat."

"Renni and Tootie will scream, Gaylen, if they find them missing."

"They will sell them. We can make sure they go where they're supposed to go," I said.

The phone rang. It was Braden. I walked out of the living room and onto the front porch, the only way to get a cell phone signal.

He asked, "Is your sister Delia with you?" He sounded confused, probably because he expected me to say, "Of course not." He knew Delia and never expected to find us spending the weekend together.

But something in his tone made me ask, "Who wants to know?"

"A guy called the house, asking for you. When I told him you were at your father's, he said he was looking for your sister. He thought you might tell him where he could find her."

"But not Cashiers. You told him I was in Boiling Waters."

There was a pause.

"I think I said that. Did I know you were in Cashiers? I can't remember. But I told him I'd pass along the message. If you see Delia, will you let her know her friend Mason Freeman is coming to town?"

I could hear him breathing.

Braden asked, "Do we know Mason Freeman? Are you all right, Gaylen?"

I told him I would call back, that Delia and I had to go. "Delia, help me cart the paintings out to the car. I'll get my things."

"We're leaving?"

"Mason Freeman might know we're here."

"Mason Freeman called your place?" Delia stared up the mountain slope at the road curving from town and meandering into the cottage neighborhoods.

I put one painted dress in the backseat, and Delia and I stacked four in the trunk, laying bed sheets between each one. I made cheese sandwiches from the leftover food. When Delia saw me packing a lunch away between the car seats, she said, "We got a quarter of a million between us, but my sister's making cheese sandwiches."

I locked up the rear of Amity's cottage. The house was a dusty cavity without her painted dresses. I turned off the lights and locked the front door behind me. Delia was already waiting in the car. "Sophie must have ratted me out," she said. "She never was fit for nothing."

I reached into the backseat and pulled Amity's taped note from the back of the painting. "Amity's friend doesn't live far from here. Let's take it to her. One less painting taking up space." The delivery of the paintings, as I saw it at that particular moment, had one useful merit. I was convinced at the time that a winding road trip would throw Mason Freeman off Delia's scent.

Luce Dawson lived in a brick and frame ranch house covered over with oaks and mountain laurel. She stood in the picture window looking out, taking a drag on her cigarette. She was a black woman, her hair combed down tight and pulled into a ponytail.

She was happy for visitors, her face registering out-and-out shock when we gave her the painted dress. "Do you know why Amity gave me this dress?" she asked.

Delia pulled out her pack of cigarettes.

"I don't know everything about my aunt," I said.

"Dolly, her sister, and me was best friends. She was killed in a car crash."

Amity had never talked about her sister. It seemed that Amity had a life she kept separate from the Sylers. *Preserved* may have been a better word.

Luce and I propped the painted dress against the wall next to the fireplace. She could not take her eyes off it. She sniffed and wiped her eyes on her sleeve. She sat next to me on the long gold sofa that gave us a view of her woody front yard. "Dolly never liked Malcolm much, and she and Amity argued when they married. I think she was afraid that Amity would move away from Cashiers. When Malcolm took the job with Weyerhaeuser, he promised Dolly that he would bring her back to Cashiers once they had saved enough money. But she died before that. Amity never got over it."

Delia laughed nervously.

"Dolly loved going to flea markets and bargain basements. She found that dress in a store along the highway. I talked her into it. She wore it often, so it was exactly how I remembered her." She put her cigarette in the ashtray she cradled in her lap. "It was the only thing I wanted. But I stopped going to see Amity. That was wrong, I guess. I never knew what came of the dress."

I asked her, "Did you know about the painted dresses?"

"I saw the one she hung over her bed," she said. "Little girl's dress. Belonged to her niece. She said that Malcolm's family was troubled. Her sister-in-law threw out one of her children's dresses, but Amity saved it."

I put down the glass of tea that Luce had given me. "Why would she throw away a dress?"

"Law, I don't know." She offered me more tea. "Amity saved that little dress as if that woman would want it back. Amity was like that, always redeeming things that got thrown out."

"Did Dolly and Amity ever speak again?" I asked.

"Amity never said. You know I might have tried to stop Amity from covering over that dress with paint. But now that I see it, dancing like that, it's like Dolly's come alive in it."

I helped Luce hang the dress over the fireplace after that.

Delia was in a lighter mood. The sun was disappearing. She talked all the way down the mountain. "I'm not surprised Mama kicked Truman out of the house, though. She tried to make me leave, but where was I supposed to go, I ask you?"

It was hard to tell if Delia was spinning another of her fables, so I changed the subject. "The next stop is closer to home. The rest of the dresses belong to relatives all out on the Outer Banks," I said.

Delia pointed, excited. "Apple stand!" Patio lights were lit up around the eave of the tourist shop roof. Delia jumped out as if she had never seen so many apples.

A man dressed in a bloodstained apron gave her a bag to fill. He apologized for the apron. "Sorry, ladies. A friend of mine brought me a deer to skin not an hour ago, and I been running back and forth from the kitchen to the stand." His breath was like rotted fruit.

I paid him for Delia's apples. He watched us trudge back across the gravel lot, but I told myself he wasn't watching us in any sort of queer manner. Before I was strapped into the seat, though, he appeared at my window. "You girls look like a nice pair. Sisters, are you?"

"What's it to you?" asked Delia.

I touched her leg.

"Fella kind of rough looking stopped at my stand right about the time I was hauling that deer out of the truck. Sure as all get out he described the two of you." He lifted up and helped me close the car door. I rolled down my window to hear him say, "Probably nothing, but I know people. He had a look about him and a bad suit, like no suit I ever seen on a man."

Delia started muttering and shaking her head.

I thanked the man and drove away. We found a small motel off the highway where we could sleep for the night. We had to share the bed. Fishermen had converged on the motel leaving nothing to rent but a single occupancy room.

When my eyes finally closed, she was giggling. She said, "We should have done this a long time ago."

7

I SLEPT LATE the next morning for the first time since we had left Boiling Waters. I shook Delia awake. There was a small mom-and-pop café close to the interstate ramp. We ate and got onto the interstate headed back to the coast.

She was reading a brochure picked up at the apple stand about a giant block of granite in the side of the Blue Ridge Mountains. Rock climbers wanted to buy the granite mass and were holding a fund-raiser. Delia did not understand the point of paying for the preservation of this giant mass of rock. I knew her well enough to know that if I explained the preservationist's creed, she would continue to argue her point, ignoring my explanation. She didn't really mean that she wanted to know the answer, so instead of answering her, I stared straight ahead at the snaking highway that we rolled along on together like a pinball.

We were nearly down the mountain, avoiding talk about Mason Freeman, when she asked, "What made you and Braden break up?"

My mind was on the granite, not Braden, at that exact moment. Delia, in her simplistic manner, fired and spoke. So I said what everyone says when they don't want to admit that they've screwed up a relationship. "We're having trouble communicating. It's complicated."

"He's cheated on you, hasn't he?"

Maybe it was our high elevation that swamped reason. I defended Braden while forgetting to watch my own back. "You've got it wrong. Braden's not perfect, but neither am I."

"I can't imagine you doing that," she said.

I could have coasted the remainder of the way down the mountain ridge without asking, "What makes you say that?"

She was quiet for the space between two mile markers. "You'd never do that, Gaylen, would you? Cheat on Braden?"

"That's an ugly question."

"But you didn't answer." She gasped, and then she pointed at me, her pointer finger spinning. "Nuh-huh!"

"You think I'm incapable of being bad, is that it?"

Delia threw back her head in glee. She laughed and slapped the top of her leg.

"Why do you think everyone is perfect?" I asked. "There's nothing about me that is essentially good."

She kept laughing maniacally.

I hated Delia more than I had ever hated her. At first I thought it was because she was laughing at me in my vulnerable state. But it was more than that. She could drink and have sex with different men and everyone expected it of her. But me, I had to make the right choices and put on a front for the Sylers and go to church alone on Sundays while Braden slept in. I was the good wife, the obedient daughter. "I'm only funning you, Delia. You're right. I wouldn't," I lied.

Delia fell quiet and then looked sad. "I didn't know what to say. You're the only hope I have that there's good in the world."

A Sunday school scripture came back to me. It must have stuck inside of me like a poppy seed in a kidney. "There is no one good. No not one," I said.

In the same manner that Aunt Renni believed that I would rise above my parents' emotional struggles, Delia believed that I was good; a good wife, a good daughter, a good person. When she was with Lee, she sent me a birthday card with an angel on the front. It was the only card she ever mailed to me. She had drawn an arrow that pointed to the halo and scrawled, "this is u." Since she was not overly fond of me and harbored a growing resentment dating back to the way we warred through most of our younger years, it seems that it would hit her that if I were truly good, the same goodness she saw me doling out to Braden or my mother would be given to her too.

The foothills were dotted with small jump-started towns that had sold their colloquial souls to franchised restaurants and strip malls. "Let's stop to eat," I said. It was already thirty minutes short of the noon hour. "But not here. Asheville."

"But you're still the person I know, aren't you?" she asked.

I wanted to tell her to pipe down, that I was the oldest, the smartest; she could never understand me. But even I did not know why I had failed my husband. I had never been able to answer Braden completely confident that I knew the answer, so what to say to her was even less clear. Revenge, I said once, because of a flirtation Braden had had with a nineteen-year-old college girl. But even that was not completely the reason. Something that I couldn't put into words had divided my soul. Explaining it to Delia while she wallowed in a curious, self-satisfied euphoria would be more painful than I imagined in my worst horrors. "I'm like everyone else, Delia; the Gaylen that people think they know and then another Gaylen."

She lit a cigarette as if she knew I wouldn't stop her. "I get that," she said.

While we took the Georgia pass up through Sky Valley ski resort on the way to Cashiers, we came back the route most tourists take, through Interstate 40. Braden told me once the Georgia pass would cut two hours off the trip. After what the apple seller told us, though, I wish that I had gone the back way home through Georgia too. Mason Freeman could be right behind us. I willed myself to stop watching the rearview mirror down the Carolina highway through Asheville.

"I need a beer," said Delia. "Something fierce."

I drove through the quaint town of Asheville and the bustling commerce around the Biltmore castle. Braden and I once stopped at La Paz for tamales. I figured Delia had tried only the canned kind. I made several wrong turns but finally turned up at the road that encircled the restaurant. I parked in the only space left open by shoppers out in full force.

We took the indoor seating although the sun had come out and the temperatures climbed into the sixties. I was more at ease hiding inside the darkened barlike restaurant.

Delia ordered a Corona while I got a club soda. She greedily gulped down salsa and blue tortillas, swigging it all down with beer. I asked for a taste of the Corona. "Don't stare, Delia," I said. I sipped her beer and tasted it with the food. I had to take several swigs before I understood the flavor that Braden once tried to explain to me. The beer was bland, but Delia liked how it mixed with the blue corn chips.

"You want one, ma'am?" The waitress had come to refresh the tortilla basket.

"I'm a sweet tea person. Don't have much of a taste for it," I said.

"Ever try a Long Island iced tea?" the server asked.

Delia laughed. She knew more about booze and boys than me in high school, so she was laughing at my lack of knowing how to order a drink. At least that's what I thought. "I'll have one of those," I said and then added, "Keep them coming."

The tamales arrived, and by then we were on our second drink. Delia was impressed with the food. The men she dated or married had never seen her as the kind of woman to take to a restaurant.

I asked her about Freddy. "What made you decide to date a married man?" I asked. "Or did you know?"

"I fell in love with Freddy. He was nice to me."

The drink was taking effect. I felt relaxed. I ordered us a bread pudding to split.

"I see the way you look at me, like Mama used to look at me, Gaylen," she said. "I know you judge me."

"Worry and judging are not the same," I said.

"No one asked you to worry about me. Did I?" She set down her empty bottle. "I did not."

The waitress cleared away the bottles and placed the bread pudding between us. "Anything else?"

Delia held up three fingers, pinky finger out.

"Another Corona. I guess you're finished, ma'am," she said to me. "Those Long Islands will put you on your back."

I thought she was kidding. "One more," I said. "Delia, did it occur to you that I don't like to see you used by the men you let into your life?"

"My choice," she said.

I knew that. But I remembered the day that Lee told her he was leaving. She was nearly violent. Mama was afraid that she would hit one of us. "Give me one reason to leave you to your own devices, Delia. I'd like to know that you're going to be all right."

"Daddy never let me figure things out on my own. He told me every move to make."

But she had gone to him for everything she could not buy with her small paycheck. Daddy owned her through the conduit of her dependency on him. "Why didn't you go and live your own life then?" I asked.

"I've had bad luck."

The waitress set the two drinks on the table and then handed me the check.

I finished my drink, not saying much of anything. I paid the waitress with the bank card I had ordered when Daddy gave me access to his account to pay his bills after he fell so ill. He sat on the edge of the leather lawyer's chair, one knee pointed at the floor, signing power of attorney over to me. I had not bought myself so much as a stick of gum with that card, so it seemed wrong still to finally spend his money on me.

I was having a bit of trouble with the signature line. "Can you drive us?" I asked Delia. She laughed at me. She led me out to the car and buckled me in. I cried, knowing it was silly. I was missing Braden and angry that he had not called. I was mad at Daddy for leaving me to take care of Delia. She drove me to a motel to sleep it off. Funny, I thought about Mason Freeman and how for that instant I was not afraid of him. "Frason Meeman's a twit," I said. She was laughing at me when I gave her the bank card, and while she parked to check us in, I reclined the seat and slept like a dead woman in the car.

When I woke up the next morning, Delia had checked us into the Inn on Biltmore Estate, a luxury suite. Braden and I shopped for a mantel clock a block away not a year before that. Braden had asked about the cost of a room and I remember him whistling, then I got uptight knowing he wanted me to say that we ought to blow our last wad and stay.

She was playing a video game, sitting cross-legged at the foot of the bed.

I crawled up next to her. "Did you realize when you checked in how much it cost to stay at the Biltmore?"

Delia pointed to the bill on the nightstand. I rolled over on my back, the room ceiling moving overhead. "You can't spend money like that," I said. "Before you know it, you'll be broke."

She had figured out the beginner level of the game. Every time a space pod exploded, it reverberated in my head.

"You tied one on, that's for sure," she said. "I was tipsy, but not nothing like you. Still didn't know until this morning I put us in such a posh place. Got to admit, it's the life."

She was wearing a hotel gift-store T-shirt with the sleeves rolled up to her shoulders. I noticed a tattoo I hadn't seen before. It was a daisy, small but palpable on the white surface of her right shoulder. "When did you get that?" I asked.

"Same time you did," she said.

I sat up, feeling like my head would burst open like a grapefruit on the highway. Pulling up the sleeve of the blouse I'd slept in, I slid off the bed and looked at the plain daisy tattoo in the mirror. The faint white petals and gold center were familiar. Delia and I dressed alike as girls, until I stopped all of that nonsense. Our last twin outfit was a white knit top stamped with daisies, Delia's favorite flower.

On the dresser top was a tattoo needle in a zipper sandwich bag. Delia saw me looking at it and said, "You wanted to save it, like it was emotional for you. I never seen you drunk before. You're a slobbering drunk, crying and hanging on me." She continued to smile and kill the Masters of the Universe.

My tattoo was on my right shoulder, the same as hers.

Delia kept laughing while losing the video game battle between the planets. Not since she was seven and losing at battle on the playground had she cared to lose. She did not care then, either.

"We should have kept driving, Delia. This isn't far enough away from Mason Freeman," I said.

"Mason Freeman wouldn't look here, would he? Why would he? He'd never think of me hiding out in a castle."

Delia had a surprising way of making sense when I least expected it.

8

IT TOOK ALL DAY to drive to Edenton. If Amity had not left one of the dresses to Boo, I might have never pulled into the pretty coastal town. I did not know what caused Boo and Thomas to leave Boiling Waters and move to Edenton.

My dim recollection of the woman the Sylers called Auntie Boo was embedded in a single memory. It was at the foot of our driveway, back in the days when my father dumped gravel down the long rutted path from our house to the road to give his car traction, that Boo and I had an encounter that seemed like nothing and everything. Auntie Boo and her husband, Thomas, lived down the street from us. Thomas liked to fish in our pond. Boo mostly stayed home, but she needed the money, so she watched Delia and me while Mother worked a shift at Weyerhaeuser. Back then everyone could get a job there.

I recalled how I sensed Boo's impatience with Delia and me. I did not understand how women judged my mother back then, so I could only sense how I was treated. The further I distanced myself from the Sylers, I noticed as I came of age, the more respect I got.

Perhaps it was not me that she disliked, I reasoned on the way to her house. But dredging up memories from the mental files dating back to when I was a kid was risky. It seemed as if even back then I knew to store whatever I saw as if somehow, later on, an adult's perception would reinterpret the memory and cough up a secret.

When my mother took the job at the lumbermill, Delia and I needed a sitter. Boo lived close by. Most of my days with Boo are still in a fog. I recall only one moment.

Boo troubled over the mud puddle that formed at the foot of our driveway where I played after a summer storm. She might have thought that my mother was neglectful for letting me play in the mud hole. Or maybe it would not have mattered what I did; she saw it as another opportunity to judge my mother. But when she found me sitting in the clay soup of summer rain, she clapped her hands at me, telling me to get out. She marched me up the driveway and then hosed me down near the garage like she might a runaway Pomeranian. If in my adult life I ran into Auntie Boo at the mall, I'd not have known her.

"Have you listened to a thing I've said?" Delia asked. She startled me back to the present.

The drive down U.S. 17 lasted for a long stretch.

"You navigated us good," I told her. "Do you ever travel out of Boiling Waters?" I asked, with a bit of forced enthusiasm. We had been driving for over ten hours. The fatigue of the road was getting to me. The sun was setting on the cold day's end.

"I been to Southport. Went to Prospect once. That's where Leland's family's from." She looked around for a café.

We crossed the Chowan River driving into Edenton. Gum trees

shadowed the brown water running beneath the Chowan River Bridge. A single herring floated atop the water's surface, its scales glistening beautifully in the dying daylight. A sign read "The South's Prettiest Small Town."

"Looks like you take this exit," she told me.

I pulled from my jacket pocket the note on which my aunt had scrawled the address of Thomas and Maurabelle Brolin, the neighbors known by the Sylers as Uncle Tom and Auntie Boo.

I drove down Broad, and that took me into Edenton's downtown district, which was characteristic of the places tourists flocked to in the summer months in North Carolina. Instead of stretching malls populated with designer chain stores, the downtown was clogged with boutiques and shoe stores, each one owned, more than likely, by some person's aunt whose sole purpose was to service the locals with handpicked brands selected by a buyer whose taste reached for something beyond that place.

Delia said, "It's getting dark. I need a smoke."

I pulled into a parking space in front of a café. I went inside while Delia stopped on the sidewalk and lit a cigarette. A waitress in jeans and an apron seated me at a table that looked out on the main drag. A church was opening up across the street. People were getting out of cars dressed in jeans, not like we dressed back when I went to church with my mother. We dressed to the nines or else stayed home.

The waitress filled my water glass. I held up the note that had been taped to the back of the painted dress. "Do you know this street?" I asked.

She pressed open the note. Turning to a woman standing behind the counter, she asked, "Bonnie, you heard of Elm Street?"

Bonnie came out from behind the counter. "Sure, hon. I'll write it down." She wrote on the back of the note while saying, "You'll go up Broad back this way, make a left on Cyprus and right on Elm. About the only Elm I heard of anyway." Turning to the waitress, she said, "Flor, you ever notice all our streets is named after trees?" She then asked me, "You from out of town?"

Delia walked in blowing out a stream of smoke. She took the chair across from me. She was wrapped in a blanket pulled from my backseat. We both ordered a steak and a potato and then ate, watching cars pull up and people streaming into the church.

Bonnie, the cashier who may have also been the owner, checked out a middle-aged couple and then spoke to me over the register. "Hon, you need to try our pie. It's banana cream, but not like you've ever tasted."

Delia said, "I'll have some. Me and Gaylen here, we just inherited a quarter million."

Bonnie looked stunned.

I lowered my voice and said to Delia, "You're not supposed to tell people that. It's not kosher."

Delia laughed, "I want to shout to the world, Gaylen. You know how long I been on the down low with Freddy?"

"What is that?" I asked her, annoyed. "Some sort of hip-hop language?"

"I heard of it," said Bonnie, now fully committed to our conversation. "My kids are in public school. They pick up all sorts of lingo."

She warmed up to Delia, ignoring me. "Girl, if you got the dough, you ought to go down to the Nail It and get you some silk wraps." She held up her right hand, showing Delia her red nails, decorated with some sort of floral markings the color of irises.

Delia examined the fringed edges of her cuticles. "I've never had a manicure. Can we go, Gaylen?"

"Delia, you have to consider more than just what you want right this instant," I whispered.

"Oh, let her have some fun," said Bonnie.

"What are we talking about?" asked the waitress. She identified herself to Delia as Flor.

"These girls have inherited a million dollars," said Bonnie.

Customers were turning around in chairs, craning their necks to look at Delia and me.

It wouldn't have done any good to correct Bonnie, to tell her that it wasn't a million. To her a quarter of a mil, a mil, it was all the same.

Flor pulled up a chair next to Delia. "I know this guy that helps lottery winners with their budgets." She stopped as if struck by a sudden thought. "Not that you won the lottery. You don't have to tell me. But anyway this guy is a money wizard. He can take your money and help you multiply it, you know, like Donald Trump."

"I'm in," said Delia.

"Could we have the check?" I asked.

We pulled away in my car and drove onto the main drag of Edenton. Delia was still looking up and down Broad to find the Nail It boutique when I spotted the street sign marked Elm. We passed a yellow bungalow and several brick houses nearly covered over with shrubs. Delia was in a good mood, having exchanged phone numbers with Bonnie and Flor.

"If you trust every person you meet," I said, "someone could take advantage of you."

"Not Bonnie or Flor, Gaylen. They're nice. You know, you'd have more friends if you'd learn to open up."

"You're too trusting."

She loosened the blanket around her neck and turned the heat up. She laughed, disagreeing with me. "When you meet a certain person, you know right off the bat you can trust that person. Don't you know anything about people?"

I was counting down the addresses. I had not rehearsed what I would say to Boo as had been my custom when meeting new people.

Delia continued in her upward emotional spiral. "First I'm going to get silk wraps for my nails and then a toe ring. You ever own one of those?"

"Never thought to do that," I said. "How about we drop all talk of spending for the night?"

"You sound like Daddy."

"Until you met Bonnie or whatever her name is, Delia, you'd never heard of silk wraps. You're too easily sold."

"You know why you cheated on your husband?" she asked. "'Cause you never allow yourself any fun."

I spotted the address but hit the brakes too hard. Delia came out of her seat, her forehead narrowly missing the dashboard. "Cripes!" she yelled at me.

"Why did you say that, Delia?" I asked. "That I cheated on Braden?" My insides felt unsettled.

"How do you think? One little, two little, three little Long Island teas." She was enjoying her power over me.

I parked the car at the foot of the driveway. "You don't remember right because you were too drunk. You're making it up."

She sat back against her seat. Whether she was second-guessing her own drunken state that night was beyond surety. Finally, she lowered her voice. "He was a college professor, you said, name of Max something or other." She closed her eyes and inhaled, reaching out to touch the place on the dash that had almost been her undoing. "Does Braden know?"

I was rubbing my temples. "He knows, Delia. That's why we're separated."

"I'm glad Daddy didn't know. He died thinking you were perfect." A strange smile came over her face. "For some reason, though, it makes me like you better."

"For the rest of the night, I want you to keep your mouth shut," I told her. "The last thing we need is you spilling your guts to Boo and Thomas. They already think our family is nuts."

"How do you know that?"

"It's complicated. I somehow remember her that way." Explaining it was too tiresome.

An outside light came on near the front door.

"Can I have silk wraps?" she asked.

"All right," I acquiesced.

She clapped gleefully. I got out of the car and shut the door, although it did not muffle the sound of her glee.

My finger had scarcely touched the old doorbell when the front door opened. A man, probably in his early thirties, pushed a pair of eyeglasses up his nose. He had an intelligent look about him in that his eyes were reflective, like a man who reads a lot. But he was far too young to be Thomas. I steadied myself by touching the doorpost. Delia's confession left me feeling weak in the knees.

The man looked at me curiously for a moment before asking me my business.

"My name is Gaylen Boatwright. My aunt, Amity Syler, knew a couple by the name of Boo and Thomas Brolin."

He opened the door the rest of the way. "Name's Joel Brolin. Haven't heard my mother called Boo, though, in years." He laughed, putting me at ease.

"Are they home?" I asked.

Joel was reluctant to answer. "My mother passed on two years ago. My father's home, but it's not a good day."

Delia bounded up onto the porch behind me. "I'm Delia," she said, not quite as flamboyant as she had been in the café. It only took one glance at Joel for her to evaluate the man standing in front of us. Joel was in a higher caste, according to Delia's system of calculating human worth. It made her more reticent, and that was a relief to me.

Joel stuck out his hand to Delia. She shook it bashfully.

I was let down to find Boo no longer alive. I hardly knew what to do about the painted dress in my backseat. "My father, Amity's brother-in-law, recently died. My sister, Delia, and I are driving around meeting family members," I said, not knowing how else to explain our sudden appearance.

"A road trip. I took one myself when my mother passed on." He stepped back, opening the door all the way. "Please come in."

He led us into a room with bookcases built into nearly every wall, save the ones with windows.

"I'd offer you coffee, but I'm looking after Dad this weekend, and I'm lousy at keeping the pantry stocked."

"Is he sick or something?" asked Delia.

"Alzheimer's," said Joel.

Over the course of the next five minutes, I said, "I'm sorry," a half dozen times while Joel recounted Mr. Brolin's slow regression into Alzheimer's. Joel's sister Beverly had been the chief caregiver for Thomas. She had taken off for the weekend, leaving Joel to fill in.

"But don't think Bev is a saint for doing it," he said. "She hates it, but what do you do? I'm a starving photojournalist and gone most of the time. She's really stuck looking after Dad," he said.

"I understand that," I said. Except Delia could never have stayed over to look after Daddy for a single night without forgetting herself and running off into the night. "I had to hire hospice care for our father," I said.

"What does a photojournalist do?" asked Delia.

"Aim a camera and shoot at opportune moments." He sat on the edge of an upholstered chair as if any minute he might have to get up and leave. He smiled at Delia.

She was wearing her eyeglasses that darkened in bright sunlight. Either the front porch light or the bright lamp she was sitting under had shaded the lenses. She looked like a small owl perched in the chair, wide-eyed and lapping up Joel's attention.

"You have to like what I do. Not a lot of money in it anymore.

The camera industry's made it easy for every Tom and Dick to point a camera and produce brilliant photos," he said.

"We don't know about being poor anymore, do we, Gaylen?" Delia interjected.

I sighed, hoping that would be enough to silence her.

"We inherited a lot of money," she told Joel.

"Is your father in bed?" I asked.

Joel glanced down the hall and then told me quietly, "If I wheel him out here, I can't promise he'll behave. Alzheimer's makes him do wild things. He peed on the TV last night because he didn't like what Katie Couric was saying. But, if you can handle it, visitors help him focus."

I wanted to see Thomas's face to see if I could remember anything about him. "I'd like to meet him," I told him.

Delia was looking at the TV.

Joel got up, and I told him, "My Aunt Amity was an artist. She left your mother a painting. I'm sure you and your sister would like to have it."

Joel was surprised. "Now I know who you're talking about."

"I'll go and get it while you bring out Thomas," I said.

I took my time about putting on my coat, waiting for Joel to leave the room. Then I ran for the car. If I timed it right, Delia would have no time alone with him to say more than she ought to say.

The painting was cumbersome to pull out one-handedly. Under the interior car light, a fleck of blue paint fluttered off the canvas onto the floorboard. I slid the canvas out and then held it upright. It was Amity's biggest painting, tall as me and three feet wide. She had painted a clothesline behind the painting. The dress was attached to look like a piece of laundry, inanimate, yet animated in the moment by a brisk wind. Boo's dress was suspended for all time as arty laundry.

I set it against the door and looked inside. Delia was laughing and talking to a much older Thomas than I had remembered, a stooped-back, silvery gray fellow seated in a wheelchair. His hair hung to his shoulders, the flesh of his face sagging from high cheekbones, typical of southerners from Indian ancestry. I turned the canvas sideways and shoved it through the doorway. "Here she is!" I yelled, hoping to draw Joel's attention away from Delia's alacritous zeal.

"Gaylen, Thomas remembers you!" said Delia.

Joel was standing behind his father still holding onto the wheelchair handlebars. He cast his eyes dubiously at me.

Thomas turned to look at me. A smile came over his face, and he said, "What a relief. You don't look like your old man at all, Gaylen. I was worried."

I propped the painting against the sofa. "Amity Syler made this from one of your wife's dresses." I explained how Amity saved Boo's dress and fashioned the painting.

Thomas looked at the painting, thoughtfully. After studying it, he said, "I know why she gave up that one."

"How could you remember?" asked Joel. "It's covered in paint."

"I remember everything. What I don't remember, doesn't matter," said Thomas. He stared out through the window for an entire minute. The backyard was mostly black, the only light a dim yellow glow shining over a neighbor's fence.

Delia laughed, nervous in the silence.

Joel tried to read the pencil-scrawled note in the corner.

I knelt to get a better look at Amity's writing. "It says that Boo saved the dress from her wedding."

"I took her to St. Augustine," said Thomas. He continued to stare out into the dark backyard.

Joel looked surprised. "When did Mom give Amity the dress?" he asked.

"She was mad at me," said Thomas. "Threatened to leave me. I guess that was her way of saying it was over, you know. She wanted to scare bats out of me like women do. It was the dress she wore when she married me."

Joel could not take his eyes off the painted dress.

"Seems like we'd only lived in Boiling Waters a year as newly-weds when we had our first big one. Your mother liked visiting the Sylers, especially their pond. I found her sitting on the bank, mad as bees at me. Only time I ever heard her swear. She said she learned to cuss from me, but it was her daddy she learned it from."

"I remember you faintly," I told him. "But mostly I remember Boo."

"You suffered the most in those days," said Thomas. "I'll say that."

Joel stood behind Thomas, continuing to dismiss his father's recollections. He kept rolling his eyes, waving away his words dismissively.

Thomas's voice grew quiet and so nearly inaudible it caused all three of us to lean toward him.

I mouthed to Joel not to worry. He had warned us his dad was unpredictable.

"The day your mother sent that boy of hers away was the day I stopped worrying for you."

Delia sat back in her chair, for once not saying anything at all.

"He makes up a lot of stories," said Joel. "Dad, I'm going to take you back and help you into bed."

"I'm not making up anything," said Thomas. "Stop talking for me, like I'm some ignorant puppet!"

I knew that Joel probably wanted Delia and me to excuse ourselves. But Thomas was wound up and unstoppable. "Is it me you're talking about?" I asked him.

"What was the name of that brother?" he asked.

"Truman," said Delia.

"Your mama took a lot of flak for sending him away. Even your Aunt Amity was ashamed of her for putting her boy out."

"Dad, that's enough," said Joel.

"I don't mind," I told him, but it was a polite cover. I wanted Thomas to spill out what the Sylers had covered up.

Thomas got quiet. A peaceful look softened the old man's face. Joel apologized for him and explained that he had told a lot of stories, none of them true, about him and Beverly. He fell asleep. Joel wheeled him out of the room.

On the way out of Thomas's house, I was trying to remember what Mother had told me about Truman. Nothing was coming, but while she complained about Truman, she never told me he had hit me or even laid a finger on me. That was not the Truman I remembered, the passive boy taking a flogging from her. I was squeezing my brain to jolt loose a fogged-over memory.

"Truman was a bad kid," said Delia, running to keep up with me.

I stopped and looked at Delia over the top of the car. "Where are we going next, Delia? I can't remember."

9

EVERY FALL MY MOTHER and father took Delia and me to the Cumberland County Fair. You don't hear much about them in cities, but fairs are still to this day a town gathering place. In southern counties that harbor a small town at the epicenter, people gather in blithe celebration of small things like new calves and home-canned piccalilli relish. The summer I turned nine, my mother schemed to win a county fair ribbon for a long-stemmed rose entry. She worked to perfect a single rose stem, blooming petals as pink as a baby's mouth. She cut away leaves and any branch that might suck nutrients and prevent that one long stem from growing straight into the sky.

We piled into the family Chevy, being told to guard our small denim purses and the cash saved over the summer. Carnies were known to be experts at picking your pocket, according to Mother, but worse, they took little girls about our age to be their wives. Delia was excited at the thought of being kidnapped and whisked into gypsy love. Mother digressed back into worry over the grand-prize ribbon. She steeled herself and all of us for the coming disappointment. She believed that only the closest friends of the Fayetteville socialites who judged the competition could win the grand-prize ribbon. I don't know if the socialites were imagined or if they really congregated with nothing else to do but knock my mother out of a long-stemmed rose competition.

While Delia headed straight for the midway and the Tilt-A-Whirl ride, I poked around, curious about what might go on behind the scenes. I wanted to know where the carnies lived and what they ate away from the saccharine stench of cotton candy. One large brown tent erected behind the livestock pavilion advertised nothing in particular, and it was curiosity that sent me wandering into its dark bowels.

Four men seated in folding chairs and wearing dress pants waved at me, urging me to come inside. I hung back, not because of potential kidnapping, but because I was surprised by their appearance. Not any one of them looked oily, as I expected a carny to look. One guy asked me my name.

"Gaylen," I said and then apologized for interrupting their meeting.

"Not at all," he said. He had cheeks small and tight as cherries, and shiny as if freshly licked. "We tell stories." He held up a ribbon and asked if I'd like to hear the ribbon story.

I knew that I should back out, but it was his kind eyes that lured me all the way into the tent.

He tucked the ribbon into both hands, made fists, and pulled his fists apart exposing a two-inch black strip of the ribbon. He called it sin. I was so glad he wasn't a kidnapper that I relaxed. It was my first time to hear a synopsis of the human condition according to church people. I could never recall exactly all of the metaphors he explained to me on his ribbon ladder to heaven of black, yellow, and green, but what I remembered best was the way he made me feel. He asked if I'd pray with him, and it being so natural, I did. When he asked, "Will you follow God from this point on?" I answered that I would, of course, although following God was a clump of mystery to me. My mother had always called me her good child. So I figured I'd not backslide. If there was one thing I had gained under the Sylers's roof, it was the ability to move through life without a ripple or a transgression.

Driving Delia away from the Brolin's house, I debated about what had happened to me along the way that changed me. I had slipped back across that ribbon, tumbling into the black more easefully than even Delia, who was the best backslider I had ever known.

"There's a bed-and-breakfast," I said to Delia. A light inside the Victorian inn made the window shades look like nodding eyes. "We can park in the back, you know, to hide the car."

Delia did not move for a moment. She stared past the inn. She wrapped her arms around her chest, cradling herself, I thought, because she was cold. Finally she said, "I done something bad, Gaylen." She kept staring out through the car window, not looking at me. "What gets into me?" After asking that, she turned and finally looked at me with the most confessional eyes she'd ever allowed.

Answering Delia was a tricky proposition. If she really wanted to know, she would be mad at me for not answering. If it was her way of trying to shed herself of the guilt of shooting Sophie Deals, then somehow I was supposed to figure out that she was speaking out loud to work through the guilt. "What do you want me to say?" I asked.

"Tell me if I'm crazy," she said.

"Delia, you've got some money now. You know you could see a doctor."

"I guess that answers my question."

I was tired. I felt angry with my mother at that moment, even though it made no sense to be thinking of her when Delia was having a crisis of the conscience.

"Does everyone think that of me? Like, when I'm not around, do people talk about me? Do they say, 'Delia's crazy'?" She paused only long enough to answer her own question. "People think that I don't know, but I do. What do they think, that I'm stupid too? Crazy and stupid ain't the same thing."

If I laughed, she'd get mad at me for that. But she contorted her face as she might have done when she was six years old. Her bottom lip was thrust out and she looked like she could club a person. But she never could hit hard, even when in a rage, because of her frail frame. Tall and lanky do not equate to taking someone down. Maybe that was why I finally laughed, because I knew that she couldn't stop me.

"You always have to make fun of me," she said. She opened the car door and pulled the blanket around her shoulders.

"Tomorrow, you have to buy yourself a coat," I said, still laughing.

"I would, but then I got to ask you," she said. "And I don't want to ask you for nothing." She slammed the car door shut and hiked across the backyard, her boutique sneakers slipping on the cold night dew.

I stepped out onto the gravel-littered parking lot. "I'll give you some money," I said, but she did not answer. "Spend it any way you want."

The innkeeper must have heard us drive up. The back porch light came on.

My phone went off playing "Loser" by Jerry Garcia. I had set the ring tone on "Clair de Lune," not being one to spend time changing out my phone's ring tone or buying rock song tones. Delia had changed it behind my back. She was sending me a message. Delia stepped onto the porch, still wrapped in the green blanket, and disappeared inside the house.

"You're not stupid," I said, too late.

Braden was finally calling. He sounded mad. Instead of asking him about it, I sat breathing into the phone.

"Your boss called. Did she call you?" he asked.

"She didn't," I said. But come to think of it, Braden was the first to call all day. "But we've been in the mountains, and I haven't had a signal."

"That agent you hired is kind of young. Your boss doesn't know how well she's managing with you gone."

"Kimberly's fine. I'm taking personal time," I said. "I never do, and I want to use it up before the year's out."

"Where are you, Gaylen? We need to get together and talk about things."

"Delia's in some trouble. Any cops come around?"

"Cops?"

"She has that drug dealer Mason Freeman mad at her." I still couldn't bring myself to tell him Delia shot Sophie.

"Let her work it out then. Take her back to Boiling Waters and drop her off. Come home. Delia wouldn't risk anything for you, so why gamble your own neck for her?"

"She's not right in her head, Braden. And now with Daddy gone, who would look after her?"

He didn't answer.

"I was going to settle her into Daddy's house. But now everything's upside down. I don't know what to do." I wanted Braden to fix things, but the last time I hoped for that was the last time we argued. "Do you miss me at all?" I asked.

"Gaylen, while you were gone I talked to the attorney."

"What about waiting on me, for us to talk it all out?" I asked. "We agreed."

"We were playing cards one night, and the next thing I knew I was signing papers."

Delia stuck her head out of the door, looking at me. I imagined the innkeeper was asking for a form of payment.

"If I tell you where I am, I want you to come here." I blurted out. "We'll talk. You know you don't mean any of this." I looked for an inn sign, but couldn't see in the dark. "I'm at an inn up the coast in Edenton."

"I'm supposed to fly a client to Concord at sunrise." Braden sounded more detached than the night he left the apartment.

"Gaylen, this woman wants money!" Delia yelled from the back porch.

"I have to go," I said. I was about to ask him again to come to Edenton. But I couldn't think of how to say it. Braden hung up. I climbed out of the car, carrying my overnight bag up the hill and stuffing the phone into the pocket.

Delia was smiling. "We are living like queens," she said.

I checked us each into a room, giving Delia her own place to sleep and me my own place to cry.

My mother was an upright woman. I lay in bed saying it, thinking about her, staring up at the Victorian ceiling made of painted-over tin squares. I imagined her triangular mouth when she was mad, talking about Delia and her endless list of transgressions. She liked talking about morals, about the haves and the have-nots of morality, like the woman who taught us girls Sunday school at the small Assemblies of God church she occasionally attended. Mother felt that women in the rank and file of church life looked down on her the same as the Sylers. Mother would say, "Her nose gets any higher, and she'll need a ladder to blow it." She liked organizing her ideals into a self-defense argument. Maybe she was preparing her case for Judgment Day, or maybe she was just tired of being put down by the Sylers.

But she included me in her self-justification; maybe I was her justification. But that's a post too big for any kid.

I felt her swell of pride when she dubbed me as virtuous and Delia as wicked. But she was as wrong about me as she was about everything else in our lives she had summarized into a list of good and evil.

I stripped down in the bed-and-breakfast room, taking off every-thing that smelled of riding in the car all day with Delia smoking. My clothes smelled of the sundry contents of my car: the bag of ap-ples in the backseat smelling overripe, Delia's leftover supper from Bonnie's café, and the cheese sandwiches still wrapped up like dead things in plastic wrap. I threw my blouse, my bra, my jeans that smelled potent after having my body compressed into them all day, and my pale yellow underwear onto the cold, flowery, linoleum floor. I stretched out across the bed, naked and crying. I turned off the phone so that I wouldn't know how long it did not ring.

As little as I had confessed to Max, he could not have known me, seeing only the side of me that coveted his pity and affirmation. I re-called his tiny ocean cottage, the sunroom where we sipped coffee and listened to the ocean by night with the sliding door open. He gave me what I wanted so that I would give a lonely professor a warm body to curl up next to.

"Are you comfortable?" he asked.

"Sure," I lied. I wore his robe over my swimsuit, a blue-striped terry-cloth covering that had aged over a decade without his notic-ing the frayed sleeves and hem. We had taken a swim near the shore. I was too afraid to go out far.

"Are you sorry you came?"

I kept looking toward the ocean, as if waiting for some good thing to come out of the black.

"I still can't believe you're here," he said. By that, he might have meant that he was shocked that he played a seduction card with a student and it worked. But I did not question him or his motives. At least, not the way I questioned Braden. "Do you think about me when you're at work? What am I like as a lover? If I were crippled, would you still stay with me?" Max got none of that side of me, just the simplistic pillow talk that does not require explanations.

Come to think of it, Braden might have liked me better if I'd given him the same safe distance.

"I'm not what you're used to," he said. "Your husband, he's young, I know."

"Maybe I don't want what I'm used to," I said but then realized what a cliché we were, sitting there trying to make the awkward seem exciting.

The heat was not working right, and the room was cold. I curled up on the bed, holding my knees against my chest. My own skin felt thin, like a veil that could not cover me up. I pulled the coverlet over me, deciding that if I died trying to freeze myself, being found naked and blue would only give Braden one more criticism to lay at my cold, lifeless feet.

I sipped a glass of white table wine that the innkeeper, calling herself Mrs. Buckhorn, offered Delia and me in the parlor after I'd checked us in. A realization came to me. I did not like white wine, even though I pretended to like it when Braden bought us a bottle for our last anniversary. I shoved the glass aside on the nightstand. Then I closed my eyes and slept, until three in the morning, got up and pulled on a sweatshirt and the Felix the Cat pajama bottoms.

A car door slammed outside. I slipped to the window and looked out. The moon was covered over, but a porch light left on turned everything in sight to sulfur. I blinked, believing my eyes weren't seeing straight, at the man holding a cardboard box and walking across the back lot. He paused short of the rear porch. He searched around the lot until he looked directly at my car. Then he picked up the pace, aiming for the porch. In the brighter light, I could see him, my husband. Braden knocked on the back door. The window rattled.

I turned on the nightstand lamp and riffled through my suitcase until I found my mangy blue house slippers. I put them on, and found myself looking into a vanity mirror, silver with longitudinal age streaks. My brown hair was falling aside my face, my cowlick exposed. I combed through my hair with my fingers and pulled it into a ponytail.

I walked out into the hallway. The innkeeper had left a table lamp turned on near the top of the stairs. The smell of smoke wafted from under Delia's door even though Mrs. Buckhorn had told us that under no circumstances was smoking allowed in a historical inn.

I ran downstairs, stubbing my foot against a table leg, trying to make it to the rear door in less than a minute. Through the door sash, I saw Braden's thinning hair aimed at the glass as if he was looking down. My face was flushed and full of blood. I could feel my veins pumping in my temples. The bottoms of my feet tingled as I slid across the floor, nearly tripping right dead in front of him. When I opened the door, he looked like a delivery boy holding a box. His hair was wet and combed to one side.

For a long and rather sickening minute, neither one of us knew what to say. I should have delayed, I thought, not rushed to meet him. In the nocturnal light, he was aged by a good five years. Braden was not the largest brother out of the two whopping men the Boatwrights had birthed. I had dated short men and tall men and always liked that he could hold me standing up without our eyes glaring straight into one another; we could have sex and fit like nesting cups. But his posture was stooped, and he looked down at me, holding a box as if he was going to hand it to me and leave.

I spoke first. "Did I tell you I was here?" I could not remember.

"An inn, you said, in Edenton. I drove 'round looking. I saw your car." He wasn't making eye contact. "You know your oil is due for a change. You missed your doctor's appointment. Want me to cut that cast off for you?"

His nose was swollen, and when he finally stepped into the harshly lit hallway, his skin looked ruddy and bruised. He handed me the box, saying, "These are your brother's belongings. Your Aunt Renni said it came to the house while you were gone. She found it on the porch; thought maybe you'd want it."

The box had been opened. When I fingered the torn tape, he said, "I didn't open it. Renni does what she wants."

The address label was stamped with an address not far from Boiling Waters, but I had never visited that town. "Who would send me this?"

"Renni said a note was attached saying that your brother had left his things at someone's house. When he was sent off, they didn't want to be responsible for keeping his things. That's what she thought."

I walked into the living room, and Braden followed. We sat near the cold fireplace. "You get in a fight?" I asked.

He stared at the floor and finally looked up at me. "Your sister's made enemies with the devil," he said. "She upstairs?"

I nodded. "Asleep."

"You never got all tangled up in her business before." He said it like his disappointment in me had grown since our last fight.

"I know." The cardboard box smelled like a house closed up too long. I placed it on the floor. "I wanted her to tell the police."

"The law would be kinder than Mason Freeman."

"Have you seen him?"

"No."

"That's a relief."

"He sent a guy with a message. Delia nearly killed Sophie Deals. If she dies, he won't stop until she's dead. Even if she lives, Delia's toast."

"Is Sophie in the hospital?"

Braden regarded me as if he could not believe we were having that discussion.

"I hate it when you look at me like that," I said.

"When a drug-dealing loser shows up to beat you up, you don't sit down and have a conversation."

I felt sick. "Was it tonight?"

"Right after I talked to you. I gave him a dose of his own, though." The Boatwright boys were known as brawlers. "I pounded him, ran him off. But Freeman won't stop there, sending a two-bit thug to do his dirty work."

"I should've come home today."

"He would have gone after you, and then I'd be in jail for killing him."

I was going to say that I was sorry for hurting him. But he did not stay long. He had flown to a nearby private strip. He had a new client to fly into Kentucky the next morning. I was only a stopover.

Mrs. Buckhorn found me asleep on the couch. On the floor were Truman's belongings and my unsigned divorce papers. She did not ask me why I was on the couch but said, "Breakfast is in the front room." "Front" meaning a small room to the side of the kitchen used for days when the inn was not full of guests.

We ate French bread and a warmed currant jelly. She cooked our eggs to order. Delia hovered over her plate, picking at her food, her hair hanging over her eyes. "You ever sleep in?" she asked.

"At a B&B you eat when breakfast is served." I had told Mrs. Buckhorn when we would get up, of course. Delia had to get some discipline about her.

"What's in the box?" Delia asked me. The box was between us on the floor.

"Something belonging to Truman," I said. I picked up the box, tucking the divorce papers under it. I pulled back the flaps. Inside was a pencil drawing of a man, shaven head, eyes like Mother's.

"That's a drawing of Truman," said Delia.

"How do you know?" I asked.

"He looks like Mama," she said. "I didn't know he was an artist."

"Maybe he didn't draw it," I said. But then she pointed to his signature. Besides the drawing, the box held a couple of pencils, a few receipts, and a locket. I picked up the gold necklace, a delicate chain that was soft against my palm. The locket was tarnished. It opened. A photo inside was of a teen girl with dark hair. Her eyes were dark too, like Truman's. She might have been sixteen, but wasn't recognizable.

"How'd you come by it?" she asked.

Mrs. Buckhorn was pouring my coffee. I waited until she went back into the kitchen.

"Braden showed up," I told her. "He said Renni found it on Daddy's porch. She drove it into Wilmington and gave it to Braden. I figure she was wanting an excuse to see him, to see if I was there or if we were really split up."

"Nosy Ned." She was still holding Truman's self-portrait. "Are you split up for dead sure?"

I did not show her the papers Braden left for me to sign.

"What will you do with this stuff?" she asked.

"You can have all of it. I don't want it," I said.

"I'll put it up. Maybe if he comes back, he'll want it."

"Why would he come back?" I asked.

"I wrote to him."

"You shouldn't have done that."

Delia sighed. She opened her mouth to speak, but her jaw slid back, and she seemed to search for words. "That was back before I knew about him."

"What do we know anyway? What Mother knew, she took to the grave."

"Maybe Renni knows or Tootie. Maybe that's why they fought with Mama," said Delia. "Because of the secrets she kept."

"Tootie tells everything she knows. Wouldn't she have said something?"

"Would Renni tell?" she asked.

Renni was not one to divulge, I thought. "They don't care about us, Delia."

Delia put the drawing back into the box, laying it facedown inside the box. Then she picked it back up. "There's a phone number on this," she said. She reached for my cell phone.

"You don't know who you're calling," I said.

She dialed anyway. Her mouth fell open, happy when a person answered. She asked the person if they knew Truman Savage. Then she sat nodding. When she ended the call, she was smiling the same as when she had power over me, when she found out about Max Swinson.

Mrs. Buckhorn came to clear away the breakfast dishes. I slid her my plate and cup and saucer with my one good hand. She stacked up Delia's plates with mine and thanked us for stopping by. That was the last I saw of her.

"It was a woman," Delia gushed. "The last time she saw Truman, she said, he was asking her for money, but she would not give him a cent."

"Was she his girlfriend?" I asked.

"She didn't say that but sounded like she was mad at him."

"He had that effect, Mother once said."

Delia picked up the phone again. She called information and asked for the number for Angola Prison.

"Why are you doing that?" I asked.

"My turn to be Nosy Ned," she said.

"I'm going to get my suitcase," I said. I went upstairs. Delia's door was cracked open. I gave her room a look-see. Mrs. Buckhorn had already stripped her bed of the sheets. Delia's purse was all that was in the room. I still had not bought her luggage or clothes other than the one set of clothes we had bought on the road. Renni told me that Mother saw to Delia and kept up her wardrobe and sent her to the beauty shop for haircuts. I was not any better at seeing after her than my father.

I picked up her purse and pack of cigarettes, collected my things, and met Delia at the foot of the stairs. She was giddy. When she followed me out to the car, she said, "You're not going to believe this!"

I let her in the passenger side of the car and tossed my suitcase in the backseat. Once inside, she said, "I left a message for a man who counsels Truman. He's going to tell me everything."

"Of course he will," I said.

"I'm smart."

"You are, you are."

10

I WAS STARTING to believe that Delia had been right about Mother, that she was a woman of secrets, secrets I hated because they had been kept from me and might have been about me. I pictured my father and mother lying in the ground, their hands over their mouths. I imagined taking a sledgehammer to their pretty little headstones.

Delia muttered under her breath, tapping the pack of cigarettes with her thumb. She pitied me for having been abandoned by my husband. "Delia, be quiet," I said. Her pity wore me down, making the minutes seem longer and the miles pass slowly.

"Here all this time I thought you was a princess, like not anything bad ever happened to you. It just shows how wrong a person can be," she said.

"You know, Delia, you have your own problems, so don't worry about mine."

"I don't no such a thing. I got me a house, all the money I'd want. I'm home free."

"Mason Freeman went to Wilmington last night to make Braden

tell him where you are. Not him exactly, but one of his cronies." I couldn't bring myself to tell her he wanted to kill her.

"When were you going to tell me that?"

"Braden fought with him. That's when the thug told Braden that Sophie could die."

She fell quiet and that was my purpose for telling her anyway. "We have another painted dress to deliver," I told her. "It belongs to Renni."

"I didn't mean to hit Sophie," she said. "I was shocked as the next person. I just hate to, you know, act like anything bothers me."

"It's how we were brought up," I said.

We drove through Williamston and on to Rocky Mount. In that town, we found a Fred's store. Delia bought more clothes and a small suitcase. We took I-95 south to the longest stretch of interstate, as far as I know, in the country, I-40.

"How do I figure out how far we are from Siphon?" asked Delia.

"See that measurement gauge at the top of the page, the distance scale? Place your finger and thumb on it. How many miles does the scale say it will measure?"

Delia fiddled around with the map. "Twenty miles."

"Hold your fingers just so. Then place them where we are now on I-95. Keep moving it down the page until you get to Siphon."

"Six and a half times," said Delia.

"About a hundred and thirty miles," I said. "If we don't speed, so as not to bring attention, we will be in Siphon in two hours."

She turned around in her seat and dragged a shopping bag from the rear seat. She pulled out and opened a large boot box. "I like cowboy boots. I'm going to buy me a horse." She bought a cowboy hat too, a pale straw hat that folded up in curls on either side. She put it on.

"Daddy never kept a horse. He should have," I said, knowing that she would have forgotten about the horse by the time we got her home.

The countryside had gone dormant along I-95. The grass was blond and flat, the pale yellow of winter fading into the brown, empty backyard kitchen gardens. A sign along the road advertised smoked turkeys for Thanksgiving. "It's nearly Thanksgiving," I said.

"Say, Gaylen, let's put on a big feed. We'll strut into a ritzy restaurant. I'll wear my cowboy boots and hat, like I'm so rich I don't care what anyone thinks."

"Sure, Delia," I said.

"Aunt Renni will be surprised to see us. You think she'll be mad we took the dresses?"

"I guess she could be. She and Tootie act like they want to share Amity's house with the family like Amity wanted. But Tootie has money problems and Renni's not much better off. I think they'll fight with the family over wanting to sell it."

"They can have it far as I'm concerned," said Delia. "It's too far to get there."

"I'd kind of like to have it around," I said. "It's a good place to go and think."

"Buy it."

"Delia, we can't keep spending money. You won't listen, though. You'll keep spending until you're back where you were a year ago."

"There you go, criticizing. I can't catch a break at all with you, Gaylen."

"I'd give anything to see you take care of yourself."

"I can take care of myself."

"I wish you could," I said, trying to hide my resentment.

"Then let me. Give me my share, and I'll be out of your hair."

"Daddy set the trust up for a reason."

"To control me like Daddy does. That's the only reason. Why else would you do it? Is it because you want my share? You think I'm so stupid you can just take it?"

It was hard not to react to her goading. "I haven't spent a cent on myself, Delia. I took care of Daddy for a year, and where were you while I was fighting to keep him well? Off you were, sleeping with a married man, breaking up a marriage."

"And hiding your own affair."

"You make me nuts, Delia! Shut up!"

"How is it any different? Why are you so good and I'm so bad? Because you keep it all a big ugly secret, like Mama kept secrets? I'm just dumb enough to let everyone know what I do." She flung her hat to the back of the car. "Maybe I'm not dumb as you all think, but so smart I'm just on to all of you. I know what you all say about me, that Delia's trash. What if I'm just happy to be me? What's the harm in that?"

The connection with I-40 stared down on us. I turned onto it, not answering Delia because I couldn't. I hated her for being right. She was chronically wrong until that moment.

The sky would not cut travelers any slack, not parting to let in a bit of sunlight, but staying fastened closed. The cold settled in, the coldest day so far. I knew that Delia needed a coat and that she would not think to go and buy it, that I would have to tell her to do it.

"Am I like Mother?" I asked.

"Are you going to yell at me if I answer?"

"I won't."

"Some ways, yes, and others not."

"How am I not like her?"

"You don't hit me. You yell, though."

"Not as loud, though. I know I'm not loud like her."

"Not as loud. Okay. But it's what you don't say that drives me out of my freaking gourd. Why is it that you and everybody else don't say what you mean? How come people hide theirselves from each other?"

A road sign advertised Siphon ahead.

"I think it's because we want to be liked."

"But not for who you are."

"No. For who we're expected to be."

"So everybody likes you because they don't know you. Where does that get you?"

"Respect and station. You move up the ladder, leave behind your old self."

"Like a snake shedding its skin."

"I'd like to think of myself as something besides a snake."

"Snakes, tramps, whores, lowlifes, liars. What's the difference?" she asked, and her voice had softened to my great relief.

"No difference."

She kept staring down at the toes of the fake reptile boots. "These hurt like the devil." She took them off.

Siphon evolved on the wet fringes of Angola Swamp in upper Pender County. Renni's husband, Tommy, Tim and Fanny's daddy, bought the little two-acre tract ten miles south of the meandering creek banks of Watermelon Run after the Vietnam War. He was a cook in the army and came home, according to my mother, with a doorknob or two loose.

Beyond the town of Siphon were the towns and island towns feeding into Topsail Sound. Below Siphon was the town of Burgaw, a place known for its spring festival and a small golf course that Braden called a putt-putt.

Uncle Tommy let Tim run wild in that place. As a boy, Tim trekked back into the Angola Creek Flatwoods Preserve surrounding the swamp, and a forest ranger was born in the boy who clambered across marshland, trophy bruises dappling his sinewy legs, calling off bird types and gigging for frogs by flashlight.

Tim was the only one who knew exactly where his daddy finally rested. Tommy gave Tim express details to sprinkle his ashes in the Chowan River beneath a cypress tree where he had caught a prize fish. Renni hung the fish over the mantle next to the photographs of her, Tommy, and, of course, Tim and Fanny.

When we pulled into Renni's driveway, my car was making a tapping noise. That set the dogs to yapping wildly from inside as if ten or more clambered against her front door preparing to devour anyone who stepped over the threshold.

"Gaylen? Is that you? Delia! I'll be! Would you look at the two o' you! Sakes, sakes, I'd never expect to see you two today." Renni tried to squeeze through the front door, her right foot raking back the dogs.

"I should have called," I said. "But we just kept driving and talking about coming here and next thing you know…"

"Next thing you know!" exclaimed Renni. "Let me fix you both a bite to eat. Come in this house!" She turned, and Delia and I followed her inside. Delia stooped to pick up a white Pomeranian with a tear-stained face. The remaining three dogs, all toy purebreds, trembled upon sight of us, their tails quivering like doorstops.

Renni prepared a midafternoon lunch of warmed-up stew and cornbread muffins. Delia put on a bit of an act, as if she had not eaten in days. "Mmm," she moaned as she ate each bite.

"Has this sister of yours not been feeding you?" Renni asked, laughing.

"Gaylen and I been living like two Hollywood stars," said Delia. "Eating, drinking, and laying up in fancy hotels."

Renni looked stunned. The simple way my father lived, she had no idea of the pay dirt he had just turned over to his daughters.

"Don't pay her any mind," I said. "She's going on, that's all. You know Delia." Fortunately Renni did know her to stretch the truth around the middle, so I relaxed.

"What brought you girls all the way up to Siphon? You working on settling Delia into your daddy's place? Fanny said you all decided Delia would move into it," said Renni.

Before Delia exploded with too much information, I said, "It's true. We're moving Delia into Daddy's house. It could use a coat of paint."

"I'm putting in a swimming pool and buying a horse," said Delia.

"Delia, you ought to go into the kitchen and fetch the banana pudding out of the fridge," said Renni, not taking her eyes off me. She told Delia where to dig serving bowls out of the cupboard and spoons out of the wobbly utensil drawer.

Delia picked up the Pomeranian, seeing as how it had formed an attachment to her. She disappeared through the kitchen door.

I sipped the sweet tea that Renni could have used for glucose.

"Gaylen, Fanny says she heard that you and Delia got some drug dealer after you. Now tell me that's not true," said Renni.

"How'd she come by that news?" I asked.

"She called your house looking for you. Said you weren't answering your cell phone, so she got Braden on the line. Braden told her, I'm sure. Poor guy. Has he come around yet? What I mean is, has he agreed to reconcile?"

"Braden shouldn't have told Fanny."

"He's still family, Gaylen."

"The last thing he gave me were the divorce papers."

"That sounds final then," she said flatly.

"I didn't sign, Renni. When I don't have my life full of Delia, I'll get this settled between us."

"How'd you come to know a drug dealer, Gaylen? It's not like you."

I rested my forehead in my hands.

"It's natural for girls to want to experiment, but most of us go for a martini."

"Renni, I'm not a teenager, and I'm not on drugs."

Delia was standing in the doorway, a bowl of pudding in each hand. She burst out laughing. "She can't hold her booze, Renni, let alone drugs!"

A smile spread across Renni's face. "Delia, how would you know that?"

"It's nothing," I said.

"You two must have tied one on," said Renni.

Delia set down the puddings and pushed up her sleeve. "We got the tattoos to prove it."

Bringing Renni and Delia together with me was no different than when my mother was tossed into their midst. I had taken Fiona's place as the new Syler zoo exhibit.

Renni pulled out the neck of my knit top. "Let Aunt Renni see."

"Absolutely not! It's nothing," I said, pulling away.

The door flew open. Three little girls ran screaming into their grandmother's living room. Behind them, in walked Fanny with a fat baby boy on her hip.

"Look who's here to see Granny!" said Renni. She scooped a toddler girl up into her arms.

"Don't get up on my account," said Fanny. "I was bored with Dill out of town. Since Thanksgiving's almost here, we came early. But Gaylen and Delia, I had no idea! This is magic, isn't it?"

She pulled out a chair next to me. Borrowing my still-clean spoon, she dug into the bowl of pudding Delia had just placed in front of me.

"You come in at a good time," said Renni. "These two went out and got tattooed."

Fanny stared at me like it was a joke.

Finally, I stretched out the neck of my black knit top and exposed the daisy tattoo on my right shoulder.

Fanny threw back her head and laughed.

"Maybe I'll get one too," said Renni.

I helped my aunt and cousin clear away the dishes. Delia curled up on the sofa and fell asleep. The dogs jumped up and tucked into balls around Delia like she was the dog Madonna.

"Braden said you missed your orthopedist's appointment," said Fanny, talking about the cast still on my arm. "Want me to cut that thing off for you?"

It took a lot of knife sharpening, Renni pulling, and Fanny cutting away at the top of the cast. Finally, the last smelly thread gave way. Renni walked it ceremonially to the trash can and dropped it in. I scrubbed the sooty color from my yellowed arm.

Renni made coffee, and the three of us took it out on the screened-in porch. Renni had decorated it with white wicker furniture and pink and blue cushions. Behind the little settee was a table with a stereo. She took a remote control device and turned on the stereo, selecting a soft country music radio station. Fanny and her mother talked about Thanksgiving, what they would cook, and some add-ons for Dill, the vegetarian.

"You and Delia are here for Thanksgiving, aren't you?" asked Fanny.

"Of course," said Renni. "You have to stay on. No need to go back to your daddy's just yet. That'd be depressing."

"It's not safe," I said, "for you to take us in. I don't know where to take Delia actually. Maybe farther up north. We have any relatives that could take her in?"

"Uncle Jackson and Aunt Noleen," said Renni. "Over in Dallas now. They've got the room too." She picked up a ceramic container shaped like a honey pot. She opened the lid, fished out several slips of paper, and handed one to me. "This is their telephone number."

I accepted it.

"Jackson's a second cousin. But we all grew up together, so he claims us," said Renni. She said to Fanny, "They'd love to take in Delia. Noleen always loves a project. Remember when they took in those orphans from Cambodia?"

"It wasn't Cambodia, was it, Mother?" asked Fanny. "They'd love to see you and help out in whatever way they could."

I listened to them working out Delia's problems.

Fanny said, "Maybe you ought to call the police, Gaylen."

"Has she mentioned her stint in the hospital?" Renni asked me.

"Who, Delia?" I asked.

"You knew that, didn't you, Gaylen?" asked Fanny. "But then you didn't see Delia, you said, for a year."

I did not know that Delia had been in the hospital. But my father had his own worries, what with his cancer. "Did Delia tell Daddy?"

Both women shrugged.

"She was standing up on a ladder, not a stepladder, but steps, actually, leading up to some warehouse materials at the furniture factory," said Fanny. "She fell."

"It was a scandal, like the factory boss thought she did it on purpose," said Renni.

"Dill knows a man who works there who said he saw Delia throw herself off." Fanny whispered, glancing through the window into the house.

Renni was nodding as if she knew more than Fanny but was holding back.

"Delia would never kill herself," I said. "She's a lot of things, but suicidal isn't one of those things."

"Not suicide," Renni whispered. "She was pregnant. Tootie said she had a D and C."

I was feeling sleepy after lunch. I laid my head back against the cushioned patio chair and closed my eyes. "You saying she had an abortion?"

"Dill said his friend said there was nothing wrong with her, that the factory doctor checked her out. But she went off to the hospital and checked herself in."

"It doesn't make sense," I said.

Renni said, "She was covering up the abortion. She told your daddy that she had been in the hospital because she had fallen at work. That was when she asked him for money to pay her hospital bill."

"Whose baby? Freddy Deals's?" I asked.

"Some black she worked with," said Renni. "What was his name, Fanny?"

"Don't say it like that, Mother. 'Black,' like you're spitting out something you don't like," said Fanny.

"Maybe I am," she said to her daughter.

"Freddy was married," I told them. "Maybe he told Delia she had to get rid of it."

Renni gasped. "Is he the one? The drug dealer?"

"His brother-in-law," I said. "His wife, Sophie, is the sister of Mason Freeman."

"Delia is on that family's hit list because she slept with Sophie's husband?" asked Renni, incredulous.

"Delia shot Sophie," I said.

Fanny turned down the stereo and was looking through the window for Delia. "This is serious then."

Renni got me a compress for my head. Then she asked Fanny if she would make sausage stuffing in spite of Dill's protest. Renni said to me, "I know it's hard for you tell us these things. But shouldering Delia Cheatham's problems is too much for any one person to bear."

"What is it about the Sylers and our secrets?" I asked.

"It's just our way," said Renni. "We look out for one another."

Since Renni's sympathy appeared to be on the rise, I asked, "Can I ask you about my brother?"

"Shoot, honey! Whatever you want," said Renni.

"Did you know him? Were you around when he lived with my parents?" I asked.

"I knew him in California and back here in North Carolina when James and Fiona moved back. We all moved out to California for a year to work," said Renni. "James made a big wad of cash. He was always a saver. He bought that little piece of land next to Daddy's place and expanded. When my daddy died, he didn't want the land divided up, so he gave his part to James. That's how they came by so much good hunting land." She was smiling about my father's conquest, but as my mother suspected, Renni had that strange glint of jealousy when she talked about Daddy's good fortune.

"Were you around when my mother made Truman leave?" I asked.

She was less buoyant. "The whole family was in an uproar," she said.

"Mother told me that he was a runaway," I said.

She cut her eyes at Fanny.

"I'll get more coffee." Fanny got up and collected our empty cups.

Renni sat forward, resting her wrists on her knees. Knowing more than I knew empowered her. "Your mother threw that poor boy out."

"Why would she do that?" I said evenly, staring at the floor.

"She was not a good mother back then, Gaylen."

"In what way was she bad?"

"Fiona gave herself to any man that came her way. I know that's hard for a daughter to hear," said Renni.

Mother's words came back to me. She had told me once that Renni and Tootie talked about her, that I could not believe anything they said.

Renni said, "When her first husband, Truman Senior she called him, left her to get away from her violent spells, she wanted a new man and fast. She married and then divorced him. I never knew the second husband's name.

"I think it was Polette, but it doesn't matter now," I said.

"So when your mother came flirting round James's place, Tootie told James to send her packing." She was holding back, and it showed in the erect way she sat, carefully choosing her words, not implicating herself.

"My mother once told me they kept their marriage a secret from the family," I said.

"Gaylen, are you sure you want to hear this? Let's talk about

Thanksgiving dinner, how about?" Renni asked, but the eager glint in her eyes gave away the fact she did not really mean it.

"You must have seen her and my brother, Truman, together," I said.

Renni sighed. "She knew none of the Sylers wanted James tangled up with her. She neglected Truman, and we didn't want James having kids by her," said Renni. Her mind had obviously traveled far enough back to make her forget that I happened to be one of Fiona's ill-fated kids. "It was Tootie that once lived next to her apartment. That was before she met James. When James visited Tootie, Fiona would come out on the apartment landing to meet him."

I had never heard my mother talk about living next to Tootie. I could see why she resented Renni and Tootie. "Did you ask Mother why Truman ran off?"

"Run off? That boy didn't run off. He was run off by your mother. We all called Fiona that day as word spread. Me, Tootie, and your Aunt Lilly. But Fiona, she said he was trouble and she wasn't putting up with his stuff anymore," said Renni.

"Did she mention me or Delia that day?"

Renni thought for a few minutes. She looked up at me as if she was trying hard to remember back that far. Fanny now stood over us with two cups of coffee. Then she stared out the window into the backyard. She stared a hole through me. "You must remember since you're asking."

"I'm trying to remember. I can't." I accepted Fanny's bitterly strong coffee.

"Where did he go?" I asked.

"I figure he went off to his daddy's in Texas."

"Mother, you never told me any of this," said Fanny.

"If you don't remember, then maybe it's best left alone," said Renni. Fanny and I left her like that, sitting alone and walking back through her maze of memory.

The night fell on Siphon. Fanny coaxed Delia and me into staying the night. Fanny put the kids to bed in the guest room. We cousins bedded down in the living room, talking about Tim and Meredith and how silly a baby would make him.

Delia went to sleep on the couch. Fanny and I made beds sitting up in two chairs near a window. I turned off the lamps, and we sat talking in the glow of a radio dial.

"I don't know what you're digging for, but have you thought about that thing you did as a little girl that worried the family?" asked Fanny.

I stared at Fanny, not knowing how to answer.

"You pulled your hair out by the handfuls," she whispered.

I felt my face flush. Of course I remembered, but I didn't appreciate her trotting out my past like we were swapping boys' phone numbers.

"I'm sorry. I shouldn't have said that," said Fanny.

The shameful feelings came back, as if Mother had walked in right that instant and caught my fingers tangled up in a freshly pulled strand of hair. "Why say it then? I wish I didn't remember."

"I'm saying it for a reason, Gaylen. Your mother took you to the doctor, worried sick over you. She tied your hands to the bed to keep you from pulling your hair in your sleep." Fanny's words were nearly a staccato. She continued tiptoeing over my life without consent.

"I'm surprised you remember," I said. If Fanny had found me naked, I'd not have felt any less humiliated.

"It scared me and Tim. We thought your mother was loony for tying you up like that."

Until the last few days, it was another of those covered-over memories that I had gratefully chosen to leave in hiding. "Mother obsessed over it," I said. "I fought her over it. It seemed unnatural." It came to me I had not so much as told Braden, but not because I did not know how he would take it. Forming the words to tell that old story made me feel small again and sick. I was turning back into a Syler.

"Don't you want to know why you did it?" she asked.

I turned the radio dial until I found an oldies station. Renni was sitting in the kitchen, and I wanted only Fanny to hear me. "You knew my parents. It's not hard to understand. I figure that I have a few short decades, and then you will have to strap me to a bed in an institution for good."

"Don't you say that, Gaylen! You are not like them," she said.

"Then why else would I pull out my own hair?" I asked.

"I'd want to know," she said.

"I asked Mother about it before she died. I asked when it started, the hair pulling. Because once I was old enough to be aware, I just stopped."

"When did she say you started?"

"Age six months."

"Gaylen, are you kidding me? A six-month-old pulling her hair? What did she think, that you needed a shrink?" Fanny reached out and took my hand.

"I was four when I finally stopped," I said.

Fanny sat forward, her eyes wide as if the sun was coming through them. "Next talk about the nightmares."

"It's always a man. He's crawling into my bed. He is the color of shadows."

"You talked about that when you were young," said Fanny.

"Renni didn't like me asking about my mother and brother, did she?"

"You have a right to ask about your own life without feeling as if you're prying." Fanny spoke with her usual self-confidence.

"I would give anything to have what you have, Fanny." I meant her assurance. But also the whole package that was Fanny. She was comfortable with love. She loved crazy, instigating Renni and even her father who had lost part of himself in Vietnam. I accepted a tissue from her. "I'm realizing how hard it is to look for a missing piece of yourself while connecting with a family that has let go of you." I cried, not sobbing, but reacting to the sense of being pulled in two.

"We didn't let go of you, Gaylen."

"Why do I feel so cut loose, then? You know how long I've felt adrift?" Even marrying Braden didn't take up the gap in my soul. "I don't have a map for finding my way back from age four, Fanny. You all have your own lives now. Here I sit demanding answers from the grave. I want to return to a single day in my life that will tell me everything. But when I try, nothing."

We pulled the armchairs together, making pillows out of our blankets. We lay our heads down on the same pillow. Fanny said, "You know what you have to do now."

"What?"

"Only one thing works for the blues."

"No, not that," I said.

"You have to. You swore."

"But I was ten and desperate to borrow your U2 T-shirt."

"You have to sing it or else die listening to Britney Spears, your ears bleeding, and your tongue hanging out."

"It's too humiliating."

"Sing the song!" she said.

Only because forced by Fanny's irresistible persuasion did I sing with her:

Sisters, we are one underneath a starry blanket
On the banks of our river, we will join in reverie
I'm your mother, you're my daughter, we are sisters in a prayer
That no guy will come between us; no guy will come between us
We are sisters
We are we.

Tim was mad at us for writing a girls-only song. He called us feminists. We didn't know about that, but we liked having our own song. Delia wrote the last line. But of course, she did not sing and only watched Fanny and me arm in arm, nearly yodeling the lyrics.

Renni kept a strange vigil in the kitchen by the window. She pulled out Tommy's rifle and sat in a chair cleaning the stock. The last thing I remember before falling asleep was the way she watched out the window, my uncle's gun resting at her side.

11

DELIA AND I stayed with Renni and Fanny through Thanksgiving. I presented Renni with her painted dress, the blue and green one that hung over Amity's sofa. She was taken aback since she had always thought of Amity as being closer to my mother. "She made that for me?" It took a morning's worth of examination and speculation before she remembered the day that Amity must have gotten the dress. "Your mother and Amity were having a yard sale. I brought over some of my things to have Fiona sell them for me. I told Amity that funeral dress was what I wore when my mother died. It made me sad to see it hanging in my closet." Renni sounded bewildered. "I was sorry I did that later. Now it's come back to me."

Friday, before heading back for a roofing job, Dill checked out the whirring sound under the hood of my car, worked it over with some tools, replaced a belt, and gave my car the thumbs-up for at least another hundred or so miles. He told us to take some of our money and buy a car.

Renni walked us out to the Neon. "I think the two of you ought to stay." She handed Delia a recipe card. On one side was the family's sausage dressing recipe; on the other was Renni's telephone number and address. "Don't lose this, Delia. If you get in trouble, you come right back here," she said.

Delia hopped into the Neon. She tossed Renni's card into a shopping bag.

"The last thing I want to give you girls, Gaylen, before I forget, like I forget everything else, is your mail," said Renni. She held out a stack of mail that took both of her large hands to hold.

"How'd you get their mail, Mother?" Fanny asked, not hiding her irritation.

"I went by James's house to check on these two. That's when I found that box on the doorstep that I gave to Braden that day and then your mail."

It was mostly old mail sent to my father, some junk flyers, but one letter addressed to Delia. But I was surprised by Renni's comment. "Did you say you saw Braden? I thought you brought Truman's belongings to my house in Wilmington?"

"That would've been a drive for me. But Braden came looking for you right about the time I was mopping," said Renni.

"Mother, please don't tell me you were cleaning their house without asking," said Fanny.

"James give me a key to check in on him when he got so sick. What's wrong with that?" asked Renni. "Someone run off and left the wash in the washer. Smelled putrid. I rewashed the load and dried it. It's folded and on the ironing board, by the way."

"We did leave in a hurry," I said.

Fanny held out her hand. "Cough up the key, Mother."

Renni kept keys dangling on a stretch band on her arm. Reluctantly, she handed me the house key. "Got those floors cleaned up better than when, well, God rest her, never mind." She closed her eyes out of respect for the woman she freely judged but never knew.

I was less surprised that Renni cleaned the house in our absence but more surprised that Braden had come looking for me.

"That husband of yours sure looked forlorn, Gaylen," said Renni.

"Did he say anything?" I asked.

"He was put out, you know. You weren't answering the phone. But he laughed when I asked him if there was any hope that we could keep him around. I think he likes the Sylers." She continued to say things that made Fanny sigh. "You get him over to my place, Gaylen. We'll feed him and get some beers in him. He'll forget the whole divorce issue."

Delia's window came fully down. I knew she probably felt a need to interject her philosophical position on Braden and me, so I said, "It's time to go," and "Delia, get your window up before you catch cold."

Fanny hugged me. She smelled like pablum and her mother's sausage dressing. The last thing she said to me was, "Come home, Gaylen. We need you back home."

But of course even Fanny had moved away from Boiling Waters to Durham.

***

Delia took the mail that Renni had given me. She sorted through it to throw away the store circulars but also to find the letter I told her had come to her.

"Why would a letter come to Daddy's house for you?" She must have still been using his house for an address.

Delia pulled out the envelope. I glanced and saw the rigid, mostly all-caps handwriting. She tore off one end and blew into it like Daddy used to do. "It's from Angola Prison," she said.

I imagined all sorts of things. Maybe something had happened and my parents were being notified of something, like Truman had died.

Delia finally said, "It's a letter from Truman."

"To you?"

"Both of us." She read in silence for the next five miles. "He wants us to send him money. Do you think he knows what Daddy left us?" she asked.

"Daddy said in his will that Truman was not to be left a single penny. Mother had told Daddy not a cent for him," I said. But I felt guilty about it. Mother never relented though.

Delia read:

Hi Baby Sisters. I got Delia's letter. Just thought I would contact you and find out what is going on with you. Mostly I kind of hope we can make peace between us. But, Gaylen, you have not written or visited. I guess you don't like me.

Delia stammered out each of Truman's crisply written words.

"I'll pull into Bojangles," I told her. "We'll get coffee, and I'll read if you'd rather me do it."

We stopped in at the chicken and biscuits restaurant. Delia skipped to a booth near the coffee island. I picked up a plate of cinnamon biscuits and two paper cups and met her at the table. She handed me the letter. I read out loud.

> Has Judge Cuvier made contack with you? I don't have any hope of proving I was set up by Cuvier without my family helping me. My life is over and I am old and sick of prison. This time I'm not getting out until I'm dead. What can I do to explain what I can't put in a letter or tell you on the phone? It's just too personal, a thing that the prison might record on a phone or read behind my back. You will have to come here where I can tell you face to face.

I said to Delia, "He wants us to come to Angola."
"Keep reading," she said.

> I am badly in need of eyeglasses. Also I need shoes real bad. Maybe you can help. I'm wrighting this a few lines at a time because my eyes are in such bad shape. So are my feet. If you call the Louisiana State Capitol they can give you the address of the Louisiana State Capitols' inmate fund where you can send money to help. I don't know who to ask but you. It's hard enough to do time without going crippled and blind, no help at all. Cuvier is the judge in East Baton Rouge Parish Louisiana who robbed and murdered my Dad, Truman Savage, in Houston, Texas, or at least had it done to steal my west Texas oil property. He can do just about anything he wants. He is part of Louisiana's corruption. He is a junky and a pimp and a murderer. He set me up on this beef to get

*me out of the way. If you don't believe me have a lawyer you
trust check his tax records for the past twenty years, and then
my Dad's tax records, and you will understand why he needed
me out of the way. Just telling you could cost me my life. I
don't want your money or help getting out. Maybe it won't
matter pretty soon. I'm getting in touch with my family chain
to deal with Louisiana and Houston. I'm calling for a Blood
Feud, and it falls to me to make the crooks pay in blood for
killing my dad and robbing me of all he kept for me. Whatever
you do, stay away from Metarie, Louisiana.*

"His handwriting is just like Mother's," I noticed. Mother read
voraciously, but it did not improve her handwriting. Truman's pen-
manship had two styles. For several lines, the letters stood straight
up. Then, as if something had tightened a screw inside of him, the
letters leaned forward, the words spilling out of him.

"That judge is after him, sounds like," said Delia.

I turned over the envelope where he had written, *Remember we
are family.*

All of the things Mother said about Truman Savage, Senior, Truman's daddy, were mostly back in the days when I was too young to
understand the foibles of a doomed marriage. I did not know much
else, other than the fact that he cheated on her. Mother told me she
walked into the kitchen from work and found him on the floor, en-
tangled with a young woman whose hair was teased and so sticky
with spray that it had gotten misshapen during sex on the floor. Truman Senior had his hand up her dress, and the two of them lay on a
blanket of Rice Krispies. Mother did not know if they were looking

for a snack and then got friendly or decided to include cereal in their lovemaking.

"If we stop at my place, we can look up Truman's daddy on the Internet," I said. "A murder in Houston is bound to make the headlines." We were not far from Wilmington. Braden was off in the wild blue yonder making a delivery, so the apartment would be quiet. I needed to be back home if only to remember who I was before Delia shot Sophie or, farther back than that, when Braden and I were still making sense. Maybe if I was lucky, I still had a job, depending on one's definition of lucky.

We were crossing Cape Fear when Delia said, "Is it safe to go to your place? What about Mason's faggy thug?"

"Braden ran him off. He'd be a fool to come back," I said.

"Hmmph!" said Delia.

Braden had gone shopping in my absence. In our closet hung a leather jacket, soft as baby's skin, but green, not because he wanted green, I was sure, but because the blue would have cost double. But it was a Dolce and Gabbana, nonetheless, hanging where his old Members Only jacket once hung.

Our last fight was over money. My apartment managing job was bringing in only a small paycheck. But it provided me with some security and a roof that Braden could not manipulate. I said that to him in an angry fit, that he could not take away my apartment. He had flown to see his parents the weekend before. I decorated the living room that weekend like I wanted. A blue vase of pink silk tulips was still on the coffee table. Mother was not much of a decorator, so I was finding my footing as Braden Boatwright's domestic partner, but within reason. Braden had his daddy's predilection for electronics and expensive accessories.

The Dolce and Gabbana might have been a revenge purchase. He had to have gotten a new credit card or some such to up and buy a leather jacket so supple that when I touched it I could see him in front of the mirror, thumbs running down the length of the lapel, rendering him helpless to pass it by.

The bed was unmade but that was no different from when I was home. Our linens were pale blue Egyptian cotton from a Tuesday Morning store. The blinds were still closed as I had liked it because shutting the sunlight out gave the room a blue glow. On each side of the bed was a nightstand. My clock was still on my side of the bed, my wedding-ring dish next to it. I opened the porcelain lid. Next to my wedding set was Braden's gold band. I had taken mine off the night of the fight, but not because I wanted it off for good. I had taken off for home because Daddy was dying and forgot it in my haste to leave. Braden must have returned home and, finding mine in the dish, tossed his ring in with mine. I took his out and slid both onto my ring finger.

I pulled the linens up over the mattress, tucking the edges under the bed, pulling the comforter across and smoothing the wrinkles. The last time we made love was the last time the sheets were washed, so it had been a good two months; more according to Braden, but we never agreed about it.

Not that I had success in the lovemaking department with Max, either. That first night at the cottage, we could not finish what we had set out to do. If Braden knew, he would have laughed. Max imagined I was looking for exotic passion. Trying to overcome his bookish persona, he played a part to try to be what he wasn't.

Max kept a lot of old possessions, one being an RCA record player. He put on the soundtrack from a movie called *Doctor Zhivago*. He laid a rose on my pillow and then propped himself up next to me with a look so uncharacteristic of him that I laughed. I had known him only in his Dockers and tweeds standing in front of the class articulating Fichte.

He got up from the bed and walked out onto his patio, having taken back the robe. He shut the door while I sat on the edge of his bed. He wanted me to tell him what I wanted. Men say that, but what they mean by it is, what turns you on? That isn't necessarily what women want.

What then did I want?

I sat on my mattress and pulled the folded part of the sheet up around my face to smell the linens. Braden's musky smell permeated the sheets, a smell of airplane engine oil mixed with damp clothing and a sprinkling of department store cologne. I pulled off the comforter, stripped the mattress and pillows, bunched up the linens, and carried them to the portable laundry room behind the kitchen.

Delia inspected a six-pack of Yuengling inside the refrigerator.

"Braden might not have stocked up much food," I said. "He doesn't cook at all."

"There's a pot roast in a casserole dish and some taters," said Delia. She pulled out the dish, a Corning Ware baking dish.

"That's not my dish," I said.

Delia rolled her eyes.

"That's not my dish."

"Ha!" She laughed.

"You're not going to eat that, are you?" I asked.

She lifted the lid and sniffed.

"You don't know how long it's been in there," I said, my throat strained from reprimanding her.

She opened the microwave oven over the stove and put the pot roast in to warm.

A neighbor shuffled past the front window. Her frame slowed and she tried to see inside through the thin curtains. She tapped against the window glass instead of the door. I opened the door, and she looked surprised. "There you are!" she said.

"Mrs. Shane," I said, "how's your apartment?" She had only lived in the one bedroom and one bath unit a month.

"That little twit of an agent, Amberlyn or whatever, doesn't respond like you," she said. "She's too preoccupied, probably with boyfriends and such. I see them come and go, males at all hours of the night, right out of her apartment. But that's none of my affair."

"Kimberly," I said, "is her name. Do you need anything?"

"It's all fixed finally," she said. "She's just not you."

"I'll be back soon," I said. "I'll drop by the office in a few and check on her."

"You're not leaving?" she said as a question. Mrs. Shane's neediness eked through her small, unimposing stature.

"I'll be back." I closed the door.

Delia pulled the nuked roast out of the microwave oven. It smelled edible, actually good. She salivated over it. "Do people knock on your door all the time?" she asked. "I'd tell that tenant to get bent."

"Tell me if the meat is tender. I can't eat tough meat," I told her.

She gouged the meat a few times with her fork tines. A bottle of cold Yuengling sat on the dining table, the sun shining through it turning it the color of goldfish. "You want one?" she asked.

"I don't drink anymore," I said. "I wake up defaced."

"What's defaced?"

"Tattooed."

"A tattoo is just a symbol of your psychic self," she said. "That Asheville tattoo artist told me we'd be back. Nobody gets just one."

"You fix us each a plate," I said. "My office is below us. I'll go check on Kimberly." I knew that I was about to face the brunt of Kimberly's frustration. Apartment offices are a magnet for hostility. There are the tenants who are lonely and in need of a shoulder to cry on. But most of the residents are either waiting to move out and buy a house or are so bad off financially that, more than anything else, they want a dog to kick. That was my usual job title, the closest dog to kick. Going off and leaving a young leasing agent to manage a rental office was like leaving a stick of dynamite in her hands with a two-foot fuse. When I opened the door, she leaped up out of my chair where she had finally holed up. "Gaylen, I don't know whether to kiss you or smack you." She threw her arms around me.

I kept apologizing.

She picked up a book of phone messages and placed it in my hands without taking a breath between listing the complaints that had been lodged with her. "The last tenant told me that he was going to sue us, I think because his bedroom smells like mold. He says he's allergic." She pointed to the maintenance man's initials. "Jake says it's the worst case of foundation mold ever."

"Offer to move him to another unit," I said. "Tell Jake that maintenance includes helping a tenant move out of a bad apartment."

"I never can think that fast. That's why you're needed back here," she said. "There is a tenant moving out first of the month. We can move him there."

"Have you heard from Mrs. Weymouth?" I asked. Weymouth owned the complex, along with several buildings in downtown Wilmington, all populated with adult students unwilling to live on campus.

"I told her that you would be back anytime, no need to call you, and that I had leased out the three remaining units last weekend," she said. "She tried to call you a million times."

"I'm buying you anything you want from the mall," I said.

She was handing me my set of keys.

"I can't come back until I get my sister back to her house," I said.

"You're not back?" Kimberly was not one to hide her disappointment.

"Delia's having it hard, and I've been driving her around to meet family, get her out of her funk," was all I told her.

"I haven't had time to even go to the bathroom," said Kimberly. "Now you're leaving again?"

She was getting to me. I had grown accustomed to having the weight of the rental office off me. It occurred to me that I was enabling Delia and maybe I had my own reasons. But seeing Kimberly standing helpless and not wanting those keys handed back to her brought me back to my place of origin. I could not lay my life on her shoulders while Delia lolled upstairs drinking Braden's beer and propping her feet on my sofa. For whatever reason I had taken her under my care, it was time I drove her home to take care of her own problems. I could hear a noise overhead, loud bass and the sound of dancing.

Kimberly looked up and said, "She sounds as if she's coming out of her funk."

I handed her back the phone messages. "If you'll work for me for a few more days, I'll make it up to you."

"Paid vacation?" She knew better. Leasing agents have no benefits.

"I'll talk you up to Weymouth," I said. I went upstairs. The door was ajar. Delia was sitting on the sofa, her face in a pillow. Braden's stereo blasted at the highest volume. I walked across the room muttering. The door closed behind me. A white guy wearing a green Elvis shirt was holding a pistol. He looked beaten around the eyes. Delia's face was red as if she had been struck.

I was made to sit by Delia on the sofa. Knowing the guy would most likely hit me too, I told him, "If you don't turn down the music, you'll have an irate rental agent knocking on our door. We're right over her head."

Mr. Elvis Shirt used the butt of his pistol to turn off the stereo.

"My husband paid good money, so watch you don't break it," I said as nicely as I could.

Delia moaned.

I pulled her hair away from her face. She needed a shampoo.

He turned his pistol on me. "Fork over the jewelry." He wanted the wedding rings.

I covered my hands.

Elvis Shirt was of the same make and model of guys Delia dated from high school up. He could have passed for husband number two or a boyfriend from the Raw Bar. He waved the gun around like he had gotten thug lessons from TV. But guys like him leave behind the isolation of the picked-on boys and become the men who knock over your neighbor's gas station. They pull the trigger because they're afraid; it doesn't mean they intended to kill you—no more than they intended to flunk algebra.

I handed him the rings.

Delia slumped back against the sofa saying, "Her mother-in-law gave that wedding band to her. It's like a family heirloom or some such."

He looked at me and said, "It's payment for what your old man owes me from the last time." He walked into the kitchen but leaned over the countertop, keeping his gun on us through the pass-through. He slid both rings onto his pinky finger. When he stooped down, his bald head reflected the counter light. He made a phone call, but he spoke in pronouns so we could not identify any names. His eyes twitched nervously.

"How did he get in?" I whispered to Delia.

"I heard a knock at the door. I thought you'd locked yourself out," she said. "He rammed me knocking me onto the floor. Then he turned up the stereo to cover up my yelling." She started crying. "He kicked me good, in my face and my ribs." She kept touching the red spot over her right cheek and then jerking away.

"Did he mention Sophie?"

"He kept saying her name as he was kicking me." She sneered. "Son of a gun wears steel-toed boots." She jeered at Mr. Elvis Shirt. "I hate you, pig!"

He scratched his head. He kept tapping his thigh, like his mind was racing. He sat down to the plate of pot roast Delia had made for me.

"See, what did I say? You're a pig!" said Delia.

I squeezed her leg.

He picked up his gun, tapping the trigger, antsy like an execution shooter.

I changed the subject before Mr. Elvis Shirt could shoot Delia and then me. "She's not right, you know," I told him.

"Don't tell him nothing about me!" said Delia. "He don't deserve to know."

I gave her a look.

"Hmmph!" She turned away.

I thought it might be helpful to appeal to his logical side. "I'm not kidding. My sister has to have a lot of care. When she shot Sophie, it was no different to her than shooting a deer."

He was shoveling the food in hurriedly.

"You kill Delia, and it won't be any different than killing a retarded person," I said.

"Liar!" said Delia. "Stop it!"

"You ought to keep her locked up then," he said.

"I ain't afraid of you!" said Delia. "My brother-in-law, Braden, he knows people. He has pull. He'll have you hunted down."

No amount of arm tapping or leg squeezing could stop Delia.

He ate my lunch, licking his fingers one after another, ritualistically. "Is that the guy who I shot this morning?" he asked. "I was wondering what to call him."

My ears were so full of air pressure I thought my head would thunder. I tried to read the way he emoted, the squints around the eyes. "Braden's not home," I said so weakly that it showed on my face. "That's not possible." My cheek twitched, and my mouth went dry. I was feeling sick. Braden had not called me all morning. If this hit man was telling the truth, I was at fault for my husband's death. I was sucking breaths when I said, "My husband's flown out of state." Then I sobbed, "You tell me you're lying this instant!"

"That's what I needed to know," he laughed. "You two are alone."

Delia coughed.

I rested my head against the sofa back. It was odd, the feelings that bobbed up for Braden right at that moment. I cried until he pointed his pistol again, telling me, "Pipe down, pretty face." He finished off my sister's Yuengling and then pilfered a second bottle out of the refrigerator. "You're not like little sister, are you?" he asked me. A tender quality came over him.

If I answered, I'd make Delia mad, and she was too pitiful looking for that.

"She got all the guts, but you got the brains," he said. "Maybe I'll do you last."

"No one's ever said that," I lied, but it was a good stall. It engaged him.

"Pffft!" said Delia.

"I guess you knew that you got the brains," he said.

"Mmm."

"You got to tell yourself the good you see in yourself. My old man never said nothing good about me," he told me. "Family will judge you. You got to listen to the voice inside you that tells you who you are."

"What's yours tell you?" I asked.

Delia turned and stretched her legs out over my lap. She laid her head against the sofa back and sighed, as if she couldn't believe I was talking to Mr. Elvis Shirt.

He calmed a bit, looking less anxious and not as insecure. "Grady is smart. I'm a good money manager. I'm saving up to buy a little house down in Meh-hee-co. I'll find a fat woman to keep me warm."

"Why fat?" I asked.

"Good cook." He got up and paced the length of the kitchen's galley.

"Makes sense," I said.

"You're a good cook too," he said. "Best pot roast I've ever had."

Delia and I looked at his empty plate. "I didn't cook it. I don't know who did," I said. "I've been gone, if you'll remember."

"Your husband then?" He was trying to read me or Delia. Finally he laughed. "Your old man's found someone else to cook for him. Nice. Nice."

"It could be our neighbor. She's a good cook and is like a mother to all of the tenants," I said. Delia was still touching her cheek. "You didn't have to hit Delia. She's not like you think, dangerous." I didn't know how to explain Delia to a hit man.

Delia sat forward. "There's a spider coming down on your head, mister, and I hope it bites the crap out of you," she said.

His hand tightened around the pistol handle.

Delia was not lying. A brown spider trolled softly down from the ceiling to land on Mr. Grady Elvis Shirt's head. It seemed he did not like bugs. He slapped at the brown recluse but only got spider silk.

"Careful, they're poisonous," I said. I had heard that a person could die or lose a limb from a brown recluse bite. Or maybe it was black widows.

He swayed back and forth, but the silk was anchored well. The spider trounced a bit but, undeterred, stayed the course, drawing closer to him when he yanked further. He yelled like a little girl. The gun spun on one finger.

I laughed.

Delia said, "Let's go!"

I couldn't think as fast as Delia. She was out the door. Grady Elvis Shirt grabbed at me. But it was not a productive move. The gun fell onto the carpet. I swung like I knew what to do, even though that was far from the truth. The gun spun away. He had to let go of me to go for the gun. Then I ran out the door and finally caught up to Delia. She had my car keys and my purse. We climbed into the Neon and drove out of the parking lot before Mr. Grady Elvis Shirt could get his bearings and make it out the door.

"I'll bet you're hungry. That Grady ate every bit of your lunch. He's a pig," she said. "Hah!"

12

WE STILL HAD NOT looked up Truman Savage Senior's murder on the Internet. Since Freeman's hit man was intent on finishing Delia and, through association, me, he would be right on us. He would follow us straight out onto the interstate. I invented the beginning of a strategic escape. "Grady Elvis Shirt would not think to look for us in a library," I said to Delia.

"Let's get out of town." Delia moaned; her cheek had swelled up like the tip of an egg.

"If we keep driving this car, remember what Dill said. Only a hundred miles or so, and then trade her in. We break down, we're out of options."

"I need an ice pack. That Grady will burn for this," she said.

Delia's sense of justice weighed on me. "What about Sophie?"

She was mad at me again. "What do you mean?"

"Mother of four, marriage falling into ruin," I said. "Shot by her husband's girlfriend. Could you burn for that?"

She buried her head under her arms. She was all arms and legs as she tried to find a comfortable position to settle into. "Find a country music station, will you?" She wanted to sleep.

I turned on the radio. Delia pulled the blanket over her. She yawned and told me to wake her up for supper.

"Where is it you think we're going?" I asked.

"I don't know." She fell asleep.

The only library outside of Wilmington and out of searching vicinity was in Southport, right outside of Boiling Waters. There was no car on my tail, no reason to believe Grady Elvis Shirt had caught up to us. I pulled onto Highway 17.

Southport was one of the last towns before driving straight into the Atlantic Ocean. Movies were made in Southport; artists sold paintings down on the oceanfront. Large container ships, so big they looked like little cities floating past, ferried through the inlet.

I woke Delia. She lay in the car a few minutes staring through the windshield at the sky over the ocean.

The town's librarian led me to the public computer station. A homeschool mother was trying to help her daughter with an assignment. But the girl's little brothers were climbing onto the chair next to them, right where I was supposed to sit. The librarian led me to another station.

Delia walked up, raking the hair out of her eyes, and said, "I'm going to the CD aisle." She left me.

I key-worded the name *Truman Savage*. Up came an obituary. I expected it to be the death notice of Truman's daddy. But instead it was his father's wife who had died. His father was listed in the next-of-kin record. Next to his name was his son's name, Parson. Truman Senior, it said, was from Pasadena, Texas.

I printed off Mr. Savage's address and phone number. I called the number and was answered by a machine. Mr. Savage had a friendly voice. *"Thank you for calling Truman Savage. Please leave a callback number."*

Delia skipped up carrying a stack of CDs. "They got the Grateful Dead," she said. "I'm getting them."

"What if we leave the state and don't come back for a while? You'll owe fines."

She turned to take the CDs back to the music aisle. Then swiveling on one heel, she said, "Did you find Truman Savage's murder?"

"He's answering his own phone. That doesn't sound too murdered," I said.

"Where, here?"

"Pasadena, Texas. You got your driver's license, don't you?" I asked.

She dug through her purse. "I left it out at Daddy's place. I forgot."

"You have to have identification for a plane ticket. We'll have to go home."

"Not home," said Delia.

"We'll hurry." She kept digging through her purse, but she had definitely left it back at Daddy's house.

"If Grady finds us, he'll not let us get a-loose a second time," said Delia.

I returned to the computer and checked flights. Delia joined me, whining about her hunger.

"How does Texas sound?" I asked.

I drove into Boiling Waters, expecting the fifty-year-old tinsel Christmas bells to be hung along the streetlights. But the bells, all replaced with green Christmas banners welcoming the yuletide festivals, were in no way, form, or fashion displayed. Sadie Farnsworthy's clothing boutique and bait shop was gone, a convenience store in its place. But the starkest change came slowly to me. I reduced speed, staring at the once-wooded acreage down Fifty Lakes Drive. Boiling Waters was home to the centuries-old longleaf pines. According to my father, the town once smelled of the turpentine and tar extracted from the trees' natural resin, a white tar. I had seen the sap flowing down a tree trunk like mother's milk. The longleaf-pine resin was the essence of the state's Tar Heel name, rising up from local history's primal puddle.

But the trees, so old they had gone to crown, were wiped from the land as if translated into some Christmas heaven; in their place, stark lots ready for subdivision development.

"Delia, wake up," I said.

She came up out of the seat. "What are you staring at?"

"The trees are gone."

"Oh that," she yawned. "Say, I'm up for coffee. You?"

We drove into the gas station for the only coffee bar in town. Fortysomething couples stood around in Nikes and Lands' End hoodies. At the front of the convenience station, flipping through a boating magazine, was Laudus, Daddy's cousin. He lit up when he saw us. "Come see, come see!" he said, laughing and holding out his arms.

I handed Delia a ten spot, and she went for the coffee line.

"I was hoping you hadn't left town for good," he said.

I stuck out my hand. He drew me close and kissed my cheek. His hair had turned white. It was as if I had sleepwalked through the days surrounding my father's burial. Suddenly nothing looked the same, not even Laudus. "Town's changed," I said. "I must have been in a daze the week of Daddy's funeral."

"It's seeping in with the money. Any place on the water draws those Birkenstocks and their Beamers," he said.

"Fifty Lakes Drive looks like a desert," I said.

"It happened almost overnight. Started by a woodpecker."

I knew about the woodpeckers. As a girl, I woke up to their ritual hammering most mornings.

"Appears we were the sanctuary for a rare bird," he said, nearly in a whisper.

"Woodpeckers aren't rare."

"This one was. They took a liking to our longleaf pines. The birds took so long to make their holes down in the tar bellies of the trees, they passed them on to their offspring." He waved at Delia who was still in the checkout line. "Don't know why the birds won't nest anywhere else, but they won't. They're disappearing with the tar trees."

"So we're a bird sanctuary."

"Town got wind of it, that a moratorium was coming down to keep the trees from being cut. People had bought up extra lots to sell, send their kids off to college. Next thing you know, the whole town's gone nuts. Trees older than the country's flag were being felled. It was sad to watch. Everyone walking around mad, neighbors mad at neighbors."

"The town looks naked," I said.

"Took the character right out of the place," said Laudus, a sad melancholy in his small, delicate eyes.

"I got me a mocha," said Delia. She greeted Laudus. "You ever had one, Gaylen? Like, chocolate and coffee mixed?" She handed me a foam cup.

I looked around the convenience store. I did not know a single person. It was like the old Boiling Waters had drifted away. A substitute town had taken its place, bringing in a hunger for things I had taken for granted.

"Town's lost her soul," he said.

I had never seen a whole town raped like that.

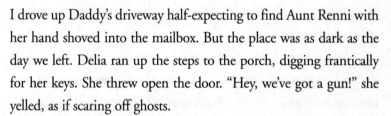

I drove up Daddy's driveway half-expecting to find Aunt Renni with her hand shoved into the mailbox. But the place was as dark as the day we left. Delia ran up the steps to the porch, digging frantically for her keys. She threw open the door. "Hey, we've got a gun!" she yelled, as if scaring off ghosts.

I went into the kitchen to wash my hands. Then I ran to my mother's bedroom and took three photographs from her bureau drawer. I tucked them into my purse. Delia wouldn't care about them anyway. When I ran back to the kitchen, I saw that the phone was yanked out of the wall. The back door was ajar, the lock bolt standing out from the door, wooden splinters on the floor. Mr. Grady Elvis Shirt had come calling.

"Someone's been in the house, Gaylen! Run!" Delia ran out of the house. I went to the door and worked the lock until I could get the door to close. I fastened the phone back into place. He had come and gone, I was sure. But the thought of it caused my neck hairs to stand up.

I ran out of the house as quickly as my sister.

Since I bought the plane tickets online while at the library, we made it to the airport and found a place to hide the car in the remote parking lot. Delia was giddy hopping onto the shuttle, it being her first trip by air.

She wheeled her little red suitcase up to the curbside check-in. We had one hour to spare before the flight from Wilmington to Houston. I led her to a travel shop, the kind that sold T-shirts and refrigerator magnets. She bought a celebrity rag and a bag of seashells she justified by saying, "For my turtle I'm going to buy." Then she reminisced, lamenting her trailer pets. "I'll bet Porter's forgot all about me by now."

I bought two cold drinks and a bag of sugared pecans. Then I checked my phone. It had been off since I had gone into the library. I turned it on and a message was waiting. I hit the redial button and got Kimberly.

"Mrs. Weymouth dropped in," she told me. "She's tried to call you all morning. You'd best call her." Kimberly sounded cool, as if she had reached the end of trying to explain me to the tenants and to my boss.

Weymouth was a nervous woman who wanted me to carry a pager, even into church, she said, although I had not gone in years. I sighed.

"My family is in a crisis," I said, not knowing what to do about the lump in my throat. I could hear my father berating me from the grave for not being responsible. Then Braden jumped into my head and nagged alongside Daddy. I had been letting go of that place since

Braden had been letting go of me, yet the dogged Syler nature had me clinging to a shipwreck of a job. Finally I said, "Kimberly, I think that it's only fair to tender my resignation."

She was quiet except for her sighing. "Mrs. Weymouth asked if I'd like your job," she finally told me. "I felt awful."

"So you told her no, right?"

Delia held up a T-shirt. The artwork was of a lusty sailor holding a nearly naked woman. "Let's get matching shirts," she said, gushing.

I shushed her, trying to shoo her back to the souvenirs.

"You just said you wanted to resign." Kimberly was defensive, her tinny voice so loud I could hold out the phone and still hear her.

"But you didn't know that I was going to resign," I said, grasping. "Are you telling me you took my job?"

"If you had not taken off without so much as a good-bye, I'd not have been so mad at you," she said. "You're not yourself, Gaylen. There's something wrong, I just know it."

"It's Delia," I said, the words not coming out as I had planned. "She's got her usual problems."

Delia looked up from the T-shirt rack. She turned and stormed out of the airport shop.

"I have to go," I said.

Delia was running through the Wilmington airport, dragging the red suitcase sideways off its coasters.

"Stop and listen to me!" I yelled.

She kept running, the shop bags flapping at her side. I could see her running alongside Sharon Creek, her bare feet brown from the bank mud, splitting the grasses open, with me running behind her yelling oaths and apologies. But she could never run as fast as me.

I caught up to her in front of a bookseller. "I didn't mean it like that," I said.

"You never paint me good to any person. Like I'm the retarded sister you got to look after." She dropped her things beside a bench and then planted herself on the seat.

I was winded. A security guard was running toward us. I looked down. "I've just stolen two soft drinks." I held up the bottles to the officer. "I'm sorry, sir! I ran out to find my sister." I pulled out some bills and handed them to him, one, two, three, four, "And keep the change," I said.

He hesitated but then took the money and returned to the souvenir shop.

"There you go again," she said. "You take off with store merchandise and blame me for it."

I sat beside her and handed her a cold drink. She was an easy mark for blame, I had to admit. "You're not the only one with resentment. I resent the fact I got to spend my life chasing after you," I said.

She opened the bottle and swigged it.

"Delia, I don't want to tell people anything about you at all. I'd rather tell them you're off in Zimbabwe or some such, saving orphans."

"Hah!"

"You act like I want to tell people that you're always in trouble. I don't."

"You're ashamed. Say it," she said.

"Make me proud then!"

"What for?"

I was finally catching my breath. I thought about her question and decided right then and there that I was going to stop blurting out easy fixes for Delia. They had not helped before and would not help now. "That's what families use for bragging rights. It's a code or something," I said. I had spent my life trying to make the Sylers proud, so what made her so special that she could just lie down and let life wash over her effortlessly? I had been hanging on to a job I hated, evicting single moms and poor students. I had gone back to school just so my father could tell his buddies at the Masonic Lodge his daughter had a university degree. But for what, I did not know. I was a wife without a husband. A student without a degree. I was a pilot who forgot how to fly. I laughed. "Honest to Pete, Delia, I don't know."

We had thirty minutes left to get to our flight terminal.

The stopover in Atlanta gave Delia time to calm herself. I took her into a jewelry shop. She tried on a pair of sterling silver earrings. You would have thought she was wearing the crown jewels.

"Nobody ever bought me such a thing," she said.

A sad melancholy settled between us. I tried to picture my father standing over a jewelry counter purchasing a gift of jewelry for Delia or my mother. It was time he did. "Let's say this is from Daddy," I said.

She hesitated.

"No lectures," I promised.

I paid the clerk and walked out onto the concourse between airport shops. The air was full of the smell of hot pretzels and the tire rubber from the carts used to wheel disabled people between terminals.

"Do you ever buy yourself anything?" Delia asked, snapping the earrings into place.

I looked at her, surprised.

"Daddy's not breathing down your neck," she said. "Indulge."

"I can if I want," I said. "It won't kill me to buy something, if that's what you mean." I went into a bookstore. I thumbed through several books, selected a novel and then a bookmark. I went next door to a sportswear store and tried on a pair of running shoes but said, "They're cheaper at the mall." The leather was soft, cradling my feet. "I'll take them," I finally said to the clerk without much more thought.

Delia dragged me to a Burberry clothing boutique. The models in the window posters flaunted pricey knits and pants. We went inside. I coaxed her into trying on a black blouse with black and white pants. She had never seen herself in that degree of style. She pulled out the shirt tag and gasped. "Four hundred dollars, oh my gosh, Gaylen!"

I checked my watch. "We've got to run and catch our flight," I said.

She dressed back in her own things.

The clerk was hanging up the pieces for Delia when I walked up to her and asked, "Can you bag those up pretty quickly?"

Delia ran out of the store, holding the designer outfit in a hanger bag and nearly hyperventilating. She followed me onto the plane snorting and laughing.

We accepted the late afternoon snack from the flight attendant. Delia was disappointed the drop-down monitors did not offer a movie.

"That's only on long flights," I told her.

She disappeared into the bathroom. She emerged wearing the Burberry outfit. "I got to get some boots to go with this now," she said.

"That's the way it starts," I said. "You buy one thing, then you have to buy another."

The silver earrings were a good match for the black and white clothes. I dozed. It was the first time I felt safe enough to go sound asleep since Delia had shot Sophie Deals. When I woke up, we were coasting into William P. Hobby Airport in Houston.

13

BEFORE CHECKING OUT the next morning at the airport hotel, I took the three photos of my mother and pinned them in a trinity inside my suitcase lid. There was the one of her as a bashful young girl and the one I remembered of her as a teen. There were common items in the teenage photograph, such as a wheelbarrow and a washtub against my grandmother's house, a spotted dog on the porch. My grandmother posed in the middle of a group of relatives. Mother stood two people away. Grandma wore a cotton dress and a black straw hat, small brimmed, but tall as a three-layer cake. Like my mother, she gardened no matter what the circumstance. Even though hard times shadowed all the relatives' eyes like sinkholes, the photo revealed a trio of begonias in clay pots on the porch steps.

Delia ranted about the hotel, criticizing the loud airplanes roaring overhead all night. So I checked us out and asked the concierge to reserve a car for me. The rental car attendant brought it right to the curb.

"We left that Grady far behind, I'll say that," said Delia. "He'll never think to look for us in Pasadena."

An old billboard advertised the Strawberry Festival from last May.

"I'll be. Here I thought they was the place for the Rose Parade," said Delia.

The gas tank was only partly full, so I pulled off of Gulf Freeway into a convenience store lot. Delia struck up a conversation with the station attendant while I selected an atlas. His name tag said, *Beefy.* "Busy place, this Houston. What do you do for fun around this place?" she asked.

"Used to go dancing down at the Cowboy Ranch museum. They shut the place down," said the young man. He had a gold-capped front tooth and wore an earring with a feather. "There's a Waffle House and a CVS drugstore on every block, but we lose the one thing that made us not like every place else."

"Why don't you open the Cowboy Ranch yourself then?" Delia asked.

He looked startled, like he'd been asleep and just got shook.

I bought Cheetos and cold drinks. Delia got a jerky just to say she got one in Texas.

Beefy asked Delia, "What's your name?"

"Delia. What's yours?"

"Todd."

"Never knew a Todd named Beefy before."

He glanced at the name tag, laughing at Delia. He was charmed by her. Men often were at first. They bought into her childish pout as if she sold it for a dollar.

I looked down and saw a large moth upside down on the floor. It was coated in ants. I tapped Delia's foot since she was about to put her foot right on it.

She jumped.

We paid and then drove onto I-45. Cars were stacked, lining up for rush hour.

"Texas is like every place else," said Delia.

"You haven't been every place else. How do you know that?" I asked.

"TV."

"What did you expect?"

"Horses, guns."

I told her to look around us at the idling drivers. "Lots of cowboy hats. Don't see that in North Carolina."

"I guess so." She sniffed the jerky. "Gaylen, you was crying in your sleep at Aunt Renni's."

So much had happened since we left Siphon. Delia jolted me back to Renni's. "I don't know why I do that," I said. "Mother used to shake me awake and ask me what was so much to be sad about. When I woke up, I didn't know. I seemed to know more in my sleep than I did awake."

Delia took out a cardboard picture of Jesus. It was the size of a pack of cigarettes and hung by a chain.

"Where did you get that?" I asked.

"Todd give it to me, probably because he slid his phone number into my hand at the same time. I'll hang Jesus up for luck." So she hung Christ over the rearview mirror.

He had a purple heart painted right over his robe.

"You think Jesus really looked like that?" she asked. "White dress, purple heart, hair like Jerry Garcia?"

"There weren't any cameras to take his picture."

"I think the purple heart means he's sad."

"He's the King of kings, Grandma used to say. Why would Jesus be sad, Delia? Because he knew he was going to die?"

"I think it was because he had to watch us running around like ants, eating each other alive. He wanted to stop us, but it was like stopping ants."

I thought about the ants on the giant moth. I did not know if that was the right analogy. I studied bugs in high school and the way they made colonies. I never read that ants were eating each other. But I imagined them down in the bowels of the earth, not knowing that a Waffle House was being built right over them. "I think he was sad because he has to look down on the earth and everywhere he looks people are asleep. So he comes down here to see who he can wake up."

Delia looked over at a car idling next to us on the interstate. A woman was driving a shiny truck. Next to her sat a man with a cowboy hat over his eyes, his arms crossed at his chest. His mouth had fallen open.

"I want to get me a Texas cowboy hat just so my friends at the Waffle House know I been to Texas," said Delia.

We merged onto I-610. The closer we got to Mr. Savage's house, the more nervous I got. It was a twisted kind of nervous, like cables of nervous and mad wrapped up around my chest. I imagined Mother and Daddy in California, but I could not see Truman. Mother once said she took me down to the ocean and touched my newborn foot to the salt water just so she could tell me I had been to the ocean. When she told me that story, it was like she had lit a torch inside of me, making me want to leave Boiling Waters and see the other side of the ocean. I could not imagine the rest of the country spread out between the place where I was born and the place I grew up. I wondered now if she did that on purpose or if she even knew what she was doing to me. But she never said what had come of her boy. Was he with her and my father in Salinas? Mr. Savage would surely know since Truman was his boy too.

Delia kept saying, "Stay straight, turn right, and turn right again," until we finally pulled up right in front of the address I had printed in the library. We got out and sidled gingerly up the walk. The house was a brick ranch, like the kind built back in the '50s. The door opened. Mr. Savage was a big man like my father. He kept staring at me as if he were reading something familiar in my eyes. "May I help you?" he asked.

"I'm Gaylen and this is Delia. Our half brother's name is Truman Savage."

"I don't know any other Truman Savage in the country. I'm the only one." He seemed proud of that, his heels lifting a bit when he said it.

Delia pulled out Truman's grade-school picture. I didn't know she had grabbed it from the house. "This is him," she said. "Our brother."

His face turned the color of a shell. "What do you want?"

I said, "Mr. Savage, you and my mother were once married." He kept staring so I said, "Fiona Chapel from back in North Carolina."

He studied me more intently, like he wanted to push me off his porch. "I left that all behind," he said. "I don't have anything to do with those people. Say, what's this about anyway? You come digging up trash around here, you'll not get anywhere with me."

I tried to assuage Mr. Savage's temper and assure him I wasn't looking to trash him. "Not at all, sir," I said. "My mother passed away some years back. But my brother, your boy Truman, he's in prison."

That surprised him.

"Could we talk to you, sir?" I asked. "We're trying to understand a few things about him."

He did not invite us in right away. But then Delia set to gibbering about our inheritance and how we were driving all over the country seeing family. Something about the words spilling out of her caused him to sigh, like he realized he could not get rid of us. So he invited us inside.

The house was decorated like everything had come from a Cracker Barrel country store. Little jars of okra and jars of cookie mix tied with ragged pink ribbons lined a shelf in his kitchen. Photographs of Mr. Savage and his wife, Gloria, and their son, Parson, were all over his house, on a fireplace hearth and next to medicine bottles on pretty little Hepplewhite tables. A miniature Christmas tree covered in faded silver and blue ornaments decorated the hearth. Mr. Savage had left it all as if Gloria might happen through the living room at any moment. He saw me looking at the tree and said, "My niece Tess worries over me since Gloria passed. She put that up. Otherwise I'd not fool with Christmas."

I took a seat in an embroidered rocker. "Your wife was Gloria. I noticed that she passed away."

He looked suspiciously at me. "How did you know that?"

"Internet."

"You looking up my business for a reason?"

"We thought you was murdered by Judge Cuvier," said Delia. She looked at Mother's ex, the two of them staring at one another, quiet as sunning gators, until I said, "My brother, Truman, wrote to us, telling us that he needed money to get an attorney and get back his father's land in Houston." I then told him what Truman had said about him. "He said you were murdered." I half-smiled. "Obviously you're not murdered."

"I'm as alive as can be. What would he say that for?"

"He wants money for an attorney," I said. "He just wants out of prison."

"Mr. Savage, my brother sounds sad. Do you ever contact him?" asked Delia.

There was a festering anger in his eyes. "I've disowned Truman. He knows why. But he's nothing but a liar, so don't ask him to tell you anything. It won't be true."

"My mother told us that he ran away from home," I said, remembering Renni's different version but playing dumb. "I'm trying to find out why."

He sat with his hands clasped, tapping his thumbs, like someone accustomed to holding together others dependent on him. I tried to imagine him married to my mother. If my father had not gone off on emotional tangents, he would be a lot like Mr. Savage: a man of few words, who, when he finally speaks, examines the words before allowing them to go public.

"The day he ran away from our house, my Aunt Renni says he came to you. Is that right?"

"Best I knew, your daddy put him on a bus," he said. "Had to. His mother, Fiona, kicked him out. There wasn't no running away to it. Don't know why she told you that."

Delia glanced at me.

"My father bought him a bus ticket?" I had not counted on my father being in on the trouble with Truman.

"Had to. Truman was only fifteen. He wouldn't have had the means."

"How long did he live with you?" asked Delia.

"A month." He pressed his hands together as if smashing a bug. "My little boy, Parson, came to me crying. The whole month Truman lived here, he was molesting his little brother." His jaw clenched. "If Parson had told me sooner…" he stopped. His shoulders lifted slightly as he breathed, while he tensely stroked his forehead with one hand. Finally he said, "But Truman had threatened him, told him that if he told, he would hurt him worse."

The room darkened. There was a change in the Texas weather.

I sighed, my head suffering the early pangs of a headache. "How do you know my mother made Truman leave?"

"Truman said she threw him out, but that didn't surprise me. She never treated him right. Of course, I always thought poorly of her as a mother, so I felt sorry for him. I'd tried to get her to let him come and live with me. If she didn't love the boy, why'd she have to hold on to him?" He got up and went for his medicine. "Pardon me, ladies. I just had a recent spell with my heart. Put me in the hospital. Got to watch my blood pressure." He went into the kitchen for water and then returned to the living room.

"What kind of mother was she…my mother…to Truman?"

"Mad as all get out. She whipped him, sometimes for no reason that I could see. But she was mad at me, mad at her mother. Fiona Chapel was mad at the whole world."

"I remember her like that," said Delia.

"I think she tried harder with us to be a better mother," I said. "I was born in California, Mr. Savage. But my parents moved back to North Carolina after I was born. Did Truman go with my mother to California?"

"He did. I tried to keep her from doing that. She had up and married one fella, but it was short-lived. Then she run off with Mr. Syler, your daddy. I told her he'd not put up with her any better than me or any other man. No man could tolerate her angry spells. She was two-timing too."

I imagined on the flight from North Carolina asking him if the dallying had been mutual. But sitting looking him straight in the eyes, I could not get up the nerve to form the words. He had an imposing stature and took a hard line on his own opinions.

"But I didn't want Truman so far away I couldn't check on him. She never listened to me. Fiona Chapel could not be told what to do. She was going to have things her way or not at all."

I said to Delia, "So Truman was living with Mother and Daddy in California. He was there when I was born."

Delia said, "Hah!"

"Fiona dropped out of contact with me after that. I moved off to Texas and married my wife. I had mailed a letter to Fiona one last time, just so Truman would know of my whereabouts. Then we had Parson. Life was finally good…until the day he showed up looking pitiful."

"My brother must have been good at gaining sympathy," I said.

"He was quite the actor. Boy could summon tears like a woman. And believable! He could work an adult like no kid I ever saw. I got my eyes opened, though."

"Did you make him leave?" I asked.

"I did. I wanted to kill him with my two bare hands, but throwing him out somehow seemed better punishment. Not twenty minutes passed and my brother Will called me from three streets away, angry. Said I was a terrible father for kicking Truman out without a dime or a place to eat. He took him right in."

"Didn't you tell him what had happened to Parson?"

"Of course not! People don't talk about such things," he said.

Delia asked, "How long did Truman stay at your brother's place, Mr. Savage?"

He looked as if the color was completely bled out of his face. "He molested all three of my brother's children: Tess, Bo, and Jana. Then my brother kicked him out."

I wanted to ask Mr. Savage again why he did not tell his brother about Parson, the same as my mother who did not tell why she kicked him out. He could have stopped it from happening. But he looked so lost, having been forced to stop and consider the past, that I kept my thoughts to myself, and they were legion.

The sun evaporated, and Houston beamed like a Mexican festival on the flat plain of southern Texas. I drove to a taco stand for a late lunch. Then Delia and I stopped in at a giant flea market before driving into Houston. I was glad to put Mr. Savage behind us. Not knowing what to expect, I had booked a flight to leave the next day.

"Truman molested us, didn't he?" Delia asked me.

"I'd like to know for sure," I said.

"Mama should have told us. We've got the right to know."

"There's got to be someone who knows for certain," I said. "Truman knows."

I felt angry but did not tell Delia the thoughts going through my mind. I imagined Truman sitting in prison, waiting to get out. I wondered if my mother had been in contact with him all of those years. In the letter to Delia and me, he had called us baby sisters. That was how he remembered us: infant girls, young and vulnerable. But I could not remember any tangible evidence of the events that transpired his last day in Boiling Waters. No matter how hard I tried, I could not picture his teen face. I tried again to remember the day he left our town. All I could remember was how he stood over my father's bed, dissecting a frog and then my mother beating him.

It was like trying to see through a painted window.

We drove up and down the downtown streets, Delia ogling the city sights and me wanting to hunt down whatever restaurants were driving me nuts with the smell of Tex-Mex and Mex-Mex.

We pulled up to the Magnolia Hotel. The valet opened Delia's door. She stepped out in her fake lizard boots and cowboy hat. Although I would not have put cowboy boots with the Burberry outfit, she somehow blended with the Texas glitz of downtown Houston. She kissed the doorman's cheek and asked him his name. He blushed and told her, "Duke." I thought it was some name all the Texas hotel people were told to say, so I did not take stock in it. She asked him if there was a vacancy, and he was certain we could get a room.

I asked him, "Where do you recommend we eat?"

"You can't beat Houston for food, ma'am. They say the food

here is like visiting one hundred and twenty or more countries. But if you want, I can make you a reservation, call you a cab. That way you won't have to find your way around."

"Give us thirty minutes, then, Duke. You pick the place." I gave him the keys, and we hauled luggage out onto the walk and checked it with him.

Delia skipped up the walk under the long black hotel awning. A woman walking a small white dog bent to scoop up her pet and step aside, wide-eyed at the sight of Delia laughing and flinging her hair. I walked past the hotel guest, smiled, and whispered, "She loves those Texas margaritas."

"Why sure, sure!" the woman laughed. "Can't blame her for that!"

Duke touched my arm. "Is your sister single?"

"Um-hm," I said.

"She's pretty as any woman I've seen," he said.

"You just have to watch, Duke. My sister bites," I said.

He turned and walked back to his post.

Delia waited near the fireplace in the lounge, touching the Christmas tree ornaments. She lifted one off the tree and held it up to the light.

I checked us into a room with two queen beds, overlooking Houston toward Galveston. By the time I checked in, night had fallen. Delia had struck up a conversation with a businessman wearing a suit and a cowboy hat. He was tall as a pine, smiling down at her admiringly.

"My sister and I are rich now too," she told him. I hooked her arm in mine to lead her toward the elevator.

"What about drinks? You promised," he said to her. His eyes traveled from her to me.

"We've already called a cab," I told him, still leading her away.

Delia fumed all the way up to the ninth floor. "He's an oil man, Gaylen. Keeps horses out on a ranch and flies back and forth to work in a helicopter."

"He told you all of that in the two minutes it took for me to check in?"

"Why you got to ruin the night? I had us double dates set up with rich brothers."

"Married, Delia."

"He didn't say he was married."

"His ring finger was white, while the rest of his hand was tanned. He took off his ring to get a date."

She looked stunned, like she had never taken Dating 101. "Still. Rich and good-looking men don't come along like that in Boiling Waters. Least not down at the Blue Water Café."

"Here's our floor," I said. I handed her a room card and demonstrated how to swipe it like a credit card. I washed up while Delia found a TV special about the Bush family.

"If I was going to be a Republican, I would vote for him. I like the way he goes in gangbusters to kick the bad guys' butts," she said. "TV's been so much better with him in the White House."

I slipped into black pants and put on some jewelry. "Since when were you not a Republican?" I asked. Delia and I were both brought up to vote for the Republican rather than the candidate. It was the Syler way.

"Lee hated Republicans."

"So you're a Democrat because of Lee and a Catholic because of Freddy Deals."

"Basically."

"He can't run again anyway, Delia." We locked up the room and headed down to the lobby. Duke had the cab waiting. He helped Delia into the backseat. She giggled.

"Take these two lovely girls to Cafe Annies," he told the driver.

I tipped Duke and he winked. I was starting to like Houston, as well as spending at least a little of the money my father had hoarded in case the world might end. The bluing dusk that settled over Houston's green city glow gave me an assurance that for this one night the world would continue, at least into the big Texas sunrise only twelve hours away.

Delia stared out and up at Houston's cityscape. I was certain we had been to Raleigh as girls, but Houston was the mother ship next to Raleigh's pod.

The Mexican driver drove through a red light, which made Delia squeal and then laugh. After that, it seemed as if he ran red lights just to hear her snort and guffaw.

"Tell me your name," she said to the cab driver.

"Benny," he said, no accent whatsoever.

Delia hooted.

"What's wrong with that?" I asked.

She kept laughing and slapping her knee until we pulled up in front of the Cafe Annie's royal blue awning. "Look, a for-real Texas palm tree," said Delia. She cocked back her hat, smiling serenely at the doorman. "Let me check us in," she begged me. "My turn, my turn to play big shot."

A foreign woman, perhaps European and blond, checked our reservations. She invited us to wait at the swanky bar until she pulled up our name. Delia ordered a margarita.

"Pinot noir," I told the bartender. I was feeling irritable, so I had to resist the urge to down the wine.

A waitress approached me. "The gentlemen seated behind you have ordered you a bottle of whatever you want," she said, a waifish twenty-something wearing a black dress and white beads.

"Tell them to keep it," I said, without looking behind me.

Delia whipped around in her chair. "That was downright rude, Gaylen."

"Don't start."

"No, let me talk for once. Here we sit like two queens in Houston, drawing good-looking men like sirens, and you run them off." She sipped her margarita and then whispered for the first time all day, "Is it because you're not over Braden?"

"That's no secret, Delia."

"Or is it Truman? The way Mr. Savage spilled the beans today, not holding back, I mean, made me sick at my stomach."

I pushed aside my glass, again deciding that I would not drink. "Does it seem like we never knew our mother?"

She asked the bartender for an extra plate of limes and then said, "That's no secret either."

"You and Mother went at it, but not us, not like she did with Daddy or the aunts," I said. I knew Mother didn't have many friends. But that was why I thought she felt a bond with me and considered me a confidant. Even at the age of seven, I felt I held a strange power over her. "Of all people, I thought I knew her. Now, starting on the drive back from Pasadena, all of these things are coming back to me. It's like she's speaking to me from the grave."

Delia said, "Hmmph!"

But something about watching Delia sucking limes while Cowboys' fans seated around the horseshoe bar cheered triggered a small fragment of something my mother said. "I remember her standing in the kitchen and telling me that she would go to her grave with the things that Truman did. But she was so irate, she intimidated me. I was a kid, and she was being loud, and I just wanted her to calm down. So I never asked her what she meant." I was seeing Mother differently now. "Those things she said about Truman were not clear, not then."

"Now you know." Delia was floating away into a mellow margarita state.

I was in the third photograph of my mother I had pinned inside my suitcase. I was eighteen months old, and she was holding me on one knee, squatted in front of my grandmother's house. She was smiling in a way that must have faded with time. I never remembered that look, not that effusive smile, not in real life, not like the one frozen in that still photograph. She was happy. That I did not remember about her without looking at that photograph of us.

I was round cheeked and laughing as if my mother and I were posing for a happy family magazine. I was so young that baldness was expected.

"But I can't prove anything. I keep trying to see Truman at our house. But there wasn't an extra room for him. There was me and you and—" I stopped.

Delia sucked the guts right out of a lime wedge.

"She made you and me sleep in a bed next to her. Do you remember?" I asked.

"Um-hm."

"But where was Truman? Did he sleep on the couch? Why did she sleep with us instead of in Daddy's bedroom?"

"She was a big nut, not sleeping with her own husband."

"Or she was keeping us close by."

"Hah!"

"I wish I would have known enough to ask before she died."

"She wouldn't have told." Delia closed her eyes, allowing the drink to trickle down her throat. Then she opened her eyes, curiously watching the bartender who was shaking a fresh margarita.

"I would've made her."

"You were afraid of her," said Delia.

I was stunned at her words. "Why do you say that?"

Delia turned around in her seat to try and pick out the men who had attempted to buy wine for us.

Things that my mother said that, at the time, seemed inconsequential seeped into my mind. *I'll never forgive that boy for the way he treated us... No one knows what he put me through.* The words fell into some of the missing slots of the past, but did not entirely fill every gap; they were just enough to leave me wanting to know the whole of the matter.

"Everybody was afraid of Fiona Syler. Even Mr. Savage," said Delia.

14

WE CHECKED OUT of the Magnolia Hotel early. Delia came out yawning and wanting to stay in bed until noon. "Our flight home leaves in two hours," I said. "And the concierge says we ought to check in early."

"What's left to go back to in North Carolina?" she asked. "Let's start a new life in Houston. I like it here. No Gradys or Mason Freemans to hold threats over your head. The pickings are good as far as guys are concerned. We got money to burn."

"You've got to stop it, Delia."

"I've never had so much."

"If we don't stop and get it in an investment where we can't spend it, it will all be gone, and you'll be no better off."

"But we had a good time," she said. "That's worth something."

Duke phoned up for our car. We waited on the walk in front of the hotel.

My cell phone rang. I answered. Braden had come home and found the apartment turned upside down. He was breathing hard, having trouble talking, but finally said, "What's happened to our place,

Gaylen? Looks like a war zone, like someone took a bat to the place. Your leasing agent, Kimberly, is frantic and wanting to know if you're alive." He did not sound easeful, nearly like when he could not find a landing strip in the dark. "Did you really quit?"

"Fired and quit," I said.

Delia twirled around to face me, staring with her mouth open.

"I hated that job anyway," I said, wondering why it mattered if Delia heard.

"You loved it," he said. "Like I've never seen you work so many hours."

"I was never off work." He really thought I loved that stinking, awful job.

The sound of someone moving furniture around or lifting broken objects made it difficult to understand him. In the background, Kimberly said, "Omigosh! I called the cops. Is she hurt?"

"I'm coming home, Braden, but that guy whose eyes you blacked is a hit man. He wants Delia really badly. I got a first name. It's Grady. I don't know where to take her, where it's safe."

"Where are you now?"

The driver pulled up with our car. Duke said, "Your carriage awaits, girls."

Braden asked, "Who was that?"

"Duke," I said.

"Do I know him?"

"I'm in Houston. Delia and I came here to try to put together some facts about my family." When he did not answer, I said, "I needed to get Delia out of town."

"Did you find what you're looking for?" He sounded melancholy and put out.

"I'm not sure," I said. There was not enough time to explain Truman Senior or Amity's dresses.

Duke took my luggage and stowed it in the trunk.

Delia slid into the open door on the passenger's side. She waved good-bye to the valet as if they were old friends.

"Are you coming home?" Braden asked.

"Grady will be looking for us. I don't know what to do." I finally told him, "He stole our wedding bands."

It took a moment for Braden to answer. "It's time to take Delia to the police," he said. I could hear sirens in the background. I imagined Deputy Bob pulling up in front of Building B on Moss Court while Kimberly ran up and down the stairs and Mrs. Shane paced back and forth on the landing.

Delia pulled down the visor and found a mirror. She dug through my purse and pulled out a lipstick. She put it on and grinned at herself.

"I agree. I'll take her straight to the police," I said.

Delia mouthed, "Let's go," through the window glass while I tried to please both Braden and her.

"The cops are here," he said. "I have to go. Call me when you land in Wilmington."

We had not pulled all the way out onto Texas Avenue when Delia blurted out, "You was fired? See, you don't tell me a thing. You're the last person I would think would be fired." She was still holding my handbag in her lap. "Me, I get fired drop of a hat. You got any mascara?" She fished through my bag like she did our mother's whenever she took us to church.

"Braden's going to the cops, Delia," I said. "He has to tell them about Grady, and that will mean telling them about Sophie." I was tired of holding back, worried that Delia would explode. "You should have told the cops from the start."

She sat up, frowning, her chin drawing up tight as a baseball. "They'll not protect me, Gaylen! They'll be waiting on me when we land in Wilmington. I'll be thrown in jail. Don't you get it? I can just hear Deputy Bob laughing his hind end off, dropping the jail key down his britches." She set to crying, so she pulled tissues out of my handbag and alternated wiping her eyes and applying little dashes of mascara to her thin, damp lashes. "I didn't mean to shoot Sophie Deals, and she's moving on with her life, isn't she? Let's all just make up and get on with things. Why is it everyone always has to blow up everything I do as if I was a mass murderer?" She kept pumping the wand into the tube and working her lashes until they were stiff and black as spider legs. "You got to take me some place far away. Mexico. Or Paris, how about? I got new clothes."

"Delia, if I hadn't started running you all over the country, I'd not have lost my job. I can't keep running."

"You have me to thank, then." She feigned sobbing. "I heard you tell your husband you hated that job."

"What else was I supposed to say?"

"You'll get another job."

"I'm so employable," I said. "I crash planes, steal airport food. I'm everyone's low man on the totem pole."

She wiped a long, dark, salty stream from her cheek. "That's why you hooked up with that professor."

"That doesn't make any sense," I said, and I was mad at her for continually bringing him up.

"He was a hoity-toity man."

"You're so off base, I can't believe it! But that's because you don't know me. How could you? Never do you try to get to know me. I'm the one always left to figure you out."

"You never wanted to be like the rest of us, Gaylen."

"What are you saying, that I slept with Max Swinson to elevate myself?"

"What does a man like that talk about anyway, I'd like to know."

"Philosophy."

"You sure know how to flirt."

"Are you saying that my stupid fling with Max had an ulterior motive?"

"I don't even know what that is."

She annoyed me to the point of losing my way out of downtown Houston. "Until we get on the plane, will you can it, Delia?" I asked. "I'll never get us out of here, and I don't want to miss the flight."

I finally saw the interstate sign and ramped into the stream of morning traffic. Most of the commuters were coming into the city while we were leaving, so I drove onto the interstate with ease. The airport sign guided me back to Hobby Airport. It was a gray morning that, according to the radio weather report, would break forth into Texas sunshine within the hour. But all I could see before me were Max Swinson's eyes the color of muddy ocean water and his slightly crooked smile. He was a bookish nerd who expressed how surprised he was when I so easily followed him out to his beach cottage. I finally hated him.

Delia was humming, not any tune in particular but a ditty that she seemed to make up.

Max hovered inside me like a funny little enigma of a man buzzing around in my head. Whether or not I was trying to elevate myself had not been so clear up until the moment that Delia unearthed it without a bit of reflection or effort on her part. My sister was wrong, but now I was left to figure out how the only good Syler girl had fallen so easily for a man who seduced me with so little effort. How well I remembered.

It was the second rendezvous to the beach cottage, and Max brought champagne. Not even good champagne, but he poured it into my glass like it had cost him a week's pay. He wore a black suit that made him look lean. The suit was fresh from the dry cleaners. I saw the tag in the collar when he laid it over the chair.

I was getting over a cold and wore so many layers it took fifteen minutes to undress. But Max never undressed fully. He kept sipping his drink and watching me. I was a floor show, but it was not like me to succumb to this brand of monkeyshines. My high school friends voted me the only girl who did not know how to flirt. I dropped my neatly folded tights onto the floor next to the blue cardigan and the knit plaid skirt.

I never felt comfortable the first time a man saw me naked. I was thin and subconsciously aware of my size B cups. I had hated puberty anyway, so when hormones trickled into my skinny frame at age nine, it filled up more of me below the waist than above. This was just another new experience with the sickening sense of discomfort that ruled over me.

Max pulled me close. It occurred to me that he had never kissed me. I closed my eyes and prepared for the kiss. I hoped his kissing me would finally rev things up between us. But he barely touched my lips. I opened my eyes, and he was holding me as if he did not know what to do next.

"Is something the matter?" I asked.

"You don't want to be here."

"I'm here. Isn't that proof?"

"You're not into me at all."

Braden had said the same thing. "You're ruining this!" I said, angry.

I sat on the bed crying. He left me there with a key telling me, "Spend the night if you want." There was a slight tremor in his voice, as if I had stolen his virility. "I'll call you."

"Delia, if you'll not bring up Max again, I'll buy you a pair of black boots. You need black for the sake of your basics." I drove into the rental car lot piecing together a plan for how I could use my share of the inheritance to finish my education and get out of Boiling Waters. But that thought was put on hold when Braden called again. The police were looking for Delia, he said, and for me. "Don't come home until I can sort this all out. Wait for my call," he told me. "And whatever you do, don't get back on that plane."

Delia was happy again.

The rental car dealer allowed us an extra day, so back we went into Houston in search of a car to keep. I told Delia, "We're not far from Dallas. I'll call Uncle Jackson and Aunt Noleen and see if they might take us in for a couple of days." I would use Renni's name and Daddy's name and hope that would open their door to us. "That will give me time to think." I was thinking of calling the Boiling Waters police but did not know how to tell Delia. Then I wondered if Jackson might help her find a job in Dallas. I could set her up with a bank account and a small amount of cash to get her started in a new life. Then I could tell Deputy Bob that she had run off and left me stranded.

But as the scheme was hatching, it was not settling well. Braden once said that it was not possible for me to lie. I thought that was true, that I knew myself. But that was before Max. The lying took over for a while until I hated myself too much to continue. But running with Delia had turned over the dark side of me again, flipping me back and forth from good to bad like a pancake.

Buying a used car in Texas was like picking shells off the beach. Every street corner, it seemed, blazed with the sales schmaltz of low auto deal claims. I drove onto a lot called The Texas Stampede. The sign was in the shape of a longhorn bull's head. The front door on the mobile office flew open the instant we pulled onto the lot. Out walked a salesman wearing a brown suede vest and a ten-gallon hat. He sidled up next to Delia and handed her a shiny marshal's badge. "It's the law around here: every customer gets the best deal in Houston." His name tag read Chris. "I'm the marshal of used cars," he said.

He handed me the keys to an orange sports car that Delia and I drove around until we were carsick. There was little room for our luggage. We tried out a second car, a Volkswagen that smelled like stale taco sauce and cigarette smoke.

Delia begged, "Please, a pickup truck, Gaylen. I've always wanted one, and look, it's marked down to twelve thousand, and it comes with a set of cookware."

"Any automobile you pick out today and drive off this lot comes with the nonstick Country Chef cookware," said Marshal Chris. "And that's a five cook-pot deal, lids included." He pressed the truck keys into my hand. "Take 'er to lunch, girls. Be our guest." He handed Delia a coupon for a bucket of chicken at a café he called the Hungry Hen. Delia grabbed the keys and the coupon and clambered into the driver's seat. I joined her inside the truck's cab.

She zipped onto the interstate, playing with the window buttons and the radio dial. "It's got a five-CD changer and a cup holder big enough for a Big Gulp," she said, a passionate connoisseur of 7-Eleven Slurpees. She spotted the Hungry Hen café sign and followed the arrows up the ramp and into the parking lot. She pulled the bright blue truck into a front-row parking slot. When a couple of men in cowboy hats glanced our way, she slid out of the truck, fake reptile boots hitting the parking lot pavement while she waved at the men as if she knew them. "Texas has a lot to offer a person," she said, walking past me through the doors.

I passed on the chicken and ordered a salad. We sat in an orange plastic booth under a sign that said "Boat on Beautiful Nacogdoches Lake."

She snuggled up next to a double-battered chicken leg, chewing and rolling her eyes. "Nobody ever give me anything for free. Except there was that time that Lee and me was down on the lake fishing. The bait shop gave us two bait cups for the price of one, seeing how the worms were going to dry up if he didn't pass them on." She smiled at the two Texans who took a booth across from us. She wiped her hands on a napkin and extended her hand across the aisle. "Name's Delia," she said to one.

"Harrison Pew, Delia," he smiled. "This is my cousin, Avery."

Avery smiled at me as if we were all being paired off by an unseen hand. He was younger and better suited to Delia. He reminded me of the type of boys at Boiling Waters High who hated school and loved shop class.

"We're test-driving that truck," Delia told Harrison. "I don't know much about trucks, like, knowing when you're getting ripped off and when you're getting a good deal."

"Avery will look under the hood for you," said Harrison.

"That's not necessary," I said, but no one listened to me.

"I just knew you were the type of guys to help us out," said Delia. "We're not from Houston."

I knew that if I did not interject some sort of distraction into the conversation, Delia would next tell them that we were wealthy heiresses hiding out from the North Carolina state police. "Where's a good place to visit around here?" I asked, figuring that Harrison and Avery were most likely not concerned with intellectual repartee.

"I like the Houston Symphony," said Harrison, glib and looking at me.

"We're not really from here either," said Avery. "We flew here from North Carolina to get away before racing season. Harrison here is a race car driver. I'm his crew boss."

"Good. Then you know all about engines and such," said Delia. She got up and walked to the door as if she knew that Avery would magically follow, and of course, he did.

"I wasn't kidding about the symphony," said Harrison. He moved across the aisle and sat in the seat Delia had just left. "I've got tickets to the Christmas concert tonight. People give me things like that all the time, but a NASCAR guy like Avery is not likely to join me."

"You don't want your tickets?" I asked him.

"Avery doesn't want his," he said. "I know you don't know me, but I'm a big fan of the Houston Symphony, a bit of a patron. I'd hate to go by myself, though." He did not try to flirt or persuade me. He said, "You look like the kind of woman who'd like to hear a good orchestra."

Harrison's eyes were not so dull and void of light. He removed his billed cap emblazoned with his name. He had a mass of blond curls that softened his looks. His temples were high, and in spite of his flannels and jeans, he looked as if he might own a black dress coat. I was about to open my mouth and tell him that I wasn't dating since I was still carrying my unsigned divorce papers around in my suitcase next to my dead mother's pictures. I said instead, "Tonight?"

Delia and I checked into the less pricy La Quinta near the interstate. It was near a shopping mall, and I needed a new dress. I found a sheath dress that fell across my hips in as flattering a manner as possible. I had shed a few pounds while running from Delia's demons.

Delia rattled on about Avery and how he saved us a fortune when he discovered a bad gasket under the blue truck's hood that had been doctored, most likely, by Marshal Chris's mechanic. He knew of a friend selling a good used sports car—a blue Miata—for a song. While Harrison and I went to the Houston Symphony, Avery would take Delia bowling, and the two of them would test-drive the friend's car.

Delia was ecstatic, not only for her bowling date, but that I had agreed. For one night, we were free of each other. But I was having second thoughts, feeling as if I was betraying Braden all over again.

"He divorced you and then told you about it after the fact," said Delia.

I sat down on the bed. "It was my fault though, Delia. I initiated the train wreck."

We sat quietly staring into the motel television. There was a battle in Fallujah and two U.S. soldiers were killed. Delia slid on a pair of flip-flops and went out for ice and canned drinks. I changed channels several times but could not get away from the war.

Harrison would come for me in one hour. He gave me his number, he said, in case I changed my mind. I showered, changed into the dress, changed out of it, reached for the phone, and then lay across the bed in my bathrobe.

Delia came through the door expecting to find me dressed. "You look awful," she said. "You having second thoughts?"

"I'm getting dressed," I said, reasoning, "I haven't seen a symphony since Braden's parents bought us tickets for our first anniversary." I burst into tears.

Delia fished a box of tissues out of the bathroom console. She lay beside me on the bed, passing me fresh tissues and wadding up the ones I used. She rolled onto her back, staring at the overhead light. "I don't think I've ever loved a man like that," she said. "Not so I just about throw up when he's gone. Lee, he did me dirty, but I liked revenge as much as I liked marriage." Her face was drawn, the face that she wore when she wanted to convince me she could be serious. "Love is a pain I get rid of. But you hold on to it, like the pain is just part of it."

"So that's what I'm left with? Love is a pain in the gut?"

"Why keep it when it goes bad?" she asked. "I'm not one for punishment."

I came up onto my elbows. "When I married Braden, it felt as if I was being carried along into marriage and then there he was sleeping in my bed every night. It became an obligation. Maybe love has to get painful before you recognize it. It's not like you think, not like you imagine." I still did not have it right, but neither did Delia. "You don't know what love feels like until you lose it."

"I'll never get it," she said. "Avery's got nice eyes. I feel something when he looks at me. I used to call it love. But it's always like that at first. Then one day I just look at a guy and there's nothing, nothing at all that feels like that first look. Listening to you, though, I don't know what else to expect. Did I ever know—with Lee, Freddy, and now with Avery?" She sat up, aimed the remote at the television, and turned it off. "Maybe I just want to have someone say nice things about me. Maybe to me that is my definition for love. Why does it have to turn so ugly?"

I handed her back the tissue box.

"You're not going out with Harrison tonight, are you?" she asked. She slumped down onto the bed, burying her face in the linens.

"I'll go," I said. "But we're headed for Dallas tomorrow. So don't grow too attached to Houston." I washed my face and dressed.

Delia found the gaming program on my phone and played solitaire.

Harrison showed up at the door dressed in black, his blond curls combed back into a ponytail.

Avery walked up behind him, his hair still wet from the shower. "You two look like you're going to a banking convention. Delia, you ready?" he asked, bored with his NASCAR boss and our symphony date. "You're missing a perfect opportunity to get creamed by me on the lanes," he told Harrison.

"I'm sure we'll live to regret it," said Harrison. He offered me his arm. We walked to the stairs, and he let me go first. Delia ran giggling around me. Avery walked around us, scratching his head. Delia would blow it with a guy like him pretty fast. That was one thing I could count on. Avery was sane enough that he would be history by morning.

As for me, I wasn't sure what I wanted.

Harrison was driving a rented classic. Braden on occasion had reserved a car like that for a wealthy client. Harrison said, "It's useless trying to eat before a concert. I hope it's all right with you. I made reservations for dinner afterward. That's a late evening."

He was so apologetic that I did not know how to take him. I wanted him to be pushy or boastful so that I would be glad for the evening to be finished. Harrison had the quiet demeanor of a monk. "I don't mind," I said.

He knew his way around Houston. He drove right up to the parking deck across from Jones Hall in the theater district. He led me through the crowd that spilled across the street and swarmed into the lobby.

"These are box seats," he said. "A friend of mine keeps them but seldom attends."

"When did you get interested in the symphony?" I asked.

"I play the violin. But it was hard to make a living at it. You have to keep five jobs going at once to keep the lights on," he said.

I must have stared at him.

"Not many of the guys know, except Avery and one other. They give me a hard time about it," he said. "Would you like a drink?" he asked.

"Club soda is all," I said.

"I don't drink either." He ordered at the portable lobby bar.

Symphony patrons—some in dress black and some in work clothes—gathered in clusters and streamed into Jones Hall.

"How often do you come to Houston?" I asked.

"My mother lives in Houston. She hates the racetrack, so I come here to see her," he said. "She was happier when I studied violin." He bought a pack of M&M's. "My first wife liked the money of racing."

"I'm divorcing too," I said.

"My ex was a good manager. She managed everything, our money, my career," he said. "But she never would just look at me and see me."

I wanted to know how long ago, but I was out of Harrison's life in twelve hours. "I needed a night away from my sister," I said. "But I don't normally date." He was still looking at me without commenting, so I said, "I hope you don't think I get picked up in fast-food restaurants on a regular basis."

We had to step aside to let a man and woman pass through. The orchestra was warming up. We disposed of the cups. Then he led us across the lobby up a carpeted staircase and down the hallway leading to the box seats.

"Not a lot of women are as quick to accept a date to the symphony. It's not your typical pick-up line," he said, a smile still fresh on his face. "Just shows you got some taste. Don't feel like you have to keep explaining yourself to me. We're two people away from home. No need to sit around in front of the television with a perfectly good city waiting on us."

Harrison was a man of easeful nature, not one to start off compartmentalizing people into categories, it seemed. He had a bit of crease around each eye, like a man ten years older than me. But he didn't talk down to me like Max had done our last night together.

I asked, "Are you Buddhist by any chance? You don't have to answer if that's too personal."

"That's all right. I'm not."

"My husband's friend is a Buddhist. He has your quiet demeanor. That's the only reason I asked," I said.

He escorted me into the hall. The red seating was less formal than most symphony halls. An usher led us to a box seat almost directly over the orchestra pit. "My mother's friend from school keeps this box seat because his mother left it to him. But they never come and enjoy it." The lights dimmed, and we sat in the padded chairs.

I reached into my purse to turn off my phone, but the phone pocket was empty. I had left it back in the room. The conductor walked out onto the stage. He introduced the pianist who would play Rachmaninoff's Third. The audience responded with high approval.

"You said 'your mother's friend from school,'" I said. "Is she a teacher?"

"Retired professor. That was what she wanted for me, to be a musician and teach college."

"Race car driving and violin playing are strange bed mates," I said.

"I know."

I settled into the concert music, trying to get out of my head the thought that this was the silliest date I'd ever had. Going on a date to be away from Delia was like going to the men's bathroom to avoid the graffiti scrawled on the pink women's stalls.

Halfway through the concert, Harrison cupped his hand over mine on the chair arm. I knew it was simply a gesture from a man away from home who needed human touch and meant nothing more. I turned my hand up and let his fingers close around mine. I felt twelve and hiding behind the cafeteria at Boiling Waters High to make out.

An older man in front of me was nodding off to sleep. I imagined his wife, who was caught up in the rapture of Rachmaninoff, had dragged him to the symphony. Harrison glanced toward him and then fixed his eyes again on the pianist.

Braden would have said something about the sleepy husband. He would have made me laugh. But Harrison actually liked the music and was most likely judging the man for his lack of musical savoir-faire.

The whole time Harrison held my hand, I could picture Braden flying through the air, through the fringes of clouds, barely visible by night. I closed my eyes and remembered the large mass of fingers taking my hand the first time. My life with him flashed forward to that night when, at a showing of *The Rocky Horror Picture Show*, I considered for the first time the picket-fence-and-kids scenario, but nothing beyond the matrimonial pipe dream because I was a marriage critic. My mother had married three times, cautioning me it was for the birds. Conflict was the warning meter in the sensitive mechanism of marriage, according to my mother. If she and my father went to battle, then there was something irrevocably wrong between them. It was only because she was aging and failing in her health that she stuck it out with my dad, husband number three.

This was the handbook of my marriage schooling.

Braden was as plain as peanut butter. He seldom read a book, knew nothing about music except the songs he listened to on Carolina Country 104.2. But I sat thinking about him and how bored he would be and the tension he would bring to the evening. I sat in the pounding driving storm of Rachmaninoff's Third, willing the clash and the fracas of Braden Boatwright back into my life. There was something inherently disturbing about me, I decided.

My first date with Braden was a night of almosts. I almost told him that I normally did not feel anything for any guy on a date. But instead I asked him if he liked his shrimp. He kissed me right inside my apartment door and almost kissed me again, but I backed away. I wanted Braden to come inside and stay because for that whole evening I never tired of the sound of his voice, even the way he repeated the punch line to a story. I never could get the words just right to make a guy want to make me the one he would take out again. Braden had almost made it out to his car when I ran after him and said, "I've had the best time tonight that I've ever had with a guy."

If it were not for me finally giving him that first come on, he might never have asked me out again. We might never have known each other the way we did that first summer. But I said it, I realized, out of an earnest response, a feeling beating its way out of my fossilized emotions.

When the symphony ended, the lights came up. I put on my own coat, walking two feet ahead of Harrison. "If you don't mind, I think I'll grab some deli food outside and take it back to my room, call it a night." I expected to be hit over the head with a Coke bottle.

"I always know how to charm a woman," he said, sarcastic but still self-abasing—so much so that I felt guilty bailing on him.

I waited up for him. "It isn't you," I said. "I'm on hold for the time being."

"I could get us a room tonight." Before I could say "no," he said, "I mean, a place where you can talk."

Of course, talk. Max had said, "Just talk." "Talk" is what men say when they mean "sex."

"Talk all night, if you want. I'll order up a coffee service. I can tell you need a friend. Just please don't go." Harrison's eyes had that effect to which Delia had alluded.

A symphony lobby employee wearing a black suit sold CDs for the pianist but also magazines, packages of nuts, cans of soda, and future concert calendars. I bought a CD along with a tin of mints.

"Let me pay for it," said Harrison. "Then let's find a quiet place. I know you've got something on your mind. I listen pretty good."

I laid down the money. Max taught me a thing or two about resistance. "I'm an idiot, and I can prove it, Harrison. But the last thing I need is to spill my guts to you." Harrison seemed like a sincere man. I wasn't judging him. But poring over the past with a man I did not know had already cost me a slightly bruised marriage. "If you could go for the car," I said. "I'll get the deli food. You want a sandwich?"

His countenance clouded. "I'll take you back to your place. We could have made a perfect memory, you know."

"I've got memories," I said. "None perfect."

The air was stiff in Harrison's car. The dropping temperature caused a mist to form inside his window glass. He grabbed a tissue and wiped the windshield in angry swipes, back and forth, squeaking against the glass as he muttered.

"If you're mad, you should be," I said.

"Don't make it easier, Gaylen. I don't need to analyze this. It was a mistake."

"I don't need another relationship in a hurry," I said.

"I did want to talk all night, in spite of what you believe," he said.

"If I say I believe you, it won't change anything." I was feeling guilty for accepting the date. "I know better, but when has that ever stopped me?"

He tucked the wet tissue beside his seat. "You are right about me."

I didn't know what he meant.

"I'm a jerk, and even if I thought you would spend the night talking, I'd hope for more. I caused my own marriage to fail."

"Me too."

"She caught me fooling around."

"Caught you?" I said it so that I sounded shocked.

"Walked in on me with someone else in the middle of the day."

"I can't imagine." And I couldn't.

He must have been overcome with a need to confess. "I don't know why I did it. Racing is like catnip to some women. But even then, it was like I was watching outside myself, standing outside a window yelling at myself to stop."

"I know that feeling." I did. It made me hate myself. I felt dirty, finally wallowing in the gutter that swallows up all Syler women.

"You do?"

I fell quiet.

"Why'd your husband leave?"

I said, "You don't have to share the top ten dirty secrets of NASCAR drivers, Harrison." I unwrapped the CD and slid it into his console. It was mostly piano, lots of runs and annoying staccato, so much so that he hit the eject button.

"Confessions are best saved for the person you offend," I said.

"I wish you'd stay," he said quietly.

"I still love my husband," I said. "You can't get mad about that or take it personally."

"I could be him tonight."

"You'd settle for that?"

"If you come over to my side, you won't go back to begging. I wouldn't make you beg." He rubbed my arm. I touched his hand. It felt warm and foreign. The body hair on his hand was blond, like electrically fired wires in the gloss of passing lights. He slowed the car, pulling down a side road. He stopped at a traffic light. There were no cars coming or going, so he pulled the stick shift into park. He leaned across the seat and kissed me. He did not kiss like Max. He was large where Max was small and sinewy. I was swallowed up in Harrison. When his arms came around me, I felt like a size two. Braden worried over my size and what I ate. Harrison said, "You feel good next to me."

"You too."

He sat back as if he had gotten an idea. "Have you ever tasted liquid chocolate?"

"I've heard of it," I said. It was odd of him to ask.

"I know a place that makes it."

I couldn't help but laugh at his cliché overtures.

"Gaylen. I'm not feeding you a line. I never met a girl like you. Think about it. We both live in North Carolina. But here we are in Houston, together. It's meant to be."

We kissed again, and I was relaxing.

"There's this hotel that I've heard about. They will send liquid chocolate up to your room with a plate of cheeses. We could order a movie, see if we like liquid chocolate." He kissed the side of my face. "It would be the first thing we try together." The smell of his sweat was filling up the car.

"I can't," I said.

Harrison had had his fill of me. He started the car and drove me back to the La Quinta. I got out onto the landing in front of the office. Christmas lights blinked across the roof of the La Quinta. They were blue and matched the moon. Because there are no mountains in Houston, the city unfolded in all directions like a kids' game board, while the moon seemed to hover over all of the lights. Inside the lobby, the old hotel attendant played a Perry Como CD that filtered out through an outside speaker. Amity used to love Perry Como, or I wouldn't have known about him.

Harrison told me good night. No kiss good-bye, though. I went to the room. Delia wasn't back yet. I turned up the heat and from a packaged mix made instant hot chocolate in the minipot. There was an old movie on TV. I fell asleep as the credits rolled.

Delia woke me up at two in the morning. I could smell her tobacco and beer. "I got to tell you something, Gaylen."

I slipped out of my clothes and put on a T-shirt and flannel pants. She dropped her boots one at a time on the floor. She was obviously happy. Then she pulled my phone from her purse. "I forgot to give this back," she said. "But Tim called. He's being deployed to Kuwait."

I wasn't fully awake yet. "He can't. Meredith needs him."

"He said she was holding up. But he is leaving in the morning." She looked at the clock on the nightstand. "In four hours."

I slid down between the sheets. "Tim can't go. He's the only goodness left in the world," I said.

"Not the only one. That's what I wanted to tell you," she said.

"Delia, what's more important than Tim going to Kuwait?"

"Avery. I've fallen for him, Gaylen."

"You haven't, Delia. It's a one-night stand."

"I've never felt like that." She whispered as if Mother were in the next room. "We made love in the museum."

"How is that possible?"

"Avery's got a friend who has a pass key for special guests who want to tour the museum after hours. It's on account of Harrison and all his connections."

"Delia, he was playing you. They had it planned. The symphony, museum privileges."

"Avery said he never met a girl like me."

"That's probably true, Delia. But he and Harrison do this all the time. Don't you know about men?"

She thought it was funny that I was giving her advice about men.

"He let me test-drive his friend Shawn's Miata. I loved it, and he said he'd get Shawn to give me a good deal. Shawn owes him. Then he drove us to the museum. I was laughing. The lights were out. Then he drove us to a back door he called a special entry. I followed him inside. I mean, I've never been inside a museum let alone inside one after dark. I felt like a burglar in a mansion." Delia said several times, "It was such a rush." She lay across her bed and in a low confessional whisper, told me, "He took me into this room of paintings. He said there was this man who had a lover named Helga. He was a famous painter and his family didn't know about her until they found like a whole basement full of paintings, all of them of her. Avery turned on a light, and there they were."

"What?"

"This whole room was full of Helga, and she wasn't wearing anything. So he asked me to be his Helga. I didn't have no self-control after that. Who would for heaven's sake? He stripped me down and next thing you know we're making love right under a picture of naked Helga. He told me that when I got back to North Carolina, he was going to buy me a picture just like that for my house."

"Did you tell him about the money?"

"I told him I'd buy him anything he wants, but what else could I say? I never made love like that. It was true passion, Gaylen." She slipped down under her linens, her fingers pulling at the long strands of dark hair like a girl spinning flax.

I turned off the light.

Delia kept sighing and then laughing. I fell asleep hearing her laugh and whisper Avery's name.

Avery's friend Shawn showed up with the used car right about the time we were coming down the stairs for breakfast. Avery did not lie about Shawn selling us his car. He parked the blue Miata right out from the landing. Delia had been driving my father's old Ford since Lee sold her car to pay off a gambling debt. She wanted the Miata like she had never wanted anything. "This is exactly the car I've dreamed about," she said, even though she had never mentioned owning one.

"Avery told me to cut you two girls a deal," said Shawn. "Eight thou, but Avery says you have to drive it to see him in Mooresville."

I had to go and find a bank and come back with the money. Delia was sitting in the driver's seat flirting with Shawn.

I asked, "Where is Avery this morning?"

"He's downtown with his boss, Harrison. He and his wife are visiting Harrison's family. They brought Avery along because Harrison's wife has been trying to fix him up with her sister," said Shawn.

Delia blanched.

"Don't you worry," he said to Delia.

"Harrison's wife wants her sister to date Avery?" I asked.

"They're close like that, but you two are sisters. I'm sure you understand sisterhood. Maura Harrison has always said she wanted Avery in her family. She's used to getting her way."

"Harrison must agree with her," I said, hoping Delia could keep a lid on her temper. "What with Avery working for him and all."

Her cheeks were flushed. She was tapping the steering wheel and looking over her shoulder at me, blinking.

"I shouldn't have said that. I don't know Harrison too well. Avery says they been married so long they're starting to look alike," said Shawn.

I signed the bill of sale, and Shawn told me that since I had bought the Miata from an individual, Texas laws allowed me to drive temporarily without tags for thirty days.

"You say you don't know Harrison too well?" I asked.

"I've been to parties at his parents' house. The Harrisons throw big parties."

"The last name is Harrison?" I asked, curling up at the toes. "What is his first name?"

"Payne. He's not big in racing yet, not like some of the other race car drivers. That's probably why you haven't heard of him. But he's talented."

"I've heard he plays the violin," I said, hoping I had not been completely duped.

"Ha! I doubt it. His family made their money in real estate. Payne and his brother were groomed for business. Stories circulate that his daddy sold off part of his grandfather's land just to help Payne finance his race car hobby." He took the keys off his key ring and gave them to Delia. "Payne Harrison knows how to play all the games to get where he's going."

I packed up our suitcases and climbed in next to Delia. She drove away without saying good-bye to Shawn. We were nearly to Dallas before she said, "Avery told me he loved me." She batted back tears and gripped the wheel, staring ahead at the southwest highway.

15

NOLEEN ANSWERED the phone, but right after she started talking, Uncle Jackson picked up. They talked back and forth to each other a lot like Amity and Malcolm did. "Jackson, it's Gaylen," she said, while Jackson talked over her saying, "Let the girl talk, Noleen. Go ahead, Gaylen."

"I'm Gaylen Syler-Boatwright. My father was James," I said.

Jackson offered his condolences.

"You say you girls are in Dallas?" asked Noleen.

"Passing through thereabouts," I said.

"You ought to stop over in Garland. Let me cook you girls a meal," she said.

I accepted, and Jackson gave me directions to the house in Garland. Delia drove into a rest stop. "You take us into the city, Gaylen. City driving makes me too nervous, and I need a pit stop anyway." She disappeared into the vending overhang.

The rest stop advertised Dallas maps and sights. I locked up the car and went inside. Tourist claptrap cluttered the aisles, advertising cans of road kill, Lone Star ink pens and flags, and toggle-head dolls wearing Dallas Cowboys jerseys.

Royal Crown Cola bottles chilled inside shiny buckets of ice. I bought two along with peanuts and a pair of white sunglasses that looked exactly like a pair worn by Marilyn Monroe.

Delia pressed her face against the glass. I waved her inside. "I met a truck driver says we're not far from Garland. He's a good-looking trucker," she said.

"Delia, don't," I said. "For the rest of the trip, no more men."

"He said he'd buy us supper in Garland."

"Noleen's making supper. You'll offend her," I said.

Delia picked up an ice-cream sandwich, and we checked out. She handed me the keys. "Want to drive?"

By the time we got onto the interstate, Delia finished off the RC and the ice-cream sandwich. "Your phone's ringing," she said. She fished it out of my pocketbook. After several "uh-huh's," she handed me the phone. "It's Truman's counselor from Angola."

The counselor called himself Buddy Fortune. His voice was soft as a woman's, like a tenor who could be a soprano. I figured that he would not be allowed to answer many questions about Truman. But I was wrong.

"I'm Truman's sister, Gaylen Boatwright."

"He listed you as his next-of-kin, Mrs. Boatwright. I apologize for taking so long to answer your call. I've been on a family vacation. What could I do for you?"

"I understand my brother is in prison for stealing cars."

"That's not correct." His tone grew a shade harsh.

"Can you tell me, that is, are you allowed to tell me what he's in for?" I asked.

"Thirteen counts of child molestation, nine counts of sodomy against a minor."

Traffic piled up behind me. When I hit the brake, the driver of the Beetle directly behind me came down on the horn. Delia tensed and clasped her seat belt into place.

I repeated Truman's offenses for Delia's sake.

"That is correct," said Fortune.

A tightness in my chest caused me to cough. "How long has Truman been in prison?" I asked.

"Thirteen years."

"How much longer in prison, Mr. Fortune?"

"Eleven more years without probation."

"Can I obtain court records?" I asked.

"All you want. It's a matter of public record," he said. "Just call the parish clerk in Louisiana in charge of criminal records."

Delia turned around in her seat, pulling an invisible horn to tease a trucker who blasted back at her.

I ended the call. "Delia, get back in your seat belt. Stop attracting attention. You are wanted for questioning. State police get a good look at you and pull us over, I'm not helping you another day."

She slid back into her seat. "Truman molested," she said. "All that time Mama said he was a car thief."

"We don't know that wasn't true too," I said.

"Mama lied all those years and never told us."

A car cut me off, and I came down on the horn. I kept hitting the horn long after it drove out of sight.

Delia grabbed my wrist, yelling for me to stop. "Gaylen, you done lost it. Stop 'fore you kill us!"

I could see my mother standing in the doorway of the kitchen. The morning sun came up behind her making her look like a saint in one of Aunt Amity's paintings. I had asked her about Truman, and she answered with a hint of pepper in her voice, "That boy did things that are unspeakable. I'll take it to my grave, the things he did." Just like that her face turned gray, wrinkled, her hair turning coarse and silver. Little pieces of her were fragmented, blowing away, out of my grasp until there was nothing left but dust sifting in the sun.

"I can drive, Gaylen. Pull over, why don't you?"

"I'm the last to know everything, Delia. But I'm the girl with the brains in the Syler family."

"How many kids you figure he hurt before they caught up with him?" she asked.

"I'm ordering his court records," I said.

"You ever met Jackson and Noleen?" she asked. Her mind wandered off, and she was watching again for truckers.

"Once when I was young. Jackson helped Daddy sober up a man, I think a cousin of Daddy's. That's all I remember. He seemed cordial."

She let back her seat and closed her eyes. There was a bit of chocolate left on her lip from the ice-cream sandwich. Sleep overtook her, and she looked like a small girl fallen asleep with not a care in her mind.

My memory summoned the shaven-headed pencil sketch of Truman that Renni left for us in his box of belongings. The photo of the brown-eyed second grader left an impression of sweetness. The shaven-headed prisoner drawing did not reveal anything. Maybe it was because he did not know himself. Or maybe it was because he did not want anyone to know him.

If I ever moved out of Wilmington, and it seemed I would be moving somewhere else soon, I decided that I might consider Garland. The historical town shops restored in ice-cream colors looked like a place cut out of a children's book. In a downtown block, a big sign advertised Christmas on the Square. Children piled out of a bus, tying shoelaces and pulling on choir robes. The urge to spend a bit of inheritance money might have overtaken me, except that a parking space was nowhere to be found.

"Delia, wake up and wash your face. You have to see this place."

She roused, pulling herself up to look at the crowds converging on the square. "Mmff!" She finger-combed her hair out of her eyes. She sat up, still in her stupor, and said, "I was dreaming about a place like I never saw, not on earth. Mason Freeman was standing outside a pair of big tall gates trying to get past the gates along with Mama and Truman. Only Truman was a little boy like in the picture. She 'as holding his hand and slapping him and mad at me the same as Mason Freeman. Except I'm inside the gate, and I got the key. I'm running back and forth teasing them all, shaking the keys at them and yelling, 'You can't get in! Not without my say-so!'"

I saw a road just like Jackson had told me I would find past the square. I turned down it.

"That would be my heaven, Gaylen. Me holding the keys and letting in who I please and keeping out who I don't want in."

"You'd send Mama to hell?" I asked.

"Is there an alternative? Like, seems like standing outside the gates watching everybody partying is punishment enough."

"Never heard of an alternative hell," I said.

"Not straight to hell then. I'd make her say she was sorry for the hateful things she said and did. But I felt sorry for Truman, pitiful eyed, like he was trapped forever holding Mama's hand and getting slapped. Maybe because he was little and not like he is now."

"Help me find Gold Dust Street," I said. We drove right past it, and I sighed.

"The last place I would expect to be is heaven, now that I think about it," she said. "Maybe they's an alternative heaven."

"You let us miss our street. Now I have to turn around." I pulled into a driveway. Finally, I headed down Gold Dust. There was the big one story house, the lawn struggling to keep its summer green in the middle of December. Jackson must have decided we needed a welcoming committee. He and Noleen walked out onto the front porch, arm in arm, posed like a couple of tourists in matching red and green outfits.

"Gaylen, is that you?" she yelled. She kept saying that first to me and then Delia until Delia giggled in a low and awkward way.

Noleen set out tables in a glassed-in back porch built by Jackson after he retired from the city of Dallas.

Jackson was big like I remembered, but his shoulders stooped from age. Noleen had dressed him up in a kelly green shirt with red sleeves matching her green pantsuit. "Here we are right on top of Christmas, and lo and behold, the phone rings, and up comes a North Carolina family. It's a blessing, that's what!" she exclaimed.

Her hair, frosted at the tips and still clinging to a permanent wave, was swept up on one side and clipped by a mistletoe barrette. When Delia commented about it, Noleen said, "I make these for teachers, women down at the Dalrymple Nursing Center, what-have-you. I'll get one for each of you girls."

I did not know what to say.

"He's got nimble fingers," she said, not taking her eyes off him.

Jackson blushed.

She took me into her bedroom and showed me a wall of photographs dating back to the '60s when she and Jackson married.

"The last thing I would expect was for you to show up, and here I am without a single picture of you and Delia. I'll have Jackson take your pictures before you leave, that's what. Then I'll add you to the wall of Sylers." She talked the whole time, pointing to photographs of her brother who fought in Vietnam, a three-legged pet greyhound that needed to be put down, fifteen or more photographs of her son, Taylor, from birth up, and an equal number of photographs of their daughter who had played soccer and danced ballet.

"Did Jackson grow up knowing my daddy?" I asked.

"Oh yes, girl! They was two peas, the two of them. Jackson called your daddy Puddin' until he was grown, on account of his love for Jackson's mother's homemade banana-cream pudding."

I had never heard my father called by that name.

She lit a candle under the photograph of her brother.

"I have a cousin going off to war. Tim."

"Not Renni's Tim?" she asked. "Pshaw! No, tell me that's not true. Tim's grown? Time has flown."

"You know him?"

"Like I know you. Of course you and your sister were so little back then. Ask Tim if he remembers Jackson and Noleen. He'll tell you about the time Jackson took him and our son fishing. They hit some rapids, and the three of them nearly drowned. The authorities found them clinging to a rock. Had to take them out of those waters by helicopter and a rope."

"I thought he was lying," I said, although I was tired of talking about Tim. Since I had finally found a talkative Syler in Noleen, I wanted to see what she remembered about my mother.

"The way those Syler men tell tales, I can understand your point. But that one happens to be true."

Delia was laughing in the next room.

I closed the door. "Noleen, if you remember me young, then you remember my mother's son, Truman."

The sound of my brother's name set her back. It was the first time she fell quiet since we had landed on her porch.

"What do you remember about him?"

She seated me in an alcove with a picture window looking out over what appeared to be naked grapevines. "Your brother was troubled. Nobody tried as hard as your daddy to bring that boy around. He disciplined him, whipped him, but he couldn't get him to come around and stay out of trouble with the law. That boy was in trouble far back as I can remember."

"Truman was in trouble with the law?"

"He worked for a refinishing shop down from your daddy's place. The refinisher had a boy who was bad news. He was the one taught Truman to hot-wire cars. I always said that was when Truman leaned too far over the rail to bring back. He seemed to get worse and worse after that. First he was sent away to his Daddy's someplace here in Texas. Next thing you know, he's back in North Carolina getting sent to Rowan Salisbury Prison. I think that was the name of that place. Anyway, it was a sad day. Your daddy was ashamed of him."

"That's when you remember him being sent away?"

"That was the way it was told to Jackson, girl. Why? You know a different story?"

"For a long time, I had nightmares. Since then I've been trying to prove what happened to me when I was young."

She clasped her hands on her stomach. "I don't follow."

"I started pulling my hair."

She gasped and then nodded, remembering. She said, "You pulled out your hair by the handfuls from the time you was a baby. That's enough to give any child nightmares. Your mama troubled over you, trying to keep your hands out of that pretty silky hair."

"But what causes a baby to pull its hair, Noleen?"

She laughed. "Your mama said one day you just reached up and found a lock. She said it was curiosity. You yelled, red-faced, as if you didn't know how to let go."

Noleen's voice was grating on me. She laughed like my mother, like women do when they don't know what to say.

"What is wrong, Gaylen? You come here for more than a Christmas visit, didn't you? You looking for answers?"

I sat up and shook my head. "Not at all. I heard you made the best enchiladas in the family."

She cackled and pushed up out of her chair. "That is the honest truth! Now you get yourself in here and let me feed you. Your bones look about ready to break. Who's been feeding you anyway? Not that sister of yours, I'm sure." She walked out of the bedroom as if I would follow. I was still in the chair when Jackson, sent on a mission by Noleen, came looking for me.

"My wife about to talk your ears off?" he asked.

"I'm just tired. I'm coming," I said.

"Don't rush. She's still melting cheese and slicing tomatoes. She's got your sister icing a cake."

I was too tired to tell him that was a bad idea.

He took Noleen's chair. "Can I tell you something I remember about you?" he asked.

Why not? I thought.

"Out of all of the Sylers, you seemed like the kid that would rise above your family's situation. Some kids in your situation, they cry and whine, needy and taking their time about growing up. But you was a strong girl, like no one was going to lead you around."

"I appreciate you saying that. But I think I lost a little of her back in Boiling Waters."

"Once Noleen and I took you to church. Delia wouldn't go. You sat right between us, and Noleen had fun pretending you were her girl. She took you to children's class, and you came out having learned three Bible verses. You won a chocolate rabbit. I never heard so much smacking. You had that rabbit eaten before we ever got you back to your daddy's house. I think you was afraid your mama wouldn't let you eat it."

"I was afraid Delia would eat it," I said.

"You remember then?"

"It's foggy."

"Don't go getting old on me. I'm the only one qualified for a senior moment."

"When you said that I would rise above the family's situation, what does that mean to you, Jackson?"

He scratched his head, uneasy. "I shouldn't have said that." His gaze drifted to the wall of photographs and then back to me.

"It's like I don't know myself because I don't know my family."

"Your daddy and his brother, Rudy, they had their issues. I always blamed the war. Now Malcolm, he was sane as Lincoln. But Renni, she said those two brothers had the manic-depressive on account of their mama had it."

"My father? He didn't tell me," I said. Neither had Renni.

"Your daddy had too much pride."

Mother had never gotten help for Delia either. "What about my mother?" I asked.

"I don't know about your mother or her past. When she married your daddy, those sisters of his told a lot of stuff on her. I never knew whether or not to believe it. But when she and your daddy would tangle, you could hear them all the way out to the pond. But I don't have to tell you that."

"Mother could yell so loud, Daddy said she could dust the lamps with her vocal cords." It was easy feeling guilty over talking about her.

"I shouldn't be telling you things on your mother."

The two of us sat staring at Noleen's floral rug, sharing a big slice of guilt.

"The last thing we need to be doing is digging up family skeletons on your folks, Gaylen. They've passed on and can't defend themselves."

"They wouldn't allow me to ask any of these questions, though. It was their way." I pondered why I allowed Mother and Daddy to intimidate me. "I should've made them tell me the truth about us and about Truman." I imagined shouting down into Mother's grave beneath the hill above Syler Pond. "How could she think I could live a life based on lies?"

"To her, it wasn't lies. It was protection."

"But I pulled myself baldheaded, Jackson! I was ashamed. I remember the shame of it. The nightmares, the way that dark man in the shadows would crawl into my bed."

Jackson handed me a handkerchief. It was embroidered with the initials JCS.

I dried my eyes.

"Gaylen, you didn't have the best starting gate. But you got so much baggage hanging off you, you're never going to get any purpose about you until you lay some of it down."

"It's the only cargo given to me, Jackson." I thought, like the top of a train car overflowing with gunpowder.

"Want to know that verse you quoted when you was with us that day at church?"

Jackson was the religious cousin. I had forgotten. "Tell me then," I decided to be polite.

"Forgetting those things which are behind, and reaching forth unto those things which are before, I press toward the mark for the prize of the high calling of God in Christ Jesus."

"I don't remember any of it," I said.

"You did and two more. It's good advice."

"Reaching forward sounds better than looking back," I said. "But a family secret has shaped me into a stranger." I knew what I had to do. "I'm going to Angola, Jackson. My brother is incarcerated there."

"I never heard that. What's he in for?"

"Molesting kids."

"What do you think, that he'll confess all to you? Men like that bury their crimes in lies. He'll never tell you and you'll leave even angrier than you are now." He helped me out of the chair. "The past is all it is, Gaylen. Gone. Who told you that what happened a long time ago could give you the shape of your life today? Forget the past and move on. Closure's the best thing in the world for you."

"You don't know the things that have happened to me, Jackson." I could not tell him, even though I wanted to tell someone. "It's like a person I don't know is sitting in the driver's seat making my life for me." Jackson didn't know me or my family as well as I had hoped. He couldn't understand something that happened outside of his own skin. It was easy for him to tell me to drop it all like it had never happened. He did not have to live with my painted-over memories.

Noleen called the dining room the red room for good cause. The walls and draperies were red as cranberries. She lit red candles down a buffet, on a serving table, and along a table candelabra. "Every place setting is a Christmas pattern from a different country. Yours, Gaylen, is from Germany."

"Did you go to Germany?" Delia asked.

"There and Sweden, Luxembourg, Spain, and France," said Jackson, fishing his billfold out of his back pocket so he could sit comfortably. He deposited the billfold and his eyeglasses on the buffet, much to Noleen's consternation. But she only gave him a look and then melted when he flashed her his melon-slice smile.

"We got family coming in soon from Biloxi," said Noleen to Delia and me. "You girls stay on. We've got the room. Out back is the cottage we built for Jackson's mother before she passed. Got a kitchen in it and even its own carport."

"Biloxi was hit hard by that awful hurricane," said Jackson. "That's where our son, Taylor, and his wife and children live now. Noleen and I took our RV down there. Took us three days before they'd let us in. Couldn't get a phone signal or e-mail. Thought Noleen would faint when they stopped us at the county line and made us set up camp outside the city."

I remembered watching the news from the sofa, unable to move, the same as when the Twin Towers were hit by terrorists. My family was not one to react when bad things happened. Instead we watched, more like it was a spectacle, like it was a place far off that made us glad to be alive. "What was it like, Jackson?"

"Like a bomb had hit the place. Some houses still set in shambles," he said.

Delia scooped bean dip onto her plate.

Noleen served up the enchiladas. "So are you girls going to stay over for Christmas?" she asked.

"Might we come back here after we go to Louisiana?" I asked. Delia blinked. "Huh?"

"I've got business in New Orleans," I said. "But if we could leave Delia's car here, say, parked in your carport, we could come back in time for Christmas."

Noleen handed the dish of enchiladas to Delia.

"If you're determined to go, then at least let your husband fly you there. I'd feel better if you went escorted," said Jackson.

"Good idea," I said. The police were looking for Delia. If Braden flew us, we could travel under the police radar.

"Braden wouldn't, would he?" asked Delia.

"I'll ask," I said. "He might."

Flying on the jet to Texas had not given me pause. But the thought of climbing back into our Embraer brought back the memory of plummeting toward Wal-Mart. Before the crash I saw my mother in the same manner that people who have afterlife experiences see a dead relative sent as a divine escort. She was dressed in a floral cotton shirt tied at the waist and walking shorts. She did like taking walks along the pond. But she was wearing my grandmother's tall black hat, and she held a key out to me. It was a delicate key, like a diary key that is scarcely able to lock up secrets.

"Gaylen," said Delia, seated in a rattan chair in Noleen's guesthouse. "Where'd you go?"

Mother's image faded. "No place. I was thinking about the crash." Braden had not answered when I called but phoned back directly. I relayed what he told me. "He's picking us up in the morning on a trip to Kansas. He asked why Louisiana. I told him we decided to visit Truman and that's where he lives."

"Did you tell him what Truman's done?"

"Not yet."

"What about Deputy Bob?" she asked quietly. "Is he onto me?"

"Braden didn't say. When he comes, ask him." I did not have the strength to juggle Delia's legal problems and Truman's secrets. The thought of getting back inside the Embraer now had me obsessing over plummeting into the Wal-Mart garden center.

"What are you going to say to Truman, Gaylen? I want to slap him. Will they let you do that in prison, just walk right up and slap a man if he deserves it?"

"Truman doesn't know that we know. Jackson says he'll never confess. If he knows we know, he'll clam up. Think of the lie he told already about his daddy."

"It don't matter. We'll make him confess," she said, making a fist.

"I want to hear the truth from him," I said. I did not believe that men like him ever apologize. But I had lived with the nightmares and the hair pulling all the way back to when I was a baby. I grew up believing that I was turning into my mother or father—not sane. Now I was discovering a new thing, that after all this time, there was a good chance I wasn't like them. "Delia, I haven't had a nightmare since I realized the truth about Truman."

"It's your psychic self adjusting," she said.

I imagined a long string of bewildered children between North Carolina, Texas, and Louisiana. That sweet smile of his and his deep brown eyes could charm. Had he charmed me? Was that the thing my mind would not let me see? Sex is a mystery to a four-year-old. If he made it something else, like a game, would I have known what was going on? Or did I realize late? Did I scream or tell him to stop? In my nightmares, I could not move, but I did feel terror. Was that me as an abused baby? I could not breathe. My heart was pounding so hard I could hear it like a drumming, banging inside my skull. My arms, legs, and torso were paralyzed, and all that came out of my mouth was the shriek of a wounded being. I felt detached from my body, tormented and begging for rescue. Did my mother walk in and think that I wanted it to happen? Did I look guilty or ashamed, not knowing about sex but recognizing the look of horror in my mother's eyes? "Delia, Truman is a devil," I said. My right hand was shaking.

"Turn on the TV to CNN. Get your mind off it," she said.

We unpacked only our nightclothes so that we could rise early and leave. Noleen made oatmeal and coffee. I had no appetite for breakfast. Jackson drove us to the Dallas airport. Braden told us to meet him outside the US Airways terminal. Delia and I checked through security and then found our departing dock. We had to walk out onto the strip lugging our suitcases, down where the parties meeting private planes were allowed to board.

When I saw him standing out on the landing strip, the cold winter wind shuffling his hair around his ball cap, I burst into tears. I don't know why I cried. But his impassive stare warmed to my tears. He held me, and I could smell the faint musk of the flight cabin still in his clothes.

"I knew this'd be hard for you. You think you can fly again?" he asked.

I never was one to cry in Braden's arms, but for that moment, I allowed it, and so did he. He wheeled my luggage up to the storage section of his plane and helped Delia board. I had gotten on without him the past few weeks, but depending on him to ferry me to Louisiana seemed like a crossing of light beams. I was surprised that we did not explode right there on the runway, but truly glad. Braden, even at his drunken worst, was never ugly and to most women a good looker. He looked like a kid standing in the cold, his nose the color of wine. He had a small brown bit of bristle on his chin, shaven clean in a square, a bit of beard that reminded me of the Wilmington students who meet for darts and beer down in Myrtle Beach.

"I'm not going to be stupid about getting back into a plane," I said. "There's a day of facing your own shadows. Today I'm getting on this plane, and tomorrow I'm meeting my personal nightmare."

Braden helped me inside, up from the last step and forward into the cockpit. He was never one to splash on much cologne; more of a soap and deodorant man, but his soap smell permeated the plane. "It's cold out here," he said, and locked the door behind us. He looked startled by Delia but mumbled a greeting that sounded weak and awkward. He told me once she looked like a wild woman to him, like a girl who would throw herself off a ledge but take three people with her.

Noleen had made us bags of traveling snacks: Christmas cookies and smoked almonds. I gave them to Braden. "Merry Christmas," I said.

He looked stunned. "It doesn't seem like a holiday, does it?"

I agreed. I felt more hollow than holy.

16

DELIA PULLED A BLANKET from under her seat and wound it around her legs. I dragged a blanket to the copilot's chair. Braden handed me the headset. I passed on it. We had come to know many pilots, but few of them flew as a married pair. But what we had held in common now alienated us.

"No, thanks," I said. The Embraer smelled new from the newly recovered front seats. Braden listened to the control tower's chatter. "We'll get clearance to leave shortly," he said, mostly to Delia.

She tore open a bag of cookies and unzipped a pouch of sliced apples, arranging the food on the seat beside her.

Goose bumps dotted my arms and legs. The cockpit warmed quickly though.

"Where's my coffee?" he asked.

I offered him mine, but he turned it down, laughing.

"There's a cranky bit of cloud cover, but once we cross the state line, there's a clear sky the rest of the trip," I said.

"I'm taking you two straight in to New Orleans. You didn't say how many days you'll stay. Three days enough?" he asked.

"Hmmph!" said Delia in a half-stupor. She curled up to sleep. "What's to do in Louisiana?" Her brief foray into travel was turning her into a road diva.

"We might need four," I said, "but I'll know by tomorrow."

"Did your brother invite you?"

"Truman's in Angola," I said.

Braden got clearance. "Prison?" He prepared for takeoff. "Your family always did win all of the prizes." When I did not respond, he said, "I don't know why I said that."

Telling Braden about my family brought out more of the bear between us.

"I remember your mother said he was once convicted of stealing cars," he said. "That was way back, though. What do you say to a brother you don't know?"

"To tell you the truth, I don't know what I'll say to him. I don't know what he looks like." I imagined him tall, sort of gaunt, with a shaven head, standing in a row of others like him, like men in an egg carton. I now knew his father was a tall man. But in his only school photo, Truman had my mother's eyes: sad, brown, and fitted into deep sockets.

"What made you decide to see him?"

"He's a monster," said Delia. She turned sideways and pulled the blanket up covering her face.

"Mother told me he ran away from home," I said. "But it wasn't true. I want him to tell me why he left."

"What's he in for?"

I recalled how Jackson's face clouded into a look of inexpressible horror. I felt responsible for both Jackson's expression and the uncomfortable change in his mood. "We'll find out for sure soon."

He took off his gloves. The traffic controller asked Braden to confirm when he had taken off. He had not commenced taxiing.

"Let's get in the air," I said.

After a thirty minute wait, the Embraer rolled down the Dallas airstrip and lifted into a cloud mist. The sky unrolled like shredded paper behind us as we nosed away from Dallas and aimed for Louisiana airspace. The ground was barely visible, ribbons of color-less plains interrupted by squares of subdivisions and tiny womb-shaped lakes carved into the land. The lake water looked black from our clouded perch, staring up at us in the middle of the cold day, dark eyes aching for sunlight and summer.

Braden did not speak until we crossed over into Louisiana air-space and a clear winter sky swallowed the Embraer. Blue sky had that effect on all pilots. It was the endless expansion of blue that soothed the eyes. As the plane veered over Shreveport, the sun came up fully like a big cosmic watch lighting up the nose of the plane.

"I remember you once said you were curious about your big brother," he said.

"He sent a letter to Delia and me asking for money." I imagined waiting nervously in an Angola visitation room until a gruff voice said, "Baby sister."

"Gaylen, think about it. Your parents have both passed. Is this some deep-seated need to reconnect with your family?" he asked.

"He's a convict. Why would I want that?"

"Why even go?"

"Reasons I can't explain."

"Why do you think he'll see you?"

I had reason to believe Truman would talk. "In his letter, he sounded like he wanted to reconnect."

"Don't give him any money."

"Mother said she didn't want to leave him anything, so he won't get money." I remembered her mailing Truman boxes of cigarettes for Christmas. She liked the way that I wrapped gifts, so the lot fell to me to wrap Delia and Daddy's gifts. But she wrapped Truman's herself, the brown-paper grocery bags cut out and measured to fit the cigarette boxes. She anxiously taped and cut paper bags in a day when security allowed home-wrapped gifts.

"What was he like back then?" asked Braden.

"Not around."

"What is he, a lifer?"

"In and outer. His counselor said we could access his court records. Should I do that first, before I see him?"

"Yes, yes, get the goods on him. I don't have a good feeling about this."

Braden was right, as he so often had been in the past. But the same imperceptible rope that pulled me into the path of a milquetoast college teacher was pulling me into Louisiana. I was mad at my mother. Daddy, I wasn't so sure about. When he put Truman on the bus, he might have believed that Truman was a victim of a beating. If Mother told him, though, what it meant to me was even worse than death. Not only had my mother known about Truman, but also my father. What else did I not know about the pair who had reared me?

That thought came back of slamming their headstones until they coughed up the truth. Then I felt guilty again. I looked back at my sister who softly snored. From the time that I was aware of the fact that I was pulling out my own hair by the handfuls, I believed that the obsession rested with me and my gene pool. Then, realizing the unstable nature of James and Fiona Syler, I did the math, assuming I would end up slurping applesauce through a straw and playing bingo with guys named Napoleon and Zeus.

The last conversation I had with Daddy, he roasted me over the fact I had moved out of Boiling Waters. I spent my whole life learning to two-step around his temper. Sometimes I would try to appease him, but I often made him worse. It was when I finally fired back, "I'm an adult, and it's time you speak to me with respect," that I seemed to jolt him into the present. I felt strangely justified, as if I had finally conquered his demons for him. Then the next trip into town, I heard that he had gone around Boiling Waters telling first one person and then another that I had back-stabbed the family. I went to him asking what I could have done differently, and that sent him into another rage. Until James Syler slipped quietly into a coma, he rose and fell in my conscious mind, my emperor one minute, my gatekeeper the next.

"What do you want to prove?" asked Braden.

"I'm not crazy after all."

"You're not like them, Gaylen. You rise above it," said Braden. He turned on his CD player. He sang very badly the lyrics to "The Parting Glass." It was an Irish funeral song.

"Braden, did we know that we would fall apart and then for so long?"

He pulled his earphones from around his neck and laid them on the control panel. "You never let me in."

I knew what he meant, but suddenly the need to confess collected in my mouth and jammed down my throat. It was a well-known fact that Sylers neither confessed nor apologized.

Braden stared ahead, saying, "I once flew for a real estate broker who had a problem with the homeless breaking into one of his high rise tenement buildings at night. They slept in the stairwells and cost him money. After a lot of expense, he figured out a way to lock them out. He had special doors made that no one could penetrate. I mean, like an army tank would have to blow them open. He said he watched on the building monitors as a homeless man ran round and round his building trying to pry open those special doors." There was a hint of relaxation in his voice for the first time since he had picked me up. "Finally, the homeless guy stripped down naked and stood out in the cold until the cops came and arrested him."

I laughed.

"He decided that if he couldn't get back to that familiar stairwell, he would settle for jail. Gaylen, I understand the homeless man. You've got these special doors on you that no one can break down. After a while, I just gave up."

I bit my lip for once.

We flew over Alexandria. The town looked evacuated from our height. It was odd to me that we could never see people. That was the loneliest part of flying, feeling like the only human that remained along the black stretches of earth.

"I don't know how to read you," he said.

Maybe his metaphor was some sort of emotional segue, but it lay like a gag in my mouth.

With Braden, I was forever on the cliff of something new. He was a good son; he flew back to see his parents when his brother crashed his motorcycle and smashed his face on a guardrail. He sacrificed his time for the Boatwrights. But I had felt the sliding flux of instability since one week after our wedding. He could put to ease the travel problems of clients from corporate pools, but a new idea would come to him and our stability evaporated. Like the time he tried to compete with FedEx. If all of his ideas had worked, he would be rich. But in the middle of developing one of his ideas, he would lose interest and then momentum. Monotony to him was the day-to-day function of poring over bills that collected on every table surface or mailing off monthly statements. Maybe his ideas were intoxicating. But the worst monotony, it seemed, was my need for safety. When he got mad, I cried. Rather, I sobbed, the same as when Daddy lost his temper.

"You haven't called much," I said. "What I assumed was a lot."

"Last thing I want to do is rehash why I haven't called."

I didn't cry. It was through dead-on determination that I didn't.

Finally, he confessed. "A man will take drastic measures to keep warm."

"Don't say it."

"I cheated."

"No more." I did not want Delia to hear.

"I don't love her." He stared ahead as if he were talking to himself. A calm settled over him. "It's nothing."

I didn't want to know her name. But numbly my mouth opened, the rope pulling me into the next minute of a painted-over life. "Who is she?"

"It won't help."

"Just say her name."

"Kimberly. Your leasing agent."

Delia stirred in her sleep. "Mmmph."

"She's a kid," I said.

"Not really."

"Shut it, Braden!" I unclamped my seat belt, crawling out of the copilot's chair to get away. Kimberly was barely of age. I recalled an edge in her voice that seeped through and the detectable erosion evident in her respect of me.

"Gaylen, where are you going? Back with Delia?"

"She's not so bad, you know. She grows on you."

"I want you to know why I'm telling you."

I knew why. The awful play that had cast me as the pathetic heroine needed a final tragic ending. But hiding places being at a minimum twenty thousand feet in the air, I sat back down. We flew over Baton Rouge and then across Lake Pontchartrain.

The landing gear dropped down, jolting the plane.

"I couldn't go through with it," he said, "I'm telling you now so we can both come clean." The confession brightened his appearance; he was buoyant, like the first time I saw him.

The New Orleans control tower broke through. A storm was headed up from the Gulf. Braden wanted to fly out before sundown. "Call me when you're ready to leave, Gaylen, and I'll be back. Do you need any money?"

Delia laughed in her sleep.

"We're fine," I said. Braden knew that my father was a hoarder when it came to his money. But matters being what they were, I had not disclosed to him the full amount of the estate. "My father's cousin Jackson and his wife, Noleen, want us to stay over in Garland for Christmas. Could you come back?" I asked.

"The folks are expecting me. They're in Florida for Christmas," he said.

"If you change your mind, let me know."

"I'll give it some thought." Braden sounded as if he meant it. He set the plane in a holding pattern until we could get our clearance to land. "When you come back, I've got more to say," he said, glancing toward Delia.

Inside the New Orleans taxi was frigid. Cold rain sloshed the windshield, running down the glass in rivulets. The cloud cover made the noon hour seem like dusk. The cab driver scarcely spoke English and kept glancing in his mirror nervously at Delia. She got off the plane and into the taxi in a state of agitation.

"The last thing I thought we'd be doing, Gaylen Lee, is walking into a men's correctional facility to confront a petit four."

"Those are cakes," I said.

She stared at me, put out with me like always.

"Petit fours are cakes. Smallish. They serve them at receptions."

The driver grunted what may have been either a laugh or a guarded reaction.

Delia blushed.

"Pedophile. Is that what you meant?" I asked.

"Whatever. The thing of it is that he could do anything to us.

Like, drag us off into a gang situation or who knows what?" She was getting excited. "We're going to need some muscle in case we got to go to Fist City."

"Let's get a hotel first. Then we'll work on getting clearance through Truman's counselor. While we're waiting, we'll go to the court-house for his trial records."

"Do they just hand them over?" she asked. "No questions asked?"

"It's a matter of public record," said the taxi driver.

Surprised, I looked at him through the rearview mirror.

"My brother is a lawyer," he said. "He's my partner in this taxi service and practices law on the side."

"Maybe he could be our lawyer," said Delia. "If we have to put the clamps on Truman, we'll know who to call."

The cab driver was suddenly very lawyerly. "If he was incarcer-ated in Orleans Parish, he was probably transferred to Angola. The records are still being sorted through since the hurricane." The dri-ver pulled down his visor. "When Orleans got flooded, they even moved women into Angola. Prison system's been a mess to unjum-ble ever since." He handed Delia his brother's business card. It was one of those make-it-at-home, computer-generated cards, a photo of the dark-skinned brother fitted into the left side, a slogan under his name. "Fast legal help. Same day bonding."

"Looks like we got us a lawyer, Gaylen." Delia was thrilled. Then she asked, "You're not from Iraq, are you?"

"India," he said, as if he had been asked often.

I called Truman's counselor, Buddy Fortune. He answered right away and said Truman had been anxious to hear from us. "Visiting hours are tomorrow starting at 8:00 a.m. Be at the front gate, and I'll be sure Truman has you signed in."

The taxi driver stopped at a hotel not far from the airport, the Windsor Court. "This hotel's offering a special tourist rate, but you have to ask for it," he told us. He put our luggage out on the walk and drove away. I checked us into a guest room and left our luggage with the hotel concierge. Then we walked out into the streets. Down one neighborhood street, it was as if the hurricane had hit only yesterday.

Delia emptied herself of all of the gloom of facing Truman when she set eyes on her first outdoor café. Café Du Monde in the French Market was lit up with some outdoor lights and was full of people who had ventured back for the holiday. I ordered beignets and two coffees with chicory. We took them to an outdoor table under the covering of the open market coffee stand where we could watch people venturing in and out of Jackson Square. The last place I expected to find solace was in an outdoor café, but there we laughed, and Delia talked about Avery and the art gallery by night. She had never seen one by day, but she talked about it as if she owned it and as if Avery might call at any minute.

The phone rang. It was Meredith. I asked her about Tim, and I knew from her tone that she was sick with worry. Tim had deployed, as Delia had told me, to Kuwait in order to cross over into Iraq. He was in a place where he could not phone home and she could not know his exact location. We could send him a box of snacks but nothing chocolate because it would melt into water. I wrote down the address for deployed servicemen.

Delia talked about the beignets when I got off the phone. But I sat thinking about Tim in a sand-swept desert, a place with no deer stand or forest lookout. But he would have his gun, the one thing about Kuwait that he would understand. He knew how to take care of himself. Meredith ought not to worry.

"Let's find the courthouse and then go and buy Tim a gift from New Orleans." We stopped to talk to a cop. He was a black policeman, Creole and guarded. Braden once told me the cops in New Orleans were laid back. I asked him where court records were kept.

"You take a taxi to 2700 Tulane Avenue, Orleans Parish Clerk of Criminal Court's office. Tell the clerk at the front desk what you need, and she will tell you where to go."

Delia finished her café au lait. "I heard about the French Quarter. We got to come back tonight so I can buy some wine, just so I can tell Avery that I have a bottle waiting for him."

I hailed a cab. When Delia climbed in ahead of me, I said, "Delia, Avery is over so stop talking about him. You'll drive yourself silly with worry."

"I know love when I see it. He'll call," she said, confident she had power over him.

Delia's head, I thought, was a playland of men and first kisses and one escapade after another where she was perpetually right and never scorned. I was actually jealous.

I gave the driver the address.

"I'm going to buy a Mardi Gras shirt and beads and a T-shirt for Avery too."

"You believe that Avery is going to call?" I asked.

"He said he would. You never believe anyone, Gaylen." She reached into my handbag and pulled out a lipstick. She lifted up off the seat and used the driver's rearview mirror to color her lips. He winked at her. She giggled.

"When we see Truman, let me do the talking," I said.

"I'm not going to say anything stupid," she said, defensive.

"I want to see what he is willing to say." I pulled out the checkbook and began adding up our receipts. The money was holding tight, but we needed to watch out for expensive hotels and room service.

"I need some clothes," said Delia. "Let's buy out New Orleans."

The historical buildings whizzed past. The driver buzzed around a horse and carriage carting a couple dressed in navy and white. They looked as if they never worried about money. Like Delia.

Before I paid the cab driver, Delia ran wildly to the street corner of Tulane. By wildly, I mean that she was pointing and leaping. "A band, a parade!" she yelled.

I followed her to the curb. The music was dark and mournful. The band Delia saw was a funeral procession. The mourners were dressed in various patterns of black, some silk and some taffeta, little black laces sewn into the hems of the women's dresses. A man in a top hat led the processional. An older man standing on the opposite corner took off his hat and bowed his head.

"When I die, Gaylen, will you hire me a band like that?"

"What if I die first?"

"Is that what you want, a band at your funeral?" she asked.

"I think, bagpipes." My great-grandfather was Scotch-Irish, and I had imagined bagpipes as a fitting end to me.

The mourners turned the corner.

I climbed the steps to the Clerk of Criminal Court's office. The sun came out for a moment, and the air was heavy and balmy. In the distance was the dark cloud bank moving up from the Gulf.

The black clerk inside asked me, "When did the trial take place?"

I didn't know.

"How long has the inmate been in prison?" she asked.

"I think eleven years. He was sentenced for twenty-four years," I told her.

"Do you have a case number?"

"Only a name. Truman Savage."

She got up and disappeared into an office.

Delia said, "Hah!"

The clerk returned and said, "We can have it tomorrow afternoon. There's a charge of fifteen cents a page. It's a hundred twenty-two pages long. Can you pay now?"

"Of course, no problem," said Delia.

I waited as if Delia might actually pay. Then I pulled out a twenty and took care of the bill.

***

The hotel desk clerk recommended K-Paul's for the taste of local fare. When we arrived on foot, the walk was filling up with patrons. The store windows were suddenly freckled by the early arrival of rain. "I'll buy an umbrella," I told Delia. I ran into a tourist shop. Food was sold in cans and bottles, cans of mix and bottles of

Tabasco, with a hundred or more types of sauces with names that sent Delia laughing. She kept picking up the sauces and saying the names out loud. "Slap Your Mama," she said, giggling.

I bought a tin of pralines, some sort of crunchy mix for Tim, and an umbrella the color of irises. Delia came up to the counter wearing Mardi Gras beads. The woman, accustomed to tourists, reached across the counter to count the bead strands. I paid for all of it, and we left and crossed the street to K-Paul's.

The service was a little slow, but we sipped red wine and Delia grinned. Outside the rain let loose, and we were glad to have gotten seated. The rain swept the remaining tourists into the lobby. The air was muggy and the smell of damp humans potent, but the restaurant was lively and loud. There was no music, odd for a restaurant in New Orleans. The tense wave of people put pressure on the wait staff, and we were served quickly. Delia ordered pork chops while I ordered the dusted crawfish tails.

I peeled off my sweater. A man at the bar was staring and smiling. It was the first time I felt checked out because of the daisy tattoo. I hung the sweater on the chair back, though, feeling a part of New Orleans. "We'll visit Angola in the morning and then come back to shop," I said, as if Truman was an insignificant part of tomorrow.

Delia filled her glass again. The rain was pounding, and we heard the sound of a whoop as more people packed into the lobby. She relaxed, while the tension of the restaurant caused me to feel unsteady. It was the same unsteady feeling I had gotten when the Embraer took off out of Dallas.

"Are you mad at God?" she asked.

"About what?"

"Truman, for one thing. Braden too."

"What would it help to say that I was?" Everyone said that when things went bad. Being mad at God was a cliché, like there was nothing else to do but that when your life got shredded. But I lay awake of late, asking questions and hearing nothing back. I went from quiet prayers to pity on nights when sleep evaded me.

Delia offered me more wine, but I declined and set aside my glass. "I'm not feeling well."

The food came, and Delia stared at the bright red crawfish in front of me.

"You can have some," I offered. I peeled one for her and laid it on the edge of her plate. She considered it first and then finally cautiously put it to her lips. She sniffed it and then, finding it pleasant, popped the tail into her mouth. "It tastes like shrimp, but not entirely," she said.

Finally, the music was turned on, holiday music, though, instead of Cajun.

"We'll buy you some new clothes tomorrow," I said, not remembering if I had already said it.

"You look pale," she said.

"My nerves haven't settled since the flight."

"The last time you flew in that plane, you was taken to the hospital."

She was right, of course, but thinking about it only made the rising tension sour. The crawfish were hot on my tongue and acid in my stomach. I sipped water and asked the waiter to bring a bowl of soup.

"When I get home, I'm going to get a job that lets me travel like we been doing," she said. Of course, she was not considering her education.

"If you want, you can go back to school," I said.

"I hate school."

"It's better if you study what you like." There was that pale fragment of tension that occurred whenever I gave her advice. I leaned back to allow the chowder to be placed in front of me. "I feel faint," I said.

"You're the absolute color of lilies, Gaylen."

The room was spinning.

Delia called for the check.

I slept until three in the morning. Delia left the television on. There was an old movie on, the actress, someone my mother liked, I thought. I slipped out of the sheets. Delia lay across the other bed still wearing her day clothes. I pulled a blanket out of the closet and tucked it around her.

My cell phone was blinking. I'd missed a call while sleeping.

Through the window, the moon was covered over but still trying hard to illuminate. The rain was subsiding. The streets were black and wet, a few people still running in and out with umbrellas.

I had gotten a headache. I went for water and pain medication in the bathroom. I listened to the message. Meredith said that Tim's unit was attacked while trying to rescue a maintenance unit. He was in critical condition. She was flying to Germany to see him. She would try to call once more before the flight left.

I wanted to call her right then. But it was in the wee hours of the morning in Colorado too. I set the alarm clock. I would awaken before her and call.

After that, I wrapped in a blanket, settled into a chair, and looked out over the city. There was a cemetery across the square. The cemeteries were all numbered, and the locals had a grasp of the cemetery numbers, but I had not paid enough attention to recall it. People are buried aboveground in New Orleans; in other Louisiana cities, the same was true. In times of flood, the caskets rose, so it was best to bury the dead in tombs. Even from the storm that had rolled in that night, water rose in the streets, so the land did not perk well. But the locals adapted in order to keep their lives. They lived life rebuilding and elevating and burying loved ones aboveground.

Truman was before me now, a few hours from me. He had established himself as a liar. The court transcripts might reveal other things about him. But what escaped me was how a boy could be sculpted into Truman's shape. What sort of adapting had gone on in the Syler family that turned Truman dark and my mother silent? The Sylers had bought a life, establishing themselves in their own minds as the happy family, Sunday morning hymn singers, and creek-bank sitters. But all the while, things floated to the surface, and I kept noticing while my mother kept burying and covering over.

I slept in the chair so that I could keep one eye on the city. It could storm again and someone needed to keep watch.

17

DELIA AND I DROVE the two and a half hours to Angola in a rental. I tried calling Meredith twice but finally left a voice message.

Delia had picked up some new clothes in a boutique early after breakfast and talked in excess about the clothes until I was getting tired of the sound of her voice.

"Have you decided what you will say?" I asked.

"Say about what? Are you talking about Truman?"

"If you don't rehearse, you could blurt out something, and I've told you how that will go. He's not our kind, you know."

"I'm not going to let you put words in my mouth," she said. She woke up surly, and even though she had lightened for a while after slipping into the new clothes, the wall was coming back up between us.

"Not words in your mouth, in your head."

She wanted a cigarette, and I told her, "You'll spoil your new clothes, and there you are looking so nice, so give the tobacco a rest, why don't you?" I pulled the folded up map from under me, the one the rental car associate had given me that he had printed off for our trip. I handed her the driving directions. "We're about to pass through Baton Rouge. Read what comes next," I said.

She studied the paper, turning it over and back and forth. "Where would we be now?"

"We're on I-10."

"It says merge onto I-110. Look, exit 155B, that's the one," she said.

"We should lunch in Baton Rouge. Who knows what's ahead, and you can't count on towns outside of the cities for good lunch spots anymore. They've all been given over to fast food."

She smelled a cigarette and then packed it away.

I passed the exit and opted for one into Baton Rouge. Right off the exit, a Cajun kitchen advertised a lunch special. We pulled in and took our lunch in a room full of locals, some in suits, but most dressed casually and sipping beer with lunch. We finished a split plate of catfish and hush puppies, and Delia took a smoke before we paid and then headed north.

Delia offered the last chocolate mint to me. "When you say that we need to rehearse what to say to Truman, what is it exactly you mean? Are we trying to catch him in another lie?"

"We want him to confess what he did the day Mother made him leave, before he got on the bus to his daddy's house in Texas."

"I'll ask him if he's been having any thoughts about us when we were girls and then get him confessing," she said, as if her imagined magic over men would work on Truman.

I felt lightheaded again. "Let's don't say anything at all about Boiling Waters. Let's ask him about his life now so that he'll get comfortable with us." We were allowed a four hour visit. I imagined that

Truman had been pent up for so long he might not be well practiced in the social graces of pretense.

After driving another hour, we crossed the county line into West Feliciana Parish. According to the map, the Mississippi River was west of us and Angola straight ahead.

The prison parking lot was well furnished with signage and visitor directions. "We're supposed to park and catch a bus into the prison," I said.

Delia stared straight ahead at the massive stretch of land. The Louisiana penitentiary was built over time on plantation property. The surrounding land was green and pastoral. "Gaylen, I've never set foot inside a prison. You know I laid awake for a while last night thinking about the police back in Boiling Waters and how they might try and throw me into just such a place."

"We don't know Sophie's condition, Delia. Don't borrow trouble." It was the first time she had gotten a genuine pang of worry, while I had thought of almost nothing else since we left town. I killed the motor. "We've been spending cash, so you'd be hard to run down."

She opened the door and climbed out, smoothing her new blouse and straightening her hair. "Whoo-ee! It's kind of exciting, facing a criminal mind like this. You think he'll remember us?"

❧ ❧

The bus packed with visitors rolled down the paved road into the gated confines of Angola. Delia engaged in a conversation with a girl from Kansas. She was such a pale girl, the kind of plump face that was outlined in pink around every orifice. White hair, too, lips painted in place with pencil and glossed like varnish. Her face was softened with tiny white hairs. She was visiting her husband and introduced herself as Virgie.

I had forgotten to tell Delia how to talk to prison visitors.

"What did your husband do?" Delia asked her.

Several women glanced at Delia and then the young woman with white hair.

"Who are you visiting?" Virgie asked, evading the question.

"He's a half brother. We don't know him too well, but he's a lifer," said Delia, although that was not true.

"Do you visit often?" I asked.

"Twice a month, all that's allowed. If you come the last of the month, then when the month rolls over the next week you can come back and that makes the visit seem longer," said Virgie.

"Hmmph!" said Delia.

The bus rolled into the lot next to a gate where prison guards waited for the visitors to disembark. The guards were tall and enticing to Delia. She grinned at one, but he did not return the smile. We were stopped at the gate. One guard gave us instructions on emptying our belongings into bins after we entered the visitor check-in. I choked down headache medication dry and then prepared to surrender my handbag and jewelry.

The group jostled forward, separating Delia and me. She was hitting it off with Virgie and not as interested in me, so she used the occasion to ditch me as was her habit when fresh blood entered the picture. I was stripped of all identification and accessories. The woman taking my belongings made direct eye contact, wanting me to know that if any item not acceptable to her passed that prison wall, I would be at her mercy.

The high ceilings and block walls of the visitor entry room were painted gray, a reminder that I was leaving the world and all color behind. I could distinguish the first-time visitors from the ones who could do the visitor intake-song-and-dance by rote. Show your ID. Clean out your pockets. Remove your jewelry and belt. Show us your shoes, as in, take them off and give us a peek into the soles. Hand over your pocketbook; handbags are still called that in the South.

My guard was female and black, dressed in a uniform the color of the room. She could clean down a visitor of trappings in less than a minute. I would not have defied her but felt the resistance seeping up. I was not a prisoner, but I had to remind myself of that as a means of self-comfort.

Delia grinned at the male guard across the counter.

His badge said, "Guitreau," and he was as fat as he was tall. "Check in all items. No jewelry or purses, no writing tablets or writing instruments, recording devices, personal belongings, photos, cameras," he told her.

She held up her arms. "I'm clean."

His eyes narrowed. "Earrings, watch."

She touched the watch face. "How do I know I'll get this back, that you aren't just going to take it?"

"Henry, escort this visitor back to the bus," he said.

"She's new," I said. "Delia, hand the man your watch and earrings."

"Humph!" she said. She unsnapped her watch, then slid the long, turquoise Texas earrings from her lobes and put them on the counter.

Inside Angola, Delia lost her power over men. She looked small, standing in the intake room and stripped of her goddess powers. "What do you make of this joint?" she asked.

We fell into line and were led out into the prison yard. There were a few benches and picnic tables. Wives and children gathered expectantly. I tried to find my mother's brown eyes in the face of each man who filed out into the yard. There were men who nearly ran, but some inward control kept them from bolting and scooping up child and wife in a delirious show of affection.

I sat atop a picnic table, and Delia took the seat beside me. A man in uniform mingled in the crowd. It must have been his job to link prisoners with visitors. "May I ask your names?" he asked.

"I'm Gaylen Boatwright, and this is my sister Delia Cheatham," I said.

"Prisoner you're visiting?" he asked.

"Truman Savage," said Delia. She looked past the prison employee.

A prisoner moved toward us, his ears pricked by the sound of his own name. He walked amiably and smiling. "Baby sisters!" He threw open his arms.

A prison employee escorting him moved ahead and approached me. "Ms. Boatwright, I'm Buddy Fortune, counselor to Truman Savage. Truman," he said to my brother, "greet your sisters."

I held up my hand in protest, but Truman put his arms around me. His white uniform had the tang of mildew and bleach. His neck touched my nose. I flinched.

Fortune turned and left.

Truman took a seat next to Delia. "You look just like you did when you were a baby. Blue eyes. Do you still like ice cream?" he asked.

Delia nodded, mesmerized.

Truman's graying cropped hair was pushed back in the front in a cowlick like mine. Lines gathered around his mouth and, of course, the eyes, brown like Mother's. While he talked, I calculated his age. If he was eleven years older than me, then he was forty.

But he looked older, like a man in his sixties. His pants bagged at the torso. He was too thin for his clothes.

"Delia, why don't you sit over here, and then I can talk to both of you," he said.

My sister complied. I felt the hair rising on my neck. Truman moved next to me. He reached up and touched my forearm as I was still sitting on top of the table. "Gaylen, you have such long hair now," he said.

"That's right," I said. "I was bald when you left."

"Delia said in her letter that Mr. Syler had passed away. I'm sorry to hear of your loss." He was cordial, like a church usher. "I hope he left you two in good shape. I know your father and my mom lived on a shoestring. Your daddy worried over money. My father did too, but he invested in oil. It was a good investment obviously."

"I'm sorry about your loss too," I said.

Delia covered her mouth with her hand.

"You have to understand the corruption strung out between Texas and Louisiana. The judges are wolves. That's why I need you to help me. We're going to need a lawyer," he said.

"I met a lawyer, and we got his card," said Delia.

"Sure, we can give you his name," I said. "He's a real ambulance chaser."

Truman said, "We're family. We have to stick together."

"Let's talk like a family, then," I said. "Do you remember our grandmother, Mother's mom?"

He said, "We were close. She loved me more like she was my mom."

"Tell me what you remember about Grandma," I said. I sat back, watching while he spoke. He never flinched or indicated he was anything less than sincere. But there was a tension in his posture and the way he spoke, his eyes looking past me; it was a speech he was giving me, careful use of language that would draw me in as an ally.

"She loved working in her rose garden. She wore big hats. Her favorite place to go was church. I went to church with her. I memorized a verse. 'Know ye not that ye are the temple of God, and that the Spirit of God dwelleth in you?' She was proud of me." His eyes misted. He turned his face away and wiped his eyes.

"I didn't know you were close to Grandma," said Delia.

Truman settled into his story. "There was this time that I wanted to buy a toy gun. Mom wouldn't let me buy toys, so I asked Grandma. She didn't have money, she said. But if I would gather eggs from her hens, I could sell them to the neighbors, and she would let me keep the money. I made a dollar and a half, enough for the plastic pistol. Then an irate neighbor knocked on Grandma's door. When she cracked open one of the eggs, it had been fertilized. A chick was inside. Grandma had me pay back the money. She was sorry that I had worked so hard and couldn't keep the money. Then Grandpa walked up, jangling coins in his pocket." Truman said to Delia, "Remember how he did that?"

Delia agreed. "He was always jangling coins in his pocket."

I was suddenly observing a story about a stranger's family, while Delia absorbed it all as fact.

"He paid me the difference, and I got the pistol." He grew quieter. "But Mom accused me of stealing it. I never stole a thing, but she had that perception of me." He said to me, "Whatever she said, she was troubled. Mom didn't mean to lie."

If Delia wanted to prattle on or agree, she held back anyway.

"There were uncles," I said. "Tell me what you remember about uncles."

"Grandma had sons and then your father had brothers. There were always uncles underfoot."

"Do you remember our uncles?" I asked.

He said, "Tell me about your life, Gaylen. What have you done with yourself? You were a smart little girl. I'll bet you went to college."

"I didn't finish," I said.

"You will."

"I plan to," I said, taken off guard. He was encouraging me as a big brother might outside Angola's walls.

"What do you like to study?" he asked. "And what was your least favorite subject, while we're at it? Math, I'll bet."

How did he know? "Algebra, least favorite. I liked literature."

"I was awful at math too," he said. At least he was being confessional.

I kept talking. "Mother was awful at math. She couldn't help with homework," I said.

"Mama yelled at me when I did math," said Delia.

"She was a yeller," said Truman.

"Loud," said Delia. "Like nobody's ever been loud."

"What about boyfriends?" he asked.

"Why, sure," said Delia.

"I married a pilot," I said.

"What about your first kiss?" he asked.

I glanced into the prison yard. The families were conversing. Laughter was rising from the gatherings of reunions. "What kind of a question is that?" I asked.

"I remember the first boy that kissed me," said Delia. "He gave me a hickey. I was twelve. I didn't even know what a hickey was."

"I'll bet you were a good kisser," he said.

"I've been told by more than one that's true," said Delia.

"I guess you have children by now," he said.

"No kids. I don't stay married long enough," said Delia.

I did not answer, so he asked me directly again. I told him, "Braden and I are separated. No children. One dog."

"I like dogs," he said. "Tell me your favorite pet growing up."

Delia waved at Virgie, the Kansas girl, across the yard.

Virgie waved her over. "Come meet my husband," she said.

Delia got up and ran to the other side of the yard.

So as to not cause a lull in the conversation, I answered, in order to hide the prickly feeling rising up my spine. "We once had a lap dog, a yapper, Daddy said. We dressed the dog in our doll clothes. He allowed almost anything. I think it's because he liked to be touched, so he tolerated doll clothes, bonnets, lace socks."

"We never had a dog when I lived with Mom," he said.

"You didn't have toys or pets. Tell me, what did you have?" I asked.

"It's kind of a fog. I don't remember much about childhood. What about you?"

"I remember some of the past," I said, trying not to give too much away. "I was four when you left."

"You cried. I remember that. You didn't want Mom yelling at me. She was mad at me again. She thought I had stolen money from her purse, but that wasn't true."

"You must have felt misunderstood," I said.

He talked more, telling one story after another. I tried to remember a henhouse in Grandma's yard. Her house was in town, not a house where chickens would be kept. But his stories were detailed. I could picture my mother angry and yelling.

"How old were you when your parents split?" I asked. "My mother and your daddy."

"I was really young. Only four. My daddy wanted custody, but Mom wouldn't hear of it. She was marrying a man. I don't remember him. He left her anyway. Then I was ten and she wanted to take me away, to California. That was when she was marrying your father, husband number three. She wanted to go away to live with him. My daddy told her not to take me away. They never could agree on matters, but especially about me."

I tried to imagine Mother married to Truman Senior. She and my father seemed married forever. I once asked my father how he proposed to her. He told me that she had proposed to him. She jumped into the conversation, arguing that she had asked him his intentions. There was that hint in her voice of something I could not determine as a child. By intentions, she meant that since he was taking liberties with her, she wanted something in writing. I pieced that together all of a sudden. Daddy shook his head at her, his way of chastening her for saying too much. Mother teetered on the edge of saying more than she should while Daddy exercised restraint. I realized now it was because of his family's disapproval of my mother.

It must have been her need to confess. Sitting in front of Truman, her hinted codes came back to me.

"Did you live in an apartment in California?" I asked, remembering what the aunts told Delia.

"It was a small place."

"What was she like back then?" I asked.

"Loud. Mad."

"There was something my aunts said about you," I said.

He seemed to withdraw. His pupils shrunk. "Which aunts?"

"Renni and Tootie, my father's sisters."

"I don't remember them," he said.

"They said that my mother neglected you."

Buddy Fortune walked casually out into the yard. He and Truman exchanged glances, and he walked on past us. Truman's shoulders lowered. His face relaxed again. "How would they know she neglected me?" he asked.

"Tootie lived two doors down from my mother."

"What did she say about me?" He was more relaxed, as if he truly did not know.

"That you came to her door asking for food," I said.

"Was that in Boiling Waters?"

"According to Tootie."

"One of your aunts hated her. Is that the one you mean?"

They all hated my mother, but I held that thought in reserve.

"When we lived alone, when I was four, we lived in Boiling Waters. There was a neighbor woman who gave me food. Maybe that is when Mom met your father. He was coming to visit his sister."

He was obviously trying to remember as much as I was.

"Did she neglect you?" he asked. "She wouldn't though, would she? She seemed different with you."

"Different, how?"

"She liked dolling you up. She dressed you in clothes passed on by the aunts. But she could sew and make anything look new."

A piece of Mother's code floated up. *I like doing for girls. Boys are trouble. I was meant to have girls.*

"What kind of baby was I?" I asked.

"Beautiful. Your uncle, your daddy's other brother, Rudy, he said you were born with curves," he said.

So he did remember an uncle. "What kind of thing is that to say about a baby?" I asked.

"He was quite taken with you."

"Uncle Rudy was gay, everyone said," I told him. Mother had said it, and also Renni.

"He was kind," said Truman.

"Most of the time, he was gone," I said. "What do you mean, 'kind'?"

"He gave me things. Not anything big or new. Just toys. I don't know where he got them. He was poor as Job's turkey. Mom was always punishing me." He talked faster, repeating himself. "I wasn't allowed toys or my own things." He started rubbing his hands.

Maybe that meant he was growing irritable with his memories. But I didn't want him to figure me out and clam up. His letter had proven him paranoid enough.

I remembered the dissection kit. "You had a dissection kit. There was a dead frog, and you were showing me how to cut it up."

"How could you remember? You were only four." That disclosure flattened his buoyant tone.

"I do."

"I remember your yellow dress," he said, and then, pleased with his own ability to recollect, he laughed, "Ha-ha! You were pretty as a daisy. Delia called you Daisy Girl." He laughed to himself, pleased that he could remember so much.

Delia lingered across the prison yard, yucking it up with Virgie.

"So you remember me at age four. What else?"

"The biology stuff belonged to Mom's sister-in-law. She used it for her biology class. I think she wanted to be a nurse. She was always reading science books. But she let me have the dissection kit. I wanted to show you and Delia how to dissect a frog."

"Why would that make Mother angry?" I asked.

"Who knew what was going to make her angry? My existence made her angry," he said.

"I'm trying to understand her. Can you appreciate that?"

"You're wasting your time."

"The woman you knew and the mother who reared me were not the same two women. What changed her?"

"You."

"What do you mean?"

"You were the first good thing that came her way."

"But what about you? Why did she not see the same good in you? You were her baby too."

"She was sixteen. I was the thing that would keep my father around, or so she thought."

"What do you think your father is doing now?"

"I told you. He was murdered."

"Start telling the truth, Truman, this instant, or I'll leave and not come back. Delia and I were planning on coming back tomorrow, but you can change that with one more lie."

"I don't con my family."

"Truman, you do." My plan to keep up a front the first day was eroding. Another Gaylen was taking over.

A guard heard us and walked toward us. "Is there a problem?"

"We're cool," said Truman. When the guard walked away, he said, "I don't know what you're up to, but if Judge Cuvier is behind this, you'll be used and then thrown away like refuse. Stay away from him. He's a murderer and a pimp. He'll suck you into his campaigns, and then you'll end up like my father."

"Tell me how you think your father was murdered," I said.

He talked for over a half hour about the corrupt judge and the plot to kill his father and take his family's land. While he talked, another memory bobbed up. Mother was telling me that Truman was not capable of telling the truth. I could see her plain as life, resurrected and standing in the kitchen, responding in her strange codes to one of my many questions about the boy erased from our lives.

He talked until a guard told him his time was up. "Are you coming back tomorrow?" he asked me.

"Same time," I said.

Delia bustled to meet me. She hugged Truman good-bye. "Virgie's got a brother-in-law, and she said he's just my type."

"Breathing," I said.

Truman laughed. "I'm glad you two came. You're a gas."

Delia talked about the prospect of a new man all the way back to New Orleans.

"What about Avery?" I asked.

"The thing about Avery you have to understand is that I think he was after my inheritance. He was one of those types that once he sniffed out money in the till, the next thing you know, he'd tell me anything."

"Good to leave him behind then," I said.

"Truman is a sweet man. I guess we had him all wrong," she said. She talked until the afternoon lull overtook her, and she fell asleep.

I fueled up in Baker and connected using I-10. On the trip home, Noleen called from Garland. She bought a Christmas ham, the honey-baked kind, she gushed. I assured her that we had to return to Garland and hoped Delia's car was not a bother. She reminded me that Christmas was only a week away. I felt melancholy hearing her talk about the holidays and her grandchildren. Her children would arrive, and Delia and I would be the spare relatives.

Braden would join his family down in Florida, and they would wrap lights around the thirty-foot-tall palm tree in the front yard. Then the boat parade and flotilla would float past on the canal behind the Boatwright's deep-water lot. Braden's daddy, Clemson, would wave at Braden and his mother, Daurie, from his boat, red-faced from vodka, wearing a Santa hat and a Jimmy Buffet shirt.

Mother had established no Christmas traditions. She blamed my father, saying that he put a damper on the holidays. Daddy seemed to sleep through Christmas, guarding the football games with one eye. His stomach packed full of beans and cornbread, only the hope of a beer roused him from his sofa.

New Orleans traffic was picking up by midafternoon. I pulled up to the courthouse and left Delia asleep. The courthouse assistant retrieved the transcript for me. I carried it to a concrete bench and opened it up.

Delia came in an hour later, the side of her face red and damp with drool.

The transcript was beside me on the bench. I could not think of what to say.

Reading Truman's trial transcript left me feeling weak. I was breathing like a guppy out of the bowl. I could only think to call Jackson, who was not at home. Delia took the transcript from me and read it while I drove back to the hotel. She kept turning the pages and saying, "He's awful," and "He should be shot." Finally she laid the transcript in her lap. "Truman sure can fool you. He must have fooled Mama and Daddy until they found him out. Then poor Mr. Savage and his wife had no idea." That was when she slammed the passenger's door with her fist. "He could have been stopped a long time ago. Why would Mama hide it?"

I pulled into the Windsor Court circle drive. A valet checked the car and helped Delia out. She slid the transcript back into the manila envelope and carried it up the hotel steps.

I accepted an offer of room service and ordered scones and tea. Windsor Court's tearoom was full, and it was impossible to get reservations that late in the day. Some of the patrons seated at the linen-covered tables were dressed in winter business attire, while others had come in from tennis. The tea hostesses served high tea from antique tea services. "We'll take ours in our room," I told the desk clerk.

"Tonight, one more time, some more of those beignets," said Delia.

"We can do that again," I said.

My phone rang just as I took a seat at the room's desk overlooking the street. Jackson sounded lively. He talked of Noleen's cooking and the fact that we would have to come or else he would never be able to eat it all. He was glad to have reunited with our side of the family and even happier that Delia and I agreed to return in time for Christmas.

I waited for the lull in the conversation that said he was waiting to hear why I had called him. I told him, "We met Truman, my half brother."

"Is he what you expected?"

"Nothing at all like that," I said. "He's a charmer." Deceptively so, I thought.

"Did he tell you what you wanted to hear?"

"No."

"Nothing at all?" he asked.

"I got the court transcript, the one transcribed at Truman's trial."

"That's got to be interesting reading."

"He's a beast, Jackson. He was planning on murdering the little girls that he had attacked. As a matter of fact, he fantasized about returning to all of his victims and burning them all in a bonfire." I had not thought until that moment whether or not he had counted me in that number.

"You need to get out of there, Gaylen. Don't go back to see him."

"Once more. I told him I'd be back tomorrow."

"It's a promise you don't have to keep."

"It's a promise I've made to myself, Jackson. I'm going to tell him I've talked to his father recently."

"Don't. Drop it. Men like Truman Savage can't handle confrontation."

"I just want to see," I said. I promised to see him in a few days.

Someone knocked on the door. I thought it was room service, but when I opened the door, I found two plainclothes policemen waiting instead. "Delia Cheatham," they said.

Delia screamed, "No, please, no!"

They walked past me and straight toward Delia. One of the cops read my sister her rights.

"Please, it's almost Christmas!" said Delia. "Let me be with my family in Texas." She explained to the cops, detectives calling themselves Turner and Murphy, about Noleen and Jackson, as if the policemen would care about her surrogate family in Garland, Texas. Delia sobbed. She began to shove her new clothes into a shopping bag, but the young cop took her wrist and stopped her.

"You can't take your belongings anyway, ma'am. Let your sister bring your things home for you." Turner, the young guy, was kind to her, as if someone had told him about her vulnerabilities. Or it could have been Delia's naive manner that softened him.

"Who ratted me out?" she asked.

I did not know what to say. I had never been good at consoling my sister. I held my arms out to her, and she let me hold her. I cried with her, and it felt strange. I had scarcely cried over my own father's funeral. "Could you dispense with the cuffs?" I asked. "Please don't lead my sister out of here in handcuffs. I'll walk her all the way to your car. Delia, tell them you won't run," I said.

It was as if I had given Delia her cue. She bolted for the door. Turner grabbed her and cuffed her wrists behind her back.

"You watch yourself, mister! My sister and me, we got us plenty of money and a lawyer!" she said, agitated with the way he pressed her against the wall.

"I'll post your bail," I promised. Her cheeks were devoid of any color, and it was the first time that I saw the reality of her crime show up in her eyes.

The young cop led her down the plush hallway as the curious hotel host wheeled our tea service around them and up the hall to our room.

Delia stared after me. She looked six years old. "I won't be able to get you a Christmas present. I was going to, you know. I swear, Gaylen! I know what you like now."

"I'm sorry, Delia," I whispered. I meant I was sorry that until now she did not know me.

"You go to that café and eat beignets, Gaylen, for us! You eat some for me! You promise me!" She was desperate, and her face shone wet under the hall lamps.

I nodded although I couldn't get out another word to her. She disappeared into the elevator with Turner. While the doors closed, a slight whimper, and then the hallway fell stone silent.

Murphy, Turner's older partner, said, "Your husband, Braden Boatwright, arranged a plea bargain. He told us where to find your sister if we would let you go. But you have to testify about the day of the shooting. The victim told us you saw the whole thing."

I pictured Delia's face looking up from the defendant's table. I could not form the words to agree with him.

"Otherwise, I got to book you too," he said. The plainclothes officer stood between me and the door, as if he did not know whether I might, like Delia, bolt.

"I'll testify." I numbly agreed. I imagined Daddy glaring at me for not looking after her more carefully.

Murphy handed me his card. "You'll need to return to Boiling Waters. Call me as soon as you get into town."

"We were supposed to be with family Christmas day." I stated it faintly, as if I was too paralyzed to talk. I was worried he might change his mind and drag me down the hallway behind Delia.

"The arraignment will be pushed up into January because of the holidays. You won't do her any good this week anyway. Just be back home the week of New Year's."

"Officer Murphy, please be careful with my sister. She doesn't always say the right things, but it's because she's not right in the head."

"Your attorney will have to sort through mental defense issues, Mrs. Boatwright. Happy Christmas."

After he left, I sat down to the teacart left quickly behind by the hotel host. I pushed aside the hot teapot.

A mother and father in the grave, a brother and sister behind bars—my family managed to end up on the dead end of the street no matter how much I fought to keep each one on the path of life and sanity.

I sat in the room until the sun went down on New Orleans and covered the city darkly enough that I could venture out without being noticed at least by the staff who I was certain were beginning to whisper about the arrest. Then I returned to Café Du Monde and sat down holding a cup of café au lait and beignets again, some for me and some on behalf of Delia. I figured that I would scarcely taste them. But the taste was heightened, and it was as if I were tasting them for the first time. It was good to know that I would not lie down on a cold jail cot that night. I had imagined it many times as Delia slept next to me in a hotel bed. But I worried over her and how the other inmates would treat her.

An older man in a dark suit seated across from me sipped coffee and waited for his wife to join him. There seemed to be a lot of older people in the square, but it was only Thursday, and not all of the party revelers turned out until after rush hour on Fridays. He was bored enough to talk to me, and he told me about the jazz band that played every night for eight dollars right down the block in Preservation Hall. I finished my coffee and the crisp hot pastries that were exceptionally dusted and walked down to find a line forming into the jazz hall. I called Braden and left a phone message and waited in line.

Meredith had not called me back. I imagined her leaving for Germany, trying to intercept the calls from Renni and the rest of the Syler clan.

Then I turned around and saw a man walking straight for me. The streetlights were dim as an old London street, but as he neared, I could see his face. "Braden, is that you?" I asked.

I felt his arms come around me. I had grown so alone in my grief over Delia, so pent up, that it came spilling out when he held me close. "I know you have your reasons, Braden, but how could you?"

"They were threatening to throw you in jail. I'm sorry about Delia," he said just into my ear and turning me away from the prying eyes of those standing around me.

"She was helpless. I couldn't do anything to help her or to keep them from taking her away. I tried to tell them about her, that she can't help what she does, or it seems she can't. Can she?" I asked.

He wiped powdered sugar from my mouth. "Beignets. Save any for me?"

"We can go back," I said. It seemed like a dream that he was standing wiping sugar from my lips and even more of a fantasy that I liked the attention he was giving me.

"Let's stay here. Where does this line go?"

"Preservation Hall."

"Oh yes! You'll like that music." He spoke quietly. "Did Delia kick up a fuss, I mean, fight them when they arrested her?"

"What do you think?"

"I wanted to get here in time to try and help, you know, maybe talk to her and prepare her, but they got here so fast. I was afraid to call you. If she bolted again, they were going to come after both of you. They threatened me over and over until I agreed or, they told me, no deal."

"You couldn't have helped her. I didn't."

"Do you want me to take you back to Garland tomorrow? I can. I've taken off," he said.

"For how long?"

"Through Christmas. You want to stay here a few days, maybe fly into Dallas, see a Christmas show?"

"Can you take off that long?" Christmas was a big season for Braden, people wanting to fly private planes up to ski resorts and down to Florida.

"I just took off, that's all."

"Tomorrow I go back to Angola. One last time."

The line was moving, and we were just inside the door, handing one of the money collectors our cash, when Braden said, "I'll go with you to the prison."

"You can't." But I was surprised that he offered to accompany me. "They make the prisoners declare all visitors' names on a list. They have to preapprove you, and there's no time."

"What's he like?"

"Truman? He's nice to meet. But it's not real."

"What's so important about tomorrow?"

"I'm going to tell him I know that his father wasn't murdered."

"Did he think that he was?"

"No, he wanted me to believe that he was a victim of a conspiracy."

"To extort money, I guess. Why tell him anything?"

"The day he left our house is a complete blank. I remember days up to it, past it, but that one day is gone."

"Are you sure you want to trust him to help you remember? How will you know if he's telling you the truth?"

"I know enough. He can't lie. I've got him over a barrel."

We filed into the jazz hall and took our seats. I took off my sweater.

"What's this?" Braden saw the daisy tattoo.

"Just a tattoo," I said, as if I had gotten a new pair of earrings.

He laughed until he saw I was not laughing with him.

"Delia has this thing for daisies."

By now Delia was flying out of Louisiana with two cops and no idea of what lay ahead. I had tried to help her see ahead from the time we left Boiling Waters, but it had not done a bit of good. No matter how much I warned and goaded her, she could never see ten minutes into the future. That is when I prayed for her. It was not a big prayer.

The trombone player was warming up. He shook his spit out on the sneaker of a young boy who rolled with laughter. We turned our attention on the band in front of us. They were playing a standard. "When the Saints Go Marching In."

18

BRADEN'S LAST WORDS to me before I left for Angola prison were, "If he so much as utters a hint of threat, you make for the door, Gaylen. Don't you take anything off him."

He had checked into an airport hotel, not certain that he would find me as he did, standing out on the sidewalk in front of Preservation Hall. Braden had his easy side, and he was exercising it well, in spite of the fact that he had aided the police in arresting my sister. Or maybe ratting her out had softened him.

"There's no need to drive all the way back into New Orleans. I'm flying into Baton Rouge, so you let me know when you're headed back, and I'll have the plane ready for takeoff," he said.

I wanted to know what to do next regarding Braden. But he made it easy to do nothing, so I accepted the three twenty-dollar bills that he slipped into my hand for gas money and hugged him. When the time was right, I would explain about the money I had come into, but for now accepting money from him was a way to appease the tension between us. I used it to buy a new pair of jeans as my old ones could be stood up in a corner. I checked out of the Windsor Court and sent for the rental car.

The drive to Angola passed more quickly the second time, and I ate fast food along the way and sipped a diet drink.

The line into Angola was long as before, but I did not see Delia's friend, Virgie. I met up with the same female guard as before who recognized me. She passed me through without a hitch, and that was a relief as I had hidden the photo of my mother and me inside my bra. It was one of the three that I had carried pinned to the netting of the suitcase on my road trip with Delia. I had seen smuggled items thrown into the trash in the security line. But I risked it for no reason other than it was the only memento that would bring back the woman we both knew. That, and I thought seeing me at the age he remembered me might trigger an honest re-sponse. It was my only plan, and I had no other in mind and could form no words for the conversation awaiting me. My whole life, I had rehearsed in advance the conversations that I deemed especially difficult. When I told my father that I was leaving Boiling Waters, I had prepared perfectly for the explosion of emotion I heard when I told Daddy and he yelled through the phone, "You'll starve with-out me looking after you, Gaylen!"

When I told Braden what had happened between me and the professor, I had taken him off to a motel, crying all the way just to say, "I've cheated." I had imagined correctly every flutter of his eyes, the limp way his head would hang, my falling back onto the bed like the last brittle leaf of fall, my hands covering my face in shame.

But as I imagined sitting across from Truman, I could not predict the words that would pass between us. He walked in line out into the prison yard in that white invisible garb they all wore. When he saw me, he broke from the line of prisoners and met me at the same picnic table under the tree.

"Baby sister, you came back. I knew you would." He grinned and spoke in a tone so soft that it was very nearly like my mother's voice the time I had flu. "You smell like cheeseburger." He closed his eyes. "Dill pickle, mustard, fries, ketchup."

"Exactly." His time inside Angola had heightened his senses. "I never eat fast food, but since running around with Delia, I seem to be breaking all my own rules." I pitied him, as he seemed to drink in the smell I brought in from the outside world.

"Where's Delia?" he asked.

"She couldn't come. She's gone home, back to Boiling Waters."

"That's odd," he said. "Alone?"

"I'll join her soon. Today, I'd like to talk about our mother," I said. But the wooden way the words spilled out made him fall quiet. I said, "I'm trying to understand her. The woman she was back then and the woman I grew up knowing were not the same."

"Sometimes I can remember her face. Not today, though."

I slid my hand over the top of my blouse where it made a V. But the guard nearby watched Truman more closely than some of the other inmates, so I did not pull out the photograph. I stalled, hoping our mundane talk would bore the guard and send him nosing around another table. "When my mother and your father divorced, how old were you?"

"I answered that yesterday. Are you all right?" The conversation made him somewhat edgy, but I only knew because of the way he kept reaching to scratch the back of his neck. He sat to the right of me and stared to the left at the ground.

"What were they like?"

"Arguing, never agreeing on anything. My father wanted her to settle down, take care of the house, take care of me. But she wasn't sure of herself, what she wanted. She could never be happy with just taking care of a kid and cooking meals."

"Did she blame you for her unhappiness?"

"You sound like my shrink."

"Did she?"

"She blamed me for breathing, for taking up space, for standing too close, for not standing close enough. I was a fly she swatted. She swatted me, slapped, poked, beat, until I was unsure of how to even walk into the next minute." His soft voice turned to gravel.

"She had a sister and three brothers who all seemed normal. What happened to her?" I asked.

"Her mother's husband was not her father for one thing. She felt like an outcast. Then when Grandmother got religion, Fiona Chapel did not fit within the correct social circles of those church women. She was untamable. By the time my grandmother got her own life right and realized that her oldest girl was spiraling out of control, she was too far gone to fix."

"I know a story about you," I said.

He came upright. "Says who?"

"An aunt. My father's sister."

"The one who hated my mother?"

"Tootie," I said.

"Yes, we talked about this. Last night, lying on my cot, I remembered her."

"Aunt Tootie who lived next to my mother in an apartment. That was before Mom met and married my father."

"I don't remember," said Truman.

"Tootie says you were about four years old. You came knocking at her door. She said that you were filthy, naked, covered in your own feces. You were begging her for food."

"I don't know why you're telling me this."

"Mother was too young to have a child. She was herself a child."

"What do you expect me to do, Gaylen? Cry?" he asked quietly.

I reached into my shirt and fished out the photo.

"A smuggler. I like the way you operate. Next time slip me one of those cheeseburgers," he said.

I showed him the photo. "This is her. She is holding me. Do you remember me at this age and her back then?"

He took the picture, looking at it, the faint Mona Lisa smile not leaving his face. "You were the prettiest baby ever born."

"I was older, though, the day you left. You showed me how to dissect a frog. I was fascinated. Delia too. We admired you. You were our big brother."

"Pretty baby sisters," he said.

"I trusted you," I said.

"Always. Why wouldn't you? I looked out for you. Not like her."

"'I'll take what you did to the grave, my mother said about you. What did you do, Truman? Tell me what happened the day Mother threw you out of the house."

He was slowly kicking one heel into the soil. "Judge Cuvier sent you, didn't he? He's trying to pin another indictment on me. Well, I'm not going to bite this time," he said.

"Tell me what happened, Truman, so I can be at peace. I've had nightmares my whole life."

"Baby sister, haven't you heard? Nightmares are our friends."

"I'm not going to rest until you tell me," I persisted.

He smiled one last time and then threw his hands up, covering the top of his head as if in pain. "Stop, Gaylen! Don't torment me! I'm not your whipping boy!" He yelled until he got the attention of the guard who had wandered away from us.

"Stop, Truman!" I said. "You're avoiding telling me, and you know it."

He wept so loudly, complained so forlornly, that the other families gathered out in the prison yard turned and stared piteously at him and deprecatingly at me. There were tears streaming down his face. He wiped his nose with the back of his hand.

"She's brought in contraband! Look, see the photograph!" he yelled, waving it under the guard's nose. "It's my dead mother! She snuck it through security to torment me!" He turned and yelled at me. "You stopped me from going to her funeral, Gaylen. You could have let me come, but no!"

I was escorted out of the yard between two guards. The photograph of my mother and me was taken and thrown into a trash receptacle. "Ma'am, this is a warning to you. You've breached the rules of Louisiana State Penitentiary, and in this state that is considered a serious threat. We allowed you here on a visit to this prison on your own recognizance. It will be a long time before you are allowed back inside, and then, only if Inmate Savage so deems your time here necessary."

I was put back on the bus and sent back to my car. I had sacrificed the only photograph of my mother and me on an empty hunch.

⁂

Braden asked me to meet him at a Baton Rouge eatery called Avoyelles and gave me the directions. I parked and found him in the downstairs café sipping gumbo. I hit the women's lavatory first, and it was inside the stall that I collapsed, crying. A waitress saw my rump on the floor and asked timidly if she could help.

"I could use a wet paper towel," I said, trying to sound as if I could handle it after that.

She handed me the towel under the stall. I pressed it against my face.

She backed away. "Do you want me to get your boyfriend?" she asked. "I think he'd like to know you're upset."

The humiliation of being ousted from Angola following Delia's arrest was the final taxing element on my constitution, but I did not want to explain my life to a Creole waitress. I walked out of the bathroom.

Since Grady had stolen our wedding bands, she had assumed us to be dating. In my weakened state, I no longer cared what anyone thought. "Just bring me a basket of crusty French bread, please," I told her. I joined Braden.

"Gaylen, you look white as a fish," he said.

"I haven't rested," I said.

He wanted to know about Truman, but I was still so angry I could not even say his name.

"I'll order you a crawfish po' boy," he said.

"Nothing more than potato soup for now," I said.

"I think it's time you went home, Gaylen. Forget Texas."

"I promised Jackson."

"You never liked to disappoint people."

"The last thing I need is for you to comment on my past behavior, Braden."

"One crawfish po' boy, one bowl of potato soup, and a green salad," he told the waitress.

"I'd never go home now, not with that drug dealer still on the loose, that what's his name with the gun and the rope. Did I tell you that he was going to kill me and Delia? The things she drags me into just leave me flummoxed. Now she's going to go to jail or maybe the asylum. Would that be worse or better?" I asked.

"I hear the asylum's better than prison. More board games… Bingo, Monopoly."

"The funny thing about Delia is that now I'm heartbroken over her arrest. I used to tell my girlfriends in high school that one day Delia would end up in jail. But it was cruel of me to say that. Am I being punished?"

We talked back and forth like that for three hours, ordering extra baskets of bread and sweet tea refills. I worried over Delia. Would they let her smoke? Would they be cruel to her? Finally Braden said, "You haven't said what happened today in Angola."

I could hardly form the words and then finally said, "They threw me out."

Braden threw back his head and laughed.

"It wasn't funny like that at all, Braden."

He kept laughing until I laughed. "One bread pudding, two spoons, two coffees," he finally told the waitress. "Daisy tattoo, almost arrested, thrown out of Angola prison."

"I've done worse than all those things, Braden. You know that better than anyone."

"Everybody takes a wrong turn," he said.

"Not ten or twenty. Not the good daughter."

"Gaylen, if it seems crazy, I'm nuts. But I like you like this."

"What on earth do you mean by that?"

"Baby, don't get mad again."

"Being a Syler is like being spawned from fish in the sewer, Braden. Not everyone is born like you, with parents who love you and give you money to start your own private plane business."

"Truth be told, that business is going down the sewer."

I was stunned. Not once had he admitted defeat; he always gave me only the sanitized news. That was part of what had been wrong with us.

"I didn't want to worry you."

"Do you blame my crash?"

"The business was sinking before the crash. But we were already fighting. It seemed easier to just let you fall asleep each night."

"But I'd rather know."

He handed me a spoon. "Between here and Texas, let's talk until there's nothing left to talk about."

I called Jackson and told him I would arrive that night, except with Braden instead of Delia. Delia, I'd tell him about in person.

We were in the air before sunset, Braden's best time to fly because he liked flying into the end of the day. He said to me, "Take the helm. There's no reason not to try." His fingers straightened out, and he let go of the controls.

"I can't," I said.

"There's a certain truth to getting back on the horse."

"There's a new list. A Gaylen list. Pilot is not on the list."

He acquiesced and took back the controls. "What made you try in the first place?"

"I thought it would bring us closer," I said.

His shoulders lowered. He was looking at me, and if I assessed him like I should have been doing all along, he was seeing something in me that was not a criticism of him. "Because you loved me."

It was true enough that I didn't have to answer.

"That was a hard load to carry, you trying to be something for me, something for your daddy, and then Delia."

I couldn't add anything, especially since he had spoken it only seconds behind my own full, personal epiphany.

"That last night when you took off for Charlotte, you were nervous. But you wouldn't back down. I shouldn't have let you go alone."

"I know. I was stubborn. Sick in the head." Guilt works a strange magic on the mind. "The thing of it was that when the plane started losing altitude, I couldn't think about anything but you and what we lost," I said. That was why I confessed my affair to him so soon after I got out of the hospital. "But I did something worse. I told you because I was tired of living with the guilt. I unloaded on you." Braden left me in the motel room alone that night. "I was hoping you would make it right between us."

He could not say anything to that.

"I grew up with two people who wanted all of the family messes hidden behind a nice story. Something that made them look respectable and good. I had no point of reference for walking around without camouflage."

"My folks, they're no better'n yours."

"Are there flying lessons for people like us?"

"You mean, like spiritual guides? I think they're all selling something on cable now."

"Oh yes," I said quietly. "Mail in $19.99, and I will send you my especially anointed prayer cloth, guaranteed to cure migraines, hemorrhoids, and brain tumors."

Braden communicated with a Baton Rouge air traffic controller. Then he said, "My father, he never took a lot of time with my brother and me. He was the most together man I ever knew when it came to his business. But he fights depression. Drinks too much. My mother goes shopping to feel better, gets face-lifts, and takes cruises, alone. That's not what you mean by flying lessons."

"Going shopping isn't a bad way to feel better."

"She keeps buying things, like she thinks it's going to bring her happiness. She has more clothes than Princess Diana did, outfits she's never worn." Braden grew more confessional than usual. "I'm thinking, what if she boxed them all up and sent all her things off to some African villagers. Maybe she could find herself again if she gave her life away."

"Have you suggested it to her?"

"How hypocritical would that be?"

"Quite."

Braden and I had not been a hobnobbing couple when we dated. But after we married, we began to socialize more and more with a certain moneyed set. Although I hadn't been a great athlete growing up, in Wilmington I'd taken up tennis. Braden rubbed shoulders with Wilmington's elite, so much so that people believed he was successful, even though his business bled red. Although we never invited any of that set into our tiny apartment, we fit in well with them. The more tennis matches I could set up from our office at the airstrip, the further I ebbed away from Boiling Waters. We both felt it was only a matter of time until we bought a home down in Honeysuckle Cove or one of those elite little waterside communities. It occurred to me, though, that not once had any of those women bothered to call and see about me over the course of my trip on the road with Delia.

"What exactly have you told our clients about us?" I asked Braden.

"It's no one's business."

"So you haven't told them we're divorcing."

"I had to hire an attorney. Word spreads. What's it matter?"

"Delia has eaten up every minute of my life since we left North Carolina. But you would think one of my friends would have called to see about me."

"They're not those kinds of friends, Gaylen. What did you expect, that they would gather and pray for you like your grandmother's quilting group?"

There was a side of me that wanted to say yes, even though I knew that wasn't how it was done on the golf course or at the elegant cocktail parties our acquaintances in Wilmington loved to throw.

"I don't have any friends, Braden."

"Don't be ridiculous."

"It's not bad, you know."

"There are worse things to realize. Is that what you mean?"

"Like losing everything you have," I said.

"You're being morbid."

"Braden, I'm going to give you something that will surprise you."

He did not say anything. Maybe it was because he knew and he was reserving comment so that he might sound wise and above my petty ideas.

"I'm going to give you your divorce. When we land, I'll sign the divorce papers," I said. It was like having an out-of-body experience.

"What if I've changed my mind, Gaylen? Your timing is off as usual."

"How will I ever know what you want?"

"What do you want, Gaylen?"

"Do overs."

The silence between us was not as awkward as in the past. I waited, but it took him several minutes to finally say, "I can't go into Garland with you. Tell Jackson that I had to go home to Florida."

"Retreating isn't going to help, Braden."

"There's something I've got to tell my father. But it's got to be in person," he said.

"Can you tell me?"

"I'll let you know how it turns out. How about that?"

We were entering Texas airspace, and everything ahead widened into an eternal unfolding of possibilities.

19

NOLEEN MET ME at the airport in dire need, she said, of one more trip into town. "Join me, Gaylen, and catch me up on your exploits in Louisiana."

The hope of Christmas in Garland sparked pleasant shopper conversations within the quaint shopping strip down on the town square called Firewheel Town Center. It was located, she said, on the turnpike, or more accurately, President George Bush Turnpike. Mothers and little league friends lined up with children for last minute snapshots with Santa. The usual husband waiting too late to buy something for the wife skulked down perfume aisles with the same hangdog posture of a disappointed trout fisherman buying fish on the way home. Desperate males eyed various holes where women's gift items might be snatched up, then swinging out a credit card, they snagged the easily spotted boxed sets, especially if wrapped in a little extra ribbon or tinsel that might make them look good to the missus.

Noleen pulled out a list she had made to purchase extra stocking gifts for her two granddaughters and a grandson. She headed into the junior's section of Dillard's department store. In the misses section, I wandered through a display of cashmere sweaters. I was selecting a pink one for Delia when I decided I liked it so well I should buy two. I witnessed Noleen greedily gathering little packets of earrings and socks the color of taffy. She never knew that I saw the gleam in her eye, the pleasure of lavishing on grandchildren what she may not have heaped on their father at that age.

Since both of my parents were in the grave, they would never know the overwhelming lust of buying excessively for grandchildren at Christmas. My father had come from a large family, but since my grandmother had birthed so many daughters and only three boys, it was left to Daddy and his brothers, Malcolm and Rudy, to carry on the family name. It was such an odd, sinking feeling to realize that the Sylers had nearly come to their end.

Mother, I imagined, might have enjoyed a grandchild. My father, however, might not have noticed, as he seemed not to notice his daughters unless one of us had gotten into trouble. I picked hair barrettes and ponytail holders off a turnstile. I carried them to Noleen and said, "These are the rage now. You have to get these."

She was thankful.

I followed her out of the shopping center into the Town Center. We watched a Christmas fireworks display, something the merchants put on every night leading up to Christmas. The temperature was dropping, and since neither of us had brought a coat, we loaded our bags into the backseat of her massive red pickup truck and climbed into the front of the cab to get warm.

"Something's happened to your sister. Tell me, Gaylen. You know you can trust me."

"She's been arrested," I said. I watched several families pass in front of the truck, laughing and drinking in the holiday like it was a stimulant.

"What on earth?"

"She shot a woman."

"In New Orleans? Whatever for?"

"Before that. It was back home in Boiling Waters. I helped her run, Noleen. I didn't know what else to do." I wished that I had been more artful in making up a story, especially after she fell so quiet. "I'm sorry I kept it from you, but you were just getting to know us. I'd hoped for a better introduction. I should be in jail with Delia. But they made me say I'd testify as a witness."

She was too stunned to drive, so we sat with the engine idling and the cab finally warming.

"The woman's brother is a drug dealer," I said, as if it somehow justified my sister's crime. "I wasn't helping her run from the police. It was the dealer. He wanted to kill her."

"You certainly carry around a load of weight, girl." She pulled on her driving gloves and geared the pickup into reverse. We circled up and then lumbered off the parking lot onto the turnpike. "What else could you do? The police wouldn't have protected her. But now they have her in jail, you say? What do they think they'll accomplish by throwing Delia in jail? That's like locking up the Easter bunny or the tooth fairy." She was a benevolent soul, much like Amity. "Where is she tonight?"

"In Raleigh, I think." The detective's card was in my wallet. But I had not thought far enough ahead to wonder where I would go to see her. "I have to go home to help her find an attorney. Her Miata...I guess I should sell it."

"It's such a pretty little car. Why don't you park it in the garage, and we'll look after it. You come back for it when things settle down."

I agreed, too numb to assemble a better plan. "This isn't the life I wanted, Noleen. I can't seem to get away from my family's volatile way of life. I see someone like you, making simple plans, ordering your life around a family meal and a Christmas tree. You make it look so effortless. How do I get from here to normalcy?"

"Every family has a broken link. But, girl, what makes you think that you're responsible for keeping your sister's life smoothed over?"

"It's what my father did. He passed it on to me."

"You can choose not to do that, to live your own life."

"Just like that? Delia will disintegrate." I imagined her, like Truman, spending the rest of her life in prison.

"People fail one another. I've failed my kids lots of times. They fail me double that. We can't keep one another from choosing to drop to the bottom of life."

"Delia's not well."

"Like your daddy and your mother."

"You knew?"

"Honey, everyone who knew them knew."

"What if Delia ends up on the streets? She could die. I'd feel responsible."

"There are people who have fewer faculties than Delia who take on simple jobs and look out for themselves. Let her try. Your daddy never let her take on enough responsibility to learn how to look after herself. You're going to have to let her go. Don't let your father rule you beyond the grave. It's time to let him go to his rest. He had his chance at life. Now you have yours."

"I have to see Delia through this trial. I can't leave her to flounder. She wouldn't know what to do," I said.

"Maybe looking out after Delia gives you purpose."

"You make it sound as if I thrive on Delia's dysfunction."

"I didn't say that."

"I do get weary of her. My mother used to say Delia would be the death of her." I knew that Mother was being dramatic. But Delia, up until my mother's last breath, was hovering over her, begging for more attention than she could give. My mother turned onto her side, turning her back to Delia, and passed away.

"What do you want, Gaylen?" Noleen echoed Braden.

A naked moment of clarity caused me to mutter, "Peace."

"Peace is an inwardly wrought work." She waited as if I might ask more. But I pondered her words as if she had just given me a box holding mysterious contents. An inwardly wrought work could mean a multitude of things. She could be handing me a platitude. I wanted what she said to be true because if it was, then it would mean that peace was something to be grasped. If a platitude, then I had had my fill of them. I hoped for it to be attainable.

Jackson held vigil over a large barbecue grill while we shopped, basting a long brisket into fork-tender oblivion. The grill was a chrome double-decker model, the kind seen set up around the parking lot of Panthers' stadium during pregame tailgate parties.

Noleen pulled a dish of fried squash out of the oven. She had prepared it earlier that day along with a sweet potato casserole. Car lights flooded the front living room. Noleen ran through the kitchen, drop-ping the dishes onto warming trays. "They're here! They're here!" she screamed, excited.

Jackson came to his feet. He retied his chef's apron, putting it on just for the sake of the grandchildren.

Their son and daughter and their respective families met at the airport and, renting a van, drove into Garland from Dallas. They piled out onto the driveway, shrieking and tumbling out with bags of Christmas gifts. Noleen helped her daughter, Constance, by taking her toddler boy out of her arms. Constance's daughters, Mimi and Sacha, were of the perfect age for the hair tie-ups and pink and pur-ple socks Noleen purchased at Firewheel Town Center. Constance looked curiously at me. It was the first moment that I felt awkward about intruding on their family gathering.

"Everyone, this is Gaylen Boatwright. Her father, James Syler, was my cousin," said Jackson.

"I remember James Syler," said Constance's brother, Taylor. "We called him Uncle James and he had two girls." Taylor was older than me, but not by much, perhaps a little older than Tim. I could not picture him at all at any of the family gatherings, but it was shortly after I started school that the Sylers stopped gathering, at least as far as my parents' invitations were concerned. He and his wife each car-ried a toddler son.

"You must be one of the two sisters. I remember you. You caught crayfish down in a stream." Taylor was friendly, and that put me at ease. But then it was easier for men to share their parents than it was for daughters.

Jackson fielded any further questions by saying, "Gaylen's father recently passed, so let's make her feel welcome…and where's my grandson?" He looked through the inside of the van and then turned around and found the boy in Noleen's arms. She handed the child to him since it was of no use to argue with him.

The girls, growing up in Idaho, wanted nothing to do with Texas barbecue, but Noleen pulled out a pan of macaroni that soothed their skittishness. I worked beside Constance seeing that everyone was served. It seemed that after I paid special heed to her daughters, she warmed to me. It was the first time, though, that I felt as if I were missing a limb since Delia's arrest.

Jackson started the dishes brigade, so I joined him, and we soon had the brunt of the kitchen cleanup under way. Constance wanted her mother's undivided attention. She drew her into the living room to take pictures near the tree. Taylor's wife, Sandra, called the children from the table to join Aunt Constance and Grammy.

I said to Jackson, "Go on and join them. I'll finish."

"Not on your life."

"Don't be a girl. You go join them. I mean it."

He took slight offense. "It takes a manly sort to work in the kitchen."

The little boy whose name I could not remember dallied in the doorway between the kitchen and living room.

"They want you in there."

"When I'm ready. I have a question for you, and now that they've cleared the room, it's my only chance," said Jackson.

"Go on."

"What makes a smart young woman like you chase all over the country like a gypsy?"

"Having an angry drug lord on your tail isn't motivation enough?"

"I heard that side of it."

"Why else would I? I had a good job."

"Everyone is looking for a place to call home."

"You don't have to worry. I'm not moving in," I said.

"Braden ever talk to you about buying a home?"

"We knew we would eventually." I still didn't get what he was saying.

"You're a pilgrim on a journey."

It came to me more than once that I was an orphan. *Pilgrim* had a more generous connotation. Pilgrims had prospects.

"Delia, she's got reason to run. The poor girl, she's got such a swarm going on in her head, she'll never know up from down. But not you. You're not the rootless soul I'd expect to find wandering place to place. I used to travel with Estate Economics before I retired my securities license and bought a bait store. There were some days I'd feel as if I would never find my way back home. The guys cut out for high finance, they lived for the road. I lived to see Noleen and the kids."

I never knew a man like Jackson existed. "I do have a sense of wanderlust. It's not like I've been miserable trailing all over."

"But if you had a home, you'd return to it. A place to hang your hat."

"I have to move out of my apartment. They don't let you keep them if you quit."

"I mean a house. A homestead. You know…a place with a yard and a couple of kids or three."

I knew what he meant, but the old homestead concept had gone by the wayside. None of our friends ever stayed long in a house. They would upsize and then, often in a panic, downsize. Or get transferred. "I don't want a house until I have the dream down right."

"What's your idea of a dream?"

"Not a big place, but some shade trees. An old house, maybe, that takes two people to fix it up. Neighbors that will join you in the backyard for coffee spur-of-the-moment. A sidewalk to take walks along. If something bad happens, the neighbors will gather and be there for you."

"I hope you have a time machine. You'll have to go back to the '50s for that." He took a stack of dishes from me and set them aside to rinse. "Do you want to tell me what happened at Angola?"

"It wasn't what I expected."

"It never is when you face a sociopath."

"He just tells one lie after another."

"I'm sorry you didn't find what you were looking for."

"I thought he would be like this caged man, cornered by me, that he would tell me what happened. I hoped he would be confessional."

"Men like Truman want two things. Money and access to more victims. Every human is just another avenue of access."

"After that, I got a hold of his court transcripts. I told you about them."

"Throw them away."

"He duct taped his victims' mouths shut to muffle their cries." I couldn't stop crying after that.

Noleen peeked into the kitchen, followed by Constance and all three grandchildren. When she found me crying, she walked me to the bedroom and sat me down. Jackson kept passing me tissues. He was bigger than life at that moment, like Lincoln sitting on his giant marble chair on the National Mall. Jackson is forever a father.

Constance and her sister-in-law herded the children out into the backyard. They did not need to know what I knew. I apologized and told Jackson and Noleen that I had overstayed my welcome.

Noleen said, "You stay here as long as you want. We have plenty of room."

Then my phone rang. Meredith was crying. She was talking so fast about Tim that it was hard to make out at first what had happened. I could not get her to stop crying. It was that kind of night.

Noleen insisted I stay all the way through Christmas. Braden called before I fell asleep and said he would pick me up the day after Christmas. He had called an attorney friend who met with Delia. She called right after Braden. The women locked up with her were cruel to her.

Meredith stayed by Tim's bedside until the morning she woke up spotting. Tim had been downgraded to serious condition. He made her fly home.

Christmas Day passed slowly, the feasting slowing and settling over Jackson and Noleen's household like a sedative.

I had witnessed one meteor shower my entire life. It was the night that Braden proposed outside the movie theater in downtown Wilmington. But Jackson assured me that I had never seen real Texas shooting stars and that his backyard would be like the big black backdrop for the show. Because of the wooded neighborhood, Noleen said, we would see it better.

I helped little Mimi on with her coat. Constance's kids were set for cold nights, coming from Idaho. I dragged two lawn chairs behind me, following Noleen who led us to the darkest woodsy corner of the yard. The sky overhead was crowned with treetops, like God made a circle with his fingers for us to look through.

Constance set her chair next to mine. She had made coffee and passed me a cup. Noleen kept saying, "Is that one?" to which Jackson would reply, "Not yet. We've got five minutes before the show." He held a flashlight over his wristwatch and seemed to believe that the meteor shower would be an exactly timed appearance. Mimi sat in his lap, while Noleen held on to Sacha. The baby had fallen asleep upstairs, and Constance was happy to find adult conversation.

Constance and I talked until the first star jetted across the sky. Mimi and Noleen giggled.

Constance said to me rather gingerly, "I heard that your cousin was caught in friendly fire in Kuwait. I'm sorry."

"That's not exactly right, but thank you. Tim is with the National Guard. They had gone into Iraq to rescue a maintenance unit that had gotten sidetracked crossing over from Kuwait. Meredith, his wife, was so frantic, she said, that she had not gotten her facts straight." I could barely breathe worrying over him. "He's recovering." All Meredith knew at first was that Tim had been airlifted to a hospital unit in some undisclosed location. She kept crying about the undisclosed location and was mad because of the secrecy she was cautioned to exercise over the phone. The cell phones were not secure, she was told, and that made her angry. Everyone up to the president of the United States made Meredith angry. I was mostly mad at Tim. He had a shattered knee that required surgery. His right arm was in a cast.

Another star trailed and then another until the sky was bulleted with them, like raindrops hitting dust.

"I don't remember Tim," Constance said. "But Taylor's older so he remembers more than me. I don't remember ever traveling to North Carolina. I wish I did."

So the night passed, and we stayed up until Mimi was falling asleep, no longer interested in the sky rockets skimming the Texas sky waters.

I was well into my REM cycle when Delia phoned. It was her one call, and she was wildly irate. "They served this awful mess of turnip greens that was runny like soup, Gaylen! Cold turkey for Christmas. Get me out of here!"

I calmed her as best I could. I nearly fell asleep with her talking into my ear until I heard the jail matron take the phone from her and hang it up. There was a distant ache, I admitted. But I fell asleep again. I could not fix Delia tonight.

20

NEW YEARS' CAME and Braden joined me in packing up our belongings to be out of the apartment by the weekend. He had fallen from favored-son status with his father after their visit. He was more lost than I. While I had spent the past week dusting off my résumé, he and his partner met on a daily basis to decide how the business would be divided up if they found a seller, but also how they would respond if it did not sell.

That left little time to discuss our floundering lives. The business's bills that had piled up over the winter would consume what little profit Braden could rake in from his share.

Kimberly said very little to me when I dropped off my extra set of master keys. I only said, "I know what you think I don't know. If you can live with yourself, then sleep soundly."

"You deserve each other," she said quietly.

That erased any doubt that Braden had broken off entirely with her. I knew what I might have said back in the fall before I had taken the road trip. But I was too exhausted to debate her.

Braden met me at the apartment door. "Joseph Fishman says that Delia will do time. Sophie Deals is irate and sounds very innocent and convincing." He had been sleeping down at the hangar. His hair was shoved under a ball cap.

"How does Delia sound to him?" I asked, although I had a good idea already.

"She sounds emotional and defensive. Most of all guilty and deceitful," he said.

"I'm going to see her again Thursday. They won't allow more than one visit a week."

"Fishman wants you to drop by his office tomorrow." Braden handed me the attorney's business card. "He'll want to discuss her attorney fees."

"There goes her inheritance," I said. "It's exactly like Daddy said, that she would find a way to lose it all." But I had imagined her money falling into slot machines at the Cherokee Casino or being invested in nail wraps or new pets bought off Craig's List.

"I got my father to pay Fishman an advance."

"Did you?" I asked. "You might have asked me."

"I thought you'd be grateful," he said.

"Braden, my father left Delia and me a quarter of a mil, divided between us."

"It will take all of her half to pay Fishman."

"Aren't you surprised?"

"Your father squirreled away money for years. I knew."

All of that time, I had not told him because I thought it would change his treatment of me for the wrong reasons. "So you've not tried to woo me back for the money, even though it might save the hangar?"

"I'm a lousy businessman, Gaylen. Why delay the inevitable?"

I made him a tuna sandwich, and we ate in the dining room over-looking the pool for the last time. We had painted the walls yellow our first weekend as a married couple. The walls had faded under the constant glare of the sunlight.

"You think you'll like having a roommate again?" he asked me.

"I met her once," I told him. "She's a pharmacist, though. Not likely to stiff me for her half of the rent."

"What's that?" he asked, pointing to the last painted dress lean-ing against the wall.

"My Aunt Amity painted dresses and framed them. The dresses meant different things to different Syler women or women who knew us. That one was for a friend of my mother's. I barely remember Effie. She had a tomcat of a temper like Mother." The canvas was five and a half feet tall. The dress was blue and posed in a porch swing. "She had cancer back then. Mother saw to her for a while. But then they parted ways as friends. Mother never said why." I slid it to the side, revealing my own painted dress. "This small dress was mine."

"You were a shrimp."

"I can't keep the big piece. I'm taking it to Effie's house this weekend. She's still alive, but living now in Wilmington. But she didn't know Mother had died." I detected pain in her voice when we spoke over the phone. "Taking her this last painted dress may help."

"There were more?"

"All delivered."

"So that's where you were all this time with Delia?"

"It was missional. Where did you think?"

"I thought you were running away from us."

"I probably was."

"Let's break down the bed first," he said.

***

I waited an hour in the visitor waiting room before I was allowed in to see Delia. I presented my identification to the captain, who then led me down a corridor to a room where inmates were given forty-five minutes to visit. The room smelled like chlorine mingled with the faint stench of mopped urine. It had been four days since I last visited Delia. She was more sedate than the first time.

"That attorney, he don't give me much hope of getting out of here, Gaylen." She was in a simpering mood and could not stop wringing her hands. She looked thinner than before her arrest. "Can't you get me a different attorney?"

"Fishman's a decent attorney, Delia. I need to tell you that it's going to take most of your inheritance to pay him."

She screamed, and that brought the jail guard into the room.

I assured him that I could calm Delia. He took a seat behind her, nonetheless.

"They don't know nothing about my trial or anything in this place. When I try to ask questions, all I get are nasty comments. These men are nasty in this place. That badge don't mean nothing. They're all pigs."

"Delia, only your attorney can answer your questions. Don't ask anyone for anything other than your phone call."

"Then the food makes me want to throw up. And look at this prison getup. Orange. What's the point of that anyway?"

"So that an escapee can be easily spotted."

"I want out, Gaylen. I'm beginning to pace."

"You're good at making friends. Try getting to know someone."

"They're all crazy in here. Not like you." She was not supposed to touch me after our initial hug. Her fingertips stopped short of mine. "I miss you." She cried.

I consoled her by saying, "You do have a good attorney. I'm going to see him tomorrow and there's hope that you'll get off with a lighter sentence because you've committed no other serious crimes."

She seemed intent on controlling herself.

"Other than mooning Deputy Bob, that is. I don't think that counts as a serious threat."

The guard laughed.

"Deputy Bob, he come to see me," she said.

"That's odd."

"Not really. He said that he felt bad for me. He can come in any-time. Have you ever noticed that he has kind eyes?"

"Delia, do you know that without a man in your life, you still have worth?"

"He's never been married. I used to think he was gay, but now I'm beginning to suspect he's been waiting for me all along."

"I put some money in your jail account."

"There's not much to buy. Cigarettes is all. I miss shopping with you. Tell me about Garland. Did you have fun with Jackson and Noleen?"

"They've invited us back. They're keeping your Miata for you."

"Precious angels! Whoever knew we had so much family that cared for us. Why you think Mama never got to know so much of our family?"

"She kept to herself."

"That's why I never want to be alone."

"But you don't have to take in every stray that comes down the road, Delia." The talk went back and forth between us until our forty-five minutes had ended. I hugged her again.

Then right outside the jail, as I was about to stop inside a café for coffee, Meredith called. Tim was being flown out of the German hospital to Maine. She couldn't meet him because the doctor had restricted her travel. "I don't want him coming home with strangers, Gaylen. Can you meet him there? Can you bring Tim home?"

I knew that Noleen might say that I was an emotional firefighter. I was learning, as she had suggested, that there were times to let people drop to the bottom of life. But other times, helping a friend in a time of need benefits the soul.

But first things needing to be first, I met the next morning with Delia's attorney, a Jewish lawyer who was very grave about her case. "Is that an act?" he asked. "Or is she legitimately off-the-wall?"

"It's not an act."

"Then we've got a perfect insanity defense. You'd have to brace yourself as your sister is placed in an institution."

"Where would she go?"

"There are state institutions. Mental health is a rat's maze in this state."

"Try to keep my sister out of prison." It was the best I could do for her, and I could not imagine my father could have done any differently on her behalf. I paid Fishman the next advance.

I drove back to the apartment. Braden, realizing our Wilmington friends were not the types to move us, ordered a moving company to pack up the rest of our things. The apartment was empty except for a suitcase with my traveling clothes and toiletries. I opened the laptop and searched for a flight deal to Maine. Meredith had given me instructions on catching Tim's flight from Maine to Colorado. I could leave the next morning and arrive three hours ahead of Tim.

I called Effie and explained that I could not bring her the painted dress until after Delia's trial. I took my remaining belongings and locked up the apartment for the last time.

The landing was quiet. There was a biting wind. I had never been so happy to move, in spite of the fact that I had yet to assimilate a plan for what might come next. But I was leaving behind an old skin. The path was not clear, but clearly to move ahead had to be a good thing.

But I had been wrong before.

<hr/>

I left for Maine the next morning with a winter storm moving up the Gulf toward North Carolina. I packed for even colder weather. My flight left on time. The weather cleared crossing over Virginia. The pilot mentioned Virginia Beach, which caused all of the passengers to look out the windows. A cruise ship was in the bay, and several sailing yachts were anchored in the deeper waters. The young man next to me was talkative. He was a freckled teenager who had a fear of flying.

"You ever crash?" he asked.

"As a matter of fact, yes."

"I knew it. I shouldn't have come."

"I was the pilot, though. I think you're safe today."

He relaxed, but reached over me and pulled down the window shade. "Didn't it make you afraid to fly?"

"For the most part, yes."

"But you got on anyway. That takes guts."

"I'm needed in Maine."

"I guess it was like a near-death experience."

"No tunnels of light. But yes."

"I saw a movie about a man who survived a crash," said the young man. "It altered his personality. He, like, got screwed up. But in the end, he decided he wanted to live."

"That makes sense."

"So do you ever want to fly again?"

"I gave up my pilot's license."

"Are you, like, religious now? Did you find God?"

"I always believed."

"Do you believe you were saved for a reason?"

"I do. I don't know what that is yet."

"Where are you going today?"

"My cousin was caught in the crossfire of a battle at the Iraq-Kuwait border. He's coming home to the States. I'm flying to Maine to ride home with him."

"That sounds like a purpose."

"It's a start."

The talk calmed him. He read a copy of *Creative Loafing* and then fell asleep. I asked the flight attendant checking seat belts to bring me a blanket. I draped it over the boy. The sun was coming up. I accepted hot coffee and a wrapped bagel from the attendant. I borrowed the boy's newspaper. *Creative Loafing* was written for an eclectic readership. I read an article about tattoos. I thumbed to the last page of the piece to see how I might have Delia's daisy removed from my shoulder. It made perfect sense that an all-inclusive article about tattoos would explain removal, but it didn't.

There was a stopover at LaGuardia. I took lunch inside a deli and then walked the New York airport mall. A bookstore clerk was pushing a cart full of sale items to the store's entry. I pillaged through and purchased a novel and a journal. Then I picked up a newspaper. A jeweler's kiosk caught my eye. I stopped and selected a pair of earrings for Delia. I tucked them into my carry-on baggage and waited back at the departure gate until my flight arrived.

The newspaper reminded me of my father sitting at his breakfast, reading the small morning paper that came once a week. That reminded me of how my mother worked at Weyerhaeuser for a time and Daddy cooked me breakfast. I was five and wanted pancakes. My mother, had she been home, might have told me to eat cereal. But not knowing how to suddenly parent two daughters, he complied each morning like a short-order cook. He made them as best he could, but they were yellow and curled at the edges. I ate them out of sympathy for him. He was anxious when he set the plates in front of Delia and me. He had lost his job and was out of work for six months. I could sense anxiety in him, as if we girls might notice the misshapen pancakes and criticize him. So as I ate each bite, I made affirming comments, such as, "Good, good pancakes, Daddy. Best ever!" Then I would chew the rubbery bite, and Delia would scowl. But that feeling never left me, of wanting to help my father feel better about himself.

I read until the plane descended on the Portland landing strip. I located the information monitors. Tim's flight would land in an hour right next to my landing gate. The pralines and crunch mix I had purchased for him in New Orleans were stuffed into my carry-on.

When the plane taxied into the gate, I stood at the portal. It was a large jumbo jet, and I expected it would take time to see him. But out he came first thing, pushed in a wheelchair by two pretty flight attendants who were doting on him.

He turned positively pale when he saw me, and then he cried and held open his arms. "Gaylen, Meredith didn't tell me you'd be here."

I threw my arms around him and held him until he could gain control.

One of the flight attendants said, "Looks like you've got your escort, sergeant. We'll go now."

The girls smiled at him and then headed across the aisle into the gift shop.

"Meredith was afraid you'd be alone. You have plenty of company it seems," I said.

He laughed.

"You've been a long time from home. I guess you want a pub. There is one down the terminal a piece."

"I promised Meredith no booze after we graduated college."

"I wouldn't tell her."

"You were always a friend, Gaylen. I would like some food, though, anything but hospital food."

I wheeled him down to the food court. He ordered seafood chowder and two hot dogs, a box of fries, and two doughnuts. "How is Delia? Staying out of trouble, I hope?"

"In jail in Wilmington." I told him what happened that day out in front of her trailer. "I tried to help her, but I think I made matters worse."

"If you loved her, then you did her good."

I had not looked at it that way.

He took a pain pill with water. "There was this private that was in my unit. Said he had a mother who was a kleptomaniac. He felt terrible when our unit was called to Kuwait. It was the worst time to leave her, he said. She was on probation, and he had moved in with her to help her stay straight. But I told him that he couldn't be around every minute to keep her from stealing. Delia's going to get into trouble whether or not you are around. But maybe in her old age she'll settle down. Even golden retrievers settle down, so why not humans? She'll remember you loved her."

"What's in Kuwait anyway?"

"Sand and oil," he said. "They even got a Starbucks there now. But it's the way into Iraq now."

"Do you want to tell me what happened?" I had been of the opinion that men coming home from war would talk about everything but the war. "If you don't want to, then don't. I don't care."

He pressed his palm into his kneecap and closed his eyes, like he was adjusting a bone or some such. He groaned faintly, but then he started talking. I must have been the first person he told his story to because it came spilling out of him like I'd hit a water main. "Some captain wanted a promotion. It was near to time for retirement, and he wanted a service medal and a bigger retirement check. Because he had never seen battle, he signed his unit out of Oklahoma up for active service. It's a big sprawling war, so there was plenty of room for more units, but his was a maintenance unit. He had imagined that with nothing to guard but oil derricks in Kuwait and a new base, Fort Wolf, he would have the glory of Middle East landscape on his record without the risk. Only problem was, because he had injected himself into the war, he didn't have a true duty station. His men were loaded with supplies for a fighting unit that had gone in to soften a region in Iraq. It was my unit. We had gone in first. The locals were unpredictable. They had no guns, but the scud missiles, if they hit close to the target, could blow a hole in the ground the size of a car.

"I was riding shotgun with the Oklahoma captain. The morale in his unit was lousy. His chaplain couldn't handle the line out the door, and the captain was down men's throats right and left. We were driving through a sandstorm, and you've never seen them like there in the desert. Sandstorms last for days. My whole mouth was like a cave. I heard the zing, and then the captain slumped over. He was hit clean through the head."

"A sniper?"

"That's the thing. Those poor people didn't have guns. Not in that remote region."

"What then?"

"It was reported as a truck accident. But, as I said, I was riding shotgun. We weren't in no accident of any sort. I knew he had men going off AWOL, mad and wanting to be back home. I think it was one of his own men." He picked at his food.

"So he was shot in the head."

"Clean and perfect shot. If a local had gotten a gun…they couldn't shoot worth crap. It had to be a trained GI. But no one would talk about it."

"What happened to you?"

"His second in command, a first lieutenant, called a halt. I was yelling for us to keep going, but he made me stand down. Like his captain, he had not seen that kind of duty. He didn't know you don't stop a convoy on the side of the road. That's when I heard the sound. It was like a scream coming at us. The scud hit the side of our truck square. I was knocked onto the road. The truck was on fire and on its side. I could hear my buddies inside the truck. Mack, my friend out of Southern Pines, he was yelling. But I couldn't get to him. My knee bone was shattered. Felt like fire coming up my leg. Then I fell asleep."

"Meredith can't wait to see you."

"She's my life."

"What are we fighting for anyway?"

"Not sand."

"Too painted-over to know?"

"It's a jacked-up war."

The flight to Colorado was an hour late due to maintenance repairs. We were placed on another plane. It was crowded, leaving the passengers in a surly mood. But because of Tim's condition and the unavailability of seats, we were upgraded to first class. He fell asleep fairly quickly, from the heavy medication, I suspected.

He awoke two hours later during the beverage service. I offered to buy the in-flight movie earphones, but he wanted to talk again. "Tell me about you and Braden," he said.

"It's been a state of limbo of late."

"He loves you, Gaylen."

"Not that he's said that, but it's something to ponder."

"What did you think, that you would go around feeling in love all of the time?"

"You do."

"I know that I'm in love. I don't feel it every minute of the day. I do today because I miss her. But love is not a feeling. It's an act of will."

"Then you should be able to fall in love with anyone."

"Don't reduce it to formula, Gaylen. You start out with the romantic notion of love. That's the lure. Then once you've bought into it, said the I-do's, it's a daily service to a person. Meredith can drive me crazy with her lists and plans. She's always revising our future. Not that it does any good. Tomorrow never turns out like you plan. She's annoying like that, so when she's in revision mode, she's not as endearing as, say, when she's out squatting over her flower bed, rump in the air. But I'll negotiate with her. Then she's buying into me because I'm investing in her. Then I feel that, and that's when I just know that I've made a deeper impression on her."

"How did you turn out so good? Sylers never turn out good."

"No one's good."

But Tim was a good man. I admired him. He was like the one good seed that drops from a plant in a dump and is blown into a field to become the true essence of its purpose. "If I can't be like Jesus, I want to be like you."

"Aim for Jesus. If you miss, it's still good."

His knee was hurting after that. He pushed his seat back down. "They patched me up in Germany, but I got more surgery when I get back home." The flight attendant kept checking on him. She felt his forehead. "He's got fever," she said.

"Look through my bag, Gaylen," he moaned. "There's stuff for fever."

There was a pharmacy inside his duffel bag. I pulled out one medication after another until he said, "That one. Give me two of those."

The flight attendant brought him water and a compress. She put a pillow under his head. Tim fell asleep again, and I sat watching him until the pilot announced our descent into Denver.

An airport escort met us at the gate. Tim asked her to stop in at a gift shop. He bought a bouquet for Meredith. The escort led us to an elevator and then assisted us by picking up Tim's luggage from the turnstile.

I placed the tin of pralines on his lap. "These are from New Orleans. For you and Meredith to share."

"New Orleans. That's one place I've not been."

"Meredith would like it."

"Would I?"

"Not so many pine trees or lookout stations."

"I won't be climbing into a lookout tower anytime soon." He sounded melancholy. His face sagged dejectedly.

Meredith waited parked exactly where she said, under the Delta sign. "Gaylen! Over here!" She walked toward us, a slight bump re-shaping her knit top. "Oh, Tim! Tim!"

Tim laughed. They embraced awkwardly, Meredith holding her face next to Tim's as she cried. He consoled her as if he would always be strong. If I had not witnessed him crying in Maine, I would have bought into his chivalrous ruse.

He pulled himself up by the car door and squeezed into the front car seat. The airport escort wheeled the chair away. I untied the cord from his crutches and slipped them into the car trunk next to our luggage.

There was snow covering most everything. I had been to Den-ver once with Braden. It was in the season between winter and spring when the grass was yellow but the temperatures still struggled to climb into a comfortable climate. On this day the weather was the type the city fathers wanted depicted on postcards. The mountains west of us looked white and hard. I slipped into my coat and pulled out gloves as well. "Good grief, Meredith! How do you live in so cold a place?" I asked.

Meredith and Tim lived in a town north of Denver, northeast of Boulder, called Longmont. It was a growing town where people had only recently started locking their doors at night, according to Meredith.

She and Tim talked about things back home more than on the war front. I stretched across the backseat and napped on and off be-tween Denver and Longmont. When I woke up, Meredith was telling Tim about the surgery scheduled for him at the veterans' hospital.

I spent the next few days in and out of their house, borrowing the car, running errands for Meredith back and forth from the pharmacy. It was a pretty little house that had climbed in value after a magazine report listed the town as one of the best places in the country to live.

Meredith checked Tim into the VA hospital on Tuesday. While she ran down to the cafeteria to buy snacks for us for the long surgery ahead, I waited beside Tim. The anesthesiologist would be in at 4:00 a.m. so the doctor had encouraged him to sleep until he was awakened. I made a bed in a chair while Meredith took the cot.

Tim sipped water, the only thing he was allowed in the hours leading up to his surgery. "Talk to me, Gaylen. I'm going nuts here."

"Everything turns out good for you, Tim." I believed that about all good people. "You'll wake up tomorrow night with a new kneecap and a new mountain to climb."

"There'll be no more climbing."

"I meant it in the metaphorical sense. But you'll still be a ranger."

"They've offered me a desk job down in the park." The residue of spiritual death was in his eyes. He was flagging, too, from so much pain medication. "I took the ranger job to be outdoors. This is a promotion, though, they tell me. More money, actually."

"Meredith says you'll be training staff. You'll be the boss."

"Giving tours, demonstrating to tourists how to watch for bear droppings." He was not expressing much enthusiasm.

"What do you tell them?" I asked.

"To carry a whistle or little bells to shake at the bear. Grizzlies aren't afraid of anything, but they hate noise."

"Is there really a difference in bear droppings?"

"The black bear, he's an omnivore. So you'll find little leaves and berries in his droppings."

"What about the grizzly?"

"In his droppings are little bells and whistles." He started to laugh and then grimaced.

"I stepped right into that," I said.

"Ha-ha!" he poked fun at me. "Grizzlies haven't been spotted in Colorado since the late '70s." He could not keep the jokes coming, though. He leaned back into the hospital pillow.

"Braden called to check on you," I said. "I told him you were grumpier than he was after his appendicitis attack. Why do men turn twelve again when they're wounded?"

"We're scared. We're no different than women."

"The next time you see Braden, give him the truth serum you seem to live on."

"Meredith gave me lessons early on. She says that if you start out telling the truth as young lovers, you'll not die when you get old but just walk straight into heaven together."

"Want to know the truth about me?"

"I know you."

I doubted him. "I cheated."

"I told you. I know."

"Braden's got some nerve. He told you, didn't he?"

"He told on himself first. He said that what you did was partly his fault. You wanted revenge, he said."

"He said it was revenge?" That surprised me. The details were so inhabited now by complications that I could hardly say what had really caused it.

It was the third trip to the cottage, and I had already decided to break it off with Max. He did not overdress this time or play a part. Instead I found him making pancakes. He made breakfast for dinner. He fed me strawberries and told funny stories. It was getting late, and I had planned to leave. But I was going home to an empty bed. Braden had flown a corporate executive to Kentucky.

Braden would never fully confess about what had happened between him and the college girl. It was boiling over inside me. I even told Max that. He avoided talking about Braden at all. Instead he seated me in a chair and massaged my neck and shoulders. He talked quietly. "I slept with Max that night because of some weird debt I owed him for listening to me."

"Makes sense."

"Why don't you hate me, Tim?"

"Too much of that floating around."

"What makes it so easy for you to love unreservedly?"

"Haven't you heard? God is love."

Until that moment, I had not applied that principle so liberally to my own flaws. I imagined an angrier God, one who disagreed with most of my decisions, who was never satisfied with any of my choices. "I think of God as a giant critic."

"You're mixing him up with your father."

The sky was growing dark. I turned on a lamp next to Tim. Meredith peeked into the room. She carried the sack of crackers and giant cookies to a table, laid them down, and then picked up a book. She sat next to Tim and stroked his hair. She read poetry aloud. Tim fell asleep, and she lay beside him in the hospital bed. They looked like they could fall asleep just like that and wake up in heaven.

21

IT WAS SNOWING OUT, and Tim was back home recuperating. I didn't know the temperature, but cold is cold in Colorado. Tim was going to get back most of his life. But it had returned to him in an entirely different shape. The physical therapist told Meredith and Tim that he would walk again without the aid of a crutch in six months.

I gave Tim a novel for a welcome home gift. "It's about a man who almost dies," I said. I thought it would inspire him to carry on.

He was propped up in his bed. The TV blared, and he stared out the window. Meredith crossed the backyard in a sprint, taking out the garbage. She talked over the fence to a neighbor, a man most likely inquiring about Tim's recovery.

Tim said to me, "Gaylen, you are slow to come out of hiding. But once you do, you'll be surprised."

"I'll find myself, you mean?"

"No. That's not it."

"Tim, like you, I'm resilient. I'll be fine."

"What does 'fine' mean anyway? It's being stuck and telling everyone you don't mind being stuck."

There was a new layer of cynicism snowing down on Tim's jolly disposition.

"Do you need your meds?" I asked.

"Tell me, were you surprised when you cheated?"

"Never more surprised."

Tim was chipping away at me again, but in his current state of misery, I let him go. It would be therapeutic for him to think that he was helping me. "It was like watching someone else going through the motions. But I felt dead until the moment that I succumbed. Suddenly my feelings were alive. It was exciting in the early stages. Better than being numb."

"But now?"

"Sheer misery, old chap."

"The human heart is deceitful."

"I understand what you mean."

"Do you?"

"Give me a little credit, Tim. I have been exposed to all things religious. My mother took me to every church in town." I said it as gently as I knew how. "I'm not a Sunday school greenhorn."

"Sunday school was a place to tell kids sunshine stories."

"You need a pill," I said.

"But God's a valley sitter. I don't hear him too good when the sun's shining. But in the valley, he comes through loud and clear."

I was hoping this was helping Tim. It seemed to place him in a better mood so I humored him.

"He allowed his creation to kill his boy. He sat and watched. That had to be hard," he said.

"It never made sense."

"It does now."

I wanted it to. "I haven't heard a word from God, Tim. What do you do when there's nothing from heaven but silence?"

"Get out of the noise, Gaylen."

I shook out his next dose and put it on the tray in front of him.

"Can you get me one of those cookies that Meredith brought home?"

"I can. Then I have to go. My sister is calling me every night. Delia is lost without me."

"I hope you help her find her way home."

The last painted dress leaned against the small bedroom wall, casting no shadow, for the night had enveloped the room. I had not noticed the smallness of the apartment when I agreed to the sublease. The young Wilmington woman named Alice Poe who was my new roommate was a career woman who, like me, had decided to rent temporarily until deciding where to buy a home. She had left me a note on the corkboard in the kitchen telling me how to set the alarm and where to park my car. She was off on a summer vacation to France, and I would have the place to myself for two weeks.

I napped on Alice's small tweed sofa, too tired to get ready for bed. My suitcases sat out in the middle of the floor. I lay contemplating where and when I would continue my education. I made a mental list that included visiting Delia in jail that afternoon and then soliciting schools for brochures. But I could not feel anything but anxious and for the life of me could not shake the nerves.

My guiding belief had been that once I had made my fortune, I would be at ease. It had not occurred to me that my father, driven by manic compulsions, was storing up a small fortune that would be my lot to manage. But the worry of how to care for the inheritance troubled me. Then there was the burden of how best to help Delia, whose money was being eaten up in legal costs. I fell asleep finally and woke at three in the morning to hear a faint shuffling noise.

Since I was unfamiliar with Alice's neighborhood, I imagined it to be an overhead sound at first. A child getting up in the middle of the night and padding across the floor might make that sound from the overhead unit. I was drifting back to sleep when a sharp sound caused me to sit up.

I stood up, and just about the time I pulled on my robe, there was a dull knock against the apartment door.

Through the window, the streetlights flooded the landing enough to expose a figure standing in the common area. A hood covered his head. He knocked again. Finally, he said, "Gaylen, it's me, Braden."

Behind him, the flow of interstate traffic whispered faintly through the copse of trees. I let him in, and he was wet from a rain mist that followed him from his apartment in Wilmington to mine.

He pulled off the damp hooded sweatshirt and left it on the linoleum entry.

"It's early," I said.

He explained the intrusion. "I woke up, and you weren't there."

"Because I'm here, Braden. I got my own place now."

"You liking it here?"

"Until I buy a house."

"Mind if I make coffee?"

"I guess not."

"Some for you too?"

"Are you staying that long?"

"A bit, if you'll let me."

I stepped aside to let him pass. "Are you okay?"

He looked around the place as he turned on the lights in the kitchen. Alice had the cute kind of tastes found in home-crafter's bazaars, every small decorative piece hot glued with a bow. "Tim, how was he? I mean, I called, but he was sleeping. They got him doped up, Meredith says."

"He's got to depend on Meredith to get around. He gets sore lying in bed. She helps him move and roll over. You could go see him."

"Yes, yes. I should do that."

"The coffee's in the fridge, just like home."

He found the bag and made a half pot, very black and caffeinated like he liked it.

"You can sit if you want," I said.

Braden took a seat at the small glass-top kitchen table. "Your sister getting any better?"

"Depends on what you mean by better." I imagined Delia in jail and I felt sorrier for her at that moment than I had ever felt. "The attorney can get her off, he thinks, on an insanity plea."

"That's a logical direction."

"She'll go into an institution, Braden. The system here is out of whack." It was all sad to think about. She was a woman beyond help or repair, but in that instant it came to me that I could love her and resign myself to the realization that if that was all that existed between us, I'd accept it. She had no gauge for loving back. My mother had believed that by withdrawing affection, she could force Delia to reach for sound reason. But Delia could not be forced to grow normal roots. She was a frail cactus incapable of roots, dependent on the desert elements for succor. "Delia will die in a place like that."

"Truth is I didn't come here at three in the morning to talk about your sister." He had always wanted to iron things out in the middle of the night.

"How about you take the sofa, get some z's, we'll figure it out in the morning," I said.

"I want to know about your brother, Truman."

"So did I, Braden. Don't set yourself up for disappointment."

"Give me one detail about him. One thing you haven't told me."

"What good is it?" I asked.

"Maybe some good. Maybe not."

"The nightmares. They were about him."

He did not say much. He filled a cup for me and then one for him. "How do you know for sure what happened?"

"I put it all together, Braden."

"How have things changed then, since you did all that?"

"Why are you here?"

"I think you lost your feelings for me, but I think they're still there."

"What's that got to do with Truman?"

"Maybe he's the cause of you losing your way."

"What's your excuse then?" I asked.

"I was mad at you."

"Mad. Is that what you call it?"

"Back to the first question. How have things changed since you chased down your ghosts?"

I knew only one thing for certain. "I don't have the nightmares anymore."

"You ever think about me?"

"Yes."

"In a good way?"

"Sometimes."

"I miss you, Gaylen."

"We're a mess together."

"Would you be willing to let me date you again, no hope of anything else?"

"You're asking me on a date?"

He pulled a book of poetry out of his shirt. He handed it to me. It was a small collection of traditional rhyming verse. But on the cover, a daisy. He touched my tattoo. "I realized you must like them."

The sky lightened, and it was morning. Braden left once I agreed to a Friday night dinner. Sea gulls flew over the balcony. I was longing for the day to pass until Delia's hearing. I walked out onto the balcony and sat down to read the book of poetry.

"Gaylen!" It was a good sound, the sound of my own name.

"Deputy Bob?" I said.

He was grinning from below as if he had won first prize at a bass tournament. The next person I saw was my husband. He was pale and looked as if he had come straight from his bed. His shirt was nicely rumpled, and the circles under his eyes gave him a desperate look that was a more comely look than I had ever seen on him. "There's a new development in your sister's case," he said.

"Sophie Deals's home was raided on a drug bust. Found a closet full of cocaine," said Deputy Bob.

"She must have come home and bolted when she saw the heat outside her place," said Braden.

"She's got to report as a witness for the prosecution in Delia's case," said Deputy Bob.

"That's good news then," I said. "Today's the day."

"Let's go for a drive before the hearing," said Braden. "Clear your head and all."

Stretching up and down the landscape on either side of the road lay a salt marsh full of an entirely hidden world of birds and marsh creatures. The long road that led out to a rarely traveled highway, except by the locals who lived along that Outer Banks inlet, gave Braden more time to talk.

"I thought today was my day to lose a sister," I said.

Braden kept telling me, "Hush. Don't talk like that."

"You care about Delia then?"

"If you do, then I do."

22

DELIA KEPT TURNING around in her chair to look at me from the defendant's table in the New Hanover County courtroom. I had been in consultation all afternoon with her lawyer. He addressed the judge, a black woman whose features reminded me of Luce Dawson. "Your honor, the defendant, Delia Patience Cheatham, would like to enter the plea of 'no contest.'"

"What are the grounds, Mr. Fishman?" asked the judge.

"The victim, Mrs. Sophie Evans Deals, has disappeared. The county sheriff's office has sought her for questioning regarding the twenty kilos of cocaine found in her house yesterday morning."

"These are unusual circumstances. Has local law enforcement considered the victim's case and how long this defendant might be held pending her discovery?"

"Mrs. Deals's husband, Freddy Deals, has been arrested for possession of illegal substances."

Delia said, "Humph!"

The attorney continued. "Freddy Deals has been interrogated and seems distressed that his wife has disappeared without telling him her whereabouts. We move that the state of North Carolina drop this case due to extenuating circumstances that would most assuredly prevent the speedy trial of the defendant, Delia Cheatham."

The judge questioned the prosecutor, who had no argument on behalf of a missing victim. The judge asked Delia to rise. Delia got up and, for once, said nothing.

"Ms. Cheatham, it seems that the victim for this hearing, who herself is being sought for criminal involvement, is nowhere to be found. It's the decision of this court that you be released on probation. As a condition of your probation, you will be released into the custody of a local county probation officer. Do you understand that it is not permissible for you to cross the North Carolina state line for the term of one year?"

"I'm home to stay," said Delia.

"The defendant agrees with your verdict," said the attorney.

The gavel came down releasing her. My sister turned and said to me, "Hah!"

I called Effie, my mother's friend. She had heard about the hearing two months earlier and was surprised I would call her at all. I told her that I would like to bring her the last painted dress. It was March, so local arteries were clogged with school traffic. Judging from the mothers backing up for the car line, Effie must live a couple of blocks from an elementary school.

I drove into town alone. She sat out on her porch waiting. I climbed the porch steps, the sun on my shoulders, my sleepy eyes hidden behind the Marilyn Monroe sunglasses I bought with Delia on our way out of Dallas.

She had prepared a plate of sandwiches: pimento and olives. I ate a finger sandwich and she talked about my mother. "I loved your mother. Fiona was the best friend I ever had. But she had this way of punishing me if I said something she disagreed with. Once, I told her that the president was going to run the country into bankruptcy. She didn't like that, so she didn't talk to me for a month. Then after that, she came around again, bringing me a cutting from a rosebush and a sack of tomatoes, and, without saying anything at all, that would square things, she thought."

"That sounds right," I said.

Effie set the painted dress up next to her porch swing. It was then I realized that Amity had painted it exactly. "I didn't know you had moved into this house back then," I said. "That's a painting of this swing, isn't it?"

"Oh yes, I moved here after my husband passed. He died of a stroke. Amity and your mother helped me move into this place. We fixed the porch swing, painted it, and then we sat sipping beers and laughing, enjoying the swing."

"Why did you part ways then?" I asked.

"Honey, that's water under the bridge." She got up and took my plate and offered me a drink that I declined.

"Everyone I've taken a painting to has told me a story about my family. My mother kept secrets, but that's not news to you, I guess."

"It was your brother that caused it, us parting ways, that is."

"Truman."

"I met Amity that day in Boiling Waters, agreeing to pick Fiona up for a girls' outing. We were supposed to go out greenhouse hopping, we called it. It's when we would drive the highways, stopping along roadside stands and greenhouses looking for new flowers to plant.

"But we drove up to her place and found her in a fight with Truman. I had seen them fight before. No one could stop her once she went after him. It was like trying to stop a bobcat. She kicked your brother out of the house. I hated that I was afraid of her when she was like that. I hid out. That was when I saw her come running out of her house, holding a child's dress. She hurled that little dress right into the barrel she used for yard waste. Her burning barrel she called it. But her phone started ringing. Before she could come back and burn it, I ran and fetched it."

"Was it mine?"

"It was your little dress, the one you had on that day. When I told Amity what I had done, she told me she would take it. She drove back to Cashiers, taking the dress with her."

"Why did my mother send Truman away, Effie? I want to know."

"I felt so awful. I drove around the block and into town when finally I saw your daddy putting Truman on a bus. I pulled aside and watched. I saw them argue. Your daddy pulled out some bills, gave him money. Then he watched him go. The only thing that boy had was a grocery sack filled with a few belongings. I was heartbroken. I never saw so much pain in a family as I saw that day. I couldn't bear to stand by and watch and do nothing. I got out of the car and approached your daddy. He was perfectly ashen. I asked what happened." She could not speak for a few minutes.

I waited, watching the school traffic passing in front of her house.

"Your daddy told me that Fiona had heard a noise in the house that day. She said it sounded like a little bird. She walked in and found you on the floor in the bathroom with his hand over your mouth. Truman was on top of you."

"Don't feel bad for telling me." I kept staring at the women in the car line, their passive expressions and the way they made phone calls to pass the time and fill up the minutes like I impassively filled the time not looking at Effie.

"I asked your daddy whatever caused that boy to go so wrong. He said that it was his brother, your uncle Rudy. He was nothing like his brother Malcolm or your daddy. He victimized that kid and then learned him to his ways. I could tell your daddy felt to blame. I did not know how long your daddy knew. People think that if they turn their backs, that bad stuff will go away. But boys like Truman keep getting worse until they're made to stop."

"Was Truman always so brutal?" I asked.

"Amity said Truman's grandmother invited her to church one weekend when she was in town. Truman sat in the back alone. Then in the middle of the sermon, that boy let out a wail so pitiful it broke her heart to hear him. I think we all thought of him as a hardened kid."

"Did she ask him why he was crying?" I asked.

"No one checked on him or asked him anything."

"Did you ever talk to my mother again?" I asked, both hands making fists in my lap.

"That was the last time."

"Did Amity know?"

"People don't talk about things like that."

I had given up on helping those who don't seek enlightenment so I didn't say anything.

"No matter what, though, I knew Amity would redeem that little dress."

"She did. I have it."

"What are you going to do with it?"

"It told me things that no one else would tell. But it's time to let it go, Effie."

"It makes sense now."

That was the last time I saw Effie. I took my painted dress down to the beach. The day was almost over. The families had gone home. I found a strip of isolated beach, away from the patches of oat grass, away from eyes. I poured kerosene across the canvas. The fuel trickled down across the folds of the dress. A piece of fabric showed through, pretty yellow dotted swiss. Truman was right about the color. Along the hem, a daisy border.

I made a pyre of sticks encircled by a ring of stones. I set fire to one corner of the canvas and then sat drawing in the sand until Amity's work of art was no more than ashes. The last thing to do was to wait for the tide. I moved back the stones. The circle was broken so the water stole in and covered the embers. Before the sun was gone, the tide was in good form, lapping hungrily until the ashes were swallowed whole into the ocean's belly.

I called Braden from my apartment. We had been dating every weekend since getting the trial behind us. "Meet me at this address." I rattled it off.

"What's up?" he asked.

"Just meet me at two o'clock today," I said.

I drove following the driving directions I got off the Internet. We had looked at several houses together, so I figured he would not be surprised at my call. I drove for miles past a lake and miles of fields dotted with buttercups. Then I turned down a long drive lined with overgrown shrubs. Then the house came next, a brick and frame farm house, a green porch out front in need of paint.

A calf loped across the acreage in a neighboring pasture.

I got out of my car, a used but newer model I had picked up at auction. From the trunk, I pulled out a bundle. The front door was left unlocked, just as I had asked the realtor to do for me. I pushed it open.

The house was empty. There was a brick fireplace in the living room, old wooden floors. I walked across the creaking planks. There was a kitchen to the side, the cabinets painted over so many times the sharp corners had disappeared. Those would be the first to go.

I walked down the hallway coming to the last bedroom on the right. I pushed open the door. On the floor I rolled out a mat and then covered it over with a white linen sheet.

From outside was the clank of Braden closing his truck door. His mirror arced off the window glass.

I lit some candles the color of beeswax and set them around the room on the floor.

"What's this about?" he stuck his head in the room.

"I think I found our house," I said.

"But what's this?" he asked. "On the floor?"

"Thought we'd test drive the room first," I said. I pulled down the window shades. "Hurry. Lock the door." I pulled the blue shirt over my head and tossed it behind me. I unzipped my jeans and slid them down. Braden kicked off his shoes. He took off his shirt and met me in the center of the mat.

I woke up that first morning after I had seen Effie and sent the ashes of that last dress into the ocean. My senses had come awake to the fact that I was no longer dead. I had forgiven my mother. I laid to rest the idea that Truman might ever confess. Whether he did or didn't was not going to change me a bit. That was when I first realized that I was no longer practicing at loving my husband as Tim had said. I lay there in my bed listening to my roommate headed off for parts unknown realizing that I could finally belong somewhere just by my act of will.

I pressed my skin against Braden's chest. His skin was sticky and warm as summer. I closed my eyes, and he kissed me like the time we kissed the night of *The Rocky Horror Picture Show.* I softly wet his lips with my tongue and then drew back. "You feel that?" I asked.

"Like nobody ever felt anything," he said.

Feelings can hurt. But when they are the most alive is when they are allowed out into the open, come what may, whether nurtured or used for target practice.

"I feel," I said.

"I know, baby." Braden pulled me down on that white mat and we made that house our own.

Friday Braden flew Delia and me into Charlotte for a date. Jackson had shipped Delia's Miata on a semitruck to a car lot where we picked it up. Delia drove us into the city. She had never owned a car outright that could not be repossessed. It satisfied me to see her in a car and a house that she owned without payments. My father had done a good thing providing for her in that manner. He just had not imagined her in anything but his old Ford.

We parked and ate in an upscale seafood restaurant in the South Park neighborhood. Before Delia went overboard in placing her order, I reminded her of her limited budget. Then she went overboard anyway.

After dinner, Braden and I walked down the street to a coffee shop. Delia stopped, posing under a tree lit by white lights. She raised her arms like a mermaid swimming upward and then she twirled. A young man coming out of a restaurant bar saw her and he asked if she would like to dance. There was a street band playing a Creedence Clearwater Revival tune. Delia kicked up her leg, her hair swinging around her head. The college boy laughed like a man smitten.

"I feel like I'm fifty," said Braden. "I never thought I would care about your sister. But the pain in your eyes as you were watching her at the hearing…I felt it. What will you do about her now?"

"I can't do much beyond setting her up in Daddy's house. I'll put a little money in her account, enough to supplement her income from Hamby's furniture." Delia was already asking me for money.

"When Bob and Johnny told me that Freddy Deals had been caught on a security camera trying to sell our wedding bands, I thought I would be sick. He had only called me once with a threat to kill you if I didn't hand over ten-K. Before I could negotiate some-thing, anything, I thought, he slammed the phone down. I called the police and that was when I felt so desperately alone."

I didn't know what to think. I didn't know Deals had threatened Braden about me. I took Braden's hand under the table. He was al-ready talking about a job interview and what he would do next week. But I didn't let go of his hand the whole time he talked.

Delia left that boy standing in the light of a streetlamp as if they had never met. I walked her over to the valet stand in front of P.F. Chang's. She said good-bye to me before heading home, back to Boiling Waters. "You love Braden now, don't you?"

"There have to be love stories, Delia. It's how we complete our dreams as women."

"You're not mad at God anymore then," she said.

"I never said that, Delia." But she could know things too with-out my telling her.

"You can't love Braden without God. Love comes from God."

"We're working things out. God and me. Braden and me."

"You and Braden still going on a trip?"

"We're going to sail a boat up the coast."

"No flying."

"I prefer the sanctity of tides."

The valet driver pulled the Miata into line behind a string of waiting cars.

I had inherited much since my father's passing. A quirky sister and a do over of my life were at the top of the list. I had set out to change Delia, but instead I had changed. The last thing I would give her was permission to be herself, not that Delia needed my permission. God would keep her, and I would trust him to watch over what my grandmother had called the little lambs.

Delia would go on being Delia. But I would go on and let those who told lies take them to their graves, if that was their greatest wish. Misery could tell lies too. I had to learn to tell the difference between my own misery and the possibilities that existed beyond its wake. I could forgive as I had been forgiven. It was proof of God, as far as I could tell. I would know him better, I decided. There was more to my pilgrim's journey than the small painful path I had just stumbled out of. As Tim said, he was more than a swirling mass of mystery. God had involved me in my search for answers, and the answer I discovered was that there is more to me than what my mother had covered over. "I love you, Delia," I said.

She skipped all the way to her car.

ACKNOWLEDGMENTS

WHEN I FIRST STARTED the journey that evolved eventually into *Painted Dresses*, I was also celebrating having been accepted into one of the finest creative writing programs in the South, the Queens University of Charlotte Writing M.F.A., led by Fred Leebron and Michael Kobre. I owe a debt of gratitude to the earliest readers, the Queens podmates and peers to whom I am grateful for their readings, late night coffee gatherings, and general writer's angst talks that helped me rethink my story and make it the best possible story for my readers. Thanks to Sherry T., Dolores A., Hannah H., Rachel M., Peggy C., Charlie R., James M., Henry "Brabham" S., Blaise W., Brook C., Dan B., Hershella S., Sam G., Moyette G., and Claudine G. Also to the faculty authors, Elissa Schappell whose generous eye helped me guide this novel, and to Jane Alison, Dan Jones, Helen Elaine Lee, Naeem Murr, and Pinckney Benedict for wise counsel.

And to those who helped along the way with research assistance, Gayle Jones at the Brunswick County Library, Robin Vore and Jeff Cloud with airplane lingo, and Linda Thornton with facts about the east coast jails. A special thanks to a special young artist, Jarrett Ernest, for telling me about your painted dresses.

And to the editorial team who tenaciously read and re-read and, along with many diet colas, kept me going and believing we could shake the truth out of covered over lives: Shannon Hill, Lauren Winner, and Pam Shoup.

ABOUT THE AUTHOR

Patricia Hickman grew up in Arkansas where she studied creative writing at the University of Arkansas. Later she moved to North Carolina where she earned an M.F.A. in creative writing from Queens University. She has written fifteen novels for major publishers such as Random House and Warner Books. Her writing is critically acclaimed by publications such as *Publisher's Weekly* and *Library Journal*. She's taught writing at UNCC and in workships around the country. She frequently speaks on national radio programs. She and her husband live in North Carolina.

Please visit www.waterbrookmultnomah.com
for the Readers Guide
for *Painted Dresses*.